30119 026 743 85 8

CIR
8/14

Undressed by
the Billionaire

SUSAN STEPHENS
AMANDA BROWNING
SUSANNE JAMES

D0727069

MILLS & BOON

All the characters in this book have no existence outside the imagination of the author, and have no relation whatsoever to anyone bearing the same name or names. They are not even distantly inspired by any individual known or unknown to the author, and all the incidents are pure invention.

All Rights Reserved including the right of reproduction in whole or in part in any form. This edition is published by arrangement with Harlequin Enterprises II B.V./S.à.r.l. The text of this publication or any part thereof may not be reproduced or transmitted in any form or by any means, electronic or mechanical, including photocopying, recording, storage in an information retrieval system, or otherwise, without the written permission of the publisher.

This book is sold subject to the condition that it shall not, by way of trade or otherwise, be lent, resold, hired out or otherwise circulated without the prior consent of the publisher in any form of binding or cover other than that in which it is published and without a similar condition including this condition being imposed on the subsequent purchaser.

® and ™ are trademarks owned and used by the trademark owner and/or its licensee. Trademarks marked with ® are registered with the United Kingdom Patent Office and/or the Office for Harmonisation in the Internal Market and in other countries.

First published in Great Britain 2013
by Mills & Boon, an imprint of Harlequin (UK) Limited,
Eton House, 18-24 Paradise Road, Richmond, Surrey TW9 1SR

UNDRESSED BY THE BILLIONAIRE
© by Harlequin Enterprises II B.V./S.à.r.l 2013

The Ruthless Billionaire's Virgin, *The Billionaire's Defiant Wife* and *The British Billionaire's Innocent Bride* were published in Great Britain by Harlequin (UK) Limited.

The Ruthless Billionaire's Virgin © Harlequin Books SA 2009
Special thanks and acknowledgement are given to Susan Stephens
The Billionaire's Defiant Wife © Amanda Browning 2008
The British Billionaire's Innocent Bride © Susanne James 2009

ISBN: 978 0 263 90497 0
ebook ISBN: 978 1 472 00818 3

05-0213

Printed and bound in Spain
by Blackprint CPI, Barcelona

THE RUTHLESS BILLIONAIRE'S VIRGIN

BY
SUSAN STEPHENS

LONDON BOROUGH OF SUTTON LIBRARY SERVICE (SUT)	
30119 026 743 85 8	
Askews & Holts	Feb-2013
AF	

Susan Stephens was a professional singer before meeting her husband on the tiny Mediterranean island of Malta. In true Modern™ Romance style they met on Monday, became engaged on Friday and were married three months after that. Almost thirty years and three children later, they are still in love. (Susan does not advise her children to return home one day with a similar story, as she may not take the news with the same fortitude as her own mother!)

Susan had written several non-fiction books when fate took a hand. At a charity costume ball there was an after-dinner auction. One of the lots, 'Spend a Day with an Author', had been donated by Mills & Boon® author Penny Jordan. Susan's husband bought this lot, and Penny was to become not just a great friend but a wonderful mentor, who encouraged Susan to write romance.

Susan loves her family, her pets, her friends and her writing. She enjoys entertaining, travel and going to the theatre. She reads, cooks, and plays the piano to relax, and can occasionally be found throwing herself off mountains on a pair of skis or galloping through the countryside. Visit Susan's website: www.susanstephens.net—she loves to hear from her readers all around the world!

CHAPTER ONE

SOME said confidence was the most potent aphrodisiac of all, but for the man the world of rugby called 'the Bear', confidence was only a starting point. Confidence took courage, something Ethan Alexander proved he had each time he faced the world with his disfiguring scars.

A change swept over the Stadio Flaminio in Rome when Ethan took his seat to watch Italy play England in the Six Nations rugby tournament. Men sat a little straighter, while women flicked their hair as they moistened their immaculately made-up lips.

Without the Bear, any match, even an international fixture like this one, lacked the frisson of danger Ethan carried with him. Tall, dark, and formidably scarred, Ethan was more than an avid rugby supporter, he was an unstoppable tycoon, a man who defied the standards by which other men were judged. His face might be damaged, but Ethan possessed a blistering glamour born of keen intelligence and a steely will. His grey eyes blazed with an internal fire women longed to feel scorch them, and men wished they could harness, but today that passion had ebbed into simmering frustration as he contemplated human frailty. How could something as simple as a sore throat lead a world-famous diva like Madame de Silva to pull out of singing the national anthem for England at such an event as this?

The same way a damaged spine could end his own career as a professional rugby player, Ethan's inner voice informed him with brutal honesty.

He'd brought in a young singer as a replacement for Madame de Silva. Savannah Ross had recently been signed to the record company he ran as a hobby to reflect his deep love of music. He hadn't met Savannah, but Madame de Silva had recommended her, and his marketing people were touting the young singer as the next big thing.

Next big thing maybe, but Savannah Ross was late on pitch. He flashed a glance at the stadium clock that counted down the seconds. Hiring an inexperienced girl for an important occasion like this only reminded him why he never took risks. He'd thought it a good idea to give his new signing a break; now he wasn't so sure. Could Savannah Ross come up with the goods? She better had. She'd been flown here on his private jet and he'd been told she'd arrived. So where was she?

Ethan frowned as he shifted his powerful frame. The execution of last-minute formalities was timed to the second to accommodate a global television audience. No allowances could be made for inexperience, and *he* wouldn't allow for last-minute nerves. Savannah Ross had accepted this engagement, and now she must perform.

This wasn't like any theatre she'd ever played in before, or any concert-hall either. It was a bleak, tiled tunnel filled with the scent of sweaty feet and tension. She didn't even have a proper dressing-room to get changed in—not that she minded, because it was such an honour to be here. Hard to believe she would soon be singing the national anthem on the pitch for the England rugby squad—or at least she would once she found someone to tell her where she was supposed to go and when.

Poking her head through the curtain of the 'dressing-room' she'd been allocated, Savannah called out. No one answered. Not surprising, in this shadowy tunnel leading to the pitch. The lady who had issued Savannah with a visitor's pass at the entrance had explained to her that what rooms there were would be needed for the teams and their support staff. Knowing Madame de Silva always travelled in style with an entourage, including Madame's hairdresser and the girl whose job it was to care for Madame's pet chihuahua, Savannah guessed the management of the stadium had been only too relieved to release the many rooms Madame would have taken up. And she was grateful for what she had: an adjunct to the tunnel—a hole in the wall, really—an alcove over which somebody had hastily draped a curtain.

And she had more important things on her mind than her comfort, like the clock ticking away the seconds before the match. She had definitely been forgotten, which was understandable. Taking Madame's place had been so last-minute, and her signing to the record label so recent, that no one knew her. How could anyone be expected to recognise or remember her? And though she had been guided to this alcove everyone had rushed off, leaving her with no idea what she was supposed to do. Sing? Yes, that was obvious, but when should she walk onto the pitch? And was she supposed to wait for someone to come back to escort her, or should she just march out there?

Hearing the chanting of the excited crowd, Savannah knew she must find help. She was about to do just that when she heard the rumble of conversation coming closer. A group of businessmen was striding down the tunnel and they must pass her curtained alcove. She would ask one of them what to do.

'Excuse me—' Savannah's enquiry was cut short as— whoosh, splat!—she was flattened against the wall like an invisible fly. The men were so busy talking they hadn't even noticed her as they'd thundered past, talking about the man they called the Bear, a man who had made his own way to his seat when all of them had been jostling to be the one to escort him.

The Bear…

Savannah shivered involuntarily. That was the nickname of the tycoon who had sent his jet to fetch her. Ethan Alexander, rugby fanatic and international billionaire, was an unattached and unforgettable man, a shadowy figure who regularly featured in the type of magazines Savannah bought when she wanted to drool over unattainable men. No one yet had gained a clear insight into Ethan's life, though speculation was rife, and of course, the more he shunned publicity, the more intriguing the public found him.

She really must stop thinking about Ethan Alexander and concentrate on her predicament. To save time she would put on her gown and then go hunting for help.

But even the sight of her beautiful gown failed to divert Savannah's thoughts from Ethan. From what the men had said about him, having Ethan at the match was akin to having royalty turn up—or maybe even better, because he was an undisputed king amongst men. Taking into account the man-mountains in the England team, the Bear was the best of all the men there, they said; he was the deadliest in the pack.

Savannah shivered at the thought of so much undiluted maleness. By the time she had wriggled her way into her gown she had worked herself into a state of debilitating nerves, though she reasoned it wasn't surprising she was intimidated, when this tunnel led onto the pitch where the atmosphere was humming with testosterone and almost palpable aggression.

The thought took her straight back to Ethan. The power he threw off, even from the printed page, made him physically irresistible. Perhaps it was the steely will in his eyes, or the fact he was such a powerfully built man. He might be a lot older than she was, and terribly scarred, but she wasn't the only woman who thought Ethan's injuries only made him more compelling. In magazine polls he was regularly voted the man most women wanted to go to bed with.

Not that someone as inexperienced as her should be dwelling on that. No, Savannah told herself firmly, she was gripped more by the aura of danger and tragedy surrounding Ethan. In her eyes his scars only made him seem more human and real.

Oh, really? Savannah's cynical-self interrupted. *So that would be why these 'innocent' thoughts of yours regularly trigger enough sensation to start a riot?*

Prudently, Savannah refused to answer that. She had no time for any of these distractions. She poked her head round the curtain again. There was still no one there, and she was fast running out of options. If she continued to yell she'd have no voice left for singing. If she put her jeans on again and went looking for help, she'd be late onto the pitch. But she couldn't let Madame de Silva down, who had recommended her for this important occasion. She couldn't let down the squad, or Ethan Alexander, the man who had employed her. She'd put her dress on, then at least she'd be ready. Or her parents who had scrimped and saved to buy the dress for her, and she only wished they could be here with her now. Secretly she was happiest on the farm with them, up to her knees in mud in a pair of Wellington boots, but she would never trample on their dreams for her by telling them that.

As her mother's anxious face swam into her mind, Savannah realised it wasn't singing in front of a world-wide audience that terrified her, but the possibility that something might go wrong to embarrass her parents. She loved them dearly. Like many farmers they'd had it so hard when the deadly foot-and-mouth disease had wiped out their cattle. Her main ambition in life now was to make them smile again.

Savannah tensed, hearing her name mentioned on the tannoy system. And when the announcer described her in over-sugary terms, as the girl with the golden tonsils and hair to match, she grimaced, thinking it the best case she'd ever heard for dyeing her hair bright pink. The crowd disagreed and applauded wildly, which only convinced Savannah that when they saw her in person she could only disappoint. Far from being the dainty blonde the build-up had suggested, she was a fresh-faced country girl with serious self-confidence issues—and one who right now would rather be anywhere else on earth than here.

Pull yourself together! Savannah told herself impatiently. This gown had cost a fortune her parents could scarcely afford. Was she going to let them down? She started to struggle with the zip. The gown had been precision-made to fit her fuller figure, and was in her favourite colour, pink. With the aid of careful draping it didn't even make her look fat. It was all in the cut and the boning, her mother had explained, which was why they always travelled up to the far north of England for Savannah's fittings, where there were dressmakers who knew about such things.

'You can't wear that!'

Savannah jumped back as her curtain was ripped aside. 'Do you mind?' she exclaimed, modestly covering her chest at the sight of a man whose physique perfectly matched his reedy voice. 'Why can't I wear it?' she protested, tightening her arms over her chest. It was a beautiful dress, but the man was looking at it as if it were a bin liner with holes cut in it for her head and arms.

'You just can't,' he said flatly.

Taking in the official England track-suit he was wearing, Savannah curbed her tongue, but she wasn't prepared to let the man continue with the peep show he seemed intent on having, and she held the curtain tightly around her. 'What's wrong with it?' she asked with all the politeness she could muster.

'It's not appropriate—and if I tell you that you can't wear it then you can't.'

What a bully, she thought, and her flesh crawled as the man continued to stare at her curvy form behind the flimsy curtain. Did he mean the neckline was too low? She always had trouble hiding her breasts, and as she'd got older she hated the way men stared at them. She would be the first to acknowledge her chest was currently displayed to best advantage in the low-cut gown, but it was a performance outfit. She could hardly hide her large breasts under her arms! 'Not appropriate *how*?' she said, standing her ground.

The man's disappointment that she didn't fold immediately was all too obvious. 'The Bear won't approve of
it,' he said, as if that was the death knell of any hopes she
had of wearing it.

'The Bear won't approve?' Savannah's heart fluttered a
warning. To walk out onto the pitch and have Ethan
Alexander stare at her… She had dreamed of it, but now
it was going to happen she was losing confidence fast.
That didn't mean she wouldn't defend her dress to kingdom
come. 'I don't understand. Why wouldn't he approve of it?'

'It's pink,' the man said, his face twisting as if pink
came with a bad smell.

Savannah's face crumpled. It was such a beautiful
dress, and one her mother had been so thrilled to buy for
her. They had discussed the fact that hours of dedicated
work had gone into the hand-stitching alone, and now this
man was dismissing the handiwork of craftswomen in a
few unkind words.

'You'll have to take it off.'

'What?' Savannah felt the cold wall pressing against
her back.

'I understand you're a last-minute replacement,' the
man said in a kinder tone, which Savannah found almost
creepier than his original hectoring manner. 'So you
won't know that a major sponsor has supplied a designer
gown for the occasion, which he expects to be worn. The
dress has received more publicity than you have,' the man
added unkindly.

'I'm not surprised,' Savannah muttered to herself. Well,
it could hardly have received less, she thought wryly,
seeing as she was a last-minute replacement. She kept a
pleasant expression on her face, determined she wouldn't
give this man the satisfaction of thinking he'd upset her.

'And the Bear expects all the sponsors, however small their donations, to get their fair share of publicity, so you'll have to wear it,' he finished crossly when she refused to capitulate.

Perhaps he would like her to cry so he could play the big man to her crushed little woman, Savannah reflected. If so, he was in for a disappointment. Because she was plump and rather short, people often mistook her for a sweet, plump, fluffy thing they could push around, when actually she could stick her arm up a cow and pull out a newborn calf during a difficult birth, something that had given her supreme joy on the few occasions she'd been called upon to do so. Her slender arms were kinder on a struggling mother, her father always said. She didn't come from the sort of background to be intimidated by a man who looked like he had a pole stuck up his backside.

'Well, if that's the dress I'm supposed to wear,' she said pragmatically, 'I'd better see it.' She hadn't come to Rome to cause ripples, but to do a job like anyone else, and the clock was ticking. Plus she was far too polite to say what she really wanted to say, which was *what the hell has it got to do with the Bear what I wear?*

Someone pretty important to your career, Savannah's sensible inner voice informed her as the man hurried off to get the dress; *someone who is both the main sponsor for the England squad and your boss.*

When he returned the man's manner had changed. Perhaps he believed he had worn her down, Savannah concluded.

'Madame Whatshername was pleased enough to wear it,' he said with a sniff as he handed the official gown over to Savannah.

Savannah paled as she held up Madame de Silva's

gown. She should have known it would be fitted to the great singer. Madame was half her size, and wore the type of couture dress favoured by French salon-society. The closest Savannah had ever come to a salon was the local hairdresser's, and her gowns were all geared towards comfort and big knickers. 'I don't think Madame's gown will fit me,' she muttered, losing all her confidence in a rush as she stared at the slim column of a dress with its fishtail train.

'Whether it fits you or not,' the man insisted, 'You have to wear it. I can't allow you onto the pitch wearing your dress when the sponsor is expecting to see his official gown worn. Putting his design in front of a worldwide television audience is the whole point of the exercise.'

With her in it? Savannah very much doubted that was what the designer had had in mind.

'You have to look the part,' the man insisted.

Of team jester? Savannah was starting to feel sick, and not just with pre-concert nerves. In farming lingo she would be classified as 'healthy breeding stock', whereas Madame de Silva was a slender greyhound, all sleek and toned. There was no chance the gown would fit her, or suit her freckled skin. 'I'll do my best,' she promised as her throat constricted.

'Good girl,' the man said approvingly.

Savannah's chin wobbled as she surveyed the garish gown. She was going to look like a fool, and beyond her little drama in the tunnel she could hear that the mood of the crowd had escalated to fever pitch in anticipation of the kick-off.

Where was she? Ethan frowned as he flashed another glance at his wristwatch. A hush of expectancy had swept the capacity crowd. It was almost time for the match to start, and he was more on edge than he had ever been. He had promised the squad a replacement singer, and now it looked as if Savannah Ross was going to let him down. In minutes the England team would be lining up in the tunnel, and the brass band was already out on the pitch. The portly tenor who had been booked to sing the anthem for Italy was busily accepting the plaudits of an adoring crowd, but where the hell was Savannah Ross?

Anxious glances shot Ethan's way. If the Bear was unhappy, everyone was unhappy, and Ethan was unusually tense.

Madame's fabulous form-fitting gown had a sash in bleakest white and ink-blot blue, which like a royal order was supposed to be worn over one naked shoulder.

Fabulous for Madame's slender frame, maybe, Savannah thought anxiously as she struggled to put the sash to better use. If she could just bite out these stitches, maybe, just maybe, she could spread out the fabric to cover the impending boob explosion—though up until now she had to admit her frantic plucking and gnawing had achieved nothing; try as she might, the sash refused to conceal any part of her bosom.

And as for the zip at the back…

Contorting her arms into a position that would have given Houdini a run for his money, she still couldn't do it up. Poking her head out of the curtain, she tried calling out again, but even the creepy man had deserted her. She peered anxiously down the tunnel. The crowd had grown quiet, which was a very bad sign. It meant the announcements were over and the match was about to start—and before that could happen she had to sing the national anthem! 'Hello! Is anyone—?'

'Hello,' a girl interrupted brightly, seemingly coming out of nowhere. 'Can I help you?'

After jumping about three feet in the air with shock, Savannah felt like kissing the ground the girl was about to walk on. 'If you could just get me into this dress…' Savannah knew it was a lost cause, but she had to try.

'Don't panic,' the girl soothed.

Savannah's saviour turned out to be a physiotherapist and was using the tones Savannah guessed she must have used a thousand times before, and in far more serious situations to reassure the injured players. 'I'm trying not to panic,' she admitted. 'But I'm so late, and the fact remains you can't fit a quart into a pint pot.'

The girl laughed with her. 'Let's see, shall we?'

The physio certainly knew all there was to know about manipulation, Savannah acknowledged gratefully when she was finally secured inside the dress. 'Don't worry, I'll be fine now,' she said, wiping her nose. 'That's if I don't burst out of it—!'

'You'll have a fair sized audience if you do,' the girl reminded her with a smile.

Yes, the crowd was wound up like a drum, and Savannah knew she would be in for a rough ride if anything went wrong out on the pitch.

As the physio collected up her things and wished her good luck, Savannah stared down in dismay at the acres of blood-red taffeta. It was just a shame every single one of those acres was in the wrong place. Madame was a lot taller than she was, and how she longed for the fabric collecting around her feet to be redistributed over her fuller figure. But it was too late to worry about that now.

'You'd better get out there,' the girl said, echoing these thoughts, 'Before you miss your cue.'

Don't tempt me! Savannah thought, testing whether it was possible to breathe, let alone sing, now she was pinned in. Barely, she concluded. She was trapped in a vice of couture stitching from which there was only one escape, and she didn't fancy risking that in front of the worldwide television audience. She'd much rather be safely back at home dreaming about Ethan Alexander rather than here on the pitch where he would almost certainly look at her and laugh.

But…

She braced herself.

The fact that she could hardly move, let alone breathe, didn't mean she couldn't use her legs, Savannah told herself fiercely as she tottered determinedly down the tunnel in a gown secured with safety pins, made for someone half her size.

Here goes nothing!

CHAPTER TWO

SHE had forgotten how much her diaphragm expanded when she let herself go and really raised the rafters. How could she have forgotten something as rudimentary as that?

Maybe because the massive crowd was a blur and all she was aware of was the dark, menacing shape of the biggest man on the benches behind the England sin bin, the area England players sat in when they were sent off the pitch for misdemeanours.

Sin.

She had to shake that thought off too, Savannah realised as she lifted her ribcage in preparation for commencing the rousing chorus. But how was she supposed to do that when she could feel Ethan's gaze in every fibre of her being? The moment she had walked onto the pitch she had known exactly where he was sitting, and who he was looking at. By the time she'd got over that, and the ear-splitting cheer that had greeted her, even the fear of singing in front of such a vast audience had paled into insignificance. And now she was trapped in a laser gaze that wouldn't let her go.

She really must shake off this presentiment of disaster, Savannah warned herself. Nervously moistening her lips, she took a deep breath. A very deep breath…

The first of several safety pins pinged free, and as the dress fell away it became obvious that the physio's pins were designed to hold bandages in place rather than acres of pneumatic flesh.

His mood had undergone a radical change from impatient to entranced, and all in a matter of seconds. The ruthless billionaire, as people liked to think of him, became a fan of his new young singing-sensation after hearing just a few bars of her music. The crowd agreed with him, judging by the way Savannah Ross had it gripped. When she had first stumbled onto the pitch, she had been greeted by wolf whistles and rowdy applause. At first he had thought her ridiculous too, with her breasts pouting over the top of the ill-fitting gown, but then he remembered the famous dress had been made for someone else, and that he should have found some way to warn her. But it was too late to worry about that now, and her appearance hardly mattered, for Savannah Ross had him and everyone else in the palm of her hand. She was so richly blessed with music it was all he could do to remain in his seat.

She refused to let the supporters down. She carried on regardless as more pins followed the first. She was expected to reflect the hopes and dreams of a country, and that was precisely what she was going to do—never mind the wretched dress letting her down. But as she prepared to sing the last few notes the worst happened—the final pin gave way and one pert breast sprang free, the generous swell of it nicely topped off with a rose-pink nipple. Not one person in the crowd missed the moment, for it was recorded for all to see on the giant-sized screen. As she started to shake with shame, the good-natured crowd went wild, applauding her, which helped her hold her nerve for the final top note.

Thrust from his seat by a rocket-fuelled impulse to shield and protect, Ethan was already shedding his jacket as he stormed onto the pitch. By the time he reached Savannah's side, the crowd had only just begun to take in what had happened. Not so his target. Tears of frustration were pouring down her face as she struggled to re-pin her dress. As he spoke to her and she looked at him there was a moment, a potent and disturbing moment, when she stared him straight in the eyes and he registered something he hadn't felt for a long time, or maybe ever. Without giving himself a chance to analyse the feeling, he threw his jacket around her shoulders and led her away, forcing the Italian tenor to launch into *Canto degli Italiani*—or 'Song of the Italians', as the Italian national anthem was known—somewhat sooner than expected.

There was so much creamy flesh concealed beneath his lightweight jacket it was throwing his brain synapses out of sync. Unlike all the women he'd encountered to date, this young Savannah Ross was having a profound effect on his state of mind. He strode across the pitch with his arm around her shoulders while she endeavoured to keep in step and remain close, whilst not quite touching him. As he took her past the stands the crowd went wild. *'Viva l'Orso!'* the Italians cried, loving every minute of it: 'hurrah for the Bear'. The England supporters cheered him just as loudly. He wondered if this compliment was to mark his chivalry or the fact that Ms Ross could hardly conceal her hugely impressive bosom beneath a dress that had burst its stitches. He hardly cared. His overriding thought was to get her out of the eyeline of every lustful male in the Stadio Flaminio, of whom there were far too many for his liking.

It crossed his mind that this incident would have to have happened in Italy, the land of romantic love and music, the home of passion and beauty. He had always possessed a dark sense of humour, and it amused him now to think that in his heart, the heart everyone was so mistakenly cheering for, there was only an arid desert and a single bitter note.

By the time Ethan had escorted Savannah into the shelter of the tunnel she was mortified. She felt ridiculously under-dressed in the company of a man noted for his *savoir faire*. Ethan Alexander was a ruthless, world-renowned tycoon, while she was an ordinary girl who didn't belong in the spotlight; a girl who wished, in a quite useless flash of longing, that Ethan could have met her on the farm where at least she knew what she was doing.

'Are you all right?' he asked her gruffly.

'Yes, thank you.'

He was holding on to her as if he thought she might fall over. Did he think her so pathetically weak? This was worse than her worst nightmare come true, and it was almost a relief when he turned away to make a call.

It couldn't be worse, Savannah concluded, taking in the wide, reassuring spread of Ethan's back. This was a very private man who had been thrust into the spotlight, thanks to her. No doubt he was calling for someone to come and take her away, nuisance that she was. She couldn't blame him. She had to be so much less in every way than he'd been expecting.

While he was so much more than she had expected...

Ethan Alexander in the flesh was a one-man power source of undiluted energy, a dynamo running on adrenalin and sex. At least that was what her vivid imagination was busy telling her, and she could hardly blame it for running riot. No television-screen or grainy newspaper-image had come close to conveying either Ethan's size or his compelling physical presence. And yet the most surprising shock of all was the way his lightest and most impersonal touch had scorched fireworks through every part of her. He'd only touched her elbow to help steer her, and had draped his jacket across her back, and yet that had been enough to hot-wire her arm and send sparks flying everywhere they shouldn't.

Her thoughts were interrupted by the young physio coming over to see if she could help. 'It wasn't your fault,' Savannah assured her, hoping Ethan could hear. She didn't want him blaming the young girl for Savannah's problems. 'It was my breathing,' she explained.

'What a problem we'd have had if you hadn't breathed!' The young physio shared a laugh with Savannah as she started pinning Savannah back into the dress. 'And I'm really glad you did breathe, because you were fantastic.'

Savannah had never been sure how to handle compliments. In her eyes she was just an ordinary girl with an extraordinary voice, and no manual had come with that voice to explain how to deal with the phenomenon that had followed. 'Thank you,' she said, spreading her hands wide in a modest gesture.

But the girl grabbed hold of them and shook them firmly. 'No,' she insisted, 'Don't you brush it off. You were fantastic. Everyone said so.'

Everyone? Savannah glanced at Ethan, who still had his back turned to her as he talked on the phone. She pulled his jacket close for comfort; it was warm and smelled faintly of sandalwood and spice. Tracing lapels that hung almost to her knees, she realised that even though Ethan's jacket was ten sizes too big for her it did little to preserve her modesty, and she hurriedly crossed her arms across her chest as he turned around.

'Okay, I've finished,' the physio reported. 'Though I doubt the pins on Ms Ross's dress will hold for long.'

'Right, let's go,' Ethan snapped, having thanked the girl.

'Go where?' Savannah held back nervously as the physio gave her a sympathetic look.

'Ms Ross, I know you've had a shock, but there are paparazzi crawling all over the building. Don't worry about your bag now,' Ethan said briskly when Savannah gazed down the tunnel. 'Your things will be sent on to you.'

'Sent where?'

'Just come with me, please.'

'Come with you *where*?' The thought of going any-where with Ethan Alexander terrified her. He was such an imposing man, and an impatient one, but with all the paparazzi in the building the thought of not going with him terrified her even more.

'After you,' he said, giving her no option as he stood in a way that barred her getting past him.

'Where did you say we were going?'

'I didn't say.'

Savannah's nerve deserted her completely. She wasn't going anywhere with a man she didn't know, even if that man was her boss. 'You go. I'll be fine. I'll get a cab.'

'I brought you to Rome, and like it or not while you're here you're my responsibility.'

He didn't like it at all, she gathered, which left one simple question: did she want this recording contract or not?

She couldn't take the chance of losing it, Savannah realised. She hadn't come to Rome to sabotage her career. She might not like Ethan's manner, but she was here on his time. Plus, she didn't know Rome. If her only interest was getting home as quickly as possible, wasn't he her best hope?

She had to run to keep up with him, and then he stopped so suddenly she almost bumped into him. Looking up, Savannah found herself staring into a face that was even more cruelly scarred than she had remembered. Instead of recoiling, she registered a great well of feeling opening up inside her heart. It was almost as if something strong and primal was urging her to heal him, to press cream into those wounds, and to...*love him*?

This situation was definitely getting out of hand, Savannah concluded, pulling herself together, to find Ethan giving her an assessing look as if to warn her that just looking at him too closely was a dangerous game well out of her league. 'It's important we leave now,' he prompted as if she were some weakling he had been forced to babysit.

'I'm ready.' She held his gaze steadily. This was not a time to be proud. She didn't want to do battle with the paparazzi on her own, and she would be safer with Ethan. There were times when having a strong man at your side was a distinct advantage. But she wouldn't have him think her a fool either.

'After you.' Opening the door for her, he stood aside.

He looked more like a swarthy buccaneer than a businessman, and exuded the sort of earthy maleness she had always been drawn to. Her fantasies were full of pirates and cowboys, roughnecks and marines, though none of them had possessed lips as firm and sensual as Ethan's, and his hand in the small of her back was an incendiary device propelling her forward.

'What's wrong now?' he said impatiently when she stopped outside to shade her eyes.

'I was just looking for a taxi rank.' By far the safest option, she had decided.

'A taxi rank?' Ethan's voice was scathing. 'Do you want to attract more publicity? Don't worry, Ms Ross, you'll be quite safe with me.'

But would she? That was Savannah's cue for stepping back inside the stadium building. 'I'm sure someone will find the number of a cab company for me.'

'Please yourself.'

She couldn't have been more shocked when Ethan stormed ahead, letting the door swing in her face. Defiantly, she pushed it open again. 'You're leaving me?'

'That's what you want, isn't it?' he called back as he marched away. 'And as you don't need my help…'

'Just a minute.'

'You changed your mind?'

Savannah's heart lurched as Ethan turned to look at her. 'No, but.'

'But what?' He kept on walking.

'I need directions to the nearest taxi rank, and I thought you might know where I should look.' She had to run to keep up with him, which wasn't easy in high-heeled shoes, not to mention yards of taffeta winding itself like a malevolent red snake around her feet.

'Find someone else to help you.'

'Ethan, please!' She would have to swallow her pride if it meant saving her parents more embarrassment. 'Can you really get us out of here without the paparazzi seeing?'

He stopped and slowly turned around. 'Can I get us out of here?'

The look of male confidence blazing from his eyes was

at its purest. When she should be considering a thousand other things—like how long before the paparazzi found them, for example—a bolt of lust chose that moment to race down her spine. His eyes were the most beautiful eyes she'd ever seen, deep grey, with just a hint of duck-egg blue, and they had very white whites, as well as the most ridiculously long black lashes.

'I'm done waiting for you, Ms Ross.'

He was off again, but this time he grabbed her arm and took her with him. Savannah yelped with surprise. 'Where are we going?'

'To something that travels a lot faster than a taxi,' he grated without slowing down.

What did he mean—a helicopter? Of course. She should have known. Like all the super-rich, Ethan would hardly call a cab when he could fly home. 'Can we slow down just a bit?"

'And talk this through?' he scoffed without breaking stride. 'We can take all the time in the world if you want the paparazzi to find you.'

'You know I don't want that!' *Okay, no reason to worry*, Savannah told herself. They would fly straight to the airport in Ethan's helicopter, from where she'd fly home. Traffic snarl-ups were reserved for mere mortals like herself. In no time Ethan would be back in his seat at the stadium ready for the second half, while she returned to England and her nice, safe fantasies. Perfect.

Or at least it was until a door burst open and the press-hounds barrelled out. It only took one of them to catch sight of Ethan and Savannah for the whole pack to give chase.

'This way,' Ethan commanded, swinging Savannah in front of him. Opening a door, he thrust her through it and, slamming it shut, he shot the bolt home.

If she hadn't left her sensible sneakers in the tunnel she might have been able to run faster, Savannah fretted as Ethan took the stairs two at a time, but now the straps on her stratospheric heels were threatening to snap.

'Leave them!' he ordered as she bent down to take them off. 'Or, better still, snap those heels off.'

'Are you joking?'

'Take them off!' he roared.

'I'm going to keep them,' Savannah insisted stubbornly.

'Do what you like with them,' he said, snatching hold of her arm, half-lifting her to safety down another flight of steps. 'And hitch up your skirt while you're at it, before you trip over it,' he said, checking outside the next door before rushing her out into the open air again. 'Your skirt—hitch it up!'

Hitch it up? The photographers would surely be on them in moments, and when that happened she didn't want to look like a...

'Do it!'

'I'm doing it!' she yelled, startled into action. But she wouldn't ruin the shoes her mother had bought her. Or Madame's dress. Slipping off her high-heeled sandals as quickly as she could, Savannah bundled up the gown, noting she barely reached Ethan's shoulder now. Also noting he barely seemed to notice her naked legs, which shouldn't bother her, but for some reason did.

'Come on,' he rapped impatiently, still averting his gaze. 'There's no time to lose.' Taking her arm, he urged her on.

Savannah was totally incapable of speech by the time they'd crossed the car park. Yet still Ethan was merciless. 'There's no time for that,' he assured her when she rested with her hands on her knees to catch her breath.

Straightening up, she stared at him. She didn't know

this man. She didn't know anything about him, other than the fact that his reputation was well deserved. The Bear was a dark and formidable man, whom she found incredibly intimidating. And she was going who knew where with him. 'You still haven't told me where we're going.'

'There's no time!'

'But you do have a helicopter waiting?'

'A helicopter?' Ethan glanced towards the roof where the helipad was situated.

He had a helicopter there, all right, she could see the logo of a bear on the tail. She could also see the scrum of photographers gathered round it.

'A useful distraction,' Ethan told her with satisfaction.

A red herring, Savannah realised, to put the paparazzi off the trail. 'So what now?'

'Now you can sit,' he promised, dangling a set of keys in front of her face.

Ah…She relaxed a little at the thought that life was about to take on a more regular beat. She should have known Ethan would have a car here. His driver would no doubt take them straight to the airport, where the helicopter would meet him and she would fly home. She was guilty of overreacting again. Ethan was entitled to his privacy. He'd taken her out of reach of the paparazzi and saved her and her parents any further humiliation. She should be grateful to him. But she still felt a little apprehensive.

CHAPTER THREE

EVEN with the knowledge that comfort was only a few footsteps away, Savannah reminded herself that this was not one of her fantasies and Ethan was no fairy-tale hero. He was a cold, hard man who inhabited a world far beyond the safety curtain of a theatre, and as such she should be treating him with a lot more reserve and more caution than the type of men she was used to mixing with.

'Put this on.'

She recoiled as he thrust something at her, and then she stared at it in bewilderment. 'What's this?'

'A helmet,' he said with that ironic tone again. 'Put it on.' When she didn't respond right away. he gave it a little shake for emphasis.

It was only then she noticed the big, black motorbike parked up behind him and laughed nervously. 'You're not serious, I hope?'

'Why shouldn't I be serious?' Ethan frowned. Dipping his head, he demanded, 'You're not frightened of riding a bike, are you?'

'Of course not,' Savannah protested, swallowing hard as she straightened up. Was she frightened of sitting on a big, black, vibrating machine pressed up close to Ethan?

'If you have any better suggestions, Ms Ross…?'

Watching Ethan settle a formidable-looking helmet on his thick, wavy hair, she mutely shook her head.

'Well?' he said, swinging one hard-muscled thigh over the bike. 'Would you care to join me, or shall I leave you here?'

She was still staring at the tightly packed jeans settled comfortably into the centre of the saddle, Savannah realised. 'No…no,' she repeated more firmly. 'I'm coming with you.' Remembering the door incident, she already knew he took no prisoners. Holding up her skirt, she hopped, struggled, and finally managed to yank her leg over the back of the bike—which wasn't easy without touching him.

'Helmet?'

As Ethan turned to look at her, Savannah thought his eyes were darker than ever through the open visor—a reflection of his black helmet, she told herself, trying not to notice the thick, glossy waves of bitter-chocolate hair that had escaped and fallen over the scars on his forehead. But those scars were still there, like the dark side of Ethan behind the superficial glamour of a fiercely good-looking man. Her stomach flipped as she wondered how many more layers there were to him, and what he was really thinking behind those gun-metal-grey eyes.

'Helmet,' he rapped impatiently.

Startled out of her dreams, she started fumbling frantically with it.

'Let me,' he offered.

This was the closest they'd been since the stadium, and as Ethan handled the catch he held her gaze. In the few seconds it took him to complete the task every part of her had been subjected to his energy, which left her thrumming with awareness. And he hadn't even started the engine yet, Savannah reminded herself as a door banged open and a dozen or so photographers piled out. Snapping his own visor into position, Ethan swung away from her and stamped the powerful machine into life. 'Hang on.'

There was barely time to register that instruction before he released the brake, gunned the engine, and they roared off like a rocket.

Propelled by terror, Savannah flung her arms around Ethan, clinging to as much of him as she could. Forced to press her cheek against his crisp blue shirt, she kept her eyes shut, trusting him to get them out of this. But as the bike gained speed something remarkable happened. Maybe it was the persistent throb of the engine, or the feel of Ethan's muscular back against her face—or maybe it was simply the fact that she had a real-life hunk beneath her hands instead of one of her disappointing fantasies— but Savannah felt the tension ebb away and began to enjoy herself. She was enjoying travelling at what felt like the speed of sound, and not in a straight line either. Because this wasn't just the ride of her life, Savannah concluded, smiling a secret smile, but the closest to sex she'd ever come.

As Ethan raced the bike between the ranks of parked cars she was pleased to discover how soon she became used to leaning this way and that to help him balance. She could get used to this, Savannah decided, sucking in her first full and steady breath since climbing on board. She felt so safe with Ethan. He made her feel safe. His touch was sure, his judgement was sound, and his strength could only be an asset in any situation. There was something altogether reassuring about being with him, she concluded happily.

When she wasn't being terrified by him, her sober self chimed in.

Ignoring these internal reservations, she went with the excitement of the moment—not that she needed an excuse to press her face against Ethan's back. As she inhaled the intoxicating cocktail of sunshine, washing powder and warm, clean man, she decided that just for once she was going to keep her sensible self at bay and ride this baby like a biker chick.

Ethan was forced to slow the bike as he engaged with the heavy traffic approaching Rome, and Savannah took this opportunity to do some subtle finger-mapping. She reckoned she had only a few seconds before Ethan's attention would be back on the bike and his passenger, and she intended to make the most of them. He felt like warm steel beneath her fingertips, and she could detect the shift of muscle beneath his shirt. She smiled against his back, unseen and secure. She felt so tiny next to him, which made her wonder what such a powerful man could teach her, locking these erotic reveries away in record time when he gunned the engine and turned sharp right.

The bike banked dramatically as they approached the Risorgimento Bridge spanning the river Tiber, forcing Savannah to lean over at such an angle her knee was almost brushing the road. As she did so she realised it was the first time she had ever put her trust in someone outside her close-knit family. But with the Roman sun on her face, and the excitement of the day, clinging on to a red-hot man didn't seem like such a bad option, she told herself wryly. In fact, who would travel by helicopter, given an alternative like this?

She was feeling so confident by the time Ethan levelled

up the bike again, she even turned around to see if they were being followed.

'I thought I told you to sit still.'

Savannah nearly jumped off the bike with fright, hearing Ethan's voice barking at her through some sort of headphone in her helmet.

'Hold on,' he repeated harshly.

'I am holding on,' she shouted back.

As if she needed an excuse.

They took another right and headed back up the river the way they'd come, only on the opposite side of the Tiber. Ethan slowed the bike when they reached the Piazalle Maresciallo Giardino where there was another bridge and, moored under it, a powerboat…

No.

No!

Savannah shook her head, refusing to believe the evidence of her own eyes. This couldn't possibly be the next stage of their journey. Or was that one of the reasons Ethan had been making that call back at the stadium, to line everything up?

'Come on,' he rapped, shaking her out of her confusion the moment they parked up.

As she fumbled with the clasp Ethan lifted her visor and removed the helmet for her. As his fingers brushed her face she trembled. Staring into his eyes, she thought it another of those moments where fantasy collided with reality. But was Ethan really looking at her differently, as if she might be more than just a package he was delivering to the airport? The suspicion that he might be seeing her for the first time as a woman was a disturbing thought, and so she turned away to busy herself with the pretence of straightening out her ruined hair. She still had her precious high-heels dangling from her wrist like a bracelet, which turned her thoughts to her mother and what she would make of this situation. Her mother was a stand-up woman and would make the most of it, Savannah concluded, as would she.

'Are you thinking of joining me any time today?'

She looked up to find Ethan already on board the boat, preparing to cast off. He leaned over the side to call to her, 'Get up here, or I'll come and get you!'

Would you? crossed her mind. Brushing the momentary weakness aside, she called back, 'Wait for me.'

'Not for long,' he assured her. 'You're not frightened of a little mud, are you?' he added, taunting her as she teetered down the embankment.

Frightened of a little mud? He clearly hadn't seen their farmyard recently. 'What sort of wet lettuce do you think I am?'

'You'd prefer me not to answer that.'

'I'm not all sequins and feathers, you know!' She kicked the hem of her gown away with one dirty foot for emphasis.

'You don't say.' Ethan's tone was scathing, and then she noticed their chins were sticking out at the same combative angle and quickly pulled hers in again.

'There is an element of urgency to this. Paparazzi?' Ethan reminded her in a voice that could have descaled a kettle.

And then car horns started up behind her. She was providing some unexpected entertainment for the male drivers of Rome, who were slowing their vehicles to whistle and shout comments at her. They must think she was still in evening dress after a wild night out with an even wilder man, Savannah realised self-consciously. A man who was threatening to make good on his promise to come and get her, she also realised, detecting movement in her peripheral vision. 'Stay back,' she warned Ethan as he took a step towards her. 'I don't need your help.'

It was a relief to see him lift his hands up, palms flat in an attitude of surrender. She had enough to do picking her way across the splintery walkway without worrying about what Ethan might do.

It was just a shame she missed his ironic stare. The next thing she knew she was several feet off the ground travelling at speed towards the boat. 'Put me down!'

Ethan ignored her. 'I can't live life at your pace. young lady. If you stay around me much longer, you'll have to learn to tick a lot faster.'

She had no intention of 'staying around' him a moment longer than she had to, Savannah determined. But, pressed against Ethan's firm, warm body, a body that rippled with hard, toned muscle... 'Please put me down,' she murmured, hoping he wouldn't hear.

Ethan didn't react either way. He didn't slow his pace until they were onboard, when he lowered her onto the deck. Having done this, he surveyed her sternly. 'The race is still on,' he said, folding massive arms across his chest. 'And I have no intention of giving up, or of allowing anyone to hold me back. Is that clear?'

'Crystal.'

'Good.'

Savannah smoothed her palms down her arms where Ethan's hand prints were still branded.

'Well, Ms Ross, shall we take this powerboat on the river?'

'Whatever it takes,' she agreed, watching Ethan move to straddle the space between the shore and the boat.

'I'm going to free the mooring ropes,' he explained, springing onto the shore. 'Can you catch a rope?'

Could she catch a rope? He really did think she was completely useless, Savannah thought, huffing with frustration. Ethan had got her so wrong. 'I might have smaller hands than you, but I still have opposing thumbs.'

Was that a smile? Too late to tell, as Ethan had already turned away.

'In that case, catch this.'

He turned back to her so fast she almost dropped the rope. It was heavier than she had imagined and she stumbled drunkenly under the weight of it.

'All right?' Ethan demanded as he sprang back on board.

'Absolutely fine,' she lied. Summoning her last reserves of strength, she hoisted it up to brandish it at him.

'Now coil it up,' he instructed, pointing to where she should place it when she'd done so.

'Okay.' She could do this. Quite honestly, she enjoyed the feel of the rough rope beneath her fingers—and enjoyed the look of grudging admiration on Ethan's face even more. But she needed to even the playing field. Ethan was dressed appropriately for taking a powerboat down the river. She was dressed, but barely. 'Do you have a jumper, or something I could borrow?'

Ethan made a humming sound as he looked her over. 'I see your point.'

Savannah felt heat rise to her cheeks and depart southwards.

'I'll see what I can do for you,' Ethan offered, brushing past her on his way across the deck. 'I must have an old shirt stowed here somewhere…'

Her nipples responded with indecent eagerness to this

brief contact with him, just as a fresh flurry of car horns started up on shore. Who could blame the drivers? Savannah thought. The sight of a decidedly scruffy girl in an ill-fitting evening dress onboard a fabulous powerboat in the middle of the afternoon with a clearly influential man of some considerable means would naturally cause a sensation in Rome. But why couldn't Ethan notice her?

'What's wrong?' he said when he straightened up, and then his stare swept the line of traffic. One steely look from him was all it took for the cars to speed up again. 'Will this do?' he said, turning back to Savannah. He thrust a scrunched-up nondescript bundle at her.

The shirt was maybe twenty sizes too large, Savannah saw as she shook it out, but in the absence of anything else to wear she'd have to go with it. Plus it held the faint but unmistakeable scent of Ethan's cologne. 'It's absolutely perfect. Thank you.' Slipping it on, she realised it brushed her calves, but at least she was decent. She pulled the shirt close and, inhaling Ethan's scent deeply, gave a smile of true contentment, the first she'd unleashed that day.

He was stunned by the sight of Savannah wearing his shirt. She looked…adorable. She looked, in fact, as he imagined she might look if they had just been to bed together. Her hair was mostly hanging loose now, and the make-up she'd worn for her appearance on the pitch was smudged, which made her eyes seem huge in her heart-shaped face, and her lips appeared bruised as if he'd kissed them for hours. His shirt drowned her, of course, but knowing what was underneath didn't help his equilibrium any. Hard to believe he had looked at her properly, critically, for the first time just a few moments ago when she'd asked for the shirt. Nothing on earth would have induced him to stare at her out on the pitch where she'd been at such a disadvantage. But now? Now he couldn't take his eyes off her fuller figure.

Savannah tensed guiltily as unexpectedly Ethan's gaze warmed. What was he thinking—that she was a fat mess? A nuisance? As sophisticated as a sheep? Before her imagination could take her any further, she took her seat. 'I'm on it,' she assured Ethan when he glanced at the harness.

She couldn't do the darn thing up. And now Ethan was giving her the type of superior male appraisal that got right up her nose.

'I don't seem to have the knack,' she admitted with frustration. Maybe because her hands were shaking with nerves at being in such close proximity to Ethan.

'Would you like me to fasten it for you?' Ethan offered with studied politeness.

As he leaned over to secure the catch for her, Savannah felt like she was playing with fire. Ethan's hair was so thick and glossy she longed to run her fingers through it. And he smelled so good. His touch was so sure, and so…disappointingly fast. She looked down. The clasp was securely fastened. 'Is that it?'

'Would you like there to be something more?'

As he asked the question Savannah thought Ethan's stare to be disturbingly direct. 'No, thank you,' she told him primly, turning away on the pretence of tossing her tangled hair out of her eyes. But even as she was doing that Ethan was lifting his overlarge shirt onto her shoulders from where it had slipped.

'Are you sure you're warm enough?' he asked gruffly. 'Only it can be cold out on the river.'

Or hot to sizzling. 'I'll be fine, thank you.' Each tiny hair on the back of her neck had stood to attention at his touch, and it was a real effort not to notice that Ethan had the sexiest mouth she had ever seen. She would have to make sure she stared unswervingly ahead for the rest of the boat ride.

CHAPTER FOUR

'Now what are you doing?' Ethan demanded. He had just opened up the throttle, and as the boat surged forward it pitched and yawed; Savannah had chosen that very moment to shed her harness, which forced him to throttle back.

'I'm calling my parents.'

'Calling your—?' He was lost for words. 'Not now!' he roared back at her above the scream of the boat's engine.

'They'll be worried about me.'

This was a concept so alien to him it took him a moment to respond. 'Sit down, Savannah, and buckle up.' He spoke with far more restraint than he felt and, after congratulating himself on that restraint, he conceded in the loud voice needed to crest the engines, 'You can speak to them later.'

She reluctantly agreed, but he detected anxiety in her tone. He also detected the same desire to protect Savannah he'd felt out on the pitch, except now it had grown. His intention to remain distant and aloof, because she was young and innocent and he was not, was dead in the water. There was too much feminine warmth too close. 'I'll speak to them,' he said, wanting to reassure her.

Savannah was right, he conceded, her parents must be

worried about her, having seen everything unfold on television. 'You can speak to them after I do,' he said. 'But for now *sit down*.' And on this there could be no compromise.

Even Savannah couldn't defy that tone of voice, and he made sure she was securely fastened in before picking up speed again. It amused him to see she had pushed back the sleeves on his overly large shirt and pulled it tightly around her legs, as if she felt the need to hide every bit of naked flesh from him. He supposed he could see her point of view. They were diametrically opposed on the gender scale. He was all man and she was a distraction. Fixing his attention to the river, he thrust the throttles forward.

'This is wonderful!' she exclaimed excitedly as the powerboat picked up speed and the prow lifted from the water.

It pleased him to see her looking so relaxed, and he even allowed himself a small smile as he remembered her jibe about opposing thumbs. There was a lot more to Ms Ross than the circumstance of their first meeting might have led him to suppose.

What exactly that might be was for some other man to discover, though, because this was strictly a taxi service to get Savannah out of harm's way as fast as he could.

Oh, yes, it was, he argued with his unusually quarrelsome inner voice.

She was only here because she had no other option, Savannah reassured herself as the powerboat zoomed along the river. She was glad she'd been able to catch the rope and prove to Ethan she wasn't completely helpless—after the debacle at the stadium she certainly needed something to go right, but she still had some way to go. She cupped her ear as he said something to her. It was so hard to hear anything above the rhythmical pounding of the boat.

'You're not feeling seasick, are you?'

'On the river?' she yelled back. This riposte earned her a wry look from Ethan that made her cheeks flame. He might be stern and grim, but she still thought he had the most fantastic eyes she had ever seen, and there was some humour in there somewhere. It was up to her to dig it out. But for now... To escape further scrutiny, she dipped her head to secure the strap on her sandals.

'You can't put those on here.'

Savannah's head shot up. 'But my feet are filthy. Surely you don't want them soiling your pristine deck?'

'I don't want them anywhere near me,' Ethan assured her, which for some reason made Savannah picture her naked feet rubbing the length of Ethan's muscular thighs and writhing limbs entwined on cool, crisp sheets.

Swallowing hard, she quickly composed herself whilst tucking her feet safely away beneath the seat. Such a relief she had Ethan's shirt to wrap around her; Madame's gown was split to kingdom come, and what little modesty she had left she had every intention of hanging on to.

But as the river rushed past the side of the boat, and Savannah thought about the flicker of humour she'd seen in Ethan's eyes, modesty began to feel like a handicap. If only she knew how to flirt...

Flirt? Fortunately, she wouldn't be given a chance. Savannah's sensible inner self breathed a sigh of relief as at that moment Ethan looked behind them. He must think they were still being followed, Savannah reasoned. She did too. The paparazzi would hardly have given up the chase. But she felt safe with Ethan at the helm. With his sleeves rolled back, revealing hard-muscled and tanned forearms, he gave her confidence—and inner flutters too. In fact the sight of these powerful arms was apparently connected to a cord that ran from her dry throat to a place it was safer not to think about.

Had she lost her grip on reality altogether?

With every mile they travelled she was moving further and further away from everything that was safe and familiar into a shadowy world inhabited by a man she hardly knew. As the boat spewed out a plume of glittering foam behind them, Savannah couldn't shake the feeling she was racing into danger, and at breakneck speed.

There were many things he could do without in life, and of all them this fluffy thing in the oversized shirt was top of his list—though Savannah could be feisty. She had a stinging retort, for example, should she wish to use it. Far from that being a negative, he found it very much in her favour. She was also a real family girl, and, given that her parents would have undoubtedly seen everything unfolding live on television in their front room she had kept a cool head and thought not of herself but of them. A quick glance revealed her checking her feet. No doubt her pedicure was ruined. She was the smoothest, most pampered and perfect person he'd ever met, and possessed the type of wholesomeness that could only be damaged by him.

Feeling his interest, she looked up. He should be glad they couldn't hold a conversation above the thundering of the hull on the water. He had no small talk for her; he'd lived alone too long. His passion for rugby, one of the roughest contact-sports known to man, defined him. The majority of his business dealings were conducted on construction sites, where he loved nothing more than getting his hands dirty.

He was well named the Bear, and the contrast between him and Savannah was so extreme it was almost laughable; only the music they both loved so much provided a tenuous link between them. Forced to wrench the wheel to avoid some children fooling around in a dinghy, he was surprised at the way his body reacted when Savannah grabbed hold of him to steady herself.

'Sorry!' she exclaimed, snatching her hand away as if he'd burned her.

He was the one who'd been burned. Savannah was playing havoc with his slumbering libido and, instead of shouting at her to sit down, he found himself slowing the boat to check that she was all right.

'I am now,' she assured him, and then they both turned around to make sure the children were okay.

As their eyes briefly clashed he was conscious of the ingenuous quality of her gaze. It warmed him and he lusted after more of that feeling. He needed innocence around him. And yet he could only sully it, he reminded himself. But he hadn't meant to frighten her, and it didn't hurt to take a moment to reassure her now.

'You're not such a baddy, are you?' she said to his surprise.

In spite of his self-control his lips twitched as he shrugged. A *baddy*? He had to curb the urge to smile. He'd shut himself off from all that was soft and feminine for too long. Living life by his own very masculine rules and preferences, he hadn't been called upon to take anyone else's feelings into account for quite some time. And a woman like Savannah's? Never. 'A baddy,' he repeated. 'I've never been called that before.'

It was as if she saw him differently from everyone else on the planet. He smiled. He couldn't help himself. Paying close attention to the river, he didn't look at her, but he knew that she was smiling too.

No sooner had he begun to soften towards Savannah than he reverted to coldly examining the facts. Did he need this sort of distraction in his life? Savannah was very young and had a lot of growing up to do. Did he want the attention of the world centred on him, when he'd successfully avoided publicity for so long? He'd gone to the match with the sole intention of supporting his friends in the England squad, and it was them who should be getting the attention, not him. He felt a stab of something reprehensible, and recognised it as envy. The days when he'd hoped to play rugby for England weren't so far away, but the past could never be recaptured. He had learned to adapt and change direction since then; he'd moved on. But the facts remained: the injuries he'd sustained during a prolonged beating by a gang of thugs had meant the club doctors had been unable to sign the insurance documents he needed to play his part in the professional game. And so his career had come to an abrupt and unwanted end.

But none of this was Savannah's fault. He might be drawn to her, but he wouldn't taint her with his darkness. He would fight the attraction he felt for her. Some might say he needed a woman like Savannah to soften him, but he knew that the last thing Savannah needed in her life was a man like him.

'I'm sorry you've missed the match, Ethan.'

The river was quieter here and he cut the engines. 'Don't worry about it. I'll watch the replay on television later.'

'But you can't detect the scent of excitement on a screen,' she said with concern.

Or feel the ravages of failure, the blaze of triumph… Yes, he knew that, but he was surprised Savannah did. 'It's no big deal.'

'Yes it is,' she said, pulling a face that made him think

how pretty she was. 'You'd be there now if it wasn't for me.' Frowning with concern, she began plucking threads from his ancient shirt.

He didn't prolong the exchange. He didn't like people getting close to him. He was a bear licking his wounds in the shadows, full of unresolved conflict and bitterness, and chose not to inflict himself on anyone—least of all an innocent young girl like Savannah.

'Watching England play must be both a passion and a torment for you.'

Why wouldn't she let it rest?

'Perhaps,' he agreed, accepting she meant no harm by these comments and was only trying to make conversation. It was public knowledge that the damage to his spine had ended his career. Lifting he could do, running he could do, but to risk another knock, another blow…

'You could let me off here, if it's quicker for you.'

He followed her gaze to a nearby landing stage. 'I could let you swim to the far bank,' he offered dryly. 'That might save some time.'

Her expression lifted, which pleased him. He didn't want to intimidate her, though his appearance must have done that already. Mooring up and calling a cab to take her to the airport was what he should do. He should let her go.

But the decision was taken out of his hands by the sound of rotor blades. The paparazzi's helicopter was still some way off, but it was approaching fast. There was no time to do anything more than hit the throttle and tell Savannah to hold on.

'They've found us?' she shouted above the roar of the engines.

Oh, yes. The race was back on. And no way was he going to let them catch her. 'Yes, they've found us,' he confirmed grimly. 'Sit tight.'

The spray was in her hair, her eyes, and her knuckles had turned white with holding on. If she'd been nervous before, she was terrified now. It was one thing showing a brave face to the world when things were going well, but the black, menacing shadow of the paparazzi helicopter would soon beam a travesty of the true situation around the world. Adding fuel to the paparazzi's fire, she was forced to cling to Ethan as he pushed the powerboat to its limits, because he was the only stable element in a world that was tipping and yawing as the currents played bat and ball with their hull.

Nothing had gone right for Ethan since she'd turned up in Rome, Savannah thought guiltily, and though he hardly knew her he had insisted on fighting her corner in spite of the personal cost to him. He must be wondering what he'd done to deserve such aggravation!

CHAPTER FIVE

As A surge of water threw the delicately balanced boat off kilter, Ethan fastened his arm protectively around Savannah's shoulders. At first she tensed, but then slowly relaxed. Ethan had no idea how profoundly his protective instinct affected her. Coming from a man as cold as he was, his smallest touch bore the intensity of a kiss. She could get used to this physical closeness all too easily. But they would soon reach the airport, she would fly home, and she would be nothing more than a tiresome memory to him. But at least the helicopter was wheeling away. 'Fuel shortage?' she suggested hopefully.

'I think you're being a little over-optimistic,' Ethan said as he powered back the engines. 'My best guess is they got the photographs they came for and their work is done.'

'How can you be so calm about it? Don't you care?'

'I don't waste time regretting things that can't be changed.'

'But they breached your privacy. Won't you make some sort of protest?'

Her heart jolted to see Ethan's lips tug in a smile. 'I hope you're not suggesting I should try to curb the freedom of the press?'

'Of course not, but.'

'But?' he pressed.

'Well, I just can't roll over.'

'You don't have to,' he pointed out. 'It's happened and I'll deal with it.'

'Okay, well, my parents are going to be devastated. What if the press are there right now, hammering on their door? Ethan, I have to call them.'

He couldn't imagine anyone else on earth in this predicament thinking of placing an international call, but he was fast learning that Savannah's first thought was always for others, and he envied the loving relationship she obviously enjoyed with her parents and would never stand in the way of it. 'I'll speak to them first to reassure them, and then you can speak,' he suggested, warming to her.

'Would you really do that?'

Her relief made him think he should have done it sooner. 'Number?'

As she recited it he punched it in to his mobile phone, and it occurred to him that Savannah must have no idea how lucky she was to have a loving family.

'You didn't have to do that,' she said several minutes later when she had finished speaking to her mother.

'I wanted to,' he admitted. 'It was the right thing to do,' he added sternly when Savannah's face softened into a smile.

'It was very kind of you.'

'It was nothing,' he argued, turning his attention back to sailing the boat. 'All I did was point out that my legal team will handle any press intrusion, and reassure your parents that they mustn't worry because you were safe with me.'

'You gave them your private number.'

'How else are they supposed to call me?'

'Well, thank you,' she said sincerely.

'Your mother seemed reassured,' he said, unbending a little. His reward was to see Savannah's face softening into a smile.

Her mother had been reassured, Savannah reflected with relief. Her romantic mother had always been a sucker for a strong man, though she preferred them safely corralled on the cover of a book or on a screen at the cinema, and kept a well-trained beta hero at home. She wondered if her mother would be quite so reassured if she could see Ethan in the flesh.

'I have another call to make,' Ethan told her, turning away.

As Ethan stood in profile his scars were cruelly exposed, and it appalled her to think one person could do that to another. But surely it couldn't have been one person—it had to have been more—a gang, maybe? She'd felt a fraction of Ethan's strength today and he was bigger, stronger and fitter than most men. What kamikaze group of yobs would have dared to take him on?

Trained yobs—professional thugs, truly evil men—was the only conclusion she could possibly come to. No casual attack could result in such serious injuries. But who would pay such men to beat Ethan so severely he'd nearly lost his life and *had* lost his sporting career? Professional rugby might be a highly competitive sport, but it was hardly a killing ground.

As Ethan finished his call and stowed the phone, turning the wheel to negotiate a bend in the river, Savannah was wondering if the person behind Ethan's beating also accounted for the darkness in his eyes. If so Ethan carried far more scars than were visible to the naked eye. 'Are we going to the airport?' she said, noticing he was steering the boat towards a tributary.

'To the airport first, and then to my place in Tuscany—just until the heat dies down.'

'To Tuscany?' She was feeling more out of her depth than ever.

'Unless you'd prefer me to leave you to the mercy of the press?'

Savannah's heart turned over as Ethan looked at her. How childish he must think her. Women would scratch each other's eyes out for the chance to be with Ethan like this, and yet she had sounded so apprehensive at the prospect of staying with him. 'I don't want to be left to that pack of hounds,' she confessed. 'But I've put you out so much already.'

'So a little more trouble won't hurt me,' Ethan reassured her dryly.

Maybe his lack of enthusiasm didn't match up with her fantasies, but what Ethan had suggested was a sensible solution. And his place in Tuscany sounded so romantic—such a pity it would be wasted on them. 'Are you sure it wouldn't be easier for you if I just fly home?'

'If you do that you won't be able to take advantage of the security I can provide. It would take me quite some time to get the same level of protection set up for you in England, which is why I've made some arrangements for your parents.'

'Arrangements? What arrangements?' Savannah interrupted anxiously.

'I decided a cruise would take them well out of the range of prying eyes.'

'A cruise?' She gasped. 'Are you serious?'

'Why wouldn't I be serious?'

'You mean you booked a holiday for them?'

'It's the best solution I could come up with,' he said, as if booking fabulously expensive trips was nothing unusual for him.

Savannah couldn't stop smiling. 'You have no idea what this will mean to them. I can't remember the last time they went away—or even if they ever have been away from the farm.'

'The farm?'

'I live on a farm.' She shook her head, full of excitement. 'You must have seen my address on file?'

'Lots of addresses have the word "farm" in them. It doesn't mean a thing.'

'Well, in this instance it means a great deal,' she assured him, turning serious. Savannah's voice had dropped and emotion hung like a curtain between them, a curtain Ethan swiftly brushed aside.

'Well, I'm pleased I've made the appropriate arrangements.'

'Oh, you have,' Savannah said softly, thinking of all the times she'd wished she could have sent her exhausted parents away for a break, but she had never had the money to do so. Their grief when they'd lost their herd of dairy cows to disease had exacted a terrible toll, and they'd only survived it thanks to the support of the wonderful people who worked alongside them. Those same people would stand in for them now, allowing them to take the holiday they deserved.

'You've no idea what you've done for them,' Savannah assured Ethan.

He brushed off her thanks, as Savannah had known he would. But because of his generosity she thought he deserved to be wholly in the picture, and so she told him

how her parents had stood by and watched their whole
herd being slaughtered—animals they'd known by name.

'That must have cost you all dearly,' he observed,
looking at her closely. 'And not just in financial terms.'

It was a rare moment between them, but Ethan scarcely
gave her a chance to enjoy it before switching back to
practicalities. He treated emotion like an enemy that must
be fought off at every turn, Savannah thought as Ethan
told her that her bags would probably arrive at the *palazzo*
before she did.

'Just a minute,' she said, interrupting him. 'Did you say
"the *palazzo*"?' Of all the day's surprises, this was the
biggest. Ethan had just turned all her points of reference
on their head. As far as Savannah was concerned, a
palazzo was somewhere people who existed on another
planet lived.

'There are a lot of *palazzos* in Tuscany,' Ethan explained, as if it were nothing, but as Savannah continued
to stare incredulously at him he finally admitted, 'Okay,
so I've got a very nice place in Tuscany.'

'You're a very lucky man,' she told him frankly.

In the light of what Savannah had just told him about
her parents' hardships, he had no doubt that was true. At
least they'd be able to put plenty of space between each
other at the *palazzo*, he reminded himself thankfully.

'Tell me about your *palazzo*.'

Finding he was staring at her lips as she spoke, he
turned away. 'Later,' he said, relieved to see his driver
waiting exactly where he had asked him to, by the landing
stage. He waved to the man as he cut the engines and
allowed the powerboat to glide into shore. 'We'll disem-
bark first, and then I'll tell you more about it when we're
on my jet.'

But she was back on the ground and in the back of a second limousine before Ethan turned to answer her questions.

'The name of the *palazzo*?' he resumed, leaning over from the front seat where he sat next to the driver. 'The Palazzo dei Tramonti Dorati.'

'That's quite a name.' Savannah laughed as she tried to say it, stumbling over the unfamiliar Italian words, acutely conscious as she did so that Ethan was watching her lips move.

'Not bad,' he said, congratulating her on her accent.

'What does it mean?' Savannah found that she badly wanted to hold Ethan's attention.

'It means "the Palace of the Golden Sunset".'

He hadn't meant to enter into conversation with her, but how could he not when she glowed with pleasure at the smallest thing? It reminded him, of course, of how very young she was, but even so he couldn't subdue the urge to tell her about a home he loved above all his others.

'It sounds so romantic!' she exclaimed, her eyes turning dreamy.

'Yes, it's a very old and very beautiful building.' He knew he was being drawn in, but he would never forget his first sight of the *palazzo*, and he'd had no one to share it with before. 'The towers glow rose-pink at sunset,' he explained, though he left out the emotional angle, which had entailed a longing to own the ancient *palazzo* that had come from the depths of his soul.

'The *palazzo* is located in a glorious valley blessed with sunlight, and the medieval village surrounding it is inhabited by wonderful people who appreciate the simple things in life.' And who had taken him to their heart, he remembered with gratitude. As he tried to convey something of this passion to Savannah without becoming overly sentimental, she remained silent and alert, as if what he didn't say told her everything she needed to know.

She confirmed this, saying softly when he had finished, 'You're even luckier than I thought.'

'Yes, well…' He left the statement hanging, feeling he'd gone too far. He wasn't a man to brag about his possessions, or even mention them.

Ethan was full of surprises. His sensitivity was obvious once he started talking about the *palazzo*. He flew planes, he rode bikes, he drove powerboats, and he had a perfect command of the Italian language. The thought that he did everything well and was capable of such passion sent a frisson of arousal shimmering through her.

Which she would put a stop to right away! Savannah's sensible inner voice commanded. It was one thing to fantasise about sexual encounters with Ethan, but quite another to consider the reality of it when she was saving her virginity for some sensible, 'steady Eddie' type of bloke, and then only when they were married.

'Are you too warm?' Ethan asked, misreading the flush that rose to her cheeks as she moved restlessly on the seat. 'I can easily adjust the temperature for you.'

Savannah bit her lip to hide her smile.

'What's so funny?' he demanded suspiciously.

What was so funny? Ethan was the man most women had voted to go to bed with, and she was the woman most men had decided not to go to bed with—that was funny, wasn't it?

'I asked you a question, Savannah.'

The easy atmosphere that had so briefly existed between them had suddenly gained an edge.

'Is it my scars?' he pressed. 'Do they make you nervous?'

Ethan had read her all wrong, Savannah realised. He was so far off the mark, she shook her head in shock. 'Of course they don't.' It was no use, because Ethan wasn't listening.

'Is that why you're trying so hard not to laugh?' he demanded.

'I've told you, no!' She held his gaze. There must be no doubt over this. She would be the first to admit she was overawed by Ethan, and that he even frightened her a little, but those feelings were all tied up in his worldliness contrasted with her own inexperienced sexual-self, and had not the slightest connection with his scars. If he thought she was shallow enough to be intimidated by them… Savannah shook her head with disgust at the thought. As far as she was concerned, Ethan's terrible scars were just a reminder that even the strongest tree could be felled. 'I see the man, not the scars,' she told him bluntly.

In the confines of the limousine his short, disbelieving laugh sounded cruel and hard.

That had to come from some memory in his past, Savannah reassured herself, refusing to rise to the bait. Sometimes it was better to say nothing, she was learning, and to persuade Ethan she was more than the fluffy girl he thought her would take action, not words. She had been raised on a working farm and knew the value of hard work. She was used to getting her hands dirty and wasn't frightened of much.

Just as well, Savannah reflected as Ethan turned away with a face like thunder to continue his conversation with the driver, because there was nothing easy about Ethan Alexander. But whatever Ethan's opinion of her, she would stand up for herself. Perhaps he had learned that much about her. If nothing else this journey was giving them both the opportunity to learn a little more about each other. What she'd learned might not be reassuring, but it hadn't put her off Ethan either—in fact, quite the reverse.

CHAPTER SIX

As THEY approached the end of the journey they sat in silence, and Ethan could sense Savannah's unease. For all her excitement at the thought of seeing his *palazzo*, she was wondering what she had got herself into. He had always been intuitive. His mother had told him he was keenly tuned, close to the earth and all its mystery. She'd told him that before the crystal sphere she'd kept next to her bed told her to marry for the fourth time, apparently. At seven years old he had begged her not to do it, believing it would be a disastrous move for his mother and for himself. She had ignored him and the marriage had been a disaster. So much for his mother's belief in his special powers. The beatings had begun the day his new 'daddy' had arrived back from their honeymoon. He'd gone away to school that September, and had been the only boy in his class relieved to be living away from home.

And why was he remembering that now? He moved so that Savannah was no longer in his eyeline in the mirror. Was it because for the first time since his rugby career had been ended he wished he could be unblemished inside and out? Was it because Savannah Ross was too innocent to know the ugliness inside him?

Realising he was only paying attention to half the things his driver was telling him, he made some token comment and started watching Savannah again. She looked so small and vulnerable, sitting all alone on a sea of cream leather. The Bentley was the right scale for a man his size, but she was dwarfed by it. And she was a distraction he couldn't afford, he warned himself, especially if he was going to remain aloof from her when they reached their destination.

Stately cypress groves provided a lush green counterpoint to the rolling fields of Tuscany, and with the sun burning low in a cobalt sky Savannah wondered if there might be enough beauty here to distract her from her main obsession—but her main obsession turned at that moment to speak to her.

'We'll be arriving at the *palazzo* at the perfect time.'

'Sunset,' Savannah guessed. A thrill of excitement overtook her fear that Ethan had not forgotten or forgiven her for the earlier misunderstanding. As the light faded his face was in shadow, so she couldn't see his expression to gauge his mood, but there was something here that had lifted it—his *palazzo*, she suspected. Following the direction in which he was looking she searched hungrily for her first sight of the building. The sky was a vibrant palette of tangerine and violet so dramatic, so stunningly beautiful, she had butterflies in her stomach at the thought of what might come next. She could sense Ethan was also buzzing with expectation, and try as he might to be stern all the time, an attractive crease had appeared in his face. He'd softened just a little. Now if he could only soften a little more and smile at her that would be a gift—the only gift she wanted.

'When we cross the river, you'll see the *palazzo* in this direction.'

As Ethan pointed towards the shadowy purple hills, she sat bolt upright, tense with expectation.

'I don't want you to miss the approach,' he said, seeing her interest. 'It's quite spectacular.'

'I won't,' she assured him as anticipation fluttered in her stomach. Something told her that this was one of those precious moments that would mean something all her life and must be cherished.

She was only half right, Savannah discovered. When it came into view the *palazzo* exceeded her expectations so far it took her breath away. Rising like something out of a legend from the mist was a winding road and an old stone bridge, and then the towering walls. A glittering snake of water travelled beneath the bridge, and as they crossed it she thought the restless eddies were like mirrored scales carrying the sun-fire to the sea.

'Now you understand why the palazzo got its name.'

Even Ethan couldn't quite keep the excitement from his voice.

'Understatement,' she breathed. The turreted spread of the Palazzo dei Tramonti Dorati appeared framed in fire, and even her fertile imagination hadn't come close to doing it justice. This wasn't the Gothic horror she'd feared Ethan might inhabit, but a palace of light, built from pink stone that might have been sugar-rock. Glowing warm beneath the red-streaked sky, it couldn't have appeared more welcoming.

'What do you think?' Ethan prompted.

Savannah was surprised her opinion mattered to him, and the thought touched her immensely—though she mustn't read too much into it, she reminded herself. 'I think it's stunning,' she told him honestly. 'The colour of the stone is extraordinary.'

'Pink?'

The touch of irony in his voice made her smile. Were they connecting at last? Just a little, maybe? But she wasn't going to push it. 'You must admit, it's unusual,' she said, trying to sound grown up about it, though the prospect of staying in a pink palace, and one as beautiful as this, would have excited anyone.

'The stone is pink because millions of years ago this whole valley was a deep marine-gulf,' Ethan explained. 'The pink hue is due to the millions of tiny shells and fossils locked in the rocks.'

'What a magical explanation.' And romantic, Savannah mused as Ethan settled back to enjoy the last leg of the journey. He might fight as hard as he could to keep his distance from her, but he had brought her to one of the most romantic places on earth. Ethan might shun everything pink or soft or feminine, but he'd let his guard down by showing her his *palazzo*. 'The Palace of the Golden Sunset,' she murmured happily as the limousine made a smooth transition from slick tarmac to the winding cobbled streets.

'Can you see the fragments of the original walls?' Ethan said, turning towards her again.

His enthusiasm was framed in a scholarly tone, but he was clearly determined to share this with her, and he didn't need to tell her how much he loved his *palazzo* when she could feel his passion like a warm cloak embracing her. 'Yes, I see them,' she said, pressing her face to the window. In some places there was little more than raised ground to show where the original walls must have stood, but at others she could see what remained of them.

They looked like blackened silhouettes pointing crooked fingers towards the blazing sky.

'Much of the structure dates from medieval times,' Ethan continued.

Like the thinking of its master? Savannah wondered. What would it take to have Ethan see her as a grown woman rather than as a singing sensation recently signed to his record label? And was she sure she wanted him to think about her that way? Wasn't it safer to remain as she was—a ward under his protection?

It was beyond the scope of Savannah's imagination to conjure up the consequences of attracting the sexual attentions of a man like Ethan, and as the limousine slowed to pass beneath a narrow stone archway she told herself how lucky it was that this was only destined to be a short stay. Any longer and she'd definitely fall in love with him.

The paparazzi would soon find another story and she'd be able to return home. But if she was so confident about that, why was she wracked by shivers of anticipation at the prospect of staying with Ethan?

Because she was tired, Savannah told herself firmly. Who could blame her for feeling uncomfortable with what lay ahead when she was pinned into a dress that felt more like a medieval torture-device than a couture gown?

'This gateway is called the Porta Monteguzzo.'

She paid attention as Ethan distracted her, and was about to answer him when, embarrassingly, her stomach growled.

'Hungry?' he prompted.

'I'm starving,' Savannah admitted, wondering when she had last eaten. And did she dare to eat when another crumb of food on her hips meant she would definitely pop out of Madame's gown and she had no clothes of her own to wear yet? 'Porta Monteguzzo,' she repeated, both in an attempt to distract herself from hunger pangs and to try again to master the musical Italian language. 'Doesn't "*guzzo*" mean "food", in Italian?'

'You're thinking of gusto, perhaps?'

She watched his mouth, thinking how well he spoke the language…amongst other things.

'Which means taste,' Ethan explained.

Or tasty, perhaps, Savannah mused as she turned to stare innocently out of the window while Ethan resumed his conversation in fluent Italian with their driver. But as they drove deeper into Ethan territory and the world he dominated, and those tall, stone walls of his stole the light, Savannah knew that, though the sight of Ethan's fairy-tale castle had thrilled her beyond belief, it had singularly failed to reassure her.

Oh.

Savannah's heart sank as she stood in the hallway of the *palazzo*. It was a struggle to marry up the exquisite exterior with this dismal space. Wasn't it wired for electricity? She could hardly make out the faces of Ethan's staff as he showed her round.

Okay, so maybe that was a slight exaggeration, but the inside of the palace was like something out of a gothic horror film—'dark and dismal' didn't even begin to cover it. It might just as well have been lit by candlelight, it was so shadowy and grim. To say she was disappointed after the stunning run-up to the building was a major understatement. But she was more concerned about the fact that Ethan chose to live like this.

As the housekeeper led the way up the marble staircase, Savannah's apprehension grew. Apart from the very real risk of missing her footing on the dimly lit staircase, the landing they were heading for appeared equally dingy. To go from fairy-tale *palazzo* to the haunted house was a huge disappointment. She only had to contrast Ethan's grand *palazzo* with her parents' simple farmhouse to know there was no contest: she'd prefer the sunny chaos of the farmhouse to this grand grimness any day.

Perhaps she should offer a few home-improvement tips, Savannah concluded as the housekeeper indicated they should follow her down a darkened corridor. 'Don't you worry about your staff tripping over the rugs?' She took the chance to whisper discreetly to Ethan.

'I can't say it's ever occurred to me,' he said with surprise.

'It would occur to me,' Savannah said worriedly as the housekeeper stopped outside a carved-oak door. 'What if someone was carrying a tray with hot drinks on it, or some glasses, and they tripped? They could really hurt themselves, Ethan. This is dangerous. There's hardly any light here at all.'

'No one's ever complained before.'

She knew she should hold her tongue, but it was about time someone did complain, Savannah thought, and Ethan's staff was hardly likely to.

The more she thought about it, the more Savannah became convinced that she must be one of Ethan's first guests at the *palazzo* in a long time. She wasn't sure exactly what she'd been expecting from a man known to be reclusive, but this was hardly the big, open house her family would have filled with light and laughter. She smiled as she thought of the cosy farmhouse back home with its rickety furniture and frayed old rugs, but it was a hundred times more welcoming than this.

The housekeeper was smiling at her expectantly, Savannah realised, quickly refocusing and smiling back.

Ethan was shifting restlessly, as if he couldn't understand the delay before the housekeeper got round to opening a door. But Savannah understood perfectly when the housekeeper finally revealed her surprise.

'*Signorina*, this is your room.'

Savannah didn't need to see the older woman's beaming smile to know that someone was keen to make her feel welcome. 'My room?' Savannah stood on the threshold, gazing in wonder. 'You did this for me?' The contrast between this well-lit space and the rest of the *palazzo* was incredible. No wonder the housekeeper had revealed her surprise with such a flourish.

'You're too generous.' But as Savannah looked at Ethan she realised he was as surprised as she was. He'd had nothing to do with it. His staff had done all this for her. They must have thrown open every window to air the room, and they had certainly lit every available light. There was a log fire blazing in the hearth, which illuminated all the beautiful old oil-paintings, and there were fresh flowers everywhere, beaming a rainbow welcome at her. 'Thank you; thank you so much!' she exclaimed, turning to grasp the housekeeper's hands.

'You bring us music, *signorina*, but all we can bring you in return is flowers.'

'What do you mean "all"?' Savannah exclaimed. 'This means everything to me.'

Tears stung her eyes as she remembered this was the sort of thing her family did for each other at home. The housekeeper had given her the one thing money couldn't buy, and that was a genuine welcome. Conscious of Ethan standing at her side, and knowing how difficult he found dealing with displays of emotion, she expressed her feelings more calmly to him. 'This is wonderful, isn't it?

You have great people working for you. I hope you appreciate them.'

He would think her presumptuous, Savannah realised, though she could read nothing on Ethan's face. But she had to say something, because his staff had carved an oasis of light and beauty for her from his cold, dark *palazzo*, and now she was eager to do the same for him.

He was shocked by his staff's initiative. All he'd done was call ahead to explain the situation to them and ask them to make a room ready for Savannah Ross. He should have known the Italians' great love of music meant they would already know everything about Savannah, and that it would have put wings on their heels when they learned he was bringing her to stay.

As his gaze embraced the room before him, he began noticing things he hadn't before, like the pink-veined, marble-topped console table where the telephone rested. He had bought it with the *palazzo*, and it was a beautiful example of a craftsman's art. Savannah was right; with the light shining on it, the furniture, like everything else in the room, was fully revealed in all its glory. No wonder she had been so relieved to see the efforts his staff had gone to for her. But the real difference here was Savannah, he thought, watching her shimmering golden hair bounce around her shoulders as she followed the housekeeper around the room. Savannah brought the light with her.

With emotions roused that he had thought were long buried, Ethan was suddenly keen to put some distance between them, so he found an excuse to leave Savannah in the care of his housekeeper. But she stubbornly refused to let him disappear so easily. 'I'm so excited,' she told him. 'I can't thank you enough for allowing me to stay here.'

'Then don't. This is nothing to do with me.' He dismissed the glowing room with a gesture.

'You're so wrong,' she assured him. 'This has everything to do with you.'

He shrugged. 'In this instance, Savannah, it is you who is wrong. This is a beautiful suite of rooms and nothing more. It has been aired and put back into use, and that is all.'

'And is that all you have to say about it?' she demanded, frowning.

'What else is there to say? I rarely come here, but it is beautiful, and I had forgotten.'

'But you never will forget again,' she insisted passionately. 'Not now the lights have been switched on.'

He gave her a look that stopped her in her tracks. It was a look intended to warn her not to go this far again. The contact between them was electric, and he let the moment hang for some reason. Anything might have happened as Savannah looked up at him had not his housekeeper coughed discreetly at that moment. It was only then that the rational side of him clicked into focus, and he took a proper look at Savannah and realised how exhausted she looked. She was still wearing his old shirt over the ill-fitting gown. She must have felt embarrassed, dressed that way when he'd introduced her to his staff, but not for a moment had she let it show. Her attention had been all on them, her only thought to make them feel special. 'Could you bring Ms Ross a robe, please?' he asked his housekeeper.

He wanted Savannah covered up. Her pale skin beneath the neck of his shirt was making him restless. She still had her precious sandals dangling from her wrist, like a child with a garish bangle, and she was scarcely taller than a child. She couldn't have eaten since that morning, he remembered. 'Take a bath,' he said briskly, 'And then use that phone over there to call down for something to eat.'

'Won't you eat something too?' she asked with concern.

'Maybe.' He dismissed her with a gesture. He had no intention of prolonging this encounter. It occurred to him then that perhaps he didn't trust himself to prolong it.

'Where will you eat?' she pressed as he prepared to leave.

He hadn't given it a moment's thought. 'I'll take dinner in my room,' he said, remembering that that was what he usually did.

'In your room?' She pulled a face, and then immediately grew contrite. 'Sorry. It's none of my business where you eat.'

No, it isn't, he almost informed her, thinking of her other comments since they'd arrived, but the fact that she looked so pale held him back.

Fortunately his housekeeper returned at that moment with the robe, which put a halt to further conversation.

He took that as his cue. 'Goodnight, Savannah. Sleep well.'

'I'll see you in the morning?' Her eyes were wide, her expression frank.

'Perhaps.' With her innocent enthusiasm she made it hard for him to remain distant.

'For breakfast?' she pressed.

'Ah…' He paused with his hand on the door, as if to say he was a much older man with many better things to do than to entertain a young woman. 'We'll see.'

'Sleep well, Ethan. And thank you once again for allowing me to stay in your beautiful home.'

Who should be thanking who? he wondered, catching

sight of the luminous expression on his housekeeper's face. 'Goodnight, Savannah.' He didn't need a second dose of Savannah's radiant face before he walked out and closed the door to know his defences had been breached.

CHAPTER SEVEN

SAVANNAH waited for Ethan's footsteps to fade before asking the housekeeper shyly, 'Do you think it would be possible to put on some more lights?' The housekeeper had been so kind to her that Savannah felt her request might have some chance of success.

'More lights, *signorina*?'

'In the *palazzo*? I mean, it's very dark outside my room, and I just thought it might be safer for you—for all of us.'

The housekeeper studied Savannah's face before deciding. 'Come with me, *signorina*.'

As they left the room together the housekeeper called to a passing footman, who looked at Savannah with surprise when he heard her request via the housekeeper. As he hurried away, the housekeeper exchanged a look with Savannah. 'You are starting a revolution,' she confided.

'Oh dear.'

'No, it's good.'

'Is it?' If only she could feel confident that Ethan would agree.

Savannah approached the first light-switch.

It took all of her resolve just to switch it on. But when she did…

'*Bellissima!*' The housekeeper exclaimed, clasping her hands in front of her. 'This is what the *palazzo* has been waiting for.'

Her endorsement encouraged Savannah to ask if they could put a few more lights on.

The housekeeper drew in a breath and then, exhaling slowly, she turned to look at Savannah. Her eyes were sparkling. 'A very few,' she agreed. 'Let's do it!'

They hurried off in different directions, snapping on light switches like naughty children, and they didn't stop until the whole of the upper floor was flooded with light.

Down in the hallway Savannah could see more lights being turned on. It was like the curtain going up at the theatre, she concluded, feeling that same sense of wonder—but the only difference here was a glorious home was being revealed rather than a stage set.

The housekeeper rendezvoused with Savannah back at her room. 'It's amazing!' Savannah exclaimed softly, gazing at the transformation they'd created.

'*Si, signorina.* You have worked a miracle.'

'A very tiny miracle,' Savannah argued with a smile. 'I only turned on the lights.'

'Sometimes that's all it takes,' the older woman observed shrewdly.

They shared a smile before the housekeeper left Savannah, after asking her to promise she would call downstairs if she needed anything more.

Well, she would need all the friends she could find on the staff, if she stood a chance of leaving Ethan's home happier than she had found it, Savannah reflected. But with all his beautiful treasures bathed in light she had to believe he would share her enthusiasm for ancient frescoes stepping out of the shadows, and carvings revealed in all their intricate detail after years of neglect.

But…would he be pleased, or would he be angry at her continued interference? She was only a guest, after all, and one that wasn't here for very long. She suspected she knew why Ethan avoided light, but her concern was for the main thoroughfares where safety was an issue. The more intimate areas like Ethan's rooms could remain discreetly lit. She could only hope he would agree it was a happy balance.

Deep inside, Savannah believed everyone needed light. And as for the *palazzo*, well, she'd already seen the results of the transformation Ethan's staff had brought about in her rooms, and their instincts were right. There should be light, love and music in such a beautiful home. There should be life at the *palazzo*.

Savannah took a long, soapy bath. Now the excitement was over, she realised how hungry she was, and until supper arrived a bath was the perfect distraction from hunger pangs as well as from the likely repercussions of her interference in Ethan's home.

Twiddling the taps with her toes, she sank a little lower in the fragrant bubbles. This story might not have a happy-ever-after ending, but she had fairy-tale accommodation for the night, and after the staff had gone to so much trouble it would have been churlish for her to refuse the setting they had prepared.

She had rifled through the full-sized luxury products on the glass shelves like a small child in a beauty salon, and now the scent rising from the steam had led her into a dream world of erotic images in which Ethan starred…

Wrapped up cosily in a warm robe some time later, she

stared into the mirror. It was so easy to imagine Ethan's dark face when she saw him in the shadows everywhere she went. It was torture, knowing he was somewhere close by, and almost impossible not to imagine him stripped and naked beneath an ice-cold shower. It would be cold water, because warm was too indulgent for him. And his bedroom would be spartan, she decided, because Ethan denied himself anything soft or superfluous— which didn't leave her with too much hope, Savannah concluded wistfully.

Rubbing her hair vigorously, she walked back into the bedroom. Kneeling in front of the fire to dry her long hair, she thought about Ethan's complex character. All he seemed to need was a clean bed and a floor to pace— perhaps with the addition of a giant television-screen in every room to catch up on any rugby matches he might have missed. Perhaps it was the legacy of those dreadful scars that made him so careless of his own comfort.

Thinking about them always made her so angry. Casting the towel aside, she began to pluck distractedly at the rug. Who would do that to him? Who could do that to a fellow human being?

Why don't you ask him? Savannah's inner voice prompted.

Because life isn't that simple?

But it could be, if she went to him, and spoke to him…

Rolling onto her back, Savannah stared up at the ornate plasterwork. All the *palazzo* could be like this, cared for and fully restored, and always welcoming. Or it could remain cold and full of shadows. How lonely it must be to live in the dark.

Sitting bolt upright, Savannah hugged her knees and, resting her chin, she stared into the fire. It didn't have to be like this if someone changed it around—if she changed it around. An impossible task, perhaps, but not if she had the help of Ethan's staff. Even this gleaming fireguard, polished to a flawless sheen, was evidence of their care for him. They had to be as keen as she was to see the *palazzo* come back to life.

Impatient with inaction, she sprang up. She hardly knew where she was going, but as she crossed the room her spirits lifted. It was such a glorious ultra-feminine space it must have given Ethan a headache just to poke his head round the door. Everything that wasn't gilded or twinkling glass was covered in silk, satins or velvet, and all in the most exquisite pastel colours. Stretching out her arms, she turned full circle, thinking it the most appealing space she had ever inhabited. She was still smiling broadly when she reached the door and opened it. 'Ethan!'

'Savannah.'

She knew immediately from his voice that Ethan was furious. She felt instantly guilty, as well as silly and awkward, standing barefoot in front of him in her towelling robe. Her lips trembled and her smile died instantly.

'What have you done?' he snapped.

Her gaze slid away. 'I was taking a bath.'

'You know I don't mean that.'

Savannah drew her robe a little closer, conscious that Ethan's stare was boring into her, demanding an answer.

'I mean the lights,' he explained. 'I take it you're responsible?'

'Yes, I switched them on. Please don't be angry with your staff, Ethan.' She touched his arm. 'It was all my fault. I did it for them, for you.'

'For me? For them? What is this nonsense?'

Tears were threatening. She had been so looking

forward to sharing this moment with him, Savannah realised, and now it had all gone wrong. Far from wanting light, Ethan craved the darkness to hide his scars. She should have known and not been so insensitive. In trying to help him she had arrogantly assumed she was right, only seeing the world from her own perspective. And now he couldn't wait to turn those lights off, or for her to leave. 'I'm so sorry—'

'You'll have to leave,' he said, perfectly echoing her thoughts. 'I can't have this sort of interference. Please pack your bags.'

'Ethan—'

'There's nothing more to say, Savannah.'

'But it's nighttime. Where will I go?'

'A hotel, the airport, somewhere—I don't care.'

'You're throwing me out?'

'Save your melodrama for the stage.'

'Says you, living in the dark!' She couldn't believe she'd said that. But it was true. She was fighting for Ethan, and where that was concerned nothing she said was going too far. But as Ethan's stony stare raked her face, Savannah realised he didn't see it that way.

'Will you pack?' he said coldly, confirming her worst fears. 'Or must I call the housekeeper to do that for you?'

'Ethan, please.' It was no use. He'd closed off to her.

As he shook Savannah's hand from his arm, he saw her tears and his heart ignored the dictates of his head.

'Please don't be angry with your housekeeper,' she entreated, adding to the conflict boiling inside him. 'You must know this is all my fault.'

Every bit of it was Savannah's fault…or her blessing. He turned his back so he wouldn't have to look into her face, but still he felt her goodness washing over him. She wouldn't stop until all the bitterness was cleaned away. She touched his arm, begging him. 'You've gone too far,' he growled, wanting even now to protect her from that black evil inside him.

She didn't argue, and instead she did something far worse: she confessed.

'You're right,' she said frankly. 'I interfered where I shouldn't have. This is your home, Ethan, not mine. I asked your staff to turn on some lights so it was safer for them, and for you. I can see I went too far with that plan when one or two lights would have been sufficient, and if you want me to leave I will. All I ask is your promise that you won't blame your staff for my thoughtless actions.'

He didn't need to see any more tears to know that Savannah was at her most vulnerable. Yet she fought on in the defence of others. He couldn't ignore that. Her appeal had touched him deeply in a way he hadn't felt, maybe, ever. He was still wondering how best to deal with this unusual situation when the housekeeper Savannah was at such pains to defend came unwittingly to their rescue.

'Something to eat, *signore, signorina*?' she said blithely when Savannah opened the door to her knock.

What perfect timing, Savannah thought, exhaling with relief as she smiled at her new friend. As her shoulders relaxed she quickly adapted her manner so as not to concern the older woman. 'Let me take that tray from you.'

'No, please, let me.' Ethan's innate good manners meant he had to step forward in front of Savannah to take the tray himself.

'Thank you, *signore*,' the housekeeper said politely, handing Ethan the tray without any sign that she had overheard their heated exchange. 'I've made enough for two.'

Hmm, Savannah thought, realising Ethan had no other option other than to carry the tray into her room. 'Let me clear a space for you,' she said, hurrying ahead of him.

To give her a moment to regroup, she rushed about, hunting for her slippers. Ethan placed the tray down on the low table between the two sofas and remained standing.

This was one consequence she could not avoid.

By the time she had found her slippers and slipped them on, she could hardly breathe, let alone speak as she came to a halt in front of Ethan.

When exactly had he become so hard and unfeeling? She had only turned the lights on, after all, which in the bright world Savannah inhabited was a very small transgression. As she ran her fingers through her still-damp hair, her face naked after her shower, he knew she was also naked under her robe. She looked nervous, apprehensive; fearful. She was certainly braced for a stinging rebuke. 'We shouldn't let the supper go to waste. That's if you don't mind...'

She looked surprised at his suggestion, as he had expected, but she quickly rallied, saying, 'Of course I don't mind. Please, sit down. You must be hungry too?'

'A little,' he admitted.

Savannah had to stop audibly sighing with relief as Ethan sat down. Maybe there was a chance, however slender, that she could change things for him before she left; it was all she wanted. But as always in the world of Savannah things never ran according to plan. She remembered that her underwear for the next day, having been rinsed out, was still hanging over the bath—large, comfy knickers included. What if he decided to go in there? 'D'you mind, if I...?' Flapping her hands, she glanced anxiously across the room.

'Not at all. Take your time,' Ethan invited.

She would have to, Savannah thought, resting back against the bathroom door. She wasn't leaving this room until her heartbeat steadied, which meant she could be in here quite some time. Ethan was full of surprises. She felt like he was giving her a second chance. But he was so complex, she had no idea what to expect next. But then she hardly knew him, Savannah reasoned. When she emerged from the bathroom, there was music playing.

'Do you like it?' Ethan asked as Savannah poked her head self-consciously round the door.

'Is it what I think it is?'

'If you think it's your first CD then, yes, it is.'

Savannah pulled back inside the bathroom, suffused with too many emotions to impose them on Ethan. She felt elated that her teachers' and parents' dreams for her had come true, and dread that Ethan only regarded her as a property belonging to his record label.

'Aren't you coming out to join me?' he called. 'Come and listen to your music.'

She could hardly refuse, since Ethan owned the record company. 'Do you like it?' she said anxiously when she returned.

'Like it? Your singing voice always makes me think of…'

Frogs croaking? Wheels grinding?

'Birds singing,' he said, settling back with a blissful expression on his face as Savannah's voice filled the room. 'Song birds,' he added dryly, without opening his eyes.

At least not crows squawking.

She should have more confidence, Savannah told herself, but in many ways she was as happy in the shadows as Ethan. In a different way, of course. But she loved nothing more than the wide-open countryside back home, and the fact that she could walk for miles unnoticed as she soaked up all the glories of nature.

'I'm glad we signed you.'

Savannah refocused to find Ethan staring thoughtfully at her. 'Thank you.' She risked a small smile as her heart drummed wildly.

'You should eat something. It must be hours since you last ate.'

Probably. She had no idea. But she would have to lean past him to take something, and she was acutely aware that she was naked under her robe.

'Here,' he said, offering her the loaded plate. 'Take one of these delicious *ciabatta*.'

'Ethan, if I've offended you—'

'Eat something, Savannah, before you faint.'

'I didn't mean to,' she finished softly. 'Sometimes my enthusiasm carries me away.'

He hummed at this and angled his stubble-shaded chin towards the plate.

'Thank you.' Selecting a delicious-looking, well-filled roll, she bit into it with relish, expressing her pleasure in a series of appreciative sounds. Even now, beneath Ethan's unforgiving eye, she couldn't hide her feelings. 'You're very lucky to have such wonderful staff.'

'Yes, I am.' And when she thought that short statement was it, he added, 'You were right about the gloom making life difficult for them. And, yes, even dangerous. And, as for artworks, I hadn't even noticed.' He paused and then admitted, 'Who would think turning on the lights could make such a difference?'

She could.

CHAPTER EIGHT

ETHAN realised how much he had misjudged Susannah when his housekeeper, having returned with a fresh plate of food, took him to one side to inform him that she was glad to see how happy the *piccola signorina* was now the lights were on.

The way the older woman had held his gaze suggested more than the fact that Savannah was a guest with particular tastes to accommodate, or even that his housekeeper liked the young singer and wanted to make her stay as comfortable as possible. It was more the type of look the older generation gave the younger in Italy—and would sometimes be accompanied by tapping the side of the nose. Naturally, the older woman wouldn't dream of being so familiar with him, but she had got her message across. He'd brushed off her inquisitiveness with a rare smile.

Some time ago he had come to understand and even envy the Italian nation's fixation with love. And how could he be angry with Savannah, when all it took to make him smile was to watch her sucking her fingers with gusto before devouring another sandwich? Savannah had transformed the *palazzo* in the short time she'd been here, filling it with good things and raising the spirits of his staff. It wouldn't last when she'd gone, of course, but she had unlocked one small portion of his heart, which was good news for his staff.

'It is a beautiful room, isn't it?'

As Savannah lifted her head with surprise, he realised he was seeing things through her eyes and how different things could be if he decided to make them so.

She'd go mad with grief if she heard that Ethan had returned to his old ways when she went home. And that wasn't overreaction, it was pure, hard fact, Savannah concluded, blushing when, having held the door for his housekeeper, Ethan remained leaning against the door frame with his powerful arms folded across his chest, watching her.

Her body reacted as if Ethan had just made the most indecent suggestion. His tight fitting T-shirt strained hard across his chest, and his jeans were secured with a heavy-duty belt. She had noticed all this in the space of a few seconds, and started nervously when Ethan moved.

'More sandwiches?' he suggested, strolling across the room towards her.

She was as tense as a doe at bay, Savannah realised, sitting straight. 'No, thank you.'

And then she decided she had better get up and clear some space on the table for all the new food, but being nervous and clumsy she moved erratically, and somehow a chair leg got in her way. Ethan called out, but it was too late, and as he reached out to grab her to stop her falling she ended up in his arms.

'Suddenly you've got more legs than a millipede, and each one of them travelling in a different direction,' he suggested.

'Pretty much,' she admitted, though the millipede analogy failed to grow on her. A better woman would have made the most of this opportunity, while all she could think was had she cleaned her teeth?

'Well, I'm still hungry,' he admitted, letting her go and heading back to the sofa.

She watched him stretch out his muscular legs, knowing she had never felt more awkward in her life. And yes—thank the dentist's warnings—she had cleaned her teeth, but Savannah Ross was about to play host to Ethan Alexander? It hardly seemed possible.

'Won't you help me?' He glanced her way as he reached for a sandwich. 'My housekeeper clearly thinks we both need feeding up.'

Or perhaps the older woman wanted to keep him here, Savannah thought, surprising herself with this reflection. They ate in silence until Savannah put down her napkin with a sigh of contentment. The hearty feed had reminded her of home.

'You were hungry,' Ethan commented, wiping his lips on a napkin.

As he continued to stare at her, Savannah's cheeks heated up. They were still talking about food, weren't they?

Of course they were, she reasoned, smoothing out her hair, or rather the tangles. What must Ethan think of her, bare faced and barely dressed? Having never entertained a man before whilst naked beneath a robe, she wasn't too sure of the protocol. And as Ethan still showed no sign of going anywhere, she suggested, 'Why don't I switch on the television?' Maybe they'd catch the news, she reasoned.

'The television?'

'I just thought maybe there would be a news report about the match…or us.' Her cheeks fired up as Ethan gave her a look. The word 'us' couldn't have carried more embarrassing weight had it tried.

'I try to escape the news when I'm here.' Ethan's tone was a chilling return to his former manner.

'But surely not items affecting your business—or world affairs—or sport?' She was running out of options, wishing she knew how to turn the clock back so she could remove all reference to 'us'.

'No,' he said bluntly. 'And, Savannah, I need to tell you something.'

By which time she'd switched on the set. Her timing was impeccable, Savannah realised, recoiling as she blenched. 'Why, that's ridiculous!' A news item had just flashed up on the screen. A news item featuring Ethan Alexander caught out, so the reporters said, with his latest squeeze, a young ingénue only recently signed to his record label.

'How could such a nice evening end so badly?' Ethan wondered, glancing at her.

Now she knew why he hadn't wanted her to turn it on. 'How can you take it so well?'

'Because I know what to expect. That's one of the reasons I came to find you. I wanted to tell you myself before you found out by some other means. But now…' Leaning across her, picking up the remote-control and pointing it at the set, he switched it off.

'Shouldn't we know everything before we do that?' Savannah exclaimed. Terrible lies were being told about them. 'Don't you care what they're saying about us?'

'Do I care about gossip?'

'Gossip? They're telling lies!'

Ethan responded calmly. 'What are they going to do? They'll soon tire of us, and in no time those pictures will be wrapped around somebody's fish and chips.'

'A famous tycoon saves the girl with the golden tonsils, blushes, in front of a worldwide television audience?' Savannah stuck a finger in her mouth to show what she thought of that. 'A story like that could run and run.'

'Gossip only hurts you if you allow it to,' Ethan told her evenly. 'And if you're going to let it get you down like this, Savannah, perhaps you should have another think about pursuing a career in the public eye.'

Were those her marching orders? She went cold immediately, thinking of all the people who had helped her along the way and who would be badly let down if she quit. 'But the press say we're sleeping together.' Surely that would get through to him?

Ethan's brow rose seductively. 'Is that so bad?'

He shouldn't tease her. Savannah's cheeks flushed crimson the moment he put the thought of them being sexually involved into her head. And why was he doing that when he had vowed not to think of Savannah as anything other than a young girl under his protection? Was it because sometimes a deeper feeling than common sense took the lead?

Before he had a chance to reason it through she begged him to switch on the set again so she could know the worst. She made him smile inwardly. Her voice was shaking with anger, not fear, and her hands were balled into fists as if she would like to punch out the screen. She was new to this, he remembered. 'You know what they're saying and so do I,' he soothed, 'So let them get on with it.'

'No,' she shot back fiercely. 'We have to issue a denial.'

'We have something to deny?' he queried, pouncing on her naivety before it had a chance to take root. Picking up the remote-control which she had cunningly reclaimed, he tossed it out of her reach.

Gradually she relaxed, hopefully seeing the sense behind his years of doing battle with the press. 'Thank goodness my parents are away,' she said, confirming this.

She looked so grateful it drove home the message that Savannah came from a strong and loving family. He couldn't shake a lingering sense of loss for something he'd never had. But her desire to go out and slay dragons soon distracted him. The expression on her face was so appealing.

It took Savannah a moment to realise Ethan was laughing. It was the first time she'd heard him laugh, without it being an ugly or mocking sound. 'What's so funny?'

He shook his head, unable to speak for a moment. 'The infamous hard man and his teenage songbird?' he managed at last. 'They make us sound like something out of a novel.'

'And I'm not a teenager,' Savannah pointed out. 'I was twenty last week.'

'Twenty?' Ethan's face stilled. 'As old as that?'

'Well, I'm not some teenage tweety-pie, if that's what you think—and I think we should sue them,' she said seriously, which only made him start laughing again.

'You can if you like,' Ethan suggested between bouts of laughter.

Using magic beans to pay the lawyers, presumably. But as she had a leading role in this mess she was determined to do something about it.

'From my point of view.'

'Yes?' Savannah stared intently at Ethan, ready to jump

into armour and fight at his side at the first sign he was preparing to take on the press.

'I think you should ignore it, as I will. Unless—' he held up his hands when she was about to leap in '—they become a nuisance, in which case I shall act.'

That was just so disappointing. She didn't want to sit back and have rubbish thrown at her. She was about to challenge Ethan's decision when a knock came at the door and her bags from the stadium arrived.

'I haven't let you down yet, have I?' Ethan demanded as she checked them over. 'And I'm not about to start now. And where this newspaper rubbish is concerned you'll just have to try something new.'

'Such as?' Lifting her head, she stared at him.

'You could try trusting me.'

'But we're trapped here,' she pointed out.

'Yes, in this terrible place,' Ethan mocked gently. 'Poor us.'

He only had to say this for warning darts of fire to attack every part of her, and each tiny arrow carried a subtle message. She wanted him, but confronted by Ethan's worldliness, and by the thought of staying under his roof, she grabbed the edges of her robe and tugged it firmly shut. 'Haven't they've got anything better to do than speculate about us?'

'They're only doing their job,' Ethan pointed out. 'We're newsworthy. You. Me. Both of us together. Now that's a real story.'

'But this isn't a real story. They've twisted the truth and made innocent photographs seem so…'

'Suggestive?'

She hadn't wanted to say that, and when Ethan looked at her a certain way she wished she hadn't. Prior to this she had been sure Ethan thought of her as a ward beneath his protection, and the thought that he was now looking at her as a woman was unsettling. It might be everything she had ever dreamed of, but as fantasy hurtled towards reality at breakneck pace she lost her nerve. Getting up, she assured him, 'Well, don't worry, if I do have to stay here for any length of time, I'll keep right out of your way.'

'How very thoughtful of you,' Ethan murmured. 'Tea?' he proposed. 'Hot and sweet, perhaps?' he added under his breath. 'It's good for shock.' He reached for the phone to call the kitchen.

Shock? He thought she was in shock? She probably *was* in shock after seeing the news bulletin, Savannah conceded. But tea? She didn't want tea. 'I think I need something stronger than that.'

Ethan held the phone away from his ear. 'Espresso?'

His face was poker straight, but his eyes were laughing at her. This humorous side of him—so unsuspected, so attractive—was unbelievably seductive. And terrifying. She had no idea how to handle a man—any man—let alone a man like Ethan. The situation was rapidly spiralling out of control. 'Gin and tonic, please,' she said firmly, thinking it might help. 'A large one.'

For a moment she thought Ethan might refuse, but then he crossed the room to the wet bar where he mixed a drink. At last he was treating her like someone over the age of consent.

'Here you are,' he said pleasantly, handing her the glass. 'I hope I got the balance right?'

She took a large swig in a pathetic attempt to maintain a confident image—and choked. Worse than choked she wheezed and choked, whilst waving her hands frantically in the air as fire consumed her gullet.

'So, you're a virgin,' he said with amusement.

She was aghast that he could tell. 'How did you know?'

Holding the crystal tumbler aloft, he stared into the clear liquid. 'You can't drink a decent measure of alcohol without…' His voice tailed away as he looked at her. 'Oh, I see. We're not talking about the same thing, are we? Well, are we, Savannah?' Ethan pressed, and, far from being humorous now, his expression was grim.

She couldn't answer. Her throat had seized up with embarrassment. In the silence that followed everything Ethan had ever thought about her seemed to grow in her mind to grotesque proportions. She was too young for him, too inexperienced, too naïve, and whatever hopes she'd ever had about them ever being together had just turned into dust. But that didn't stop her wanting him, it just pushed him further away, because Ethan was so principled he would never even think of making love to her, believing her innocence was under his charge.

A virgin? *A virgin!* Ethan recoiled inwardly. This made the situation so much worse. How much worse he could hardly quantify in thought, let alone words. Savannah was only here to enjoy his protection, yet until a minute ago he had arrogantly contemplated seducing her. She was still so young, and his first thought must always be to protect her. He had to hang onto that thought now if he was to save her from the greatest danger of all, which was him—the very man who was supposed to be taking care of her.

'Ethan, please don't be angry with me,' she begged him as he made for the door.

'Angry with you?' He was bemused she could think that. 'Goodnight, Savannah.'

'Ethan, please.'

He was halfway through the door when she ran towards him. 'Sleep well,' he said, closing the door firmly behind him with Savannah on the other side. He didn't trust himself to wait and listen to her reply.

She sat on the bed for a long time after Ethan left. With her arms pressed tightly on the top of her head, she knew she'd made such a hash of everything and that she didn't have a clue how to make it right. She had known for some time now that she loved Ethan. How could she care for anyone as deeply as she did for him and not love him? But he still frightened her. She had played a foolish game of make-believe. The first time Ethan had noticed she was a woman, she had taken fright, and now his principles meant they could never be together. *Well done, Savannah*, she congratulated herself; there'd be no encores here.

Climbing off the bed, she went to stare into the mirror. What did Ethan see when he stared in his? He lived his life in spite of his injuries. He had triumphed over them. Or had he? Was she only seeing Ethan's public face? Did those scars torment him when he was alone? Because she cared about him, she couldn't stop thinking about it. How could she leave Tuscany and Ethan with so many things unresolved? She would go to him and speak to him. She would reason with him in the hope that when she went away they could at least be friends.

The fact that she didn't have a clue what she was going to say was immaterial, Savannah thought, tugging on her jeans. This was just one of those moments when doing nothing wasn't an option. She refused to have Ethan think she was repulsed by his scars, or that she made a habit of accepting hospitality and then changing everything

around for her host. Caring about someone came with responsibility, which meant she couldn't turn her back on
him. And as this might be her last chance to search
beneath Ethan's public persona, and find the real man
underneath, she had no intention of wasting it.

CHAPTER NINE

Maybe the fates had decided she deserved a bit of luck, Savannah concluded as she followed a group of servants carrying fresh towels and a tray with a pot of coffee on it. There couldn't be that many people staying at the *palazzo*, surely?

All she cared about was finding Ethan, and as she waited, concealed in the shadows while one of the servants knocked on a door, she thrilled at the sound of his voice. Finding him filled her with relief.

She waited for the staff to come out again, and when their footsteps had died away she came out of hiding and cautiously approached the door around which they'd been clustered. The handle yielded all too easily, and as she pressed the door open a crack she could hear the shower running.

Opening the door fully, Savannah slipped inside. She found herself in a mannish-looking sitting room where the scent of good leather and books was overwhelming. She looked around. Okay, so now what? There was hardly anywhere to hide. As she had suspected, Ethan's tastes were plain. The floors were polished wood, and the sofas were dark-brown leather. The walls were lined with books and not much else, other than some vibrant modern paintings.

Originals, Savannah noted with interest, signed with a letter B that had a diagonal line through it. She could imagine what a psychologist might make of that. And as for the content: frightened, wide-eyed children without faces or proper form. The paintings were brilliant—but, in the same way Edvard Munch's *The Scream* both fascinated and repelled, these paintings were deeply disturbing. And there were shadows in them…lots and lots of shadows.

Were the paintings an autobiographical account of Ethan's childhood?

She'd bet her life on it. And this window into his psyche was both more illuminating and far worse than anything she had imagined. That he had immense talent was in no doubt, and as another type of artist she found that bond between them reassuring—though everything else about the paintings troubled her and told her she was right to be concerned. Listening, she was reassured to hear the shower still running. What other secrets could she uncover in the time she had?

She wasn't here to pry, but to sense things, Savannah told herself, remaining motionless in the middle of the room. And then the water stopped running. And she was completely exposed. She braced herself. All the clever words and questions she'd been preparing for Ethan deserted her. But when he didn't emerge from the bathroom curiosity got the better of her. Tip-toeing to the door, she peeped through a crack. Sensation streamed through every inch of her at the sight of Ethan standing in front of a mirror with just a towel around him.

He was magnificent.

Although his scars were far, far worse than she had thought, she had never seen anyone half so virile or appealing. His legs were beautifully shaped and muscular, and his naked torso was everything she had dreamed of. The extent of his injuries, of his scarring, only proved it was a miracle he had made it through, and the thought of the pain he must have experienced cut her like a knife. He was twice the man she'd thought him. And more.

Savannah jumped back in alarm as Ethan thrust his fists down on a marble counter-top. For a moment she thought he'd seen her and that that must have prompted the angry action, but then she realised he was leaning over his braced arms with his shoulder-muscles knotted and his head bowed, as if the sight of his own body had disgusted him. She knew then that everything she had feared for him was true: Ethan's injuries had scarred more than his body, they had scarred the man.

'Savannah?'

She gasped out loud as he wheeled around.

'Savannah! I'm speaking to you!'

The ferocity in his tone made her back away.

'What do you think you're doing here?'

'Looking for you...' She backed away, hands outstretched in supplication. 'I knocked, but you didn't hear me.'

'You didn't hear the water running?'

'I heard it, but.'

'You didn't leave immediately?'

'No, I.'

'You what?' he flashed across her. 'Wanted to try out your amateur psychology on me?' As he spoke his glance swept the paintings which he knew she must have seen. 'I thought so,' he spat out with contempt when she didn't reply.

'Ethan, please.'

'I thought we'd agreed you'd stay away from me?'

'Did we?' Her voice was trembling. 'I don't remember that.'

Straightening up, Ethan dipped his head. His stare was menacing.

'Stop trying to intimidate me.' If only her voice would stop shaking.

'Then tell me why you're here.'

'Like I said, I was looking for you.'

'Because?' he prompted harshly.

'I wanted to speak to you.'

'And so you sneaked into my room?'

'No!'

'Go back to bed, Savannah.'

'No.' She shook her head. But how was she going to put all her thoughts and impressions into a few short sentences when Ethan would never give her the time? Shorthand was her only option. 'I care about you.'

'You care about me?' Ethan's laugh was cold and ugly. 'If you only knew how infantile that sounded.'

'Caring for someone is infantile?' Savannah threw up her hands. 'Then I'm guilty.' The feelings she had developed for Ethan were so deep and so complex, at this point she had nothing to lose. 'I'll admit, I'm not good with words.'

'No, you're not.' Grabbing his robe, Ethan threw it on, belting it to hide his mutilations from her gaze. 'Get out of here, Savannah.'

'I'm not going anywhere,' she informed him stubbornly.

'Must I throw you out?'

She wanted to run as far and as fast as she could from the expression on Ethan's face. He had turned so angry and dark, and so utterly contemptuous of her. 'You wouldn't—'

But her voice wobbled and Ethan pounced. 'Can you be sure of that?'

'I'm absolutely sure you would never hurt me.' Standing her ground, she stared him full in the face.

'Have you finished? Can I continue with my evening in peace now?'

'I've not nearly finished!' Like a cork in a bottle her frustrations had been tamped down long enough. 'You can't dismiss me. I'm not a child!'

'You certainly look like one to me.'

'Then you're not looking closely enough. I'm a woman, Ethan, a woman with feelings; a woman who won't let those feelings go just because you say I must.'

Ethan's answer was to curtly angle his chin towards the door. 'And now I'm asking you to leave.'

'I'm not going anywhere.'

He tried sweet reason. 'It's been a long day and you should be in bed.'

Savannah shook her head. 'I'm not a child you can order to bed. All I want to do is talk to you.'

'Well, I'm right out of conversation. Now, get out of here. Out!' He backed her towards the door. 'Try to get this through your head, Savannah…' Bringing his face so close she could see the amber flecks in his steel-grey eyes, Ethan ground out, 'I don't want your company. I don't want your conversation. And most of all I don't want you snooping around here, spying on me.'

'I'm not spying on you,' Savannah said, raising her voice too. 'And if it's these you're worried about—'

Sucking air between his teeth, Ethan knocked her hand away, but, ignoring him, she reached up anyway. Touching his face with her fingertips, she traced his cruel scars. 'I don't see them.'

'You don't see them?' Ethan mimicked scathingly. Rearing back, he turned his face away.

'No, I don't.' Savannah flinched as Ethan walked past her. And flinched again when, having poured a glass of water and drained it, he slammed the glass down so hard she couldn't believe it hadn't smashed. 'It's no use you trying to shut me out, because I'm not going anywhere, Ethan.'

He remained with his hostile back turned to her. Perhaps she had gone too far this time. Ethan's massive shoulders were hunched, and his fists were planted so aggressively on a chair back his knuckles gleamed white.

'Bad enough you're here,' he growled without looking at her, 'But you should have told me you were—'

'I'm sorry?' Savannah interrupted, reading his mind. 'Do you mean I should have told you I was a virgin?' She waited until Ethan turned to face her. 'Are you seriously suggesting I should have said, "how do you do, my name is Savannah, and I'm a virgin"?'

'No, of course not,' Ethan snapped, eyes smouldering with passion. 'But if you'd given me at least some intimation, I could have made arrangements for you to stay elsewhere.'

'In a nunnery, perhaps?' Savannah cut across him. 'In a safe place with a chaperon?'

'And this isn't safe, and I don't have a chaperon.'

'Correct.'

As they glared at each other it soon became apparent that neither one of them was prepared to break the stand-off.

'And if I tell you I feel quite safe here with you?'

'And if I tell you that the rest of the world will put a very different construction on your staying here with me?'

'But I thought you didn't care about gossip?' she countered.

'I care how it affects you.'

'From the point of view that I'm signed to your record

company as the next *young* singing sensation, which means I must appear to the world to be innocent?'

Ethan took her barbed comment with far better grace than she might have expected. It was almost as if they had got the measure of each other, and for once he was crediting her with some sense—though he drew out the waiting time until her nerves were flayed and tender. Relaxing onto one hip then, he thumbed his chin as the expression in his eyes slowly cooled from passion to wry reflection. 'That's a very cynical attitude for a young girl to have.'

'How many times—?'

'Must you tell me you're not the young girl I think you are?' he supplied in a low voice that strummed her senses.

'If I'm cynical,' Savannah countered, 'Surely you're the last person who should be surprised?'

'I'm going to say this as clearly as I can.' Ethan's voice held a crushing note of finality. 'I don't want you here. Please leave now.'

She waited a moment too, and then said, 'No.'

'No?'

'No,' Savannah repeated. 'You're asking me to believe I must do everything you say. Well, standing my ground where you're concerned might not be a big thing in your world, or easy in mine, but it has to be a whole lot better than agreeing to be your doormat.'

'Have you quite finished?' he demanded.

'I've barely started,' she assured him, but even she could see there was little point in pursuing this if she couldn't persuade Ethan to see her in a different light.

And she couldn't. He pointed to the door.

Lifting her head, she wrapped what little dignity she had left around her and walked towards it—but when she reached it she just had to know: 'What's wrong with me, Ethan?'

'Wrong with you?' He frowned.

'Is it because I'm not pretty enough, not desirable enough, or is it the fact that I'm not experienced and savvy enough when it comes to handling situations like this?'

'Savannah, there is no situation—other than my increasing impatience with you, which means there may soon be a situation, and it will be one you won't like.'

Walking over to the door, Ethan opened it for her. 'Goodnight, Savannah.'

Ethan felt nothing for her and she had no answer to that. She was so lacking in female guile, she had no tricks up her sleeve, and it was too late to wish she'd learned them before she'd come here.

'What do you think you're doing?' Ethan demanded when she turned around and walked back in the room.

If he wanted her out, he was going to have to throw her out, and something told her he wouldn't do that. Now she just had to hope she was right.

He shook his head. 'Savannah, you are the most difficult, the most stubborn—'

'Individual in the world aside from you?' She held Ethan's gaze along with her breath, and sent a plea into the ether. If there was anyone listening out there, anyone at all…

'I was about to say, the most annoying guest I've ever had. You will have noted my use of the past tense, I hope?'

'You can't just dismiss me.'

'Watch me. Out,' he rapped, employing the full force of his laser stare.

'Why are you so angry all the time?'

'Why are you so slow to take a hint?'

'Well, clearly my experience of men is somewhat limited, but if you'd just allow me to—'

'To do what?' he cut across her, eyes narrowed in suspicion.

'Spend time with you?' Savannah trembled as she clutched on to this last all-too-brittle straw.

Ethan's laugh was scathing. 'You must think I make a habit of courting trouble. Out.' He pointed to the door.

'Can't we even have one last drink together?'

'Gin and tonic?' he mocked.

'If you like.'

'I don't like. Now, go to bed.'

He closed the door with relief. Leaning back against it, he let out a groan of relief. Mentally, physically, he was in agony. He shouldn't even be thinking this way about Savannah. And now he knew she was a virgin he had even less excuse—though how to stop erotic images of her flooding his mind was something he had no answer for. He wanted her. Wanted her? He ached for her. The urge to lose himself in her was overwhelming him, but he couldn't feed on perfection, or drain her innocence to somehow dilute the ugliness inside him.

That was a wound of such long standing he doubted he'd ever be rid of it. It had taken seed in him the day he'd realised his mother had chosen his stepfather over her seven-year-old son, and had germinated on the day she'd seen his bruises in the bath. Instead of questioning them, she had told him she'd take his bike away if he wasn't more careful. Had she really believed the buckle marks on his back had come from a fall? That bitterness was in full flower by the time he'd been ready to make his own way in the world, and those dark secrets had stayed with him. Would he share a legacy like that with Savannah? Not a chance. She was like a ray of light with her whole life in front of her, and he would do anything to protect her. He would do nothing to stop that little candle throwing its beam around the world.

Pulling away from the door, he thrust his hands through his hair with frustration. He wanted Savannah. He wanted to make love to her. The most important thing to him was that Savannah remembered the first time she made love for the right reasons.

He tensed, hearing her footsteps returning. That sound was shortly followed by a tap on the door. 'Yes?'

'Ethan, it's me.'

'What do you want?' He tried to sound gruff. Had she forgotten something? He glanced round the room, already knowing it was a vain hope. He opened the door. She looked like a pale wraith beneath the lights she had insisted on, and they were blazing full in his face. He hardly cared or noticed these days when people turned away from him, but he noticed tonight that Savannah didn't flinch. 'What do you want?' he said wearily.

'You…'

Her voice was so small he couldn't be sure he'd heard her correctly.

'I want you,' she repeated. 'I want you, Ethan.' She held his gaze as she paused, as if she needed to prepare herself for the next step, and then she whispered, 'Will you make love to me?'

He was already closing the door. 'Don't be so silly.'

'I'm not being silly.'

The door was stuck. And then he realised she put her foot in the way. He wanted to laugh at the sight of

Savannah's tiny foot in his door, but, seeing the expression on her face, he knew this was no time for laughter.

'Please, can I come in?' she begged him.

As she looked anxiously up and down the corridor, he knew the answer to that had to be yes. He wouldn't let her make a fool of herself in front of the servants. 'All right,' he agreed, opening the door wide enough for her to slip through. He would soon sort this out. He would tell her it must never happen again and then send her on her way.

But as he closed the door she rounded on him. 'Ethan, what do I have to do to make you see that I'm a woman?'

Noticing Savannah's hands were balled with frustration, he reached out. She reached out too. Whether he intended to hold her off or pull her close, he wasn't sure, he only knew they tangled and collided, and when she closed her eyes he dragged her close and kissed her.

She was trembling like a leaf by the time Ethan pulled away to cup her face and stare into her eyes. This was everything she had ever dreamed of and more. Ethan was everything she had ever dreamed of and more, and his kiss sealed the meeting of two lovers who had to have known each other for longer than one lifetime, and who needed the immediate reassurance of pressing every fragment of their flesh against each other. As she gazed up at Ethan, with all the love she felt for him shining in her eyes, she could have sworn he asked her, 'Are you sure?'

'Yes, I'm sure,' she whispered back.

CHAPTER TEN

HE TASTED heaven when he kissed her. Dipping his head, he kissed her again, deepening the kiss, always acutely conscious that she was so much smaller than he was, and vulnerable—the very thing that held him back.

'Why did you wait so long?' she murmured when he released her.

Because keeping her safe had been paramount. Because he had feared the dark forces inside him might express themselves in contemptuous energy. He should have known Savannah's joyful innocence would defeat them. And now he felt nothing but the desire to cherish her, and to have one night; a night in which he would bring her the ultimate pleasure.

'Ethan?' she prompted, sensing his abstraction.

'I haven't forgotten you,' he murmured, sweeping her into his arms.

Her clothes slipped away in sighs and smothered laughter, and Ethan's kisses drove her remaining fears away as she clung to him, hidden from the world by the spread of his shoulders and the width of his chest. She wasn't even sure how she'd come to be naked, only that she was. And she wasn't embarrassed by that, because

Ethan was there to take care of her, and everything he did or said made her strong. He hadn't even touched her intimately, and yet every part of her was singing with awareness, and she only knew how it felt to soften and melt against him. She clung to him, asking—for what, she hardly knew. She had so much to discover. She had everything to learn.

Ethan carried her across the room to the bed and laid her down on it, where she rested with one arm above her head on a stack of pillows in an attitude of innocent seduction. The linen felt cool and crisp against her raging skin, and she was lost in an erotic haze when she noticed Ethan moving away. 'You're not leaving me?' She sat up.

'This is wrong.'

'What do you mean, "wrong"?' She was blissfully unaware of how nakedly provocative she was to him. 'What's wrong about it?' Now her cheeks were on fire. 'Do you still think I'm too young for you?'

'Correct.' Ethan sounded relieved that she had given him an out. 'Get dressed, Savannah.'

Grabbing his arm, she pushed her face in front of his. 'I won't let you do this.'

'You have no choice.'

'No choice but to be humiliated?' Her voice broke, but Ethan still shook himself free. As he stood looking down at her she thought he had never seemed more magnificent. Or more distant. 'Why?' She opened her arms. 'Why?' she repeated softly. 'Why are you doing this to me, Ethan? Why bring me here at all?'

Because he had thought mistakenly that for one short night he could forget. But the seeds of doubt had been planted deep inside him when his stepfather had assured him in hospital that no one would ever want to look at him again. That message had been driven home when his mother had recoiled from her own child. Was he going to inflict that same horror on Savannah when she saw his others scars? Knowing they were the answer to finishing this, he turned his back so she could see them. The scars on his face were bad enough, but those on his back were truly horrific.

'What are you doing?' she demanded. 'If you expect me to exclaim in horror, you'll be disappointed. These scars make no difference to the way I feel about you.'

'No difference?'

'They don't change what I feel about you in here.'

Savannah's hand rested over her heart. He tried dismissing that with a shrug, but she called him back.

'The damage might be all that others see—but I see you, Ethan.'

'Me?' he mocked unkindly.

'Your scars don't change a thing for me, except that—'

'Yes?' he cut across her, certain now that he must have destroyed her argument.

'They keep us apart,' she finished softly.

Just when Ethan needed her to be strong, she was crying for him, and for what he had lost.

'Dry your face and leave me, Savannah,' he said harshly.

'I'm not going anywhere. Your scars don't frighten me.'

'Then you haven't looked at them properly,' he assured her.

'Oh, but I have,' she argued, seeing inside him more clearly than she ever had before.

'Look at me again,' he suggested in a voice that broke her heart.

There was only one way past this. Kneeling up on the

bed, she reached out while Ethan stood tensely, like a hostile stranger. But little by little the conviction in her eyes drew him to look at her, and she traced his scars with her fingertips, traced the tramlines that criss-crossed his back and which looked as if they had been carved by a serrated knife. She traced each one of them with her eyes and with her fingertips, until she reached his beloved face.

'I revolt you,' he said confidently. 'You don't need to pretend.'

'I don't need to be here at all,' she pointed out. 'Oh, Ethan, you couldn't possibly revolt me. You amaze me.' Ethan's scars would always be a hideous reminder of the cruelty one human being could inflict on another, but they didn't make one jot of difference to the way she felt about him.

'How can I make love to you?' Ethan demanded. 'How?' he repeated with the same passion Savannah had shown him, and when she didn't reply he cupped her chin to make her look at him.

'The usual way?' she suggested softly, and because she loved him so much she risked the ghost of a smile. 'Just don't look to me for any pointers.'

Ethan thought her so cosseted and protected she couldn't tolerate anything that wasn't perfect, when nothing could be further from the truth, Savannah realised as he stripped off his clothes. 'You think my world is all concerts and evening dresses, lace and perfume?' She reached for his hand and laid her cheek against it. 'I was brought up on a farm with straw in my hair, wearing dungarees, and that's where I've always been happiest. I can take reality, Ethan, in rather large doses.'

'So reality like this doesn't trouble you?' Ethan wiped one hand roughly down the scars on his chest.

'Please don't insult me.' As she turned her face up she was aching with the need to wrench the demons out of him. Placing her palms against his chest, she kissed her way slowly across it.

'Don't,' Ethan said, tensing, but she wouldn't stop, and finally he dragged her to him.

Those scars, terrible though they were, didn't even begin to scratch the edges of his power. Ethan was like a gladiator in some ancient etching, wounded but triumphant, and she was hard pressed to think of anything with more sex appeal than that. But inside his heart there was nothing, Savannah's tender inner-self warned her. Yes, she answered back, Ethan's heart was cold, but she had to hope that in time her love would warm him. 'I want you,' she murmured, staring up at him.

'I want you too…more than you know.' And that was true, Ethan realised as he teased Savannah with almost-kisses. She was tender and precious, young and vulnerable, and he would never hurt her. And maybe her innocence was the last hope he had to heal those scars he couldn't reach.

'So, are you coming to bed?' she whispered. Holding his hand, she sank back on the pillows and threw back the covers. 'Don't be shy.'

He laughed. She was so funny and sweet. She had stripped herself bare for him in every way, proving she trusted him, and he would never betray that trust.

As Savannah snuggled lower in the bed, waiting for Ethan, knowing he might change his mind again at any moment, she started having fears on a more practical level. His size alone filled her with apprehension. He must have sensed it, for as he stretched out on the bed at her side he said, 'I think you're nervous.'

'A little,' she admitted, in a shaking voice that betrayed her true feelings.

'There's no need.' He stroked her arm into quivering anticipation, and as she looked into his eyes he promised, 'I would never hurt you, Savannah.'

How could he not? Ethan was so much bigger than the average man—bigger than most men—plus he possessed the power and the stamina of a natural athlete. She'd been around a farm long enough to know that nature allowed for this sort of unlikely coupling, but she wondered now if in some extreme instances such things weren't possible. This was without doubt an extreme instance. She might be plumper than she wanted to be, but she was small and soft compared to Ethan. There was nothing soft about him. He was huge and hard.

Expecting to be soothed and reassured, she was surprised when Ethan moved so quickly to pin her beneath him. And now he was straddling her with his powerful thighs, and she was completely at his mercy while he murmured erotic, outrageous suggestions in her ear that made her squirm with excitement.

'Better?' His lips were curving with amusement as he stared into her eyes.

There was passion in his eyes as well as humour, and she was reassured to a point beyond fear. 'Much better,' she admitted. With Ethan's thighs pressed close against her sides, there was nowhere else on earth she'd rather be. But still she asked for one last reassurance. 'You won't hurt me, will you?'

His answer was to kiss her tenderly until she relaxed, and then he deepened the kiss, which made her want to do anything but relax. Lacing her fingers through Ethan's hair, she tried telling him by her eagerness alone that her nerve endings were screaming for his attention.

'There's a lot more to you than meets the eye, Ms Ross,' Ethan murmured, smiling against her lips.

Savannah stared boldly at Ethan's mouth, shivering with sensation as his kisses migrated down her neck. 'What are you doing?' she asked, writhing with pleasure when he reached the most sensitive hollow above her shoulders.

'Exploring,' Ethan murmured.

The feeling when he teased her nipples was beyond description, and while he suckled and teased the sensation travelled through to the core of her being, until it was impossible to remain still. Ethan could have done whatever he wanted with her, and yet he never once made her feel vulnerable, other than to put her at risk of overdosing on pleasure. Bucking against him, seeking contact, she moved restlessly on the pillows as she assured him, 'I can't take any more of this.'

'So, shall I stop?'

'Just you dare,' she warned him, seeing the laughter in his eyes.

'What's your hurry?' he demanded when she pressed against him.

'You,' Savannah complained fiercely. 'You're my hurry.'

'Then it's time for you to learn a little patience.'

'I don't want to learn patience.' She shivered with delight as he ran his hands down her naked body. 'But, if I do,' she proposed, 'can we do this again?'

'If you're good.'

'I'll be very good,' she assured him. And as he pulled away to look at her she pulled him back. She didn't have sufficient strength to compel Ethan to do anything, but for now the pleasure machine was at her command. 'No more teasing,' she warned him.

'What, then?' His lips were tugging with amusement.

'Make love to me…' And she was deadly serious.

CHAPTER ELEVEN

HE PROTECTED them both, and then touched her in a way he knew she would like. As she moaned beneath him, inviting more of these touches, he feathered kisses down her neck.

He hadn't guessed he could be quite so gentle, or Savannah half so passionate. She brought out the best in him, more than he'd ever known he had, and as she clung to him, crying out his name, moving against him and driving him half-crazy with desire, he held back, knowing he had found someone who could reach him at a level no one else could.

That it should be a young girl like Savannah both surprised him and stirred his conscience. This was the start of a new chapter in Savannah's life as a woman, but when tonight was over he would have to end their relationship. But for now…

Listening to her beating time with her voice to the music of their pleasure, he knew he had never known such extremes of sensation. Gathering her into his arms to stare into her eyes, he brought her to the brink and tipped her over, staying with her through the ecstasy as she enjoyed the release she had been searching for. When she quietened and snuggled in to him, he felt sure as he gazed into her drowsy face that time was playing tricks on them and that they had known each other much longer than one night. It was a short step from there to knowing Savannah should be with someone who could give her the kind of life she deserved.

'Ethan, where are you?' she murmured, reaching up to touch his face.

'I'm still with you,' he murmured.

'No, you're not,' she argued softly, with barely the strength to open her eyes.

She was right. He was in a dark place he wouldn't take her. Dipping his head, he kissed her deeply, and before she had a chance to question him further he made love to her again.

Savannah lay awake for the rest of the night, pretending to be asleep in the early hours when Ethan left her. She didn't know him well enough to call him back. That struck her as funny and a little embarrassing, because she might not know him but she loved him. And loving him meant she understood his need for space. What had happened between them, what they'd shared, had been so much more than either of them could have expected. Of course, Ethan would need space to consider the changes this must make to his world. The changes to her world were immeasurable. Ethan was her man and her mate, and she had welcomed him inside her body with triumph and excitement. Ethan knew everything about bringing her pleasure, and they had been as one until pleasure had consumed them.

Only one worrying incident had tarnished the night. Ethan had drifted off to sleep after they'd made love, but after a few minutes he had thrown up his hands, as if to ward off a blow. It was some buried memory he couldn't bring himself to share, she guessed, and it hurt her to think of him locked in a nightmare where she couldn't reach him. She had to believe there was a key to breaking that destructive cycle, and that she held that key.

Turning her face into the pillows, Savannah inhaled Ethan's scent. Exhaling softly in the darkness, she turned on her back as contentment consumed her. Her whole being was drenched in a warm, happy glow. She had expected to feel different when she gave herself to a man, but she hadn't expected to feel quite so complete. She couldn't wait to see the same look of happiness in Ethan's eyes, and, as the lilac light of dawn was stealing through the heavy curtains, there was no reason why she shouldn't go and find him.

Stretching her arms, Savannah welcomed the new day with a heart full of joy. It was a new and better world with Ethan in it. She had never believed in love at first sight, but now she did. She'd heard that opposites attracted, and she'd proved that to be right. She was deeply in love, of that there was no doubt, and after last night it couldn't be long before Ethan told her that he loved her too.

He had left Savannah sleeping, and now he was avoiding her at breakfast, choosing instead to start the day with a dawn jog around the extensive grounds surrounding the *palazzo*. But even after that he craved more exercise to clear his mind. He moved on to the gym and after taking an icy shower he swam. As he powered down the Olympic-sized swimming pool there was one thing on his mind: Savannah. He could not get her out of his head.

Did he love her?

The thought was too fantastic to contemplate. He wasn't entitled to love anyone. His stepfather had drummed that into him from the start, and over the years he had come to see that it was the one thing the man had said to him that made sense.

CHAPTER TWELVE

HE DRESSED in the changing rooms just off the swimming pool rather than return to his private suite of rooms where Savannah would still be sleeping. Snapping his watch into position, he prepared to face the day. Heading out of the leisure facility, he made straight for his office. This wasn't a relaxing room where he could watch sport in comfort, but a cold, flickering world where he kept a handle on his business empire. He had this same facility in all his houses. No one was welcome to join him, because this was his techno-version of an ivory tower. He sat in the swivel chair absorbing a blizzard of information, and realised immediately he'd been away too long. He had to go to Savannah now and update her on the current situation. Of course he'd take legal measures to protect her from the braying paparazzi, but the sooner she could leave Italy the sooner she could break free of his shadow and get on with her life.

Savannah ran down the magnificent staircase, consumed by excitement at the thought of seeing Ethan. She could see his servants bustling about in the hallway, and knew that one of them would be able to tell her where he was. She didn't even try to hide her beaming smile, and was half-afraid everyone would guess she was in love with their *gran signore*, and half-afraid they wouldn't. She approached the first young man who smiled back at her to ask him where she could find *Signore* Alexander.

Signore Alexander was in his office as usual, the young man told her, adding that if she would like to wait out on the terrace he would make sure breakfast was served there, and that *Signore* Alexander would be told she was asking for him.

'Thank you!' Savannah exclaimed happily. She must look such a sight, she realised as the young man smiled back at her, but she hadn't wanted to waste a single moment on make-up or drying her hair. After her shower she had quickly thrown on her jeans and a casual top, and left her hair hanging loose and damp down her back. This was a whole new world to her. Catching sight of the house-keeper, she waved, and when the older woman came over to see if Savannah needed anything she took the chance to ask a few discreet questions about the paintings on Ethan's walls. As she expected, the housekeeper told her that Ethan had indeed painted them, but they had never been exhibited as far as the housekeeper could remember.

She'd expected that too, and asked if it would be possible to open more windows. 'And I'd like to pick some flowers, if that's all right. I'd love to fill the *palazzo* with flowers—if I'm allowed to.'

'*Signorina*, we have a hothouse full of flowers—and that's before you even start on the garden—but no one ever picks them.'

'Oh, perhaps I shouldn't.' It wasn't her house, after all, and she'd made enough changes.

'Perhaps you should,' the housekeeper encouraged. 'Why don't I show you where the vases are kept?'

'Are you sure Signore Alexander won't mind?'

'I'm sure the *palazzo* can only benefit from your attentions, *signorina.*'

With her fresh flowers newly arranged in the centre of the table, Savannah settled herself at the breakfast table on the terrace to wait for Ethan. Last night was still framed in a rosy glow. Her world had been turned upside down over the past twenty-four hours, and it was a very beautiful world indeed, Savannah thought as she gazed across the emerald parkland. There was a lake at the *palazzo*, as well as formal gardens, and with wooden shutters framing the sparkling windows and vivid bougainvillea tumbling down the walls, the ancient palace was like something out of her most romantic fantasy.

Savannah's gaze returned to the floral arrangement on the table. She had picked the flowers herself and had placed them in a vase. It wasn't much of a gift, on the scale of the things Ethan owned, but it was a love token given with sincerity.

'It's good to see you've made yourself at home.'

'Ethan!' In her euphoric state it seemed to Savannah she only had to think of Ethan for him to appear. 'You startled me,' she admitted, still clutching her chest. She sank down in her chair again, not wanting him to think her too excitable—or, worst-case scenario, too much in love with him. If he thought that it might prompt the unwanted opinion that she was too young to know what she wanted yet.

'I didn't mean to startle you. Perhaps you were daydreaming?'

'Perhaps I was,' she admitted shyly.

'No reason why you shouldn't. I want you to enjoy your short stay here.'

Savannah paled at Ethan's mention of a short stay. So last night had meant nothing to him. Of course it hadn't meant anything to him, Savannah realised, breaking up inside. Ethan was a sophisticated man, and she was...

What? A fool?

She was a farm girl from the depths of the country. And perhaps that was where she should have stayed.

She had jumped to so many conclusions, and all of them wrong. This man was not the tender lover from last night, but a stern and formidable stranger who was currently staring back at her as if she were a visitor she barely knew, and whom he was kindly putting up for the night.

'Do you have everything you need?' he said.

Not nearly, Savannah thought, following Ethan's gaze to her empty plate. 'I was waiting for you.'

'There's no need.' He appeared restless, as if he didn't even want to sit down.

'Is something wrong?' she asked him.

'I need to speak to you.' His voice, his manner, was a return to their former, professional relationship.

'It's not my parents, is it?' That at least would make a horrible sort of sense.

'No. They're both well,' he reassured her. He reached out a hand that didn't quite make it to her shoulder. 'Do you mind if I sit down, Savannah?'

Did she mind? It was the wrong question from the right mouth. 'Of course I don't mind.' Her heart squeezed tight. She was tense all over. 'Would you like some tea? Can I pour it for you?'

'I don't want anything, thank you.'

Normal, everyday things should make a crisis manageable, shouldn't they? It didn't work for her. Ethan hadn't even glanced at the flowers she'd picked for him. and now she braced herself, certain there was worse to come.

'The paparazzi are at the gates, Savannah.'

How right she was! 'Here at the *palazzo*?' She couldn't believe it. The stab of distress she felt at the thought that Ethan's privacy had been breached, and that it was all her fault, was terrible.

'You mustn't be alarmed,' he said, misreading her expression.

'Alarmed? I'm concerned for you.'

Ethan wasn't listening. 'If you stay in the grounds and let me handle them, you'll be safe. Savannah,' he said, staring at her intently, 'Trust me. I won't let them near you.'

All the ground she'd gained had been lost. Ethan thought she couldn't handle it. He was going to mop up the mess she'd created without her help. No wonder he'd cooled towards her. He'd had time to think, and had concluded she was a liability. A man who guarded his privacy as Ethan did must be eager to be rid of her. 'I can't tell you how sorry I am.'

'Sorry?' he cut across her. 'Please don't be. You have nothing to apologise for, Savannah. You've done nothing wrong.'

Other than to fall in love with him. Ethan was all concern for her—not because he loved her, but because she was under his protection—and he would do anything it took to keep her safe. Savannah knew she shouldn't want more than that, but she did. 'What can I do to help?'

'Stay out of the way?' Ethan suggested.

So she was to be compliant, invisible and ineffectual? She had never longed for the farm more. At least there she could have shown Ethan another side of her. It seemed now that was a side of her he would never see.

'The only problem, as I see it,' he observed, thoughtfully thumbing his stubble, 'Is that you'll have to stay here a little longer.'

He couldn't have made it clearer. There never had been any long-term plans where Ethan was concerned. That was the price she must pay for playing the game of love without the necessary credentials. 'But I can't just sit here. I have to do something.'

'The best thing you can do,' he said, 'is stay out of my way.'

Ethan was right; what did she know? Life on a working farm was great, but it wasn't the best apprenticeship for this world of celebrity. Whatever Ethan did now would be swift and decisive. He'd deal with the press and then he'd come back for her, by which time she must be ready to leave.

He returned to his office where he immediately contacted his legal team. He wanted them to draft an injunction to keep Savannah safe and free from harassment by the press when she left him, which must be soon now. She preoccupied his thoughts, and he missed her already. He'd noticed the softening touches she'd made—the dust sheets had all been removed and the *palazzo* had been thoroughly aired. There were flower arrangements in many of the rooms, punctuating the ancient artefacts and imbuing the *palazzo* with fresh life, he reflected, tapping his pen on the table top as he waited for his call to connect.

He had to stop this! He was relieved when his call connected, and he heard the cool, impersonal voice of his lawyer on the other end. Savannah was a real danger to the status quo in his life. She had made him look at things that had never mattered to him before—frescoes, carvings, and all the incredible paintings he'd inherited when he'd bought the *palazzo*. She was a Salome of the arts, he concluded, whilst firing instructions at his lawyer. Savannah had beguiled him with her voice, and then enchanted him with her innocence and naivety, tempting him beyond the logical and factual to appreciate the beauty and emotional wealth locked in the treasures he owned. Raking his hair into a worse state of disorder than before, he signed off, determined that Savannah's qualities would never be compromised. Thank goodness he'd recognised in time the imperative of putting a stop to this fantasy of loving her, and had brought cool legal minds to bear on the problem instead.

A few short words and his lawyer had got the picture. In fact, his lawyer had seen all the pictures. As he stowed the phone, he relaxed. Back in a familiar world without emotion, he could focus on the facts. Savannah's welfare meant everything to him. His feelings towards her might have muddied the water for a short time, but that was over now.

Over…

He still had her music. Picking up the remote-control, he turned on her CD. As Savannah's voice floated around him he found it impossible to remain tense—impossible to forget how very special she was, and how at all costs he must protect her.

At *all* costs, he reminded himself, as he left the room to make sure that Savannah had the chance to live her dream.

She wasn't good with make-up. In fact, she was useless, Savannah concluded as she peered into the mirror. She was back in her room and, having packed, she supposed putting on make-up before she left was all about pride. She was going to leave the *palazzo* with her head held high, and not looking like some washed-out waif. But a good technique with make-up took more skill than she had. Professional make-up artists had worked on her for the photo shoot for her album, though when she appeared on stage she could pile on the slap with the best of them; no subtlety required. But she hardly ever wore make-up off-duty. It would frighten the animals, she concluded wryly.

Well, she would just have to do, Savannah decided, having pulled her face this way and that. With no outfits to choose from, she was wearing jeans and flip-flops. But at least she had combed her hair, and she was wearing the pretty, lacy cardigan she always packed to wear over her evening gown to keep her warm in the wings while she was waiting to sing.

Moistening her lips, she attempted a pout and quickly gave up. You could put the glitz into the farm girl, but you could never take the farm girl out of Savannah Ross.

And thank goodness for it. She'd need every bit of grit she had to part from Ethan and act as if it didn't hurt like hell.

After instructing his lawyers, Ethan went outside and issued a statement to the press. He went back to the office, and had barely walked through the door when he saw Savannah's face staring out of one of the monitors. It was so unexpected, he stood transfixed, and then realised one of the reporters had somehow managed to elude his security staff and had accosted Savannah as she was coming out of the bedroom on her way across the court-yard. She was going to say goodbye to his staff in a typical act of kindness, he realised. His eyes narrowed as he took in the scene. Far from running scared, Savannah had the news hound by the elbow and was showing him the door. From the tilt of her chin he gathered she was about to send the man off with a flea in his ear. But were more opportunists hanging around? He was already through the door, this time with a look of murder in his eyes.

One reporter she could handle, but a jostling crowd…

CHAPTER THIRTEEN

HE WAS mobbed the moment he stepped outside the door by the paparazzi. Now that they'd seen Savannah leaving his private rooms, he would struggle to deny that anything was going on between them. Whatever Savannah had told them must have been good, he concluded as the reporters formed an arc around him. He gave them a look and they went scattering back. They had agreed to leave, and had been caught out. The photographers remained a safe distance away from him, hovering like slavering hyenas as they bumped each other shamelessly in an attempt to capture both him and Savannah in the same frame. He hadn't looked at her directly yet, but he was deeply conscious of her standing close by him. He made no attempt to close the gap. He had no intention of compromising her, and would keep his distance until he'd had his say.

'Is it true you and Ms Ross are an item?' one of them asked. 'I thought you told us that Ms Ross's welfare was your only concern.'

So, what had she told them? He had no way of knowing. His only concern was to protect Savannah and prevent scandal blighting her career. They had spent the whole day avoiding just this situation—but when she gave him a look that said her brave act of ejecting the reporter from the palace grounds had gone badly wrong, and she was sure she had just shot her reputation to hell and back, he moved swiftly into damage-limitation mode. He had two options: he could deny a relationship, and make Savannah look like a fool if she had said something different, or confirm one and bring her firmly under his protection. There was really no decision to be made. As he strolled over to her an air of expectancy swept the reporters, and as they fell back he put his arm around Savannah's shoulders.

For a moment Savannah couldn't get her head round the fact that Ethan was standing next to her. And not just standing at her side, but supporting her. The shock of feeling his arm around her shoulders must have gummed up her brain, she concluded as he gave her a reassuring squeeze. She knew this must just be an act for the benefit of the press, but it was a pretty seductive fantasy.

'I never saw you as a security-guard before, Ms Ross,' Ethan murmured. 'But you handle yourself pretty well.'

Savannah felt a rush of pride and relief as she identified the reporter she'd firmly ushered out of the grounds standing in line with the others. They were quite a team, she thought wryly as Ethan dealt effortlessly with the hail of questions—much good it would do her as far as her non-existent romance with Ethan was concerned!

'One question at a time, ladies and gentlemen, please.' Ethan raised his free hand to bring everyone to order, and she noticed how his relaxed tone of voice set everyone at ease.

'I'll answer all your questions. At least—' Ethan tempered with a glint in his eyes '—those I am prepared to.'

This made the reporters laugh, and as Ethan turned to glance at Savannah she felt her body respond. 'Of course, I can't speak for Ms Ross,' he added, with another of those dangerously addictive, reassuring squeezes.

As the noise of conversation fell Savannah realised how tense she had become. Pressed up hard against Ethan, she had grown as stiff as a board. Ethan, of course, had no such inhibitions, and was perfectly relaxed in the spotlight. He felt great—fantastic, in fact—warm, strong and in control. The first surprise he launched was to announce that she had his full authority to say anything she wanted to say about their relationship.

Their relationship?

'Not that Ms Ross needs my authority to do so,' he added with an engaging shrug. 'She's got plenty to say for herself.' Ethan's eyes were darkly amused as he turned to her for confirmation. He went on to agree to answer three questions. After which he was sure they'd all want to get away. 'So choose wisely,' he added, which brought another chuckle from the crowd.

He'd got them in the palm of his hand, Savannah realised. The female reporters were practically panting to be first to ask him questions. They might as well have called out, 'Choose me! Choose me!' she thought tensely as a forest of red-gloss-tipped hands shot up. How were they supposed to resist Ethan's wicked smile when it was sending seismic signals through her own system? And something told her this was just the tip of the iceberg where Ethan's charm offensive was concerned.

So, was she jealous? And since when? Since she realised she couldn't have him. She might not be able to have him, but did she want other women going there?

Now she was supposed to convince him she knew this was only an act for the press. Well, she'd give it her best shot.

The first question came from a young woman, who moistened her lips and arranged them in a pout before asking him, 'So, do you deny there is a relationship between yourself and your protégée, Ethan?'

'Not at all,' he said. 'Why should I?'

'But Ms Ross said—'

He didn't even blink, though he couldn't have had a clue what she had said. 'Miss Ross was trying to protect me...' As Ethan turned to look at her and his voice softened, his eyes held everything she could have hoped for.

Except sincerity, Savannah registered, meeting Ethan's gaze and holding it so that he was in no doubt that she knew this was all pretence. He got the message loud and clear. There was more humour in his gaze than anything else— humour and warmth—which was a devastating combination in such a dark, forbidding man, and all the warning she needed to keep her feelings for Ethan in check.

'So you and Ms Ross *are* an item?' the same girl pressed.

'Take care.' Ethan cut in like this was a game. 'That's your second question. Don't you think you should give someone else a chance?'

Reluctantly, the girl stepped back.

'*Are* you and Ms Ross an item?' A well-known wily reporter from a national television-station asked the same question, with more relaxed laughter.

'Ms Ross has already given you her answer—and, before you ask me to confirm what she's said, please think about your stories and how you're going to flesh them out. The tycoon leaving the stadium with his star performer can only be old news now, right?'

Ethan's audacity made Savannah gasp. Was he going

to write the press release for the reporters? From hunted to hunter in the space of a few seconds was not bad going, she reflected, even as the wily reporter pressed his lips down in acknowledgement of a worthy foe. 'But you must admit it's a great headline?' he said, launching his own fishing expedition.

'Is that question two or three?' Ethan's eyes were glinting with challenge, and Savannah knew he was enjoying this. Everything was a game to Ethan, a game he was determined to win.

'Will Ms Ross be staying at the *palazzo* with you for long?' The reporter waited patiently for Ethan to reply while the rest held a collective breath.

'As long as she likes,' Ethan said, turning to look at Savannah when she started to protest.

Okay, so she was only trying to defend Ethan's dignity—forget her honour; he clearly had. Pulling her tight, Ethan kissed away her protest, leaving her trembling like a leaf and everyone else gasping. 'Which means Miss Ross might be here quite some time,' he announced.

By the time Ethan released her she was fit for nothing, and even the reporters were still reeling with surprise that the famous recluse had come out. Ethan, of course, was completely unmoved, and continued his verbal jousting as if nothing unusual had happened.

So, what was he was up to? Disarming the press with more truth than they could handle? Even she wasn't naïve enough to believe that. His behaviour towards her had to be an act. She should have known better than to try and fight Ethan's battles in his own back yard. He was hardly the type to let her take over.

As cameras swivelled to take a better shot of her, Savannah's arms flew up instinctively to shield her face, and in that same moment Ethan stepped in front of her. 'We have a deal,' he told everyone firmly. 'And I expect you to honour that agreement, as I shall. I answer your questions, and in return you respect our privacy.'

Ethan's back cut off Savannah's view of the proceedings, but her pulse pounded a reminder that Ethan was a warrior who wouldn't allow her to stand alone. That didn't mean he felt the same about her as she felt about him, just that he was a natural born protector. She longed to tell the press that, whatever the future held for them, she adored Ethan Alexander and always would.

'And your third and last question?' Ethan prompted, reclaiming Savannah's attention as he drew her close.

'How long do you expect this *liaison* to last, Ethan?' the reporter asked him, making the word liaison sound sordid.

Savannah felt Ethan's grip change and soften, instead of growing angry, and she realised that she could have walked away from him at that point, had she wanted to.

'Don't you think it would be more chivalrous if you addressed that question to Ms Ross?' Ethan's tone was neutral, almost as if he was condoning the reporter's scathing tone. But as the reporter turned to her Savannah felt very strongly that Ethan had played some clever move.

'Well, Ms Ross?' the reporter demanded.

Before she could answer, Ethan held up his hand. 'You've had your three questions,' he pointed out wryly.

As a clamour of protest threatened to break out, Ethan smiled at her. 'Why don't we pose for an official photograph?' he suggested.

'Are you serious?' Savannah said incredulously, still reeling from Ethan's killer move.

'Never more so.'

As Ethan's mouth quirked with familiar humour,

Savannah realised she trusted him. It was that simple and that complicated, she thought, taking her place standing at Ethan's side.

That was the signal for the photographers to rush to grab the best positions. They called for them to look this way and that, and fortunately smiling came easily to her. It wasn't that hard to pretend she felt good pressed up close to Ethan, and when the photographers asked them to change position, and he brought her in front of him with his arms loosely slung around her waist, she could have happily stayed there for ever. How hard could it be to rest her head against the chest of the man she loved with all her heart?

'There's just one more thing, ladies and gentlemen of the press,' Ethan announced when everyone had had their fill of them. 'And my lawyers have mailed this information to your editors,' he added. 'My legal team has drafted an injunction protecting Ms Ross. It was placed in front of a judge this morning. Everything that falls outside what I have told you will be jumped on. And, of course, this order will protect Ms Ross when she leaves here and picks up her career. She will not be harassed or there will be legal consequences. She will be left alone.'

He didn't need to say more, Savannah realised, taking in everyone's expression. There wasn't one reporter there who was prepared to risk an expensive libel case that might put their job in jeopardy. Ethan had acted swiftly and effectively to protect her.

'But you've told us very little,' the wily older reporter complained. 'Other than the fact that what we have on you and Ms Ross is old news.'

As they looked at each other both men knew this was the end game. There was nothing left for the reporters to do but to pack up and leave. They did so without further comment, but as they reached their vehicles the older reporter turned and tipped his head in Ethan's direction, as if acknowledging another man at the top of his game.

'With the lives we both lead, it's almost inevitable that our paths will cross again,' Ethan explained as they watched the reporter walk away.

'And you don't mind that?'

'Challenge always gives me a buzz.'

So Ethan's life would go flat now. And she hadn't been much of a challenge for him, had she? Savannah reflected, remembering she'd practically begged Ethan to make love to her.

His phone rang and he had to turn away to take the call. 'Will you excuse me?' he said politely.

Savannah waited.

'The England manager,' Ethan revealed, sounding pleased. 'The boys won their match and would like to come over for a celebration.'

'Oh, that's great news!'

He looked at her sternly. 'I was about to say, but—'

'But what?' Savannah cut in again.

'But, in case you hadn't noticed, I don't do entertaining.' Having slipped the phone into the pocket of his shirt, Ethan started walking back towards the *palazzo*.

'But I do,' Savannah called after him recklessly.

'You do what?'

Ethan stopped so abruptly, she almost ran into him again. 'I do entertaining,' Savannah explained, staying a safe distance away. 'In fact, I love entertaining.' The prospect of humiliation was very real, seeing as she was supposed to be leaving the *palazzo*, not arranging a party for Ethan. But what did she have to lose? 'So, if you need a hostess, you've got one.'

'No.' Ethan quickened his step.

'No?' Prompted into action, Savannah ran after him. 'Why not?'

'For the obvious reasons.'

'What obvious reasons? Ethan, please, just wait and listen to me.'

'I said no, Savannah. Thank you for the offer, but there isn't going to be a party here. Half the *palazzo* is shut up. It hasn't seen the light of day since I bought it.'

'Well, what a good excuse to open it up. It can be done, Ethan, just like my room.'

Shaking his head, he strode away from her. 'I've got business appointments.'

'I could handle everything for you.'

'You?' He didn't break stride as he headed back towards the *palazzo*.

'Yes, me,' Savannah said patiently, scurrying along at his side.

'The boys can come over for a quiet kitchen-supper.'

She felt like punching the air.

'But I don't do celebrations.'

'There's always a first time.'

'That's a popular misconception put about by an optimist,' Ethan informed her, speeding up again.

'You wouldn't even have to be there,' Savannah added hastily, forced to run to keep up as they crossed the court-yard. 'Unless you wanted to be there, of course,' she added, seeing Ethan's expression darken.

'If I agree to anything at all, it will be a quiet meal or-ganised by my staff. And an early night for everyone,' he told her sternly, reaching for the door.

'Oh…I'm sure the squad will enjoy that.' Savannah pulled a face Ethan couldn't see as he lifted the latch on the big wooden door that led through to the utility rooms at the back of the *palazzo*.

'So, what are you saying?' He swung round to confront her. 'You want to stay another night?'

It would have been nice if he'd wanted her to. She swallowed her pride. 'If it would help you, yes; I'm prepared to do that.'

Ethan's hum told her nothing, his expression even less, but she wasn't done yet. This was one straw she wasn't going to lose her grip on. 'You helped me. I'd like to help you.' She gave a nonchalant shrug. 'It's the least I can do.'

The very least.

CHAPTER FOURTEEN

'MY STAFF won't need your help with a kitchen-supper,' Ethan pointed out.

'I'd like to do a little more than that for the squad.' And when Ethan threw her a hard stare she added, 'Don't look so suspicious, Ethan. I'm not going to turn it into a bacchanalian romp.'

'I should hope not.' He held the door into the hallway for her.

'Just some good food and hospitality.'

'A kitchen-supper,' Ethan confirmed, which wasn't what Savannah had in mind at all. There was that cobwebby old dining-room to be brought out of wraps, just for starters.

'Either way,' she said, curbing her enthusiasm as more ideas came to her, 'we should consult with your staff first, as this is very short notice for them.'

'At the start of this discussion, tonight wasn't going to be an event my staff would need notice for,' he pointed out.

True, but she had learned when to speak and when to say nothing—and what was it people said about actions speaking louder than words?

* * *

She wasn't going to build any bridges with marshmallow and fluff, Savannah reflected, rolling up her sleeves to help Ethan's staff prepare the neglected dining-room. Beneath the dust sheets the furniture was still beautiful, and the upholstery, in a variety of jewel-coloured silks, was as good as new. Ethan had carved his own narrow path through the glories of the *palazzo*, looking neither left nor right, she guessed, until he'd reached the suite of rooms he had chosen to occupy.

Later that day as Savannah straightened up to survey the finished dining-room she joined Ethan's staff in exclaiming with delight. The transformation from spooky and dark to glittery and bright was incredible. But would Ethan share their pleasure, or would he be furious? Having given his tacit consent to a quiet evening in, he would hardly have expected her to expand that brief quite so radically. But the old *palazzo* deserved an airing and the England squad certainly deserved this.

Savannah thanked each member of the household by name before they left the dining-room, knowing she couldn't have done any of this without them. She had been accepted by the people who worked for Ethan, and their smiles were so warm and friendly that she felt quite at home. Which was a joke, because this was not her home. In twenty-four hours she would fly back to England and never see it again. That was her deadline for convincing Ethan that this scene of warmth, comfort and welcome didn't have to end when she left, and that it was better for everyone who lived in the *Palazzo dei Tramonti Dorati* than cobwebs, shadows and dust.

Taking one last look around before she left the glowing

room, Savannah thought of this as her one chance to give Ethan an evening to remember, as well as to restore the heart of his *palazzo* before she returned home.

Ethan's chef excelled himself, working non-stop in the kitchen, and when the housekeeper had finished lighting all the candles Savannah thought she had never seen a lovelier room. With its soaring ceiling and deep, mullioned windows, the flicker of candlelight, the long, oval dining-table dressed with fine linen, sparkling crystal glasses, and Ethan's best silver cutlery brought out of storage for the occasion, it looked quite magnificent. Ethan had sent a message to say he had been detained on business and to start without him. What he would think of her opening up the dining-room when he was expecting to hunker down in the kitchen, she could only guess. It wouldn't be good news for her, Savannah thought, but what mattered more was that Ethan saw the possibilities here. There was a palpable air of excitement amongst his staff, and at their urging she had even gone mad and donned her neglected pink gown for the evening.

Feeling a flutter of excitement at the thought that all that was missing now were the guests, Savannah slowly turned full circle one last time to take everything in.

He was annoyed at being late, but it couldn't be helped. The meeting had run on longer than he'd thought. The England squad was already here. He'd seen their coach in the courtyard. He could hear the sound of male laughter as he strode across the hall. He ran up to his room to shower and change, eager to get back down and support Savannah. There was too much testosterone floating around for his liking. It was only on his way downstairs again that he realised the sounds he could hear were not coming from the kitchen, but from the dining-room. He frowned as he retraced his steps across the hall. The room had been shut up for years…

A manservant opened the double doors for him with a flourish, and as he stood on the threshold he was momentarily stunned. The scene laid out in front of him showed the oak-panelled dining-room fully restored to its former glory. It was a haven of colour and warmth, and the sound of fun and laughter drew him in.

If Savannah had chosen to be a theatrical designer rather than a singer, she couldn't have conjured up a more glamorous set. But in the centre of that set was the centre of his attention: Savannah, looking more dazzling than he'd ever seen her.

Looking…There were no words to describe how Savannah looked. With her soft, golden curls hanging loose in a shimmering curtain down her back, she looked ethereal, and yet glamorous and womanly. She was playing hostess to the squad in a stunning pale-pink gown that fitted her voluptuous figure perfectly. This was no child, or some wanton sex-kitten displaying her wares in front of a roomful of men. This was a real woman, a woman with class, with heart and light in her eyes, a woman he now remembered was accustomed to working alongside men on her parents' farm, which explained her ease of manner. That was what made it so easy for his friends on the squad to relate to her, he realised.

'Ethan…'

Seeing him, her face lit up, and as she came towards him he realised he had expected to be shunned after the churlish way he'd treated her, but instead she was holding out her hands to invite him in. She was more than beautiful, he realised in that moment; Savannah was one of those rare people: a force for good.

'Come,' she said softly. 'Come and meet your guests, Ethan.'

His attention was centred on her after that moment, and though he was quickly immersed in the camaraderie of the team he was acutely aware of her every second.

The boys in the squad laughed goodnaturedly, and made him admit that what Savannah had organised for them was a whole lot better than a quiet kitchen-supper. He agreed, and eventually even he was laughing. What Savannah had done for the team had made them feel special. She made him feel special.

It thrilled Savannah to see what an inspiration Ethan was to the younger players. Everyone showed him the utmost respect. At Ethan's insistence she was sitting next to him. She couldn't bear to think this was the last occasion when she would do that.

'Here's to England winning the Six Nations,' he said, standing up to deliver the toast. 'And here's to the only one amongst us without a broken nose.'

It took Savannah a moment to realise Ethan was raising his glass to her, and as everyone laughed and cheered he added, 'To our gracious hostess for the evening, the lovely Savannah Ross.'

'Savannah Ross!' the squad chorused, raising their glasses to her.

Savannah's cheeks were crimson, but Ethan hadn't finished with her yet. 'Would you sing for us?' he murmured discreetly. As his warm breath brushed her cheeks her heart beat even faster. She was touched by the request, but terrified at the thought of singing in front of a room full of people, all of whose faces she could see quite clearly. There was no nice, safe barrier of blinding footlights to hide behind here.

'I'm sure you don't want to hear my rendition of Rusalka's *Song to the Moon*!' She laughed, as if the aria's romantic title would be enough to put him off.

But Ethan wasn't so easily dissuaded. 'That sounds lovely.' He looked round the table for confirmation, and everyone agreed.

As the room went still, Savannah wondered could she do this? Could she sing the song of the water-sprite telling the moon of her love for one man? And could she do that with Ethan staring at her?

Help him in dreams to think of me...

'No pressure,' Ethan said dryly.

Pressing her fingertips on the table, she slowly got up.

Silvery moon in the great, dark sky...

Savannah hardly remembered what happened after the opening line, because she was lost in the music and the meaning of the words. She didn't come to until she heard everyone cheering and banging the table. And then she found Ethan at her side. 'Did I—?'

'Sing beautifully?' he said, staring deep into her eyes. 'Yes, you did.'

She relaxed and, laughing as she shook her head in exaggerated complaint, raised her eyes to the ceiling for the benefit of the squad. 'What can you do with him?'

'What can *you* do with him?' Ethan murmured, but when her quick glance brushed his face she saw his expression hadn't changed. It was always so hard to know what Ethan was thinking.

'Our only difficulty with Ethan,' one of the players told her, 'is that he refuses to consider anything that has his name, a team, a ball, and a rugby pitch in the same sentence.'

'Leave it,' Ethan warned goodnaturedly when he overheard this comment.

Savannah kept her thoughts to herself. But didn't everyone know Ethan's injuries had prevented him from further involvement in the game? He just couldn't risk one of the man-mountains landing on top of him. Tactfully, she changed the subject. Tapping her water glass with a spoon, she offered to sing an encore if the boys would help her with the chorus. And as she'd hoped that soon took the spotlight off Ethan.

After murdering every song they could think of, the players retired to bed, while Savannah insisted on changing and staying behind to help the staff clear up. 'It's late,' she told Ethan, 'and everyone's tired. We've had a wonderful evening, thanks to your staff working so late, so I'm going to stay and help them.'

'Then so will I,' he said, giving his staff the night off.

'I never thought I'd have the courage to sing in front of such a small group of people,' Savannah admitted as they worked side by side, putting the room to rights.

'You could certainly see the whites of their eyes,' he agreed wryly.

But none of them had eyes as beautiful as Ethan's, Savannah mused, keeping this thought in a warm little pocket close to her heart. 'You gave me the courage to do it,' she admitted.

'Then I'm pleased if your short stay here has helped your confidence.'

Savannah didn't hear any more. The warm little pocket shrivelled to nothing. She'd been trying to tell Ethan they were a great team, but it had fallen on deaf ears. And if that was all he thought this incredible time had meant to her she really was on a hiding to nothing. But at least she could stop worrying whether she had given away too much, singing her impassioned song to the moon, Savannah reflected sadly, for just as Ethan's talent for inspiring people and for his art was wasted so was her love for him.

'You were great tonight,' he said, reclaiming her attention as he toed open the door to carry a tray to the kitchen. But just as her heart began to lift, he added, 'I'm really glad we signed you, Savannah Ross.'

She was still flat when Ethan returned with the empty tray. 'Well, have we finished?' he said.

'Looks like it,' Savannah agreed, checking round. 'What?' she prompted when Ethan continued to look at her.

She would ignore that look of his. Memories of their love-making sent an electric current shooting through her body; she'd ignore that too. What she must do was leave the room. 'Excuse me, please.' She avoided Ethan's gaze as she tried to move past him.

'I thought you might want a nightcap.' One step was all it took to block her way.

That was the cue for her willpower to strike. She wanted Ethan to make love to her one last time, though in her heart she knew sex would never be enough; she wanted more; she wanted all of him.

But, if sex was all they had, what then?

CHAPTER FIFTEEN

'It doesn't usually take you so long to decide, Savannah.'

True, Savannah accepted wryly. The way Ethan had pitched his voice, so low and sexy, was sending her desire for him into overdrive. 'Water's fine.'

What was she doing? So much for her intention to retire to bed and think chaste thoughts! She'd sold out for a glass of water, and now Ethan showed no signs of moving out of her way.

He wanted her. He loved her. Savannah had impressed him tonight in every way, but what he felt for her was so much more than pride in her achievements. She had filled his home with light and laughter, and he could never thank her enough for that. She'd worked as hard as any member of his staff to make his friends feel welcome. She'd mixed well with the men and had known where the boundaries lay and how to impose a few of her own without causing embarrassment. She'd told him more about the farm and her life there, and he only wished he'd had the chance to see it before their lives diverged. But at least she was leaving on a high note. He would never forget the way that men with battered faces had treated her like a favourite sister, and how much trouble she had gone to for them. And how she had looked so beautiful, and yet not once had flaunted her appeal. In fact, quite the opposite; she seemed totally unaware of it.

'It was a great night, Ethan; let's not spoil it now.'

'Spoil it?' he queried.

'You know I have to go tomorrow.'

So let's not draw this out, she was telling him. And, yes, he should let her go. 'It was a very good night,' he agreed, fighting back passion. But there were forces inside him that overruled his modern take on the situation. She was his. He wanted her. He loved this woman. The desire to possess Savannah overwhelmed him, and as she sensed the change in him and her eyes darkened he dragged her into his arms.

This was wrong. This was fool's gold. This was also the only thing on earth she wanted right now. She put up a token resistance, pressing her hands against Ethan's chest, but as she stared into his eyes and he murmured something decidedly erotic she gave in. Ethan understood the needs of her body and how to turn her on in every way there was. He knew how to extend her pleasure until she was mad with it, mad for him, and now all expectations of sleeping alone and dreaming chaste thoughts were gone. She groaned softly as he teased her with his lips, and with his tongue and teeth, reminding her of what came next. He felt so hard, toned and warm as his hands found her breasts. And he tasted of warm, hungry man— clean, so good, and so very familiar. And she'd missed him in the few hours they'd been apart.

But she shouldn't… They mustn't…

Her hips were already tilting, thrusting, inviting, while

Ethan was backing her relentlessly towards the door. She waited until he slipped the lock before lacing her fingers through his thick dark hair and making him her prisoner. 'Shall we be captives here for long?'

'As long as it takes,' he promised huskily.

And as he brushed her lips with his mouth, and she sighed and melted, she murmured, 'Kiss me.'

'Since when do I have to be prompted?'

Since never. Savannah purred with desire, and then gasped as Ethan swept her into his arms and carried her across the room. 'What do you think you're doing?' she murmured as he laid her down on the rug.

'A nice, soft rug is so much kinder than a table, don't you think?'

Savannah's cheeks blazed red as she understood Ethan's intentions were to take her any place, any time, anywhere, much as her fantasies had dictated. 'Why didn't I think of the rug?' she murmured, arcing towards him.

'Because you've still got a lot to learn?'

'Everything,' she corrected him happily.

'So, I'll teach you. Where would you like me to start?'

'Right here…' She placed his hand over her breast, and uttered a happy cry when he turned her beneath him.

Holding her wrists loosely above her head, Ethan dealt with the fastening on her clothes. She loved it when his big, warm hands cupped her buttocks, subjecting her to delicious stroking moves as he prepared her. She loved to feel those hands caressing and supporting her as he positioned her. She loved everything about him—the wide spread of his shoulders, the power in his chest, and the biceps flexing on his arms when he braced himself above her. She felt protected and loved. She wanted this, needed him—needed Ethan deep inside her so she could forget she had to leave him in the morning. Wrapped up in passion, she wound her legs around him and lost herself again.

His intention had been to take Savannah to bed and make love to her all night, but here, in front of a crackling fire in the candlelit room she had made beautiful, there were all the romantic elements she could wish for, and he wanted to give her the full fairy-tale romance. All that had ever stood in the way of that was his cold, unfeeling heart, but for tonight he had the chance to hold Savannah in his arms while she slept, and he wanted to remember how she felt in his arms, and how she looked when he held her safe. He wanted to keep her safe always. *Safe from him.*

He knew what he must do, Ethan accepted grimly. Easing his arm out from under her, he kissed Savannah awake like some prince in a distorted fairy-tale. There could be no happy ending here. She smiled at him groggily. Reaching for his hand, she brought it to her lips. As she gazed at him her lips moved, and the dread that she was going to say 'I love you' made him kiss her again, but this time not to wake her, but to silence her. He wouldn't lure her into his cold, dark world, but the moment he released her she asked the one question he had been dreading most. 'Ethan, tell me about your scars.'

He turned his face away for a moment, cursing his arrogant assumption that Savannah could ever be distracted from her purpose. She touched his face to bring him back to her, but he pulled away. 'What do you want to know?' he said coldly.

'Everything.'

Everything? The word echoed in his head. If he would

save her from him, he was blindingly certain he would save her from *everything*.

'Ethan, why is it so wrong for me to want to be close to you when we just made love? I want to know who did this to you and why. Surely you can trust me enough to tell me that?'

She had no idea. How could she? He removed himself a little more, both physically and mentally. 'I can understand your fascination.' He spoke in a murmur as he reasoned it through, his mind set on other occasions when he'd suspected the questioner had obtained some sort of foul, vicarious thrill out of the violence.

'Fascination?' Savannah's voice called him back. 'Ethan, you don't know me at all. How can you think me so shallow?'

'Aren't all women shallow?' The bitterness burst out of him before he could stop it.

'I don't know what kind of women you've met in the past,' Savannah countered hotly. 'And I don't want to. But I can assure you I'm *not* shallow.' Her voice was raised, her body tense, and her gaze held his intently—but after a moment she froze, and a change came over her. 'Is your mother behind this?'

Every part of him railed against this intrusion into the deepest part of his psyche. 'How could you know that?'

'Because I can't think of anything more terrible than betrayal by a mother, and whatever wounded you to this extent has to be that bad.'

'You know all about me in five minutes?' he demanded scornfully.

'I knew you from the moment I met you.' She said this with blinding honesty 'From that second on, Ethan, I knew you.'

For the longest moment neither of them spoke, and then he told her some of it.

'One man did this to you, Ethan?' Savannah's face contorted with disbelief, and her eyes betrayed her bitter disappointment that Ethan didn't trust her more than that.

'I don't believe you. I can't believe this was some random attack. There isn't a man alive who could do this to you.' Her eyes narrowed in thought. 'Unless you were unconscious at the time—were you unconscious? Did someone drug you to do this?'

'It would be a cold day in hell before that happened.'

He must have been attacked by a gang, Savannah reasoned. The way Ethan had described his stepfather, the man had been a cowardly weed who wouldn't have had the strength to hold Ethan down and inflict such terrible injuries.

'Can we drop the subject?' he snapped, jolting her out of her calculations.

'No, we can't,' she said bluntly. 'I want the truth, Ethan—all of it. We just did some very adult things, and it's time you stopped treating me like a child.'

CHAPTER SIXTEEN

ETHAN'S naked torso looked as though a pitchfork with serrated edges had been dragged back and forth across it several times. 'A gang of men must have done this to you,' Savannah insisted, sure she was right now.

'You tell me,' Ethan snarled, 'Since you seem to know so much about it.'

The tension in him frightened her. Wound up so tight, he surely had to snap. But she wouldn't let it go. She couldn't let it go. If she couldn't reach out now and touch him, she never would. She went for his machismo with all guns blazing. 'If a gang of thugs attacked you it's nothing to be ashamed of.'

'*Ashamed?*' Ethan roared, exactly as she'd hoped. 'You think I'm ashamed?'

His fury filled the room, but as the window of opportunity opened she climbed through it. 'What am I supposed to think if you won't tell me?'

'May I suggest you don't think about it at all, since it's no concern of yours?'

Savannah's heart was hammering in her chest at the thought of what she'd started, but if Ethan held back now there was no hope for him—for them. 'If we mean anything to each other.' She could see the black void in Ethan, but stubbornly she kept right on blundering towards it. 'If you can't trust me.'

He was already reaching for his shirt. 'Get dressed,' he said, tossing her clothes onto the bed. He couldn't wait to leave her. She'd gone too far.

Savannah dressed quickly, determined to finish what she'd started, and with everything half-fastened and hanging off her shoulders she raced to the door. Pressing her back against it, she barred his way. 'Tell me—tell me everything, Ethan. I won't move until you do.'

He looked down at her from his great height as if she were an annoying flea he might choose to flick out of his way. She braced herself against the look in his eyes, and against the knowledge that Ethan could always use the simple expedient of lifting her out of his way. His expression assured her he had considered that, but to her immense relief he eased back. Several seconds passed while they measured each other and then he started speaking.

'A gang of men attacked me with baseball bats. When I was unconscious they cut me.' He said this with all the expression of a man reading out a shopping list. 'Are you satisfied, Savannah?'

'Not nearly.' She felt so sick she could hardly stand. 'Why did they do that?' she demanded.

'Don't push it.'

'Why?'

'I don't talk about this—not to you, not to anyone.'

He held her gaze, unblinking, until she was forced to look away.

'You were lucky to survive—'

'I said I don't talk about it.' His expression had turned to stone.

'You were lucky to retain your mobility. There must be many who have not been so fortunate.'

'Savannah,' he growled in warning.

'Or who have lived to tell the tale.'

'Comprehend this,' he snarled, bringing his face menacingly close. 'I don't want your understanding, and I sure as hell don't want your pity.' Pulling back abruptly, he unlocked the door and left the room.

She had prepared for this, but, even so, Savannah was stunned for a moment. The energy from Ethan's fury still rang in her ears, disorientating her, but she rallied quickly. Chasing after him, straightening her clothes as she ran, she followed him up the stairs. The lights had been dimmed as the staff had gone to bed, and tall, black shadows crossed with Ethan's, joining them by a tenuous thread. Driving herself to the limit, Savannah took the stairs two by two.

Catching hold of her as she came up to him on the landing, Ethan swung her round. 'Do you and I speak the same language?' he demanded, trapping her against the wall.

She fought him, warned him to get off her and railed at him, but Ethan stole each impassioned word from her lips with a kiss.

'Hiding the evidence of your arousal?' Ethan taunted, as when he released her she stood with the back of her hand across her mouth.

'I love you. Of course I respond to you. I have nothing to hide.' She pulled her hand away, revealing her love-swollen lips. 'Why do you hide your pain from me, Ethan?'

'My pain?' Ethan laughed. 'Spare me the psychobabble.'

'Is it too close to home?'

He greeted this with a contemptuous sound.

'So now you return to your ivory tower,' Savannah observed. 'And I go home?'

'It's safer for you there.'

'Safer,' Savannah repeated, shaking her head. 'There's no compromise with you, is there?'

'No,' Ethan confirmed.

'Then by those same rules you have to accept I won't give up on you.'

As the light played on Ethan's hard, set face, he folded his arms and leaned back against the door.

Ethan continued to stare at her with his dark eyes slumberous and knowing Savannah wanted him to seduce her all over again. He held a dangerous power over her, she realised, and that power was addictive. The pleasure Ethan could deliver was unimaginable, and she would never get enough of him. But with his warm, hard body possessing her, the realities of life would always be shut out. 'I won't leave until you tell me how you got those,' she said, refocusing determinedly.

He laughed. 'You're refusing to leave my house?'

'What's the worst that can happen, Ethan—you tear up my contract?' His eyes narrowed with surprise, as if that had never occurred to him. 'Your life is far more important to me than a recording contract.' The moment this was out in the open, Savannah felt naked and vulnerable. She would give up everything for Ethan, she realised, and now he knew that too. If he laughed at her now, everything was over.

Ethan remained where he was, with his arms folded, quietly watching her.

She pressed him again about his scars. 'Please,' she entreated, holding out her hands to him.

'Believe me, you don't want to know,' Ethan said, shifting position.

It was a start; it was a chink of light at the end of the tunnel and she groped towards it. 'Perhaps you think I'm too young to share this with you, though not to take to bed?' she suggested.

Ethan shrugged, and in the same monotone he'd used before he told her about the beatings that had started when he was little, and had gone on until he was too big for them, when his stepfather had employed a gang of thugs to finish the job. His stepfather's timing had been impeccable, she learned. He had chosen the week Ethan had heard he'd won a coveted place on the England rugby squad to finish the job.

'So I would never play again. And, as a bonus, he had me scarred.'

Ethan's early life had been so very different from her own, Savannah could hardly take it in. But it made everything clear, she realised as he went on. 'Before his arrest my stepfather and mother came to visit me in hospital. He must have wanted to be certain the job had been completed to his satisfaction before handing over his money, I imagine.'

Savannah's stomach churned at the thought of so much evil. 'Go on,' she prompted softly.

'His main purpose was to ensure no one would ever look at me again without revulsion, and who better to test this on than my mother?'

'I can't believe your own mother would turn from you. Surely that was the very moment when she would draw you to her heart?'

'Your experience of childhood was very different to mine. Let's just say my stepfather got his money's worth.'

'No, let's not,' Savannah argued fiercely. 'He failed. If anyone notices your scars, you make them forget. You have a bigger heart and a bigger presence than your step-father could possible imagine.'

'And there's a grisly fascination about me that makes me irresistible to the ladies?' Ethan interrupted dryly. 'Yes, I know that too.'

'Don't you dare suggest that's how I feel, because it's just not true. You're more of a man than anyone I know. And, as for your stepfather…' Savannah's rage was all the more vivid for being contained. 'The little worm!' she managed finally.

As Ethan's eyes flickered she poured her love into him. There was just a single step dividing them and she took it. Winding her arms around his neck, she stared into his eyes. 'I can't leave you like this.'

Gently untangling her arms, Ethan pulled away. 'Give up on this, Savannah.'

'Never!' But she could feel him withdrawing into himself, and she didn't know how to pull him back.

'Goodnight, Savannah.'

She heard the note of finality in his voice, and as Ethan turned away she wondered if she would ever be able to forget this moment and what might have been, or close her heart to the possibility of love.

Savannah's eyes were still drugged with sleep when her searching hands acknowledged an empty bed. Of course her bed was empty. Ethan wasn't here. Ethan never had been here in the way she'd wanted him to be, and last night he had made it clear he never would be. Fumbling for the light switch, she grimaced when she saw the time. He must have been up for hours saying goodbye to his friends, and hopefully, she wasn't too late to do the same.

When she entered the dining-room everyone cheered.

'What?' Savannah said, smiling as she stared around. Ethan's stare was boring into her, but she couldn't ignore those happy faces round the table.

Ethan's voice curled round her, underscoring her sense of loss. 'Your CD just debuted at number one on the classical charts.'

Number one? She should feel something. This was what she and the team behind her had been working towards for years. Her career was important to Ethan's record company, Savannah registered numbly, so she was pleased for him.

She had everything to be grateful for, she told herself firmly, prompting her reluctant facial muscles into a smile.

'We'll want your autograph before we leave,' one of the players teased, understandably oblivious to Savannah's troubled state of mind.

'And could you sign this for my sister?' asked another. 'My sister dreams of being a singer like you one day.'

Savannah jolted round immediately. 'I'll do better than that,' she offered. 'Piece of paper, anyone?' Ethan tore a sheet from a pad and handed it to her. Resting it on a magazine, she scribbled something and handed it to the player. 'Give this to your sister. It's my telephone number. Tell her to ring me. I'll give her any help I can.' Who knew more about dreams than she did?

Playing a role helped her get through the rest of the morning, and then the happy hostess standing at the leading man's side waved off the team.

Ethan waited until the coach was out of sight before asking Savannah to accompany him to his study.

'What's this?' Savannah said as he handed her an envelope. She gazed in dread at it, as if it contained the ashes of her future.

'It's your first-class ticket home.' His stare was un-swerving, and the fact that he'd put acres of desk between them wasn't lost on her. Closing her fingers around the envelope, she wanted to say something, anything, but the words just wouldn't come.

'I didn't think you'd want to travel back with the team.' Ethan had put her welfare first again, Savannah registered dully, as if he were her business manager rather than her lover. 'And I thought you should travel home in style.' He said this as if that style was the panacea for all ills.

'Travel home in style?' Savannah repeated.

'My chauffeur will take you to the airport, and from there you'll—'

'Ethan,' she cut across him. 'I don't need a chauffeur to take me to the airport, and I don't need to travel home in style.'

'There's around an hour until you leave.' He might not have heard her. 'It shouldn't take you long to pack, should it?'

Some toiletries and two evening gowns? 'No, it shouldn't take long.'

'Good. That's settled, then. And I don't want you worrying about the paparazzi.'

Ethan was nothing if not efficient, Savannah thought, already anticipating his next reassurances concerning security, guards and alarms.

'So you'll be fine,' he finished.

If that was all it took, Savannah thought wistfully, ex-pressing her thanks. Learning what she had about him, she could understand why Ethan's heart had grown so cold, but not why he refused to embrace the chance of love.

'Okay?' he said with one of those brief, forced smiles people used to bring an encounter to an end.

'Okay,' she agreed with the same false gusto.

Ethan had his fists planted on the desk and was leaning towards her, as if keen to underline his concern. Savannah thought she knew why. She was the valuable property of Ethan's record company, and it made sense to protect her. This was no personal relationship, other than in her self-deluded head. She stuck the envelope in the back pocket of her jeans, and when Ethan looked as if he was waiting for her to say something more she managed, 'First class? Exciting.'

'My apologies. I couldn't free up the jet for you, because I need to use it.'

'No problem,' she assured him. If Ethan wasn't with her who cared where she sat? But…more leg-room with the heart ache? She'd take it. 'I'll get ready, then.'

What more was there to say? Should she beg Ethan to let her stay on? And, if he agreed, could she ever soften him?

The reality of a man who had proved to be absolutely untouchable chilled her to the core. It was better to leave now before she said or did something she'd regret, Savannah concluded. She loved Ethan with all her heart, but in his eyes she could see not even a flicker of encouragement. Having thanked him again for the arrangements he'd so kindly made for her, she did the only thing possible and left.

CHAPTER SEVENTEEN

HE LISTENED to the limousine crunch across the gravel as it carried Savannah to the airport, waiting for the rush of relief that never came. She had sought him out immediately before leaving to thank him for his *hospitality*. His hospitality? When she'd left him to go and pack, he'd sat brooding in his study, supposedly finalising a bid for a country home in Surrey, but his thoughts were all of Savannah. He wouldn't inflict himself on her, which was the only reason he let her go. She was young and idealistic, and in time she'd come to see he was right. He was glad she had gone, he brooded, gazing out of the window at a view that was no longer perfect without Savannah in it. Perhaps if he repeated that mantra long enough he would come to believe it.

He pictured her face and remembered her parting words: 'You have a beautiful home, Ethan; take care of it. And start painting again.' She had smiled hopefully at him as she'd said this, adding, 'You have a real talent.'

For the macabre?

'Yours is the talent,' he'd told her.

'Paint some happy scenes, Ethan, and don't hide them away—put them on display.'

It was shorthand they both understood for 'keep the lights on'.

Savannah had done more than bring the *palazzo* to life, she had held up a mirror to his life, giving him a tantalising glimpse of how it could be. Which was all the more reason to set that pure heart free. He wouldn't weigh Savannah down with his dark legacy. Savannah deserved better than that, better than him, and with her career going from strength to strength there was no reason why she couldn't have it.

It was like the bottom falling out of your world twice, Savannah concluded as she closed the front door on the bailiffs. She was still reeling from her parting from Ethan, and had barely been back at the farmhouse in England five minutes when the two men had knocked at the door.

It was like a black-comedy sketch, she decided, crossing the room to put the kettle on the Aga; a very black comedy-sketch.

'Your parents have taken on too much credit, love,' the bailiffs had told her when she had assured them with matching determination that they must have got the wrong address. Unfortunately, the two men had had the right address and there was no mistake. They had shown her the legal documents they'd brought with them, and she had checked out the court order line by hateful line. The only reason they'd cut her a bit of slack was because they had wanted her autograph.

Understanding they were only doing their job, she had given them that before going to the bank to take out enough cash to send them away happy.

As she nursed her mug of tea, Savannah could only be thankful she hadn't got round to spending a penny of the money from her first royalty-cheque before she'd left for Rome. At least she had been able to put that money to good use now. But how could this have happened? She had asked herself this same question over and over again. How could her parents' world fall apart like this in the space of a few days?

But it wasn't a few days, Savannah reflected, walking to the window and staring out bleakly at the well-kept yard. It was years of paying for the best teachers, the best gowns, and even the lovingly polished second-hand grand piano in the dining-room. It was years of sacrifice for her. And she hadn't seen it before. She had grown up taking such things for granted—the golf club, the tennis club, all the right places and all the right clothes—and all these things cost more money than her parents had, or could make from the farm.

'We've seen it all before,' one of the bailiffs had assured her as he'd taken an inventory of her parents' possessions. 'And not just in the leafy lanes where the people with money live, but more and more frequently on working farms just like this one.' He'd paused then and looked at her as if even he, collecting money from hard-stretched individuals for a living, had never quite got over the calamity that had hit the farming community.

Foot-and-mouth, Savannah reflected bleakly. The disease had devastated the countryside and the people that lived there, killing their cattle, killing their dreams. So many farmers had been forced to adapt or go under. Blinking away her melancholy, she forced her mind round to practical issues.

The court order still stood, and it was up to her to get this mess sorted out before her parents returned from their cruise. Returning to the kitchen table, she sat down to make a list. But as she stared at the page of jottings in front of her she realised she could only raise half the money needed. And if she didn't come up with a solution by the end of the month the bank would foreclose and there'd be no farm. Heartache reminded her of Ethan. Briefly she considered asking him for a loan, but quickly discounted it because he would never let her pay him back. He might have the riches of Croesus, but that money wasn't hers to dip into. No. She would find her own solution.

An unexpected phone call provided Savannah with an equally unexpected opportunity, but not one she could take up. 'I'm the last person on earth who has any influence over Ethan Alexander,' she explained to the senior official from the Rugby Football Union. But the man from the governing body of English rugby was persistent, and as he went on talking Savannah thought she saw an opportunity that might just turn out to be the saving of them all.

'And I said no!' Frowning, Ethan sprang up from his swivel chair and began to pace the long-suffering floor of his study. 'My rugby days are over. You know that,' he snapped at the official from the RFU. 'Yes, what I'm saying is your suggestion is out of bounds. I can't possibly make it fly for you—and no is my final answer. *What?*' Ethan ground his jaw as the man kept on talking. 'No, I didn't know that—when did this happen?' His expression turned grim as he listened to the official's account of a recent news item he'd missed due to a business trip. He might say no to a lot of things, but he would never turn his back on Savannah.

'No' could no longer be his final answer.

* * *

Almost exactly a month later Savannah stood on a newly levelled field at her parents' farm, waiting for Ethan's helicopter to arrive. She had anticipated this moment, spending many sleepless nights planning for it—planning that had included closing off part of her heart that would never be brought into service again.

Everyone had rejoiced on the day Ethan had agreed to be patron of the rugby academy set on her parents' farm. Savannah had quietly celebrated, knowing it marked his return to the world. From the moment Ethan had given his agreement, things had moved quickly. Savannah had persuaded her parents to enter into a long-term lease with the RFU for the use of some land, and that money had saved the farm. She couldn't have felt more passionate about this opening today for all sorts of reasons, and the only anxiety she had was seeing Ethan again. As Ethan's helicopter cast a shadow over the field, she told herself she could handle it, and what better time than this? Everything was in place, and even the local mayor had accepted her invitation to cut the ribbon outside the new clubhouse. But seeing his face at the controls undid all her good intentions. Ethan helped so many people, and yet the one person Ethan seemed incapable of helping was himself. This would be their first face-to-face meeting since they parted in Tuscany, and she loved him as much as ever. But this was no time to be nursing a broken heart. The project was far too important for that. And now she must greet the guest of honour.

He saw her immediately. Even amongst the crowd of excited children and local dignitaries, she stood out. Savannah had real presence, and the place she still held in his heart drew him to her.

Though she should be in Salzburg giving a recital today, he remembered, not standing on a rugby pitch dressed in a track-suit and trainers with her hair drawn back in a simple ponytail but never looking more beautiful. Right now she was running on the spot, surrounded by a group of youngsters, as if sport was her only passion now.

He was hugely disappointed, but the love he felt for Savannah would never change. He had come because he would do anything on earth to help Savannah and her family, and this scheme she'd dreamed up benefited everybody. Which was so like her. Savannah Ross might be the most irritating woman he had ever met, but Savannah always put others before herself.

The next few hours were going to be tough training for a life without Savannah, but where that was concerned he hadn't changed his mind. He was still scarred and she was still beautiful—inside and out. Some things never changed.

As he ducked his head to clear the rotor blades he caught a glimpse of her pale face angled towards him at the edge of the field. Was she smiling? He hoped not. He hoped she would only remember the distance he had put between them before she'd left Tuscany. He didn't want to see a look of love in her eyes. He wanted to know she had moved on.

They would never have worked as a couple, he told himself firmly as he strode towards her. How could he live with someone with no sense of responsibility? Though the fact that Savannah had broken her contractual obligations had surprised him. This youth project was vital, but she didn't need to be here. She had sacrificed a great career move, and in doing so had put herself at risk of having her contract terminated.

Now he was within touching distance, he registered

explosions of sensation. He didn't trust himself to shake her hand, and was glad when the current manager of the England squad intervened. He moved on with relief, spearheading the group responsible for making this day a reality, conscious that Savannah was behind him. *As beautiful as ever, with her skin as flawless as porcelain, and her eyes...*

He breathed a sigh of relief as he approached the line of local dignitaries, but as he fell into easy conversation he was conscious of Savannah's wildflower scent coupled with her breathy laugh. But she'd let his team down, he reminded himself grimly, and anyone who did that let him down. As she'd shunned her engagement to sing in Salzburg to be here, Ethan was under pressure from his team to end her contract.

His heart lifted when he met the first youngster on the scheme, and he recognised the same determination to succeed he'd had blazing from the boy's eyes. It was more than possible that one of these boys would play for England some day, and he knew then that that even without Savannah's involvement this was the type of project he would gladly give his last penny to.

'But this time your money isn't enough,' one of the officials told Ethan goodnaturedly, glancing at Savannah, who had joined their little group for confirmation of this.

He didn't need his attention being drawn to Savannah when he was conscious of her every second. His attention might appear to be focused on the RFU official, but he was communing with her on some other level. His feelings towards her were as turbulent as ever, but he could understand now why she was so reluctant to leave the countryside for the anonymous bustle of the opera world. However prestigious that world might be, it lacked the honest goodness of the soil, and the unspoiled beauty of these rolling fields and ancient trees. The delicate tracery of lush, green hedges and dry stone-walls surrounding her parents' farm created a quintessentially English scene, and one which he was even buying into with his purchase of the adjoining land. But even as a result of everything he could see here Savannah shouldn't have broken her agreement and let people down.

He was snapped out of these thoughts by officials ushering him into the recently erected club-house for tea. As he turned he found Savannah at his side. He steeled himself. What he had to say to her wouldn't be easy, and so he greeted her formally before glancing towards the private office where they wouldn't be overheard. 'Could I have a moment of your time?'

'Hello, Ethan,' she said softly, reminding him of another occasion when his fast-ticking clock had ruled out the space for proper introductions. He felt a pang of remorse for then, for now, for everything that could never be. And what was he thinking? Was he going to take her aside and tell her she'd lost her contract on this wonderful occasion for which she was largely responsible? Was that his way now? The look in Savannah's eyes contained a disturbing degree of understanding. She knew him too well. She knew that once his mind was made up there could be no turning back, but as she turned to walk ahead of him he did wonder at the flicker of steel in her gaze.

He launched in without preamble, listing all the reasons why breaking her contract to attend the opening of a training facility that had nothing to do with her career was unacceptable. She stared at him throughout with little reaction other than a paling of her lips. He always gave right of reply in these circumstances, and when she didn't speak up immediately he prompted her.

He was shocked by the way Savannah's face contorted with fury, and then she croaked something unintelligible at him. 'If you'd just calm down,' he said with dignity, 'Perhaps I'd be able to understand what it is you're trying to say.'

She made a gesture, like a cutting motion across her throat.

'That's a bit over-dramatic, isn't it?' he commented with a humourless laugh.

'I've lost my voice,' she half-huffed, half-squeaked at him.

Every swear-word in the book flew through his head then. He'd been so wound up like a spring at the thought of seeing her again, he hadn't even paused to consider all the facts. So a sore throat accounted for her no-show in Salzburg.

'Please forgive me,' he said stiffly. He couldn't blame her for the way she was looking at him. He never made mistakes, and therefore lacked the technique to account for them. Or maybe he did make mistakes—maybe he had—and maybe the biggest mistake of all was his under-estimating Savannah. She was an integral part of this training project. He'd learned from the officials at the RFU that this training facility was all Savannah's idea, and that she had come up with the plan of leasing part of her parents' land to the club so they could have a proper training-facility for the youth squad, as well as all the other local youngsters who wanted to come along and taste the sport. There were scholarships and training programmes and grading examinations the various groups could work towards—funded by him, but all of it dreamed up by Savannah.

More silent swear-words accompanied this thought, with the addition of a grimace and a self-condemning shake of the head. 'Savannah, please accept my apologies, I didn't realise…'

If he had expected benediction and forgiveness, he was out of luck. Spearing him a look, she spun on her heels and left him flat.

CHAPTER EIGHTEEN

HE FOUND her in the cosy farmhouse kitchen where she was standing by the Aga, drinking a steaming glass full of something aromatic. She barely looked up when he walked in, and, other than stirring her brew thoughtfully with a stumpy cinnamon-stick, she didn't move.

'Savannah.'

Her eyes were wounded and her mouth was both trembling and determined when she did turn to look at him. She gestured for him to stay away from her, but since when had he ever taken orders? He stopped short halfway across the kitchen when he saw the tears in her eyes, and his guts twisted at the thought of what he'd done.

'Savannah, please.'

She shook her head and gestured that he should stay away from her.

'I had no idea. I just got back—I came straight here.'

She shrugged her shoulders, and made a sound that showed more clearly than words that she couldn't give a fig what he did, and her blue eyes had turned to stone.

'I should have double checked my facts before wading in, but I just wanted to…'

Her finely etched brows rose in ironic question.

'All right, then,' he admitted, raking his hair with stiff, angry fingers. 'I just wanted to see you. There, I've said it.'

She huffed.

'Savannah, please.'

Lifting her tiny hand, she used it to push him away.

He wasn't as easy as that to get rid of.

How was she supposed to have a go at him when she couldn't even speak? Gestures and angry looks only got you so far—and that wasn't nearly far enough where Ethan was concerned. 'You can't just walk in here and act like nothing happened.' She wasn't sure how much of that Ethan got, seeing as she could barely force a sound that wasn't a squeak out of her infected throat.

'You should be out there, enjoying your success,' he said, confirming her impression that he hadn't understood a word of what she'd said. She pulled a face. What was the point going outside without Ethan? The scheme needed him—and not just to give it a popular face. She needed him to take on a fuller role than that, but right now her angry look was telling him: *you're a selfish, egocentric brute, Ethan Alexander, and I never want to see you again.*

But Ethan remained undeterred. 'So, just as a matter of interest, who is taking your place in Salzburg?'

'Madame de Silva,' she managed to husk.

He smiled, remembering Savannah had looked sensational in Madame de Silva's slinky gown, which was another reason he'd been only too eager to drag her off the pitch. But while he was reminiscing the wounded look returned to Savannah's eyes. 'But Madame couldn't look half as beautiful as you do right now in your tracksuit,' he assured her gently.

And before he could stop himself he dipped his head

and kissed her very gently on the lips. He thought for a horrible moment she was going to push him away. She was certainly crying again; he could feel her tears wetting his face, and he could taste them.

'You'll catch it,' she warned, her eyes wide with concern when he released her.

'Your sore throat, do you mean? I certainly hope so,' he said, kissing her again.

She wasn't nearly finished with saying hello to Ethan yet, as he released her when the door opened and everyone piled in. In typical English spring fashion the rain had chosen that moment to pour down, and there wasn't enough space in the club house or even the large marquee her parents had erected to accommodate everyone who had turned up for the opening ceremony.

Ethan quickly went about introducing himself to her parents, and then Savannah watched him mingling easily with everyone else. They had a marvellous team of workers on the farm, some of whose families had lived on the land adjoining theirs for generations. It was thanks to these lifelong friends that Savannah's parents had been in a position to accept Ethan's offer of a cruise, and she was glad he had the opportunity to meet them and thank them personally. Maybe Ethan could never be part of her life, but perhaps he understood now how special her life on the farm was, and how family and friends were a precious and integral part of that life.

As Savannah watched Ethan ease his powerful frame through the crowd of noisy visitors in the cosy farmhouse kitchen, it wasn't possible to think of him as the same man she'd first met. When he came out to socialise he radiated friendliness. Perhaps that should be her next project. If she could bring youngsters with similar injuries to

Ethan's into contact with him, he could give them the confidence to live their lives to the fullest.

Was she only dreaming, or would that really be possible? The first step would be persuading Ethan to take a full part in the scheme…

She would just have to try a little harder, Savannah concluded, passing round the savouries she'd baked. 'Ethan.' She caught up with him by the window, where he was holding a conversation with the local mayor. It was so hard to make him hear her with a scratchy voice. 'Excuse me,' she squeaked politely. 'Do you think I could borrow you for a moment?'

'Would you excuse me?' Ethan asked the mayor politely.

As soon as they found a space, she launched right in, 'Ethan, we need you.'

'You're speaking again?' His facial expression ran the gamut from relief to wry to mock-weary in the space of a breath.

'Happily, my voice is coming back,' Savannah agreed, ignoring Ethan's groan. She couldn't sing the praises of hot water, honey and lemon stirred with a cinnamon stick highly enough.

'Sorry?' Ethan dipped his head very low until his ear was level with her mouth. 'You'll have to speak up; you're still croaking,' he teased, turning Savannah's ailment to his advantage.

'If you think you're going to distract me with that wicked look…' He probably would, she realised.

'Go on,' Ethan prompted.

'We need you, Ethan,' she said, not messing about. 'And not just for a flying visit every now and then.'

'Ah…' He looked down at her sternly, but he was smiling inwardly as he remembered the house he'd bought close by. He'd see Savannah, though what she was proposing for the scheme was a step too far for him. He couldn't let the youngsters see his scars and put them off their game. 'You've touched on the one subject I'm not prepared to discuss,' he said flatly, and when she squeaked at him he put up his hand. 'Are you quite sure your throat is getting better? Only I can't tell you how peaceful it's been since you lost your voice.'

'Well, I found it,' Savannah assured him firmly. 'And it's getting better all the time.'

'No,' Ethan said flatly when Savannah put her proposition to him outside the club house by the fence. 'How many times do I have to say no to this idea of yours?'

'As many times as you're asked—until you say yes,' she told him steadily.

'Savannah, I should warn you, I don't succumb to pressure.'

'There has been the odd occasion,' she reminded him brazenly, using tactics she should be thoroughly ashamed of but wasn't.

'Don't you know you're playing with fire?' he warned, seeing her eyes darken.

'Am I?' she asked. She was all innocence as she angled her face towards him. 'Perhaps that's because I'll stop at nothing to get you properly into this scheme.'

'Well, I never thought you'd sink this low,' Ethan murmured with his lips very close to her mouth.

'Then you have a great deal to learn about me.'

Dragging her close, he kissed her again.

'Though I have to admit,' she admitted breathlessly when Ethan released her, 'That I usually try to make sure that when you and fire are concerned there's no one else around.'

Breaking off to say hello to some of the England squad—who, dressed in kit, were leading a group of youngsters out onto the pitch—he couldn't have agreed more. The moment he turned back to her, she said, 'I won't give up, you know.'

'I think I guessed that much,' he told her, drawing her after him.

'Where are you taking me?'

'Somewhere we can talk privately and your enthusiasm can be harnessed.'

'Sounds lovely,' she murmured as he helped her over a stile.

'It will be.' Vaulting over the same stile, he took her by the hand and led her waist-deep through a field of long grass.

'Well, I think we can talk here,' she agreed when he finally stopped in the middle of it.

'You can talk if you want to.'

'Ethan…'

Love, contentment and unimaginable happiness…as well as a nice, dewy meadow freshly watered by the rain. 'Thank goodness, you're underneath me,' Savannah murmured groggily to Ethan some time later.

'I didn't want you getting grass stains on your nice, new track-suit,' Ethan mocked softly as they recovered.

'Why worry? The sun is shining now and I'll soon dry out.' As she outlined Ethan's sensual mouth with her fingertip until he threatened to bite it off, Savannah wondered whether this was the right time to broach the subject at the forefront of her mind or not.

'Well?' Ethan pressed, knowing she had something on her mind.

'Well, what?' she said, pulling on her innocent face. 'Why must you always be so suspicious of me?'

'I might only have known you a short time, but I know there's usually something brewing when you have that look.'

She hesitated and then said bluntly, 'When you sprang over that stile...'

'Yes?' He wasn't going to help her.

'Well, I just thought, with your back and—'

'Oh, I see.' Moving his head, he dislodged her teasing finger. 'You want to know how I can do something like that when I can't play rugby. Or, more importantly—at least as far as your scheme is concerned—why I won't help out with the coaching.'

'Yes,' Savannah admitted, wriggling away from him and sitting up. Truthfully, she had a lot more in mind for Ethan than the occasional coaching session. She wanted him to take a much fuller role in the scheme for which he had already proved to be an inspirational figurehead.

'It's only weights landing on my back I have to be careful about,' he explained. 'My legs are fine.'

'Then...' Hugging her knees, she rested her chin on them, staring up at him.

'Then?'

'Stop pretending you don't know what I mean. And stop growling at me,' she added when Ethan made a mock-threatening sound. She fixed a stare on him. 'If there's nothing wrong with your legs, there can't be any reason why you can't take part in the training programme—just part-time, of course,' she added before Ethan could get a word in. 'Plus, the occasional guest appearance would make all the difference.'

Having buckled his belt, Ethan sat up beside her and

swung Savannah onto his knee. 'Is that what all this has been leading up to?'

'Not all of it,' she admitted truthfully.

'Well, at least you've got the decency to blush,' he observed dryly, drawing her into his shoulder.

'You still haven't given me your answer, Ethan.'

'Well, why don't I do that now?'

It was some time later when Ethan drew Savannah to her feet. As he helped to brush grass and twigs from her clothes, she sensed something had changed.

'My answer is no,' he told her quietly, confirming her worst fears. 'How can I let those kids see my scars? They'll see nothing else—they won't concentrate on the game, on my coaching—I'd hold them back.'

'No, you wouldn't.'

'For the last time, Savannah, no coaching sessions.'

Seizing his hands, she stared into his eyes. 'What if we brought other youngsters here—youngsters with disfigurements like yours—would you do it then? Would you bring everyone together so that no one was an outsider?'

She had silenced him and touched him as only Savannah could. 'I'll think about it,' he promised, silencing her in the most effective way he could. 'Now, will you be quiet?' he demanded when he released her.

'Of course I will,' Savannah agreed, tipping her chin to stare lovingly at him. 'The moment you agree.'

CHAPTER NINETEEN

THE REST of the day passed in whirl of activity, with Savannah and Ethan falling naturally into the role of host and hostess. They were a good team, Savannah thought, smiling across the crowded club-house at Ethan. No, she'd got that wrong—they were an excellent team—but she must stop looking at him as if she had to convince herself he was really there. She was feeling more confident he would agree to a little coaching. Hadn't he said as much when they were making love in the meadow? Or was it coaching her he'd had in mind? Time to pin him down, she decided as people started to drift off home.

When Ethan came to her he raised both her hands to his lips. Had the tender lover returned to her? She had to believe that was so. Conscious of her mother and father watching them from the other side of the room, she sighed with pleasure as Ethan brushed her cheeks with his lips.

'It's been a wonderful day, Savannah,' he told her gently. 'Thank you so much…'

'It's nothing,' she murmured. She was still staring up at him, feeling like she could fly.

'I want to thank you on behalf of everyone,' he added,

still holding her hands in his firm grip. 'And I promise to give serious thought to your suggestion.'

But? She could hear a 'but'. 'Thank you, Ethan.' Savannah's smile faded. There was something wrong. She could see no answering warmth in Ethan's eyes, just a rather detached interest. 'You're not going to take an active part, are you?'

'I'm the patron, and I've already donated a large amount of money.'

'I'm not talking about money, Ethan, the scheme needs you—hands-on you.' There was something else, Savannah suspected—something Ethan hadn't told her.

He released her hands. 'Anything else at all, you only have to ask.'

'I am asking. If everyone else can find time, why can't you?'

'You know why,' Ethan said grimly.

No, she didn't—and now he was being drawn away. She'd monopolised him too long, and all the people who had been waiting to say goodbye to him were jostling for his attention. She waited on tenterhooks until he was free again and then pounced. 'Ethan, look at me.' But there were more interruptions. How hard was it to do this in public when you were trying to capture the attention of the most important man in the room?

Ethan freed himself this next time. He'd seen her concern and he crossed the room to her side. 'Tell me,' he said.

'Everyone needs your magic,' she said. 'Just look around you…' There was a group of youngsters clustered round the team captain. They might be with one hero, but they were all looking at Ethan, the most formidable man in the room, with awe-struck stares. 'They need you. Just a few hours of your time, Ethan. They rate you so highly.'

'You know my position.'

'No, I don't!' Savannah exclaimed. 'Your scars? They know about your scars—they don't even notice them. What else is holding you back?'

Ethan's eyes narrowed. 'What makes you think there's anything else?'

'I know you, Ethan.'

'Enough,' he said sharply, leaning close. Putting his arm out, Ethan rested his clenched fist against the wall so that Savannah's face and his were shielded from the crowd. 'I'll do anything I can for these young people.'

'Then give them your time. Or can't you bear the thought of being on the same pitch as a bunch of enthusiastic amateurs? Aren't they good enough for you, Ethan?'

He knew she was goading him, reaching deep, and that she didn't believe it for one moment. 'Savannah,' he warned, his mouth almost brushing her lips now.

'No, I won't be quiet,' she replied, confirming his thoughts. 'You're due a wake-up call.'

'And who better to give it to me than you?' He didn't wait for her answer. Freeing the latch on the door behind her, he backed her through it holding on to her while he closed the door behind them, and then frogmarched her across the yard.

And still she peppered him with accusations. 'You paint wonderful pictures and hide them away—that's one precious gift wasted. You're an inspiration, a positive role-model for young people and a force for good—a second—'

Savannah gasped as Ethan thrust her through the entrance of the hay barn. Slamming the door shut, he shot the bolt. 'This time I talk and you listen,' he said. Bringing her in front of him, he held her firmly in place.

'I live my life causing the least inconvenience I can to everyone around me.'

'You mean you're stuck in the past and won't even glance into the future?'

'I'm sure my business analysts might have something to say about that,' he said with all the confidence of a hugely successful tycoon.

'Your business analysts? And I bet they keep you warm at night.'

'You don't know me, so just leave this——'

'I know enough about you to care.'

As her voice echoed in the lofty barn they both went still. Ethan's eyes were so dark and reflected a truth so terrible Savannah almost wished she hadn't brought him to this point. 'What is it, Ethan?' she said, reaching out to touch his face. 'Who did this terrible thing to you?' They both knew she wasn't talking about his scars.

Ethan moved his head away.

'And this time tell me,' Savannah insisted gently. 'Don't insult me with some pallid version of the truth because you've decided I can't take the facts. I can take anything for you—share everything with you—good and bad.'

Everything hung on this moment, Savannah realised, and yet all she could do now was wait.

After the longest moment, Ethan shrugged. 'My step-father beat me.'

She knew that.

'When I grew too big for him to beat me, he paid others to do it for him.'

She knew that too. 'Go on,' she prompted softly.

'There is no more to tell.'

No more Ethan wanted to tell, perhaps. 'I don't believe

you.' Her voice barely made it above a whisper, but he'd heard her.

Ethan stared over her head as the seconds ticked past, and then he revealed his innermost demon. 'When I had recovered from the accident I visited my mother to try to heal things between us. Whatever had happened in the past, she was still my mother, and I had to believe she didn't really understand what had been going on.'

As Ethan stopped speaking Savannah felt the pain of his disappointment so keenly she didn't even need to hear the rest, but she knew she had to let him say it.

'She had known,' he said in a voice pitched low. 'My mother had known all along. She knew all of it.'

What hurt Savannah the most was that she could still hear the surprise in Ethan's voice. For a moment she found it impossible to speak or even breathe, and could only communicate the compassion she felt for him with her eyes.

'She told me I got in the way… She said I was always in the way, and that she wished I had never been born. She said she never wanted to see me again, which I could understand, really.'

'No!' As Ethan made a dismissive gesture, Savannah caught hold of his hand and held it firmly. 'No, Ethan, no; that's not right. You must never think that. You did nothing wrong—not then, not as a child, not ever.' She understood now why Ethan kept so much hidden. Having been betrayed by his own mother, how could he ever reveal his feelings to anyone again? He had to know she was here for him on any terms, Savannah determined, and that part of the bargain said she would be strong—even strong enough to let him go, if that was what Ethan really wanted.

But as he shifted position, and she saw his wounded

face set in that distant mask, she knew she had to give their chance to be together one more try.

'What better scheme than ours to bury those demons in your past once and for all? What greater triumph could you have, Ethan?'

Ethan remained silent for the longest moment, and then he murmured with a flicker of the old humour, '*Our* scheme?'

'Why not *our* scheme?'

'Because you seem to be doing pretty well on your own.'

'But we can do so much more together.' She waited for his answer, tense in every fibre of her being.

'Is that right?' he said dryly, flicking a glance her way.

At least they'd made contact, Savannah thought with relief. 'I'm sure of it,' she said fiercely.

'So you've found a way out of the darkness?'

The glint was back in Ethan's eyes—and that was more than a relief, it was a reminder of their first night together at the *palazzo*. He had come back to her. Seizing his hands, she brought them to her lips. 'We'll get through this,' she promised him.

'I already have.'

'Then you have no excuse.'

'Not to shine a light?' As Savannah smiled, he wondered how he could ever have been foolish enough to imagine life without her.

'I need you, Ethan,' she told him passionately. 'We all need you.'

'Well, I don't know about everyone,' he admitted gruffly. 'But you've got me, Ms Ross—and for keeps.'

'What are you saying, Ethan?'

'I'm saying that I love you, and that I want to be with you always.'

Savannah swallowed deep as Ethan looked at her. 'I take it you'll be staying on, then?'

'Even a rugby match couldn't keep me away from you,' Ethan assured her. 'Unless England was playing, of course…'

EPILOGUE

THE SUN blazed down from a clear, blue Tuscan sky, and there were no shadows on the day that Savannah married Ethan. The world's press had gathered in the exquisite ancient city of Florence for what everyone was calling the celebrity marriage of the year.

For the farm girl, and the tycoon better known to the world as the Bear, this was quite an occasion, Savannah thought. As the bells rang out and the crowd cheered, it was a struggle to wrap her mind around the fact that she really was married to the man she adored. Standing on time worn steps next to Ethan outside the Basilica de Santa Maria di Fiore, a cathedral church only exceeded in size by St Peter's in Rome, she only had to see the guard of honour formed by the youngsters Ethan now made time to coach on a regular basis to know that miracles did happen—and that, yes, dreams did come true.

'All right?' Ethan murmured, squeezing her arm.

Better than all right. She adored him. He was without question the most wonderful man in the world. And apart from making her so happy he had extended the reach of the training scheme—which had meant leasing more space from her parents in order to house the office of the newly expanded training business, saving the farm, as well as giving them the little luxuries they'd lived so long without.

And her recording career? Well, she'd just signed a contract to complete a new album, and after that studio work and the occasional personal appearance at the world-famous opera house Glynebourne in Lewes, Sussex, just down the road from Ethan's new home that adjoined her parents' farm. He'd told Savannah she was to have her cake and—for the sake of the large family they planned to have—to eat it as well. Their mission, the newly married couple had decided, was to fill all of Ethan's homes with love, laughter and lots of light—and if possible with a rugby team of their own.

'You look so beautiful,' Ethan said, standing a little behind Savannah so the crowd had a good view of her.

'And you are the most beautiful man on earth.' To her he was and always would be. Now Ethan's inners scars were healed, he had no blemishes. 'And I love you,' she said.

'More than life itself,' Ethan agreed, smiling into Savannah's eyes. 'Now, let them have a good look at your dress.'

Oh, yes, her dress… Her very special dress in ivory silk, lavishly embroidered with seed pearls and thousands of twinkles that sparkled in the sun. It had been lovingly made for Savannah by her regular team of seamstresses in the far north of England, who knew a thing or two about showing off the fuller figure to best advantage. Who else would she have chosen to make her wedding gown, to ensure there wasn't the slightest chance she would suffer a wardrobe malfunction similar to the one that had brought the crowd at the Stadio Flaminio to its feet in Rome? In this dress her assets were displayed to full advantage, a fact that had not gone overlooked by her adoring Bear.

'Cover yourself, woman,' Ethan growled as Savannah's silk-chiffon veil billowed back and away from her naked shoulders.

'If I don't, will you carry me off and keep me safe as you did on the day we first met?' Savannah asked him.

She managed a solemn face for as long as it took her to ask Ethan that question, and as his mouth tugged at one corner he allowed, 'With one small change.'

'Which is?'

'I wouldn't waste so much time before taking you to bed.'

'Is that a promise, husband?'

'You can count on it, wife,' he murmured as they posed for pictures.

'Then I may just have to stage-manage a wardrobe malfunction.'

'And I might just have to put you over my knee, and—'

Ethan paused, seeing the official photographer was hopping from foot to foot.

'Smile, please,' the man begged, indicating that a formal pose, rather than a lover's confab was called for.

He barely had to ask.

THE BILLIONAIRE'S
DEFIANT WIFE

BY
AMANDA BROWNING

Amanda Browning still lives in the Essex house where she was born. The third of four children—her sister being her twin—she enjoyed the rough and tumble of life with two brothers as much as she did reading books. Writing came naturally as an outlet for her fertile imagination. The love of books led her to a career in libraries, and being single allowed her to take the leap into writing for a living. Success is still something of a wonder, but allows her to indulge in hobbies as varied as embroidery and bird-watching.

CHAPTER ONE

Sometimes the world could change in an instant. One moment everything was exactly the way you planned it to be, and the next it had become a place you barely recognised. This was how it was for Aimi Carteret that sultry summer evening, and it was the second time it had happened in her sometimes turbulent life.

Just moments before the second cataclysmic event that was to cause such havoc occurred, she was sitting at the large dining table of Michael and Simone Berkeley, enjoying the friendly banter. Beside her sat their son Nick, a man of genuine warmth and kindness. He was a renowned surgeon, like his father, and his father before him. Opposite were Nick's sister Paula and her husband, James Carmichael.

Six months ago Aimi had been employed by Nick to organize his hectic life. Besides operating, he had lecture tours, guest appearances on all forms of media, and had even begun to compile a family history. She worked from the study in his home, but did not live in. That was something she never did. Her work and her private life never overlapped.

Not that she had much of a private life, but that was by choice. Her life had changed dramatically nine years ago, and the mad social whirl she had enjoyed to the fullest had been left behind and never regretted. Guilt had sobered the outrageous teenager, and she had vowed to turn herself into someone she could be proud of.

She had thrown herself headlong into studying history at university, but making a career out of it had been hard. So she had learned all the skills she needed to become a personal assistant, and had been temping for a high class agency ever since. Coming to work for Nick had allowed her to use her grounding in history, and help him with his research. She had, after much hard work, found a niche for herself where she was able to feel a degree of peace.

If her old friends could see her now, they would barely recognise her, Aimi thought to herself. She didn't wear make-up, when once she had used it to enhance her large green eyes, always kept her shoulder-length blonde hair smoothed into a pleat at her nape, and pre-ferred smart suits and casuals to modern fashions.

When she had been at university, she had even worn glasses. Plain glass, of course. They had been a ploy used to keep people at a distance. She had been at university to work, not play. Her playing days had ended with a tragedy she would never forget. All she had wanted to do was blend into the background and be left alone.

It seemed strange now to remember how outra-geously she had once flirted with the opposite sex. Having inherited her looks from her actress mother, Marsha Delmont, Aimi had had no trouble attracting men, and had enjoyed their company, but she had never taken them seriously and never had any deep relationships with any of them. Her life had been about having fun, but after Austria and the terrible events that had happened there, that had all ended. She had spent the years since proving she could be a person of value.

Her life was the way she wanted it. She was here in her official capacity as Nick's assistant, but his parents had welcomed her into their home in the country as a friend. The plan was for her to look through the books and papers in the study for relevant material for Nick's book, but all Nick's family would be coming to a barbecue tomorrow, for their annual bank holiday weekend get-together, and he had insisted that she join in the festivities.

Sitting at the table, listening to the conversation, sometimes taking part, she was glad she had agreed to come. This was how normal people behaved with each other, and it was a poignant reminder for Aimi, who had once thought endless shopping, wild, glamorous parties where drink flowed like water and everything was loud laughter and music was the only way to live. That Aimi would have considered this deadly dull, but the Aimi of today bitterly regretted that she hadn't wised up sooner. Such was the benefit of hindsight. It showed you what might have been, and damned you with the knowledge that you could never go back.

In those final few minutes before her world would be knocked off its axis and sent spinning into space for a second time, everyone was laughing at something Paula had just said. Aimi found it so funny, her eyes were watering and her stomach ached. It was as she was using her napkin to wipe her eyes that the distant chime of the front doorbell permeated the room.

Simone Berkeley looked at her husband in mild query. 'I wonder who that could be,' she said to the room at large.

'Were you expecting anyone, Mum?' Paula asked, only for her mother to shake her head.

Moments later, they all heard the sound of footsteps coming towards the room and everyone looked expectantly towards the door. It opened seconds later and a tall, dark-haired man stepped into the room, grinning at the sea of faces.

'I hope you left something for me, you pack of gannets!' he exclaimed cheerfully, and his remark was met by cries of delight.

'Jonas!'

The family immediately leapt to their feet as one, leaving a bemused Aimi to swivel round in her seat and examine this late arrival. She had heard of Jonas Berkeley, of course, the oldest son, who owned a high-powered company and lived a jet-set lifestyle which took him off to all corners of the globe. His name was often in the newspapers, sometimes for his work, but more often for the latest woman in his life. Naturally he had an open invitation to the family gathering, but nobody had expected him to be able to make it. Hence their surprise and delight.

Her own surprise was her response to him, which was totally unexpected. The instant she laid eyes on him, something stirred in the depths of her. All her senses appeared to leap to attention, as if her whole being recognised and responded to something in him. His laughter as he greeted everyone sent shivers down her spine and the rakish sparkle in his startlingly blue eyes dried her mouth.

For all her wild youth, Aimi had never actually experienced such a blatantly physical response to anyone in her twenty-seven years. She was suddenly made very much aware of the blood pulsing through her veins and the rapid beating of her heart. All at once her smile faded away and it was then, as Jonas Berkeley glanced from one member of his family to another, that their gazes locked.

She could actually see the moment when he was stopped in his tracks, and her heart lurched anxiously. Something elemental forked through the air between them, only to be broken when his sister claimed his attention, yet there had been time enough to see the predatory gleam which had entered his eyes. Shocked and disbelieving, Aimi turned away, pressing a hand to her stomach.

Oh, my God, she thought dazedly. What had just happened? Silly question, Aimi, you know darned well! She had just experienced the pull of an immensely strong sexual attraction, and her whole body was quivering as a result. It was the very last thing she had expected, for she had worked hard to keep the attractive, outgoing side of her nature under control—to be the complete antithesis of her former self in every way. Which was why she had eschewed all forms of romantic entanglement. No man had ever made her control slip.

Until just now, that was. Without a word he had broken through her defences, making her feel things she did not want. She didn't know why it had happened now, only that she had to make rapid repairs so the damage did not show. Telling herself to be calm, she breathed slowly until she felt in control again. Now she should be able to give the appearance of calmness, although in reality she was still trembling inside.

A hand touched her arm and she jumped, looking up to find Nick beside her.

'Come and say hello to my brother. I'm eager for him to meet you,' Nick invited, and Aimi's heart fluttered anxiously at the thought of looking into those amazing eyes again so soon. However, there was one little part of her that needed to check out if it had really happened or if she had imagined it, so she smiled, as if the ground hadn't just rocked, and stood up.

As she took the half a dozen steps to where Jonas Berkeley stood within the circle of his family, Aimi had the weirdest sensation that she was walking down a pre-destined path. A momentary sense of caution whispered, *Go back*, yet a stronger force kept her moving. She couldn't stop her eyes from rising to meet his and, the instant that happened, once again the air seemed to become positively charged, making it difficult to breathe properly.

'OK,' Nick declared, noticing nothing amiss, and made the introductions. 'Aimi, this strapping fellow is my brother, Jonas. Tall, handsome and disgustingly wealthy, he's also a bit of a Casanova, so you have been warned. And this young woman is my indispensable assistant, Aimi.'

Jonas's teeth flashed white as he smiled directly into her eyes and held out his hand. 'Hello, Nick's indispensable Aimi. I'm very pleased to meet you,' he greeted her in a voice whose low timbre was an unexpected delight to her ear.

Aimi gasped silently, more than a little unnerved to know she was still feeling the full force of the man's charisma, despite her hasty repairs to her defences. He oozed supreme male confidence and sexual allure, and it was stunning. Knowing she was not as cool as she would like to be, she hesitated fractionally before taking his hand, and knew she had been right to do so when his fingers closed around hers. The contact sent a wave of tingles up her arm and throughout her system, causing the tiny hairs to rise. Her faint start was absorbed by his hand, which tightened on hers momentarily.

'I'm pleased to meet you, too,' she returned politely, glad to hear that she at least sounded normal. Easing her hand free, she coiled her fingers into her tingling palm. 'Nick talks of you often.' It was true, though he had never said what a charismatic man his brother was. Probably because he never saw him that way. Women would see a whole different side to him. A side she would have preferred to remain in blissful ignorance of! Whilst she might admire a man's looks aesthetically, she tried to never allow herself to be moved by them. Today, though, something was going badly wrong and she didn't like it.

'Ah, that would be the reason my ears have been burning lately,' Jonas joked lightly, his mouth tweaking into a boyish grin. 'So, how long have you been working for Nick?' he asked and, as he did so, his eyes took in the grey pencil skirt and white blouse she was wearing, despite the stifling summer heat. There was a quizzical glint in his eye when he met hers again.

'Six months, give or take,' Nick informed him, smiling at Aimi. 'I tell you, everyone could do with an assistant like her!'

His brother looked from one to the other. 'Is that so? Do I detect more than just a working relationship here?'

he enquired, and Aimi got the distinct impression that it was not an idle question. He wanted to know just how involved his brother was.

Nick laughed and shook his head. 'Good Lord, no! Nothing like that! She's brought order to the chaos of my life. Isn't that right, Aimi?'

'I do my best,' Aimi agreed uncomfortably, wondering if Nick realised he had just as good as told his brother she was not off limits. From the wry amusement in Jonas's eye, he knew it, and knew that she did, too.

'What made you decide to visit this weekend? Did you find yourself between women?' Nick asked with a surgeon's precision, and Aimi had to stifle a sudden urge to grin.

Jonas raised a lazy eyebrow at her, ignoring his brother, and smiled. 'Delicately put, Nick, as always. I did happen to find myself with an unexpectedly free weekend. But I don't think it's going to be as disappointing as I first thought!'

Fully aware of what he was implying, Aimi's eyebrows rose. She might not play the field any more, but she hadn't forgotten how the game was played. 'Oh, I'm sure it will be,' she insisted, smiling back coolly.

His head tipped. 'You think so? Funny, I usually find something to keep me amused.'

Nick snorted. 'Typical Jonas! Don't you think it's time you grew up? You're thirty-four. You should be looking to settle down and start a family.'

'I'll leave that to you. I'm happy with my life the way it is.'

'At least I'm looking! You just keep dating those beautiful airheads! What on earth do you see in them?

You can't even have an intelligent conversation with any of them!' Nick insisted doggedly.

'Shame on you, Nick!' his sister broke in on what appeared to be an old argument. 'Jonas can date whatever sort of woman he likes. Just because he's bound on cutting a swathe through the female population doesn't mean he won't settle down eventually. He'll do that when he's good and ready.'

Jonas sighed in the face of such heavy-handed criticism from his nearest and dearest. 'Thanks for making me sound like a heartless Lothario, Paula.'

Paula quickly pressed a kiss to his cheek. 'Of course you're not heartless, but you *are* a Lothario. I love you, Jonas, but I have to admit you have a cavalier attitude towards women that stinks. What you need is to fall in love with a woman who doesn't want you for a change!'

'That's my girl,' Jonas exclaimed dryly. 'I wouldn't expect anything less of the sister who waded into a brawl to rescue her little brother!'

'Oh, yes, she saved me all right!' Nick responded aggrievedly. 'Then launched into me for getting into a fight in the first place!'

Everyone laughed at that, and Aimi was relieved the focus of attention had passed on to someone else.

'Come along, everyone. Let's sit down again before our dinners get cold,' Simone Berkeley chivvied them back to the table. 'Jonas, you sit next to Paula. I want to hear all about what you've been doing lately.'

Moments later a place had been laid and a full plate set before him. Back in her own seat, Aimi discovered, much to her chagrin, that Jonas was now sitting directly opposite her. It meant it was impossible not to see him whenever she raised her head. Even looking down, she was vitally aware of him. His presence in the room was an energy her errant senses registered in minute detail. Ignoring him was simply out of the question and her eyes had a will of their own, watching him from under her lashes whilst she ate. Thankfully, he chatted away with his mother so she was able to study him with a certain amount of freedom.

The first thing she noted was how black his hair was, then the strong set of his jaw. Yet his lips spoke of sensuality. She wondered how they would feel, and immediately wished she hadn't as a delicious shiver swept over her. Aimi closed her eyes and took some more steadying breaths. She had to get a grip, and as quickly as possible. She prided herself on her cool demeanour and needed it to be working perfectly. It would never do to let Jonas see he could affect her in any way.

From what she had just heard and seen, she knew the man didn't need any extra encouragement when it came to attracting moths to his flame. However, he was going to find this particular moth had an impermeable heat shield. He might have a reputation for going through women like a hot knife through butter, but not this one. She was simply not available.

Opening her eyes, Aimi felt her confidence strengthening. She was not a weak woman, at the mercy of her senses—she was stronger than that. Bolstered, she was about to eat more of the delicious food on her plate when she felt the hairs on the back of her neck stand to attention. Her nerves skittered and, unable to ignore it, she glanced up to find Jonas watching her, the look in his eyes highly provocative.

Their gazes locked for a fleeting moment before Jonas smiled knowingly and looked away. It was long enough, however, to set her heart pounding. She chose to believe it was from annoyance, ignoring the small voice that wanted to say differently. Nor did she have to ask herself why he had looked at her like that, for she knew the answer. The man was no fool, and had sensed her initial response to him. But that moment was gone. She would not let anything slip again.

With her mind settled on that point, she raised her head again and began taking an interest in the general conversation, just as she had before Jonas had arrived. Once or twice she caught his eye, seeing mocking amusement there, but she was alerted now and didn't react to it. Finally, after the strangest hour Aimi could ever recall spending at a dinner table, the meal was over.

'Let's have coffee on the terrace,' Simone suggested, dabbing her napkin against her throat. 'Maybe there will be a breath of air out there. It's so hot, it's positively stifling!'

The country had been in the grip of a heatwave for some days now, and it didn't look like ending any time soon. Naturally, the whole family were only too happy to go outside, where looking down the garden towards the ornamental lake made them feel cooler immediately.

'You must be glad to get out of the city this weekend, Aimi,' Michael Berkeley remarked as he handed round the coffee his wife was dispensing.

Aimi took her cup with a wry smile. 'Oh, yes! Though my apartment is air-conditioned, on nights like these it doesn't seem to make a difference. Working in your study will be much better than in some musty old archives.'

'I thought you were my brother's assistant. Are you moonlighting as an archivist?'

The question came from Jonas, and Aimi steadied herself before turning to him. It was just as well she did, for she discovered he had made changes to his appearance since eating dinner. He had removed his jacket and tie, loosened the top buttons of his shirt and rolled up his sleeves, which gave him a totally different look. In his suit he had been suave and very much the international businessman; like this he looked ruggedly male and quite stunningly sexy.

It all registered on her senses and, after what had happened just a short time ago, it didn't really surprise her that her mouth went dry. Fortunately she had the foresight to take a sip of her coffee to moisten her lips before answering him. 'I'm not moonlighting. I'm helping with the research for Nick's book.'

'Nick? That doesn't sound very professional to me,' Jonas goaded, and Aimi smiled faintly.

'You might be the type of employer who insists on formality, Mr Berkeley, but your brother prefers a friendlier atmosphere,' she replied coolly, and he grinned appreciatively.

'Call me Jonas. I never insist on formality here,' he declared, and Aimi realised she had not helped herself. Now she would have to call him by name, or look a fool. 'So you're a researcher as well.'

'She's good at it, too,' Nick immediately piped up in her praise. 'Not surprising when she's got an honours degree in history.'

Jonas inclined his head towards Aimi in a gesture that showed he was duly impressed. 'A multi-talented woman. No wonder Nick snapped you up. If history is your first love, why aren't you working at one of the museums or institutes?'

'Unfortunately, those kinds of jobs don't come along often and, as I've become used to eating three meals a day, I had to do something else,' she informed him smoothly.

'So, history's loss is my brother's good fortune,' Jonas returned, equally smoothly. 'And ours, too, of course. Otherwise we would not have had the pleasure of your company this weekend.'

'You'll see very little of me, I'm afraid. I'm here to work,' Aimi pointed out, mighty glad to be able to do so.

Jonas looked surprised. 'Surely Nick doesn't intend to keep your nose to the grindstone whilst the rest of us party?' he challenged, giving his brother a disapproving stare.

'Of course not. Aimi knows perfectly well I expect her to relax, too,' Nick came back promptly, and she smothered a sigh of exasperation.

Jonas smiled, and his eyes were dancing. 'I shall make it my business to see that she does, then.'

Aimi could feel her spine tense at the suggestion, and it took all her effort to keep her expression calm. 'Don't bother,' she refused politely, to which his smile broadened.

'Oh, it's no bother. It will be a pleasure.'

The only sign of her annoyance was a brief flaring of her nostrils. She knew she could not make any further protest, but would make sure to avoid him wherever possible. Meanwhile, she caught sight of the amusement in his eyes and felt compelled to respond.

'What line of work are you in, Jonas?' she enquired, finding it curiously hard to make his name emerge naturally. 'Or have you made so much money you don't need to work?' she added, referring to what Nick had said when introducing them earlier.

He seemed to find that amusing. 'I buy up ailing companies and try to improve their health,' he answered simply, and she frowned at the caveat.

'What if you can't?'

Jonas smiled and, because it was totally natural and free of mockery, it lit up his face, causing Aimi to catch her breath yet again at the twinkle in his eye. 'Then I break them up into saleable parts.'

'Making a tidy profit on the way,' Nick added. 'Remember me telling you he was disgustingly rich?'

It sounded good, but Aimi could see a flaw. 'Making money is one thing, but what about the people? The workers? What happens to them if your cure fails?'

Jonas didn't appear in the least annoyed by being asked to justify his actions. 'They stay with the company wherever possible. This is about turning a company around, changing bad management into good. If everything goes well, everyone wins. When I have to break one up, we do our best to find alternative employment within our group. Does that meet with your approval, Aimi?' he queried sardonically, and Aimi nodded, smiling wryly.

'Of course. If I sounded disapproving, it's because not everyone in your line of work has a conscience,' she returned calmly. 'I apologise if I was rude.'

His lips twitched and now the gleam was well and truly back in his eyes. 'There's no need. You were only saying what many others think. However, it's good to know there's something about me you find attractive.'

Now that had her eyes flying to his, her lips parting on a tiny gasp of surprise. The bold challenge, right in front of his family, knocked her off balance, as did the sardonic amusement glittering in those blue orbs that dared her to respond. However, Aimi was not given to running away. Taking a breath, she moistened her lips, and her senses rocked when she saw his eyes follow the movement. Then his gaze lifted, and for a vital second the irony was gone and she could see heat there. Scorching. Elemental. Of course, as soon as he saw she had seen, his lips twitched, and she knew she had been played by a master. Which gave her all the more reason to reply.

'Are you fishing for compliments, Jonas?' she taunted with gentle mockery, and laughter erupted around her.

'Sounds like it to me,' James Carmichael interjected. 'That has to be a first!'

Everyone started teasing him, which he took with remarkable fortitude, an attitude which she *did* find attractive—amongst other things. She had always liked a man with a sense of humour and the ability to laugh at himself. Yet that changed nothing. She was not interested in whatever games he had in mind. Sitting back in her seat, she withdrew from the fray and concentrated on drinking her coffee.

The gentle ribbing continued for some time, until Jonas changed the subject. 'How many are coming to the barbecue this time?' she heard him ask his mother, but the answer was lost, as she took the opportunity to regroup her thoughts.

Aimi recognised that she was dangerously close to getting caught up in the miasma of the senses that was sexual desire, and she found that unsettling. From the moment she had vowed to change her life, no man had registered on her radar. In the beginning she had been too haunted by what had happened to feel anything but, as the healing process had gone on, she had turned the radar off deliberately. She hadn't wanted to be attracted to anyone, to find happiness in a loving relationship, for it deepened her sense of guilt to feel so alive. So well had she done the job that she had thought her defences were impermeable, but a few moments in Jonas's presence had destroyed that belief. Even now it went on. Unseen, Jonas called to her and the whole of her being responded. It was so strong, even the hairs on her skin stood to attention. The sheer intensity of it was staggering.

She didn't want to feel it, didn't want to be so aware of him, but her body wasn't obeying the rules. All she could do was try to block it out as best she could. Once the weekend was over, that would be the end of it.

She tuned back in to the conversation in time to hear Paula announce that she and her husband were going for a walk around the lake if anyone was interested in joining them.

'I could do with a walk,' she said, jumping at the chance, and looked at Nick. 'Will you join us?'

'Paula will only nag me if I don't,' he pretended to grumble as he stood up, and his sister poked her tongue out at him.

Aimi braced herself to hear Jonas declare his intention to join the group, but it didn't happen and she let out a tiny breath of relief. Though she forced herself not to look round, she could feel one pair of eyes on her back as they walked away.

It was marginally cooler down by the water and she and Nick strolled along, side by side, enjoying each other's company, following the other couple. Eventually Paula and her husband disappeared around a bend, leaving her and Nick alone momentarily.

'It's much better here,' Aimi declared, thankful for some respite from the heat—the tangible one and that given out by a pair of fathomless blue eyes.

'Jonas and I used to play on the lake when we were kids. We built a raft and would pretend we were ship-wrecked sailors. Of course, we weren't allowed to do it until we could swim. Jonas had different interests then,' he added somewhat pointedly, making her look at him.

'What do you mean?' she couldn't help but ask, and Nick rolled his eyes.

'That was before he discovered girls. Tall ones, short ones. Blondes and brunettes. All of them beautiful, and all of them madly infatuated with the handsome devil. He's never had to fight for a woman in his life. They take one look at him and, wham, they topple into his arms like ninepins! It's all too easy. He'll never settle down. Why would he, when he can have any woman he wants?'

Aimi had known the moment she had seen Jonas that he would be a hit with the ladies. She shivered inwardly as she thought again about the instant reaction she had experienced. 'No wonder you call him a Lothario!'

Nick laughed. 'He doesn't treat women badly. On the contrary, he's generous to a fault. He just never gives anything of himself. It's all purely physical. He's my brother, and I wouldn't wish him harm, but he could do with falling hard for someone, just to learn a lesson.'

'Not everyone wants to settle down,' she ventured,

knowing that such a situation was not on the cards for her. Once she had envisioned herself with a husband and children, but that dream had vanished a long time ago.

Nick came to a halt and, when he turned to her, she could see the frustration he was experiencing. 'Of course not. It isn't that. Jonas has lived a charmed life. Everything has come easy to him. He needs a reality check. Basically, he needs to know he's human like the rest of us.'

'You mean he needs to suffer,' she proposed, smiling just a little, and Nick grinned, an action that heightened the resemblance between the two brothers.

'Sounds awful, doesn't it? It's going to take someone pretty remarkable to do it, that's for sure.'

Aimi sighed as they began to walk on. 'I'm not sure you should be telling me all this,' she remarked uncomfortably, but Nick shook his head.

'On the contrary, you're the one who most needs to know,' he declared, bringing her head round in complete surprise.

'I don't see why,' she refuted, wondering what he could mean.

Nick tutted in a rather parental fashion. 'Of course you do, so just you remember what I told you when the pressure gets turned up.'

She glanced round at him curiously. 'Whatever do you mean?'

This time Nick favoured her with an old-fashioned look. 'Aimi, you're a beautiful green-eyed blonde, and Jonas isn't blind. Be careful.'

Aimi was both alarmed that he should realise what his brother was doing, and warmed that he cared enough

to warn her. Yet he need not have worried. 'I'm afraid
your brother will be wasting his time. I have no intention of being his entertainment for the weekend. Thank
you for caring, though.'

'I wouldn't want to see you hurt,' he told her, and she
smiled wryly.

'I won't be, because I don't plan to get involved with
him,' she added reassuringly.

'I'm sure that's what most of his conquests said,' he
countered with a grimace and Aimi stopped walking and
looked at him.

'Please don't worry about me; I'm going to be fine.
I've known men like your brother before, and I'm
immune to them.' It was almost true. Jonas, however,
was a different kettle of fish, and he had taken her by
surprise. He wouldn't do so again.

Nick studied her face, and what he saw there convinced him he could relax. Maybe she was right, and she
was immune. She certainly had defences like he had
never seen. 'I'll say no more, then,' was all he said, and
they continued on their way.

CHAPTER TWO

IN HER bedroom later that evening, Aimi pushed the windows wide to gather in what breeze there was, but the warmth already trapped inside her room made her feel hot and sticky all over again. Kicking off her shoes, she reached up and removed the pins that held her hair in place and the blonde locks tumbled in waves over her neck and cheeks. It felt good to let it loose, but tomorrow it would go back up again, reinforcing the look she had worked hard to maintain over the years.

In the mirror she could see the natural waves of her hair softening her features, making her look vibrantly young and alluring—carefree almost. It sent out a message that jarred on her nerves. She wasn't that person any more. Would never allow herself to be her again. It was part of her self-imposed penance.

Turning away from her reflection, she walked into the bathroom to take a cooling shower. Feeling marginally better, she dried herself on a fluffy towel and slipped into a thigh-length silk nightie. Turning off the light, she stretched out on top of the bed. However, it proved impossible to sleep, and not just because of the heat. Alone in the humid darkness, time passed slowly and her thoughts inevitably travelled back to that moment when she had first seen Jonas. She could visualise the sheer power and magnetism of him. Just thinking about it set her nerves tingling.

'Damn!' she exclaimed in exasperation, shooting up into a sitting position. 'Stop it, Aimi!' Yet for once her brain refused to obey. It played over the look in his eyes when their gazes had locked, and once again heat swept over her with such stunning force that her stomach muscles clenched in reaction.

That had her scrambling off the bed and padding to the window to draw in deep gulps of warm air. Yet it didn't help. The memories were too powerful. Too stunning. When she closed her eyes, she could almost feel the brush of his gaze on her lips as her tongue sought to moisten them, and she groaned helplessly.

'For heaven's sake, Aimi, get a grip!' she muttered to herself. 'You're not going to do this! So what if the man oozes sex appeal? You cannot allow yourself to be drawn into the flames. He's a playboy. All he wants is a body in his bed, and that isn't going to be you!'

Aimi dragged a hand through her damp hair and sighed. Lord, it was hot! Even the water in the shower had been tepid. She longed to feel something cool against her skin and, with sudden insight, knew just where she could find it. Moments later, she had slipped on her silk robe over her nightie and was padding barefoot down the stairs, the robe flying out in her wake like the wings of an exotic bird. Her destination was the large modern kitchen, and she was relieved to find she had it to herself when she passed through the door, closing it behind her. There was no need to turn on the light, for the moonlight gave the room a silvery glow.

It took a few minutes of quietly searching through drawers and cupboards before she found what she was looking for—a napkin, which she took to the counter beside the larder-style combined refrigerator and freezer. There was a delicious blast of coldness when she opened the freezer door, seeking out the bag of ice cubes. Taking a handful, she wrapped them in the napkin, closed the freezer and sat down at the table, sighing with pleasure as she drew the ice-filled napkin over her skin.

They were moments of pure bliss and she almost purred as she wondered why she hadn't thought of this before. Propping her feet on another chair, she hummed to herself as she lazily cooled herself down. Which was why she was miles away when the abrupt sound of someone tapping on the window made her almost jump out of her skin.

Her head shot round and, to her complete surprise, she saw Jonas standing outside the kitchen door.

'Oh, my God!' she gasped faintly, suddenly aware of the picture she must make, sexily draped over two chairs and wearing next to nothing. Her instinct was to rush off, but he was gesticulating to the door, clearly wanting to come in. There was nothing else she could do but put a brave face on it and comply. With a grimace of dismay, she set her napkin of ice down and padded over to the door to let him in, holding her robe together with one hand.

'Thanks,' he said, the moment he was inside, locking the door again. 'I thought I was going to have to sleep on the lawn,' he added with wry humour, which faded when he turned and looked at her standing in the moonlight, seeing her state of dishabille properly for the first time.

'Now that's a sight I don't see every day!' he breathed seductively and with obvious pleasure, whereupon Aimi hastily tied the belt of her robe and folded her arms as his blue eyes roved over her, causing her body to respond in a way he would easily recognise. She was as mortified as it was possible to be to have been caught this way. When he finally looked her in the eye again, there was a wicked gleam in the blue depths and a sensual curve to his lips. 'Were you expecting me? I hope so—you definitely have my attention,' he queried in a voice that vibrated along her nerves like the purr of a contented cat.

'Naturally, you would think that!' she shot back instantly, finding it incredibly hard to keep her composure. She felt unusually edgy and ill at ease. 'It was hot, so I came down for some ice. I didn't expect anyone to be about at this time of night. What were you doing out there?'

Jonas drew a hand through his hair, ruffling it rakishly, and she had to stifle a groan as the way he looked registered on her senses. She wondered if it was a calculated move or pure happenstance. Whatever, the effect was the same.

'Like you, trying to cool down after a hotter than expected evening,' he responded with more than a dash of irony. 'I went down to the pool soon after you went off for your walk, and fell asleep. I was trying the doors and windows, and that was when I saw you, draped across the chairs, wearing that provocative bit of nothing.'

'You should be thankful I was here; otherwise you would have had to stay outside,' she told him with all the firmness she could muster. 'And my clothes are perfectly respectable,' she added for good measure, which drew a rakish laugh from Jonas.

'Oh, I'm thankful all right, and there's nothing wrong with what you're wearing. You look good in it, and that's the problem. How the hell am I supposed to sleep now?' he charged sardonically, eyes gleaming flirtatiously.

Her heart lurched in sudden anxiety because the same thought had occurred to her. 'You shouldn't say things like that to a family employee. It's hardly appropriate,' she returned swiftly, determined to keep the moral high ground at all costs.

The moonlight made it easy to see the way one of his eyebrows rose mockingly and the sardonic twist of his lips. 'Drop your arms, Aimi, and we'll talk about appropriate behaviour,' he taunted, and Aimi felt heat scorch her cheeks at the knowledge that he had seen her body's response to him before she could hide it.

She watched speechlessly as he walked to the table and opened up the napkin of ice she had been using. Taking a cube, he rubbed it around his neck as he turned to look at her.

'That was a caddish thing to say!' she exclaimed in an attempt to sound outraged, and he laughed unrepentantly.

'I'm sure my brother just got through telling you I am a cad!'

Aimi immediately came to Nick's defence. 'He did no such thing!'

Jonas didn't look as if he believed her. 'Really? Remind me to thank him the next time I see him,' he said mockingly, allowing his gaze to roam over her from head to toe. Propping himself against the edge of the table, he crossed his feet and grinned provocatively. 'You know, that bit of nothing you're wearing leaves just enough to the imagination.'

Aimi drew in a ragged breath, knowing she ought to be able to handle the situation, yet finding it hard to remain aloof. This was the heat Nick had been talking about. It was pretty potent, and the sanest thing would be to get out of the kitchen. 'This is pointless,' she said shortly. 'I think we should just go to bed.'

Something wicked flashed in his eyes. 'Now that's really cutting to the chase!' he drawled sardonically, and she kicked herself for choosing her words badly.

'I didn't mean it like that,' she corrected hardily.

'However tempting the prospect might be, hmm?' he murmured softly and in the quiet of the night the words echoed like thunder, sending shockwaves through her system.

'You have some nerve!' she gasped faintly, and Jonas laughed seductively.

'I think you *should* go to bed, Aimi, before the need to know undermines your resolve,' he advised.

To say she was unsettled would be an understatement, and it made her respond in a way she never would have otherwise. 'What resolve?' she queried rashly, and Jonas shook his head and sighed.

'You know already. I'm talking of your resolve to have nothing to do with me,' he answered softly. 'That was the conclusion you came to during your walk, wasn't it?'

'God, you're arrogant! My resolve to have nothing to do with men like you was made years ago, not this evening,' she declared scornfully, and he looked amused.

'Men like me?'

Her eyes narrowed as she looked him up and down, doing her best to make it obvious she found him wanting in every department. 'Men who think they can have everything and everyone they want, just by asking. I have nothing but contempt for you.' It wasn't strictly true, but she was fighting a rearguard action here.

'If that is the case, why do you respond to me?' he asked softly, pulling the rug from under her feet.

Aimi held on by the skin of her teeth. 'I do not respond to you.'

That produced a soft laugh. 'I could prove you wrong, but it's late and we're both tired. I suggest you go upstairs now. We'll continue this fascinating conversation tomorrow.'

'We'll do nothing of the sort!' Aimi shot back tautly.

'By the way, I love your hair like that. You should wear it loose more often. It's very feminine, very sensual,' Jonas declared in the next instant, and her hand immediately rose to touch it.

Aimi realised she had forgotten all about it; having him see her with her hair down was like an invasion of privacy. Feeling more vulnerable than she had for many years, Aimi decided she had had enough and that a dignified retreat was in order. However, as she went to walk past him on her way to the door, her foot hit a wet patch on the tiles and slid out from under her. With a gasp of shock, she flailed around for something to hold on to and suddenly found herself caught by a pair of strong hands and hauled in to Jonas's powerful chest.

'Easy. I've got you,' he declared into her hair, but she scarcely registered him for her senses, now that she was safe, were being bombarded by the heady male scent of him, combined with the solidity of his powerful chest. It was a sensory overload that had her tipping her head and looking up at him through stunned eyes.

Jonas met that look and, though his eyes gleamed hotly, his mouth curved with wry humour. 'I think what you're thinking right now is highly inappropriate for a family employee,' he declared ironically, pushing her upright but not letting her go.

Dismay washed over her as she realised just how totally she had betrayed herself in that one gesture. What she wanted to do was run away from those knowing eyes, but what she did was tilt her chin at a belligerent angle. 'Keep your hands to yourself,' she commanded bitingly, shrugging him off, and walked away. It was hard not to hurry to the door, but she managed it and went out without a backward glance.

Out in the hall, breathing raggedly, she stared at the closed door. She had just made a complete fool of herself. To find herself experiencing an unwanted attraction to the man was one thing. To let him see it, quite another. Something about him just kept getting through her defences, and she didn't like it. Not one little bit.

Aimi berated herself all the way up to her bedroom, where she spent a restless hour trying to sleep. Before sleep finally claimed her, however, she had promised herself that she would keep well away from Jonas for the remainder of the weekend. It shouldn't be hard to do, as she was here to do research. She doubted very much if he was the type to spend much time in a library. A harem, maybe, but not a place full of musty books!

One thing was certain—no matter what he thought,

she was absolutely not going to be the next notch on his bedpost! She had worked too hard for too long to achieve this level of peace with herself to surrender it now.

The new day dawned as hot and humid as the last. Though she had managed to get some sleep, Aimi didn't feel the least bit rested, for Jonas had invaded her dreams, haunting them with tantalising possibilities. It seemed as if, waking or sleeping, she was being pulled by her senses into dangerous waters, and the current was incredibly strong. The man was too attractive for his own good, and it didn't help to remember how he had broken through her defences with incredible ease.

As she took yet another lukewarm shower, she considered the situation a little more logically. What had really happened, after all? She had discovered she was powerfully attracted to a man and that he was attracted to her. That didn't mean she was going to fall into his arms! Jonas might be an extremely attractive man, but she had known a lot of attractive men before and been able to resist them! But since that awful day she hadn't looked at a man with interest and, with a strength of purpose she hadn't been aware she'd possessed, she had simply shut down those feelings and emotions. So Jonas was going to be out of luck. She had come here to work, and that was all.

Taking comfort from that thought, she stepped out of the shower and dried herself off. Choosing what to wear wasn't a problem; she had packed only the bare essentials. Two skirts and a few blouses. Nick had told her to include a swimsuit, which she had done, but she did not expect to wear it. Today she chose her cream pencil skirt and a pale blue short-sleeved silk blouse. She slipped her feet into comfortable shoes and swept her hair back into its pleat with the ease of long practice. Smoothing the material of her skirt over her hips, she examined the view in the mirror. She looked cool, efficient and out of reach—just the way she liked it.

She was twitching her skirt into place when there was a knock on the door.

It was Nick, and he smiled as he stood in the doorway of her room. 'Good morning, Aimi. You're looking amazingly cool,' he greeted her, and her eyes crinkled as she laughed wryly.

'I don't feel it, I assure you,' she observed lightly, reaching up to sort out the collar of his polo shirt, which had gone awry.

'Well, just looking at you makes me feel cooler,' he returned charmingly, and she sighed, shaking her head.

'Nick, Nick, you're almost as bad as your brother! You must have gone to the same charm school,' she declared, grinning at him, totally unaware of anyone approaching.

'Morning, Nick,' Jonas greeted his brother and, when Aimi gave a start of surprise and glanced round, he nodded to her, lips curving into a provocative smile as he ran his gaze over her like a caress. 'I like the skirt, Aimi, but, all things considered, I prefer what you were wearing last night,' he said with a soft laugh before walking on.

She stepped back from Nick, feeling her cheeks grow warm. His remark, innocent-sounding as it was to anyone else, immediately brought back memories of what had occurred in the kitchen last night.

Nick frowned at his brother's retreating back. 'Hey, what did that mean?' he called out after him.

Jonas didn't miss a stride as he threw his answer back over his shoulder. 'You'd have to ask Aimi,' he advised, and jogged down the stairs.

Nick turned to her, eyebrows raised. 'What did he mean? You weren't wearing anything fancy last night. Have I missed something?'

She winced, knowing where his thoughts were going. 'Your brother was referring to later on. He had been locked out, and I just happened to be down in the kitchen when he was looking for a way in. That's all.' Looking at him, she saw the sceptical expression he was wearing and sighed. 'I happened to be in my nightie and robe.'

Nick let out an exasperated tut. 'Aimi, I warned you to be careful. He's my brother, and I love him, but when it comes to women...'

She squeezed his arm reassuringly. 'I know, but give me some credit. I'm not going to fall for his line of charm. I came here to work, and that's all,' she reassured him. Last night was a mistake which wasn't going to happen again.

Nick pulled a wry face and sighed. 'Sorry. I'm just a bit over-protective. You work for me so I feel you're my responsibility. I won't have Jonas playing his games with you.'

Aimi was warmed by his caring, but he didn't need to worry. 'Don't worry. Let's go down to breakfast and afterwards you must show me the library.' Working had always been a good way to distract her thoughts.

They followed in Jonas's wake, entering the break-fast room together, to find it empty. Maisie Astin, the housekeeper, was just bringing in fresh coffee and hot croissants to set out on the sideboard.

'Good morning!' she greeted them brightly with a cheery smile. 'Everyone has been eating outside today. Help yourselves, and let me know if you need anything else.'

'Thanks, Maisie. What would you like, Aimi?' Nick asked as he picked up a plate.

'Some of Maisie's melt-in-the-mouth croissants and coffee sounds perfect,' she decided, exchanging smiles with the other woman, who disappeared back into the kitchen.

'I'll bring it out. You go find a shady spot,' Nick ordered, leaving Aimi with nothing to do but wander outdoors.

Of course, then she wished she hadn't because the only person at the table was Jonas. Had he not looked up, she just might have retreated indoors again, but, as if some invisible sensor had alerted him to her presence, his head came round and he looked directly at her.

'Deciding whether it's safe to join me or not?' he challenged sardonically, and Aimi was compelled to walk forward.

'Not at all,' she denied blithely, smiling as if nothing had passed between them mere hours before. 'I was just enjoying the view.'

His lips twitched. 'Ditto,' he responded, and the lazy meander his eyes took as they ran up and down her body told her his view had nothing to do with the garden. It caused her heart to skip a beat and her nerves to start tingling as if he had actually touched her.

Irritated by a reaction she currently seemed to have no control over, she favoured him with a long-suffering look. 'You're wasting your time, you know,' she told him bluntly, keeping her voice down, not wanting Nick to hear. 'I'm not going to take the bait, however attractive the lure.'

One eyebrow rose mockingly. 'How many times did you have to tell yourself that last night?' he taunted, and she drew in a sharp breath.

'Once was enough. You're not that irresistible,' she shot back equally mockingly, and Jonas laughed appreciatively.

'You know, you're supposed to cross your fingers when you lie like that,' he cautioned, never taking his eyes off her for a second as she approached. She was so conscious of it that breathing normally was no easy matter, and she wasn't used to that.

Having reached the table, Aimi dropped on to a chair opposite him. 'Contrary to what you might think, I'm not in the habit of telling lies,' she corrected, feigning an ease she was far from feeling. Just being near him made her feel tense and unsettled.

Jonas raised that eyebrow again, to good effect. 'Really? Now I would have said most women are natural born liars.'

'That's a huge sweeping statement. Your jaundiced view was caused by a bad experience, I presume,' Aimi declared with heavy irony.

'It's a jungle out there,' he returned with a wicked grin, and Aimi knew that she would never forget that particular look as long as she lived.

'And men aren't liars?' she challenged scornfully, knowing she could name a dozen at least. 'It would be easier to think the moon is made of cheese!'

Jonas relaxed back into his chair, crossing his legs at the ankles. 'Now that sounds like the voice of experience talking. Is he the reason you dress the way you do?'

He was so far wide of the mark that Aimi almost laughed. 'I dress to please myself, not a man,' she was quick to point out.

He looked at her thoughtfully. 'Is that so? Are you trying to tell me nobody ever gets to see the exotic lingerie you wear? That would be a crying shame!'

Memories of those moments in the kitchen last night made her wince inwardly. 'My clothes are none of your business. I would not have gone downstairs had I known you were there.'

'Then I would have had to spend the night down by the pool, and never have got to see you in that mind-blowing confection of silk and lace. It's imprinted on my memory even now.' Jonas shifted, bringing one leg up to prop his ankle over the other knee. 'Seems to me, I know something about you that no other man does. Under that starchy exterior you like to wear satin and silk. What other secrets do you have, I wonder?'

'None that you will ever know!' Aimi shot back curtly but, instead of responding, Jonas merely smiled as he watched her.

'What happened to your hair last night? You weren't wearing it up in the kitchen,' he observed, and her nerves gave a giant leap.

'I don't sleep with my hair pinned up,' she explained calmly, only to see his smile broaden.

'You know what I think, Aimi Carteret?'

'Your thoughts couldn't interest me less!' she retorted witheringly, making him laugh.

'I think you practice to deceive.'

That was too close to the truth for comfort. 'Like I

said, your thoughts are of no interest to me. *You* are of no interest to me!'

'Whilst you are of considerable interest to me,' Jonas countered smoothly. 'I find myself thinking about you all the time.'

'How boring for you!' Aimi said, and he laughed— a sensual sound that sent goose-bumps down her spine.

'Oh, I have the feeling that you will never bore me, darling Aimi.'

The unexpected endearment sent a shockwave through her system, and her breathing went awry. 'I am not your darling.'

'Not yet, I agree,' he conceded, but his assertion didn't make her feel any better.

Goaded, her temper rose. 'Never!'

He looked her directly in the eyes before speaking. 'Ah, you should never say never. I discovered that myself last night. I would have bet good money that I would never find it hard to sleep in my old bed, but last night proved me wrong. I was terribly restless,' he explained with a wicked grin, mayhem in his eyes.

'You can't possibly blame me for that,' Aimi argued, as her nerves responded with a now familiar skitter. It was as if her defences had totally vanished, leaving her open to react to everything he said or did. She didn't understand how they could have abandoned her now, when she needed them most.

'Can I not?' Jonas countered, lips twitching with barely concealed humour. 'You were the one who raised my blood pressure,' he remarked sardonically, taking another mouthful of coffee from the cup on the table.

Somehow Aimi contrived to maintain her cool expression. 'My blood pressure didn't need lowering. I went to bed and slept dreamlessly,' she added for good measure, mentally crossing her fingers at the lie.

'Hmm,' he murmured doubtfully, running his hand over his chin. 'There's more to you than meets the eye.' Aimi merely raised her eyebrows. After a moment Jonas continued, 'Did you know I was supposed to be in America this weekend? Fortunately, the meeting was called off at the last minute.'

'Much to everyone's delight,' she remarked dryly, and something flashed in the recesses of his eyes.

He laughed. 'Nicely done, Aimi. Very tactful. It's no wonder Nick speaks so highly of you.'

'I do my best,' she replied smoothly, not bothered that he recognised what she was doing, just grateful she had the skill to draw upon.

'Ah, here comes the cavalry,' Jonas declared dryly, and Aimi glanced round to see that Nick had appeared with their breakfast. 'Not a moment too soon, eh?'

Nick had overheard that remark and, as he placed her cup and plate before Aimi, he glanced at his brother. 'What's not too soon?' he queried, frowning, and Jonas grinned at him.

'Your arrival with the food. Aimi was getting ready to eat the table.'

'Sorry I took so long,' Nick apologised, and she shot Jonas a warning look.

'You didn't. Jonas is pulling your leg.'

'He has a habit of doing that,' Nick confirmed wryly.

Jonas's lips twitched and he sat up straighter. 'Actually, I was flirting with Aimi, and she was giving me a hard time.'

'Good for you, Aimi!' Nick encouraged her, giving her a wink. 'There are too many women who fall into his arms at a click of his fingers already!' He took the chair next to her and started to wolf down his breakfast. Aimi followed suit, and silence fell over the table.

'What time are the hordes descending?' Jonas asked some time later.

'Midday onwards. Then it's the same old drill. Dad will be doing his usual cremation job on the bangers and burgers!'

Jonas grinned and glanced at Aimi. 'Have you been to one of our beanfeasts before?'

She couldn't help smiling at their amusement. 'No, this is my first,' she admitted. She was a little nervous about meeting the family. Finding herself amidst a group of strangers had been commonplace once, and she had thrown herself into the party mood with enthusiasm. Since that awful day, though, the thought of laughing and having fun had seemed wrong. How could she ever do that again, as if nothing had happened, when she was the one at fault? She couldn't and live with herself, so she had avoided parties, and her so-called friends had slowly drifted away. These days she preferred small, intimate dinners with people she knew well.

'Then you're in for quite an experience!' Jonas told her with droll humour, breaking her introspective mood.

Nick clicked his fingers. 'Hey, do you remember when…'

Aimi tuned out as the brothers took a humorous trip down memory lane. Sitting back in her seat and slowly eating her last croissant, she watched them both closely. They were very much alike. Both were handsome men, but Nick's face had softer lines. His hair was dark brown, whilst Jonas's was black. Nick exuded warmth, gentleness and caring, yet it was Jonas's more rugged lines that drew her attention.

Quite unexpectedly, Aimi found herself wanting to reach out and trace the lines of his face, to commit them to memory. Which was a ridiculous thing to be thinking. She did not want to remember him. The sooner they parted company, the better. Yet, as soon as the thought entered her head, one small part of her suddenly felt lost. She looked down at her coffee cup, frowning in yet more confusion. What was it about him that touched her? Good Lord, he only wanted one thing from her. Yet…there was just something about him.

The sound of laughter made her tune back in and she looked up to see Nick doubled up with mirth and Jonas grinning from ear to ear. It brought a smile to her own lips and an odd twist to her heart.

A piercing whistle cut into the laughter and made all three look round. Michael Berkeley stood at the end of the terrace, beckoning to them.

'Come along, you two! I need some muscle to set up tables. Get a move on!'

With wry looks at each other, the two brothers got to their feet obediently.

'Dad likes marshalling his troops,' Nick remarked fondly.

Aimi grinned at his expression. 'Have fun!' she teased and, as he walked away, caught Jonas's eye. The mocking look was back. As her stomach lurched, she raised an eyebrow questioningly. 'Was there something else?'

'Just this,' he said and, walking round the table, bent

to drop a swift kiss on Aimi's cheek before she could prevent it.

'Hey!' she exclaimed, whilst her pulse did a skittish pitter-pat. The feel of the brush of his lips on her skin took her breath away, it was so stunning.

Jonas was unrepentant. 'I have to have some fun. Consider that a little something on account!' he riposted neatly and followed his brother, leaving Aimi speechless.

She was left watching his rear view, and quite a view it was. Damn the man, he was just about perfect to look at. Broad-shouldered, with slim hips and long, powerful legs. There was no point trying to pretend otherwise, few men could compete with him. Of course, she immediately berated herself for noticing, when she was trying to keep these wanton wayward thoughts about him out of her mind.

She would have to try harder. Much, much harder. Bad enough that he was occupying her thoughts; she could not allow him to tempt her into breaking the solemn promise she had made. She had to resist.

CHAPTER THREE

IN AN effort to do that very thing, Aimi quickly finished her breakfast, then went indoors to find the library. It was a wonderful room, full of shelves of leather-bound books that called to her. For the next few hours she happily browsed, making notes of the books she wanted to dip into for the information Nick required. Finding a diary written by Nick's great-grandfather, she took it to a chair where she tucked her feet up under her and was soon lost in another world.

Nick found her there much later. 'There you are!' he exclaimed as he entered the room, and Aimi looked up in surprise. She had been so lost in the writing she hadn't heard anything.

'Did you want me?' she asked, hastily sitting up, swinging her legs down and slipping her feet back into her shoes.

'Yes, the rest of the family have arrived. We'll be eating soon,' he told her as she stood up, and Aimi's heart sank.

'Honestly, Nick, your family don't want a stranger in their midst. I'll be much more use to you here.'

'The books can wait,' he said, removing the diary from her fingers and setting it down on a table. 'I want you to have some fun this weekend, too.'

He would not be gainsaid and, without further protest, Aimi allowed herself to be ushered out of the house and into the garden. The barbecue had been set up by the pool, and that was where the family had congregated. Nick introduced Aimi to the various groups around the tables. Everyone made her feel welcome and were genuinely fascinated about the book she was helping Nick to research. In a very short time, Aimi was able to relax and, instead of going through the motions of acting as if she were enjoying herself, was actually doing that very thing. She said as much to Nick when they had a brief moment to themselves.

'My family are good people. I'm glad they've made you feel comfortable.'

Aimi glanced around her, seeing the large group of laughing, happy people through new eyes. It had taken a long time, but today she was discovering that she could actually enjoy herself without feeling guilty. The sky hadn't fallen in, nor the world come to an end. She didn't know why today had proved to be different from all the other days, but for the first time in aeons she had been able to put her burden aside for a few hours and simply live for the moment.

'Thank you for insisting I join you,' she responded with a smile, and Nick gave a tiny bow.

'You're very welcome, I'm sure,' he quipped and, as they moved on, Aimi's heart felt that tiniest bit lighter. Of course it wouldn't last. Later, reality would return, but for now she accepted this strange new sense of freedom without question.

It was while they were chatting to one of his cousins that Nick's beeper sounded. Though it was his weekend off, as a specialist surgeon he was often on call for emergencies.

'It's the hospital,' Nick informed her, recognising the number of the caller. 'I'd better take it inside. I won't be long.' He gave her a rueful look before striding away.

Aimi remained where she was, chatting until the conversation turned to a subject she knew nothing about, and then her attention wandered. She was watching the antics of two of the children when a movement drew her gaze. Her heart skipped a beat when she realised she was looking at Jonas, who was strolling along talking to a much older man.

She knew she ought not to look, but somehow she just couldn't tear her eyes away. He appeared totally at ease, laughing at something the other man said, and the sheer pleasure on his face made her catch her breath.

'That's Great-Uncle Jack,' one of the women at the table said, almost making Aimi jump. She looked round immediately.

'Sorry?'

'With Jonas. He used to be a sailor, and has loads of old yarns about his adventures. The children love him,' the woman explained with a friendly smile.

'Ah, yes,' Aimi murmured faintly, deeply relieved the woman had mistaken the source of her interest. 'I don't think I've met him yet.'

'Then you're in for a treat. Look, we're going to get

something to eat. Are you coming?' the woman invited, but Aimi shook her head.

'I'll wait for Nick. He shouldn't be too much longer.'

The others wandered off to join the mêlée for food, leaving Aimi alone for the moment. Of course, she immediately looked for Jonas where she had last seen him, but the two men were no longer there. No amount of searching brought him into her view again, and her heart sank. That was when she asked herself just what she thought she was doing. Had she gone completely insane? This won't do, Aimi. It really won't do, she castigated herself.

She stood up, deciding to go and join the queue after all. Anything to take her mind off the wretched man. Yet, as she turned, she found herself looking straight at him over a sea of seated people. Before she could move, and as if he could feel her eyes on him, Jonas glanced round. Their eyes locked and once more the intensity of the connection staggered her. This time, though, there was an added extra. It was a physical pull which silently urged her to close the distance between them. That blue gaze seemed to be saying, *I know where you want to be, and all you have to do is come to me.* Her lips parted on a sharply indrawn breath, and she saw the upward curve of his lips as he smiled faintly.

'There you are!' Nick's voice, speaking from right behind her, caused Aimi to spin round hastily, her heart thudding like mad.

'Oh, Nick!' she exclaimed, her head feeling alarmingly woozy, partly from shock and partly from what he had interrupted. 'You scared the life out of me!'

Nick immediately frowned in concern. 'I'm sorry, Aimi. You were miles away!'

Lord, how she wished she really was miles away! Aimi thought. A million miles from Jonas and the sensual spell he was weaving around her! Maybe then she could think clearly and get off this seesaw she had been riding since she first set eyes on him. He was a temptation she simply had to resist with every ounce of her strength for if she didn't, how could she ever look herself in the eye again? She had failed Lori once; she could not do so again.

Keeping that thought in mind, Aimi made a concerted effort to put Jonas from her mind by concentrating on Nick instead. 'What did the hospital want?'

'They needed to let me know about an emergency case that came in. They might need me to operate, so they wanted to put me on standby. They're monitoring the situation, but it doesn't look good. I should know in a few hours. Sorry, Aimi, but I think I will have to go back tonight.'

Aimi nodded understandingly, for it was the nature of his job. 'Never mind. At least you got the chance to see your family.'

'I knew there was a good reason why I hired you. You take everything so calmly; nothing seems to throw you,' Nick observed with awe. Aimi very nearly laughed at that, for his brother was playing the very devil with her vaunted calm. Unaware of what she was thinking, he urged her towards the tables of food. 'Come on, let's get something to eat. I'm famished, and I don't know when I might get to eat next.'

Aimi allowed herself to be steered away but, as she did so, she couldn't resist taking one quick glance backwards. Jonas was still watching her and she looked away hurriedly, her nerves leaping. Oh, Lord, she prayed silently, please make this weekend go quickly. Before she was tempted into doing something really, really stupid, which would jeopardise everything she had achieved.

Fortunately she was rescued by the massed ranks of the Berkeley family. Once a mountain of food had been eaten, the family got down to the serious business of the afternoon—playing games. It culminated in a form of rounders, with men against women, and created an uproar of laughter, for the rules were informal at best and each point fiercely contested. Aimi found herself laughing until her sides hurt and her jaw ached. It was all good fun and by the time it came to an end in the early evening everyone was exhausted. Gradually the other family members began to drift away again, back to their own homes, and peace descended upon the house once more.

Nobody felt like eating a heavy dinner after all that food, especially with the heatwave still holding sway. Fortunately, Maisie had prepared a light meal of salad and quiche, which she'd left in the fridge before she went home to her own family. There was much teasing whilst they ate a late supper. Contested runs were rerun with plenty of noise and, with very little effort, Aimi was able to concentrate on that, not Jonas, who sat mere feet away. Even though her senses were spine-tinglingly aware of him every second, she was pleased with herself for not showing it.

The meal over, Aimi and Paula volunteered to wash up, whereupon Nick and James agreed to wipe. They had barely done half of it, though, when Nick's beeper went off again. He used the phone in the kitchen to answer it and, from the one-sided conversation they could all hear, it was pretty clear he was going to have to go back to London. When he hung up, one look said it all. Aimi quickly dried her hands and went over to him.

'It's critical now? You must go straight away?' she asked, slipping back into the role of his assistant in an instant. 'Should I clear some of your calendar?'

'I'll let you know about that. Hopefully, it won't be necessary. The thing is, I don't know what to do about you. I need to go straight to the hospital from here, and I won't be coming back. How will you get home?'

'That's not a problem. I'll bring her back with me on Monday,' Jonas declared, and they all turned to discover that he had come into the room silently and was standing just inside the doorway. Aimi's instinctive response would have been a polite refusal, but Nick was too quick for her.

'That's a great idea, Jonas. You can have some extra time here for research that way, Aimi.' He looked at her with a relieved smile which made it impossible for Aimi to disagree, much though she would have liked to.

Resigning herself to spending another two days in Jonas's company, she took a steadying breath and smiled politely at him. 'Thank you. That would be kind of you,' she said, and didn't miss the gleam that came and went in his eyes.

'You're welcome.'

Nick rubbed his hands together, thoughts already on the task ahead of him. 'OK, so that's settled. Now I must get a move on.'

'I'll help you pack,' Aimi declared decisively, following him.

It meant she had to brush past Jonas in the doorway

and, though she tried to stop herself, she could not help but look up at him as she did so. There was a wicked gleam in those blue depths that caused her to catch her breath. Caught, her gaze wanted to linger, but she forced herself to look away quickly. She had the distinct feeling that, had she not, she could well have lost herself.

Not surprisingly then, she was in a state of some agitation as she helped Nick gather up his things. She hid it from him, for the last thing she wanted was for him to worry about her when he should be concentrating on his work. It took barely fifteen minutes, and then he went down to say goodbye to his parents and the other members of his family. Aimi walked outside to wave him off.

She stared after the disappearing tail-lights of his car and, when there was nothing more to see, she made her way back to the kitchen to discover, much to her consternation, that Jonas was the only one there. Standing by the draining board, he was wiping a plate with the ease of a man who had done so many times before.

'Oh!' she exclaimed, totally disconcerted by his presence in what she had thought would be the one place he would rarely venture, and came to an abrupt halt just inside the door. 'Where are the others?'

Jonas shrugged carelessly. 'Outside, I would imagine. I said we'd finish what was left.' He nodded in the direction of the sink whilst continuing to wipe the plate with the tea towel.

Aimi groaned inwardly, for this was exactly the type of situation she had been hoping to avoid. To put it bluntly, Jonas Berkeley was temptation on two legs and, whilst she knew she had the strength to resist most forms of temptation, he was a different matter altogether. Like the siren's song in old mythology, there was something about him which called to her on a totally primitive level. How he made her react without uttering a single word was something she had never experienced to this high degree, and she had thought she knew everything there was to know about herself. To discover she was wrong set butterflies careering around in her stomach.

She groaned to herself, and felt as though she was trapped between the devil and the deep blue sea. The washing-up needed to be finished, and she couldn't just walk away from the task she had started, for then he would know he had her on the run. So she took a steadying breath, walked back to the sink and began to wash a cup. A small silence fell and she felt compelled to break it before it grew into a monster.

'I suppose, in your line of work, you're used to volunteering people for things,' she remarked with heavy irony, and was pleasantly surprised to hear Jonas utter a soft laugh.

'I call it delegating. I pay my staff a good wage to do what I ask,' he informed her, resting his hip against the counter so that he could watch her and still wipe the crockery.

Very much aware of his regard—it was impossible to ignore the way her heart began to thump—Aimi kept her attention fixed firmly on what she was doing. 'They never rebel?'

'On occasion, and I will listen to their opinion, but in the end the decision remains with me. I have a core of loyal people who have been with me for many years.'

'Hmm. You did say you pay well,' she couldn't resist

saying, looking around to see what else had to be washed, and discovering only one last cup.

'That's a very cynical attitude. I prefer to think they enjoy the work.' Having cleared the draining board, Jonas waited for the cup she was washing.

Aimi held it out to him. 'Well, of course you would,' she replied with a wry look. Jonas smiled as he reached for the cup and as he took it his hand touched hers. Already on edge, Aimi gasped, instinctively jerking her hand away, then watched in horror as the fine china cup fell to the floor, shattering on the tiles.

'Oh, my God!' she gasped in distress. 'I'm so sorry!' Without thinking, she squatted and reached for the nearest pieces.

'No! Don't!' Jonas commanded, attempting to prevent her, but it was too late. The glass-like shard had already cut into her finger, causing her to cry out in pain. He muttered sharply, bending down to pull her to her feet. Taking her by the wrist, he held her hand under the cold tap and ran the water. 'I thought you would have known better!'

Wincing as the cold penetrated the cut, Aimi pulled a face. 'I wasn't thinking,' she defended herself, which received a grunt in reply.

'That was patently obvious. Let's have a look.' Turning off the tap, he wiped the cut with a fresh linen napkin he had produced from a drawer. 'Hmm, it looks clean enough. Fortunately, it isn't deep. Here, keep that pressed on the cut whilst I get antiseptic and a plaster.'

Shaken, Aimi didn't protest, but did as she was told. She knew she had been foolish, but her dismay at dropping the cup had been amplified by the way she had reacted to his touch. Stupid, stupid, stupid!

Jonas's return halted her self-castigation and she watched as he bent over her hand and made sure the area was dry before putting on some cream and fixing the plaster. It brought his head closer to hers and in a flash her attention was diverted to the blue-black waves of his hair. She breathed in slowly, the fingers of her undamaged hand itching to run through the dark locks. To know the feel of them.

Lost in her wayward thoughts, she was only vaguely aware of Jonas finishing the task—until, through the sticking-plaster, she was stunned to feel the brush of his lips on the covered wound. She blinked, coming back to the present, only to have her breath taken away when, a moment later, those same lips pressed a burning kiss to the palm of her hand.

'What are you doing?' she gasped faintly, her heart suddenly pounding in her chest.

At the same instant Jonas raised his head, a roguish gleam in his eyes. He did not release her hand; instead, his thumb continued a stroking caress. 'Something I've been tempted to do all weekend. Kiss you,' he declared in a voice as dark and sultry as a passion-filled night.

In the space of a heartbeat, Aimi was struggling. His voice and his touch had her senses spinning out of the stern control she placed over them. She stared at him, almost mesmerised. 'You go too far!' she protested, but there was no power in it.

His lips curved into a knowing smile as his eyes slowly, sensually, quartered her face. 'On the contrary, this is nowhere near far enough, and you know it, darling,' he corrected huskily, causing her nerves to leap wildly.

'Don't presume to know what I'm thinking!' she refuted his claim, even as her ears delighted at the sound of the endearment rolling off his tongue.

Jonas laughed softly, at the same time reaching up to run a finger along the fullness of her bottom lip. 'It's no presumption. I know. We both do. We've known exactly what the other was thinking and feeling from the moment we met.'

Which was the very last thing Aimi needed to hear, for it was true. However, at the same time it was enough to rouse her defences, giving her a breathing space to gather her forces to fight the tremendous urge to give in. 'I know nothing of the sort. I've done nothing to encourage you in this wild fantasy,' she exclaimed, but his laugh was mocking.

'Aimi, you know you don't need to do a thing! We connect on a totally different level.'

Another shockwave swept through her, for the level he was talking about was the one she had sworn would never see the light of day again. Now a sick despair replaced all other feelings and she backed away, drawing her hand from his, thankful he made no move to stop her. 'Well, we're going to get disconnected, because I'm not going to listen to any more of this!'

'Running away won't change a thing. We both know we want each other. It's in every breath we take, every heartbeat.'

Oh, God, she knew just what he meant, and not wanting to feel it didn't make it stop. The sensual pull was stronger than anything she had ever come across, and the desire to explore it a burning ache inside her. She hadn't thought it possible she could want a man with such intensity that she was tempted to forget all the promises she had made to herself after she had lost Lori.

It was the thought of that traumatic time which brought her chin up. 'Maybe it is, but I'm not going to get involved with you, Jonas.' One thing didn't have to lead to another if she remained resolute.

'That sounds good, but we both know you don't mean it,' he came back, taking her breath away.

'Of course I mean it! Why wouldn't I?' she challenged him, and he shook his head, laughing wryly.

'Because this wanting isn't going to go away that easily. It has to burn itself out, and there's only one way to do that. Which is why you and I will have an affair very soon,' he declared with such certainty she could only stare at him speechlessly.

The trouble was, every word he uttered increased her growing sense of inevitability. Yet there was nothing inevitable about it, she rallied instantly. She did not have to follow the path that seemed to stretch out before her, however enticing he made it look. Jonas might be dashing and charming, but she didn't want him in her life. There was no way she could allow him to tempt her into undoing all the good she had done, simply for the fleeting gratification of indulging in a highly sensual affair.

'I wouldn't hold my breath if I were you,' she told him bluntly. 'I'm never going to have an affair with you.'

'Never say never—it's a red rag to any red-blooded male,' he warned her softly.

Aimi tipped her chin defiantly. 'You'll be wasting your time trying to change my mind.'

He smiled sardonically. 'We'll see. I like a challenge. I think you'll prove to be the best one I've ever had.'

That comment sent a wave of anger crashing through her. His arrogance was beyond belief. 'Stay away from me, Jonas.' Aimi followed up that command by spinning on her heel and marching out of the door. Who did he think he was, telling her she would fall into his arms whenever he clicked his fingers? What a nerve!

Fuming, she knew she could not join the rest of the family. Her nerves felt as if they had fire ants crawling all over them and she needed to get away, find some privacy where she could catch her breath and think. Because her defences had just been breached again, and with even less effort than before. She needed to do some repair work—fast.

With that one thought in mind, Aimi took herself off to the library. She didn't bother to switch on the light, but sank down into one of the comfortable leather chairs by the fireplace. Leaning back against the plump squabbing, Aimi examined the initial source of her present dilemma. Her hand still tingled from the brush of his lips and when she closed her eyes she could feel once again the heat in them as they'd brushed over her flesh.

As she did so, the thought flashed into her mind that, if the internal mayhem she had experienced was the result of a simple kiss, what would something more passionate make her feel?

Half of her knew what the sensible thing to do was, but when he touched her it was her old sensual self who took control. It was an unexpected turn of events, yet, realising where her weakness lay, she knew she had to keep her distance. All she had to do was survive the next couple of days without letting him get close to her and she would be fine. Once she was away from his magnetic influence, the attraction would fade away to nothing. The old Aimi would retreat and the present one would feel more like herself again.

Sighing, she prayed for time to go fast. She needed to get back to the calm she had worked so hard to achieve. Only then would she feel safe.

CHAPTER FOUR

Surprisingly, Aimi slept better that night, probably from sheer exhaustion. She had rejoined the family on the terrace eventually, but Jonas had not been there. Aimi hadn't asked where he was, just breathed a sigh of relief. Now it was morning again, and yet another scorcher.

It being Sunday, the family went to church, but Aimi chose to remain behind. She breakfasted with them but, when they went off to change, she took her notepad and pencils along to the library to continue with her research. Yet, even with the French windows pushed wide, the room felt hot and airless. She persevered for some time, then tossed her pencil aside with a sigh of frustration. It was just too hot.

Thoughts of the cool water of the pool invaded her mind and she wondered if she dare risk it. She figured she had an hour or two before the family returned, and that was plenty of time to take advantage of their absence. It didn't take much more to persuade herself and within minutes she was nipping up to her room to put on her swimming costume under her skirt and blouse. Wrapping sunscreen and a book in a towel, she hurried down again and out through the back door.

Shedding her clothes by a lounger set in the shade of an umbrella, she slipped into the blissfully cool water, closing her eyes the better to experience the pleasure. It was wonderful, and she hummed to herself as she slowly floated across the pool on her back. She lost track of time, so she had no idea how long she had been there when there was a loud splash to her right. Water cascaded over her and she quickly came upright, wiping her eyes as she trod water and looked round to see what had happened.

Down the far end of the pool, a dark head emerged and she knew at once that Jonas had happened. As she watched, he glided to the wall, turned and swam back towards her with a front crawl that produced very little splash. Though she tried not to think it, his power in the water was impressive to watch, seeming to take no effort at all. He stopped when he reached her, grinning at her as he swept his hair out of his eyes.

'Sorry if I disturbed you. I tried not to,' he apologised, eyes twinkling with his particular brand of roguish humour.

It wasn't his swimming that disturbed her, but his presence in the pool. 'I didn't know everyone was back,' she replied, trying to keep her cool and some distance between them.

'Back?' Jonas queried with a raised eyebrow, narrowing that gap with strong movements of his arms and legs.

'From church.' She backed a little further and felt the side of the pool behind her, blocking her retreat. Cursing inwardly at the position she had got herself in, Aimi raised her chin and stared at him.

His smile broadened as he watched her predicament. 'Oh, I never go to church, except on special occasions. Which is why you have the pleasure of my company this morning,' he explained and, as they both trod water, one of his legs just happened to brush against hers.

Aimi knew it was deliberate, but that didn't stop the shockwave which swept through her system. Her lips parted as she drew in a sharp breath, but unfortunately a small wave washed in at the same time and suddenly she was coughing and spluttering.

The next thing she knew, Jonas's arm was round her, his legs tangling with hers as he supported them both with one hand on the pool edge.

'It's OK, I've got you,' he declared reassuringly, though with an edge of humour that was not lost on Aimi.

'You did that on purpose!' she charged as soon as she was able to.

'Would I?' he came back mockingly, and she blinked at him.

It was at this point that she realised she was actually holding on to his shoulders and the tanned skin was so smooth and tactile, her hands were itching to wander. She clamped down on that at once, but then became aware of the strength of his arm around her waist, and that set off a whole new load of fireworks in her nervous system.

'Of course you would!' she shot back pithily, trying to push herself away from him, but he was as immovable as a mountain. She gave up before she made herself look even more ridiculous. 'You can let me go now; I'm fine,' she told him, but he merely smiled.

'That's OK, I'm quite comfortable like this.'

She was sure he was, but she was not. OK, the rebellious part of her that had emerged in the last two days said she could have stayed like this for a long time, but that wasn't the point. The idea was not to be in his arms under any circumstances, putting temptation beyond reach. This was not a good start. Especially as the lower halves of their bodies were entangled like a lover's knot. It conjured up erotic images that did nothing to help her fight her attraction to him but, even as she groaned silently, the means of gaining her freedom came to her.

So, instead of fighting, she smiled at him. 'Jonas,' she said in a sultry voice that the old Aimi had once used to great effect. It made him look into her eyes.

'Yes, Aimi, darling?'

The endearment almost curled her toes, but she resisted it. 'It may have escaped your notice, but my knee is very strategically placed. If I were you, I'd let me go,' she added equally softly, raising her eyebrows to enhance the point.

Jonas let out a soft laugh. 'So it is. Would you do it, though?' he mused, then saw the threat of mayhem in her eyes and relented. 'You win,' he declared, letting her go, and Aimi quickly swam away towards the steps.

Her nerves were skittering as she climbed out of the water, the memory of being held so close to him sending vital messages to her brain, which she did her best to tamp down. She was very much aware of his eyes on her as she walked round to her lounger and towelled herself off. Damn it, now what did she do? She could leave, but that would only convince Jonas he had rattled her. The only thing she could do was stay and bluff it out.

Which was why she gave all her attention to applying the sunscreen, then settled back to read. However, her determination not to look at him was thwarted by the fact she could see him swimming back and forth over the edge of her book. Slowly the book dropped as she watched his powerful form cutting through the water. It was mesmerising, and it was only when he eventually came to a halt that she became aware of what she was doing, bringing the book up again hurriedly.

Minutes later, she caught sight of him out of the corner of her eye. He had left the pool and was heading in her direction. The vision of his lean male body, tanned and glistening with water in the sunlight, closed her throat and dried her mouth. Lord, he looked good enough to eat, she thought helplessly. His black trunks left little to the imagination, and she could feel herself melting in the face of so much maleness. Everything that was feminine in her responded to him, and it was incredibly hard to draw her gaze away before he reached her.

'Good book?' Jonas enquired lazily as he passed by.

'Very,' she replied, though for the life of her she couldn't have said what it was about.

She heard him moving around for a while, then he must have lain down, for she heard him sigh. Peeping round the side of her book, she saw him stretched out on a lounger a few yards away. At least if he was over there, he wouldn't be causing her any problems, she decided, and returned to her book. However, when she realised she had started to read the same page half a dozen times, because she was so busy listening for him, she gave up, closing the book with a snap and tossing it aside.

Sitting up, she adjusted the lounger so she could lie down, then stretched out on her front, resting her head on her arms. Soon the warmth and the quiet made her start to drift off, so it came as a huge shock to suddenly feel hands on her back, gliding up towards her neck. With a gasp she tried to get up, but those same hands urged her back down.

'I'm just putting sunscreen on your back,' Jonas informed her calmly, continuing to smooth his way from her neck to her waist. 'You'll burn in this heat.'

Aimi bit down hard on her lip as his fingers trailed along her ribs, coming dangerously close to her breasts. A bubble of hysteria lodged in her throat, for she was already burning and the sun had nothing to do with it. Lord, she wished he would stop, for his touch was driving her crazy! Jonas, however, seemed intent on taking his time and when he did finally stop she almost groaned. Whether from relief or disappointment it was too close to say.

'There, that should do it,' he declared. 'Unless you want me to do your legs?'

'No!' she refused, a little too quickly. 'I did them myself. Thank you,' she added in a choked voice, keeping her head turned away from him.

'OK. Now you can do my back,' he went on easily, and now she did turn to look up at him.

'What?'

Jonas stared down at her, his expression as innocent as the day was long—only she didn't believe it for a second. 'Do my back for me, would you?' he repeated and, taking her agreement for granted, strode back to his lounger and stretched out on his front.

Sitting up slowly, Aimi reluctantly picked up the sunscreen. A battle began to rage inside her. On the one hand, she knew she should refuse, do the sensible thing, but on the other, the wanton part, which she had controlled for so long, but which had somehow escaped from its icy prison, saw an opportunity to explore the inviting planes of his tanned flesh. It was this part which eventually won the silent argument and, as she crossed the space between them, she ignored the warnings of her reserved self.

Kneeling down beside him, she squeezed the cream into the middle of his back, then took a deep breath and started to smooth it on with her palms. She meant to be quite professional about it, but the instant she touched him there was no way she could remain detached. His skin was firm, yet silken, and the motion of her hands highly erotic. She soon lost track of time, indulging herself in the freedom of the moment.

'Mmm,' Jonas sighed with evident pleasure. 'That feels good. You have wonderful hands. I could get used to this.'

His voice was little more than a sensual growl, but it brought Aimi swiftly back to her senses. What was she doing? she asked herself, horrified. The heat that rose in her cheeks was mercifully hidden by the heat of the day, as she quickly finished the task and sat back on her heels. 'That's it,' she declared, preparing to rise. She needed to get away from him before she did anything else.

Jonas came up on his elbow, catching her wrist before she could move away. 'I haven't thanked you yet,' he growled, pulling her towards him as he spoke.

'Stop it, Jonas,' Aimi protested, fighting to keep her balance, but in the blink of an eye he rolled on to his back and she could only go with him, collapsing on to his chest.

Eyes gleaming with mischief, he slid his free hand around her neck and urged her mouth down to his. Aimi tried to hold herself away, but he was far too strong for her. His lips took hers with stunning sensuality. This was no tentative beginning. It was a lingering kiss that stirred the embers of their mutual passion. His mouth claimed hers, demanding an equal response, which she tried to deny him, but forces stronger than anything she had experienced before decreed otherwise. For aeons she was lost in the heat of his lips and the glide of his tongue. The more she gave, the more she wanted, and it was only the raucous cry of a crow as it flew over that eventually brought her back down to earth with a bump.

Pushing herself away, Aimi stared down into eyes that gleamed with wry humour and something more profound. Her stomach churned with self-loathing that she had once again given in to the selfish pleasures that had once ruled her life. It turned her blood to ice. 'I think you've thanked me quite enough,' she said, rising and moving away from him as she did so. 'Next time just try saying it.'

'That wouldn't be as much fun.' Jonas laughed, watching her pad back to her lounger and lie down on her front, turning her head away from him. 'You enjoyed it, Aimi. Don't pretend you didn't!' he called over to her but she ignored him.

Wincing, she closed her eyes, because the truth was she had enjoyed it. Kissing Jonas had been an incredible experience, and not one she could forget. Over and over, those moments played in her mind. Every sense she possessed had been heightened by the scent, touch and taste of him, just as she had known it would be. The man was an irresistible lure, yet somehow she had to try to resist him, for he was only interested in the fun of the chase. She could not allow herself to be yet another trophy for him.

She had to remember the reasons she had renounced the old Aimi all those years ago. It was so that she could live with herself and what she had done. Unfortunately, the old Aimi had broken bounds and got away from her for a moment, but she would conquer it in the end. She knew it was only a skirmish. There would be harder battles to fight before this was over. She had to be strong, because otherwise how could she live with herself?

Sighing, she willed her body to stop reacting to the male mere yards away. She would not throw herself into Jonas's arms, for he would only use her to amuse himself and she was worth more than that. Much more. This was the main thought in her mind as she finally began to relax, eventually slipping into sleep.

When Aimi awoke a little while later, Jonas had disappeared, and it proved just how ambivalent her emotions now were, that she had to tell herself she was relieved. Gathering up her things, she made her way back up to the house, thankful that the family had not yet returned. A quick shower washed away the signs of her swim, but she wished it were as easy to put the genie back in the bottle. Outwardly she might look calm, but inside she was in turmoil as she thought of the kiss she had shared with Jonas. It made her feel unsettled, and she didn't like it. To combat the feeling, she made sure that her outward appearance was as plain as ever—every single strand of her hair was tied into its pleat and the pins were secured in place. It wasn't the strongest armour, but it was all she had to fight both the inner and outer battle.

She spent the rest of the morning ensconced in the library again, and this time made herself concentrate. Pretty soon she found she had been able to put a pair of dazzling blue eyes out of her mind. She lunched with the family on the terrace, a little surprised that Jonas did not join them, but at least it gave her more time to settle her composure for when he did turn up.

Aimi worked until it was time to go upstairs to wash and change for dinner. As she examined her meagre wardrobe, she had another instance of her ambivalence when she found herself wishing she had something other than skirts and blouses to wear. Immediately her mind's eye saw a picture of Jonas grinning at her, knowing she had changed for him, and her spine stiffened as she fought down the wanton urge. She was not going to fall back into the old ways, when dressing to attract a man had been as normal as breathing. She was a different person. A better person, who was above such things. Which was why, when she climbed out of the shower and dried herself, she put on her royal-blue skirt and her sleeveless white silk blouse.

Her hair smoothed into its pleat and looking cool and efficient, her reflection was a necessary boost for her will-power. The woman in the glass looked as if she could handle anything. But could she? a traitorous voice asked. Aimi had considered herself beyond temptation, but Jonas was proving her wrong. Even now she was still thinking about him, which was a bad mistake, for that brought with it memories of that kiss and the storm it had aroused inside her.

Groaning at her own stupidity, Aimi turned away from her reflection and took some steadying breaths.

You can do this, Aimi. Just remember how hard you've worked to get where you are. Think of Lori, and all you promised her you would do to make up for what happened. Be strong. Be strong.

Some minutes later she was just slipping her feet into her comfortable pumps when there was a rat-a-tat-tat on the door. Surprised, she opened it, only to find Jonas outside. He was wearing a crisp white shirt that brought out the intense colour of his eyes and his hands were in the pockets of smart dark trousers. The effect was definitely easy on the eye and she groaned inwardly. Her senses registered him on levels she had forgotten she even had!

Now he favoured her with one of his trademark wicked smiles. 'As Nick is no longer here, I thought I would escort you down to dinner,' he explained his presence smoothly. 'Are you ready?'

'I think I can find my own way downstairs,' Aimi refused the offer with lashings of irony. However, Jonas was not about to be thwarted.

'I'm sure you can, but my parents did their best to instil a sense of good manners in all of us, so you shouldn't refuse my chivalrous gesture,' he countered, eyes dancing and a grin hovering around his lips.

Realising she was going to look ridiculous standing there arguing with him, Aimi reluctantly stepped outside and closed the bedroom door. 'And there was I, thinking the age of chivalry was dead!' she mocked, heading for the stairs at a brisk pace. Jonas easily fell into step beside her.

'You're a hard woman to please,' he complained, and she laughed sardonically.

'Actually, I'm quite easy to please. If you were to go away, that would please me greatly,' she shot back quickly, and almost jumped when his hand came to rest under her elbow as they descended the stairs. For so light a touch, she felt it to the very depths of her.

'We both know that's not true, darling. I have a pretty good idea what would please you greatly, but leaving isn't it,' he added in a sexy undertone, and Aimi's nerves did a series of somersaults.

It was hard to hang on to her composure when it was under such a strong attack, but she managed. 'Did your parents teach you to be outrageous, too?' she returned smartly, whereupon he laughed huskily.

'No, that was all my own doing.'

He was good at it, too, she thought waspishly. 'Yes, I'm sure it was.'

'You do that very well,' Jonas remarked easily, and Aimi glanced round at him, frowning.

'What?'

'Disapprove,' he enlightened her, and it was her turn to laugh.

'That's because I do disapprove of you,' she insisted firmly.

Jonas brought them to a halt as they reached the bottom of the stairs and turned her to face him. 'Doesn't stop you wanting me though, does it, Aimi?' he challenged, holding her gaze.

To say she didn't want him would be futile, for the man wasn't a fool. He could read women with diabolical ease. 'It will stop me getting involved with you, Jonas.'

He shook his head, supremely confident. 'No, it won't. It will add spice to our affair. I'm looking forward to it.'

Irritated beyond measure, mostly because the resurgent part of her knew he was right, she jabbed an admonitory finger into him. 'Listen to me, Jonas Berkeley…'

His smile would warm a winter day. 'You know, you really are beautiful when you're angry.'

Full of helpless rage, Aimi almost stamped her foot. 'Stop it!'

'I wouldn't, even if I could. I'm smitten with you, Aimi Carteret, and I don't intend to stop until the fever raging inside me dies down.'

As declarations went, it was a show-stopper. It certainly stole Aimi's thunder. She shook her head dazedly. 'What about what I want?'

'That's the beauty of it. We want the same thing, so why don't you simply accept it? I promise you, you won't be sorry.'

Oh, he was golden-tongued and so persuasive—was it any wonder women fell for him in droves? Which was all the spur her pride needed to make sure she didn't do the same.

'You are the most pig-headed man it's ever been my misfortune to meet!'

Jonas started them moving again. 'You won't think so when you know me better.'

'I know you as well as I intend to,' Aimi declared shortly, relieved when they entered the dining room to find the family gathered there. She immediately went to talk to Paula. Her whole body was trembling and her heart was racing. She felt besieged, under constant attack from all sides, totally dismayed by the rapid disintegration of her defences these past few days.

Fortunately, Jonas didn't follow her. Unfortunately,

now that Nick was absent, Jonas had been seated beside her, so her respite was short-lived. However, he was the very soul of charm and wit, helping the conversation flow easily around the table. She had to admire his ability to put everyone at ease, and knew it was that very same charm which managed to find a way through a woman's defences. As she ate the perfectly prepared food, Aimi had to admit, albeit grudgingly, that there was a lot to like about Jonas Berkeley—if you ignored the fact that he was a womaniser and a playboy.

As was the family habit, they had coffee on the terrace, and conversation turned to this and that. Aimi asked Simone about her passion for family history and pretty soon they were lost in the intricacies of Simone's family. Aimi found it fascinating, so much so that for a while she quite forgot about Jonas—until he spoke.

'You should show Aimi the family Bible,' he suggested to his mother. 'I'm sure she would be interested. It's a hundred years old at least.'

'Would you care to see it?' Simone asked her, and Aimi nodded.

'Certainly. We have nothing like that in our family.'

Simone immediately turned to her son. 'Take Aimi to the library, Jonas. You know which shelf the Bible is kept on.'

'I'd be happy to,' he responded with a smile, getting to his feet and looking enquiringly at Aimi.

This was not quite what she had intended when she'd accepted the offer, but there was little she could do, so she rose with every appearance of pleasure and followed Jonas into the library. Crazy as it seemed, it felt as if everything was conspiring to bring her and

Jonas together. Even her own pulse had increased its rate in expectation of heaven knew what! Things she wanted, yet didn't want to want. Like the feel of his lips on hers again.

The library was only marginally cooler than the rest of the house, even though it was on the shady side. After ushering Aimi into the room ahead of him, he closed the door, then crossed the room to push open the French windows. The light was beginning to fade, but he switched on a green shaded library lamp which sent out an intimate golden glow.

Aimi watched him from the middle of the room, which had somehow managed to shrink in size so, although Jonas was by the window, it felt as if he were right beside her. Electricity began to hum in the air around them. She could feel it taking her breath away and her awareness of him grew exponentially.

Jonas, meanwhile, had gone to one of the book-shelves Aimi had yet to search and lifted down a large leather-bound tome, which he set on the table near the lamp. Looking up, his eyebrows arched as he saw her some yards away.

'You won't be able to see it from there,' he pointed out, and Aimi finally went to join him. 'Here, you open it,' he invited, allowing her to get to the table in front of him. Of course, once she was there, he closed the gap, his body brushing against hers as he watched over her shoulder.

Aimi did her best to concentrate on the Bible, opening the cover to see that lines of names had been entered there in a fine copperplate hand.

'The third name down is interesting,' Jonas remarked, reaching around her to point to the entry, but Aimi barely saw it, for the brush of his warm breath against her neck sent shivers down her spine. 'Can you read it?'

Read it? She couldn't even remember the alphabet! All she knew was that if she turned her head the smallest fraction, her lips would touch his. 'Not really,' she lied, her voice sounding unreal to her own ears. 'It's very small.'

'There's a magnifying glass around here some-where,' he murmured, looking around. 'Ah, here it is.' He reached over and, as he did so, his cheek brushed hers. Aimi gasped and Jonas went still, turning his head just enough to look into her eyes. 'Is something wrong?' he asked softly, and the gleam in his eyes told her he knew exactly what he was doing and its effect on her.

'No, but I think we should rejoin the others,' she managed to croak out, feeling her lips tingle as he watched her mouth whilst she spoke.

'But you haven't looked at the Bible yet. There's more to see,' he added with sweet persuasion. 'You know you don't really want to leave.'

The old Aimi didn't. The one who had lived life to the full and loved with equal enthusiasm. But the one who knew mistakes had to be paid for still struggled to maintain control. Yet it was taking every ounce of strength she possessed not to turn into his arms and let the heady waters of physical attraction wash over her. Nobody had ever made her feel this need, this urgency. She was being drawn to it like a moth to a flame, knowing she could get seriously burned, yet transfixed by the promise of warmth.

Almost at the point of drowning, Aimi raised a hand to push herself away. 'I have to go,' she declared, knowing she sounded desperate, but not caring right then. 'I have to get some air.' She couldn't breathe in here. He was taking all the oxygen away. With the last of her strength, she moved away and Jonas made to follow her, only to be brought up short by the sudden loud ringing of the telephone. He had to answer it, and that was when Aimi made good her escape.

She disappeared through the French windows as she heard Jonas speak into the telephone receiver. This brought her out on one side of the house, from where she could cut through the shrubbery and head down towards the lake without being observed. She felt like an animal in flight, and her heart pounded with every step she took. Yet, even as she extended the distance between them, she could feel the siren call urging her to go back. What she wanted was behind her, not out here.

However, she knew that not everything she wanted was good for her. She had seen the effect of such self-indulgence, and had vowed it wouldn't happen again. So she headed for the quiet of the wood, hoping to find solace for her restless senses. Only there was no peace to be found, even in the rose-shrouded gazebo tucked away at the far end of the lake, overlooking the water.

Holding on to one of the wooden posts, she closed her eyes as she admitted she was fast losing the battle to resist Jonas. Wanting him was a fire in the blood that could not be quenched. For all her intentions not to get involved, right now the thought of not seeing him again was like a fist tightening on her heart. If that was unthinkable, then another thing was also true. It had been too late to walk away unscathed from the moment she had first set eyes on him. He had stirred her old self into life again and, no matter how she fought her nature, that self was not about to be denied.

The sound of a footstep broke her thoughts and made her eyes fly open. As if in a dream, she turned towards the entrance. Jonas stood there and it felt to Aimi as if the air around her gave a low, soft sigh. She watched as he stepped inside, instantly shrinking the small building and stealing the sultry air, so she could scarcely breathe.

'You followed me,' she said without surprise.

'You knew I would,' he declared huskily, and he was no longer smiling. 'I'm drawn to be wherever you are. You feel it, too.'

Aimi took a ragged breath. 'Do I?'

Jonas took another step, which brought him inexorably closer. 'It's quite stunning, isn't it, this thing between us? We felt it from the moment we met.'

'Did we?' she challenged, holding up her hand to keep him at bay, but he merely kept on going until her hand was touching his chest. Resting over his heart. There he stopped, and looked down into the depths of her eyes.

'Oh, yes. You know your skin screams to know the touch of mine,' he breathed hotly, and her heart lurched. 'It's the same for me. I cannot walk away from you, Aimi. Not yet. Neither can you run from me.'

'You don't know me that well,' she whispered brokenly, even as her fingers splayed out, feeling the heat coming off him. Without thinking about it, her other hand rose to join its mate, allowing her to feel the strength of his powerful chest and the heart beating beneath it.

'I intend to know you better,' came the soft reply, and she breathed in deeply.

A part of Aimi knew she should make some attempt

to stop him, yet she couldn't. After all the things she had just told herself, the need to know was overwhelming. Her brain shut down, leaving only need to take control. She could feel herself starting to tremble as she looked up at him, and the fire in his eyes held her mesmerised. Then, as his head lowered, it was as if the whole world held its breath. When his mouth met hers, the earth shifted on its axis, never to return to the same spot again.

She felt the touch of his firm lips throughout the whole of her body. It was the most incredible thing. Every sense she possessed came alight in that one instant. Hunger stirred and in a flash the smouldering coals of desire surged to life, sweeping over them, burning them up. There was no way back. Jonas claimed her mouth with a growl of male satisfaction and, with a low groan, Aimi responded, parting her lips to accept the thrust of his tongue. It was wild and hot, one kiss fuelling the next until it was impossible to say where one began and the other ended.

It was pure potent physical attraction and for endless minutes neither could do anything to control it. They were like puppets tossed into a maelstrom of aching need that had surfaced after days of captivity. They had opened the Pandora's box of attraction, drowning in the hidden delights. There were no barriers, no restraints. They were free at last to indulge the needs driving them on.

When the first wild rush of excitement subsided, they drew apart, breathing hard, eyes revealing the power of what they had just experienced.

'Oh, God!' Aimi groaned softly, dropping her forehead until it rested under his chin. 'I had forgotten.' It had been so long since she had allowed herself to feel anything, it was almost like the first time all over again.

'That it could be like this?' Jonas queried thickly, one arm drawing her close to his body, the other hand slipping the pins from her hair until it was a blonde halo that he slid his fingers into to frame her head. 'Heaven help me, so had I.' He sounded surprised—shocked, even.

Aimi was hardly listening. With every breath she could breathe in the scent of him, and the tanned flesh of his neck was temptingly close. All she had to do was turn her head and her lips made contact, sending shivers down her spine. Then her tongue snaked out, flickering over his skin, and her whole sensory system went into overdrive as she heard Jonas catch his breath. But there wasn't enough of him to touch. She wanted more. In an instant her impatient fingers were tugging at the buttons of his shirt until she could push the silk aside and claim her prize.

Not that she had much time to indulge her need to know the taste and feel of him, for Jonas's fingers closed on her hair and urged her head back so that he could see her.

'You're driving me insane,' he declared gutturally, plundering the aching arch of her throat with lips that burned.

Aimi clung on to his shoulders as her body started to turn molten. The strength went out of her legs, but Jonas easily took her weight, easing them down to the floor so that they were kneeling in each other's arms. Then she felt his hands unbuttoning her blouse and pushing it aside, tugging at the silky fabric until it dropped to her waist, revealing the honey-coloured silk of her bra. One long-fingered hand claimed the aching mound of her breast and instinctively she arched her body towards him, her head falling back as she closed her eyes and savoured the scintillating pleasure. His hands moved over her, teasing aside the barrier of silk, blazing a path that his lips followed, until his mouth closed on her engorged nipple, suckling, and she groaned helplessly as her senses went spinning.

By this time there wasn't a sane or sensible thought between them. There was only room for what they could feel and, like pebbles on the beach, they were helpless as each succeeding wave washed over them, drowning them in sensual pleasure. Clothing was tossed aside with fine disregard as they strove to be ever closer and discover each other. They tumbled to the floor, limbs entwined, their passion for each other as hot and sultry as the night around them.

Yet the sheer urgency of the desire which had engulfed them meant that this was to be no long drawn out, lazy lovemaking. They were driven by a purely primal need to reach the goal their bodies craved. Aimi only knew that every erotic kiss, every scorching touch was driving her insane. She longed to feel him inside her. Craved it so that, when Jonas finally slipped between her legs and thrust into her, she cried out at the stunning sensation of being one with him.

Jonas went still. 'Aimi?' he asked in a voice thick with passion. 'Did I hurt you?'

She shook her head swiftly. 'No. I'm fine. It's just…been so long,' she whispered, not wanting to talk right now.

He looked as if he wanted to say more, but she tightened her arms around him, digging her fingers into his back, using his own need against him. He began to move again and within seconds there was no room for anything other than their wild ride towards release. It came like a white-hot explosion, causing both to cry out at the sheer wonder of it. Holding on to each other, they rode the shockwaves of pleasure until even that ended. Then, replete, they slept.

CHAPTER FIVE

A LONG while later Aimi stirred, frowning in confusion as the world slowly made itself felt. Why was her bed hard, and her pillow firm yet warm? As she puzzled over that, an owl hooted almost over her head and finally she realised she wasn't in her bedroom, but outside.

That was enough to have her shooting upright into a sitting position. Stunned, she realised that not only was she naked, but so was the stirring male form beside her. As Jonas slowly opened his eyes, everything came rushing back to her. The moments in the library, followed by their heated lovemaking here in the gazebo.

Her stomach lurched and she felt sick. How could she have let this happen? Dear God, she had spent years distancing herself from the person she used to be, and now, at the drop of a hat, she had tumbled to the floor and allowed Jonas free rein with her body! Just as the old Aimi would, she had let her senses rule the moment. Had gloried in it, in fact, and it was not a comfortable thought.

She hadn't been able to fight her most basic instincts. After all she had gone through, she should have been able to walk away from him, so why hadn't she? Sitting there, in the heated darkness of the gazebo, she was forced to accept what was plain to see. Because she had wanted it to happen. Because she had wanted to feel alive again. To experience the warmth of being with another human being. Yet not just any person, only Jonas.

'Come back. You're miles away.' Jonas's low voice broke into her uneasy introspection.

She turned and looked down at him, seeing the gleam that entered his eyes and the curve of his lips as he smiled. Reaching out a hand, he caressed the curve of her back. She felt that touch in every part of her and her instinct was to lean back against it. She tried not to. Tried to be strong.

'Hmm, your skin is soft, like a peach,' he murmured, coming up on an elbow to test the feel of it with his lips.

Though it was almost like a physical pain to do so, Aimi pulled away. 'Stop,' she ordered, knowing she should leave and go back to the house. Jonas had other ideas.

'Stop?' he challenged with a soft laugh, trailing a line of kisses up to her shoulder, then to the tender skin at the base of her neck.

She knew then just how weak she really was, for helplessly she arched against his touch, unable to summon the strength to leave. Then his free hand framed her face, turning her head so that he could claim her lips in a lingering kiss.

'I don't want this,' she tried again as his lips moved on, her lashes dropping over her eyes as he found the sensitive spot below her ear.

Jonas chuckled throatily. 'I can tell.'

Aimi drew in a sighing breath. 'We can't stay here. You have to stop.'

'I don't think I can,' he whispered as he trailed a line of kisses along her jaw line. 'You'll have to stop me.'

Her eyes opened as he reached her lips again and, as soon as she looked at him, all sensible thought flew from her head. Stopping was the last thing she wanted to do. She placed her hand over his heart, feeling the steady beating under her palm. Ignoring the small voice of caution, she allowed herself to be controlled by her reawakened sensuality. Her lips curved into a smile.

'I've changed my mind.'

With a laughing growl, Jonas sank back to the floor, taking her with him. Neither of them heard the owl hoot from its perch in the tree outside.

An hour later Aimi carefully eased herself out from beneath Jonas's arm and rose to her feet. Gathering up her clothes, she quickly put them on again, then stepped over to the doorway. All was quiet outside, as if nothing monumental had happened in this beautiful place. She turned to look at Jonas's sleeping form and her heart turned over. He looked softer in sleep, his defences down, and just watching him caused a ball of emotion to expand inside her. Making love with him had been the most perfect experience of her life. He was a magnificent lover, but it was more than that. Somehow being with him had made her feel…complete in a way she hadn't felt for a very long time. She had been alive.

And then a memory forced its way to the front of her mind. It was of her best friend, Lori, laughing at her in the sunshine at the top of the ski slope that last winter. They had been eighteen, the world their oyster. They had both known then what it felt like to be alive, but Lori never would again. Aimi's hand tightened into a fist, her nails cutting into her palm. So what gave her the right to feel it now, when a better person couldn't? Because a man had broken through her defences and shown her how incredible sex could be with him? That was not good enough. Nothing would ever be good enough.

What she did now, having crossed the line and given in to temptation, Aimi simply did not know. Which was why she knew she could not linger here any longer. She had some serious thinking to do, and there was no way she could run the risk of Jonas waking up before she had made up her mind about what she was going to do. So, careful not to make too much noise, she hurried down the steps and headed for the path around the lake that would take her back to the house.

Safely in her room, for the first time she locked the door. Without turning on the light, she sank down on to the edge of the bed and dropped her head in her hands. Into her mind came Nick's warning of danger, and she closed her eyes in despair.

'Oh, Nick, look what I've done,' she said out loud, and could picture the look on his face. After all her fine words, she had allowed herself to be seduced by his brother.

What on earth was she going to do? She knew now what it was like to make love with him, and there was no way she could forget it. Lord, how she regretted those moments of weakness. Why Jonas? Why now? Because she had been overthrown by emotions stronger than her sense of guilt. Her desire for Jonas had been too powerful to deny, and she honestly didn't know if she could manufacture defences strong enough to withstand him. She only knew she had to try, because she had given her word to Lori.

Aimi took a sighing breath, pressing a hand over the fluttering nerves in her stomach. There would be no more. She would fight this thing. She could be strong. The mistake didn't have to be compounded, so long as she kept faith with herself. Finally she felt the anxious fluttering in her stomach die down and a sense of calm settled around her.

Her mind made up, Aimi summoned up the energy to shower and slip into her nightie. The heat tonight was even more unbearable than the previous ones, and there was scarcely a breath of air coming in the open windows. Aimi tossed and turned on top of the bed, the heat the least of her problems. Eventually, though, sheer mental and physical fatigue made her fall asleep. However, the dreams she dreamt were as hot and sticky as the night.

Dressing in her ubiquitous skirt and blouse the following morning, Aimi carefully pinned her hair into its pleat. She had to use new pins, getting a flashback of Jonas taking the old ones out of her hair in the gazebo last night. Fortunately she had enough, because she was not going to go back to the scene and retrieve them. Her memories were vivid enough without that!

Once she could look herself in the eye in the mirror without wincing, Aimi was ready to face the day. She descended to the ground floor, where all was still silent, it still being early. The housekeeper must have been busy, though, for the windows and doors were already open. Aimi stepped out on to the terrace, her spirits buoyed by the sight and sound of the birds searching for their breakfast. Leaning against the low wall, she watched their antics for quite a while before suddenly the hairs on the back of her neck stood up, alerting her to the fact she was no longer alone.

She half turned, knowing exactly who she would see. Her radar was specifically designed to pick up on one man. Jonas stood in the doorway, his expression thoughtful as he observed her. Their eyes met briefly and she could feel his trying to probe hers, trying to see beyond the contained front she exuded. When he failed he walked towards her and she turned back to the view, not wishing him to get even the smallest hint of how her heart turned over at the sheer pleasure of seeing him. 'Hey, what happened to you last night?' he asked as he slipped his arms around her waist. Automatically her hands came up to try and remove them, but he resisted her efforts with ease. 'I missed you,' he growled as he pressed a kiss to the spot where her pulse fluttered like a trapped bird.

Aimi felt the touch throughout her whole system, and fought the urge to let his strong body take her weight. 'I was tired so I went to bed,' she responded coolly. That was better. Cool was good.

Jonas turned her around, and she could see the deep frown between his eyes. 'What's wrong?'

Her eyebrows rose. 'Wrong? What could possibly be wrong?' she charged with a dash of mockery.

'You tell me,' he returned, still frowning. 'Last night you were all heat and passion. This morning you're…'

'Back to normal?' she put in for him, adding a faint laugh for good measure. 'What did you expect?'

He stepped back a fraction. 'Not this.'

Somehow Aimi managed to look amused, but it was by no means easy. 'Was I supposed to be all over you like a rash because you managed to break down my resistance?'

Jonas clearly didn't like her tone. 'Actually, I thought you would welcome the idea of spending the day together.'

Aimi shrugged, determined to put on a show of indifference that would keep him at bay. 'I can't help what you thought, but I'm here to work. Besides, what more could you possibly want? You had me. Now you can add me to your list.'

It could have been her imagination, but for a moment she thought Jonas actually looked taken aback. It vanished beneath a heavy frown. 'What the hell are you talking about?'

Once again she shrugged, as if it was all too much bother, whereas actually her nerves were jumping about like crazy. She was not enjoying this at all, yet she had to press on. 'Look, you saw me, you wanted me, you had me,' she spelled it out for him. 'End of story.'

His eyebrows rose at the blunt way she had said it. 'It's far from being the end, Aimi. What about the little fact that it had been a long time between lovers for you? You should have told me,' he charged her, and Aimi felt the colour flood into her cheeks.

Put on the defensive, she folded her arms so he couldn't see her hands tremble. 'And when would I have done that?'

A muscle flexed in Jonas's jaw, then he sighed and dragged a hand through his hair. 'I take your point. I just wish I had known.'

Aimi shifted from foot to foot, wishing he would drop the subject. 'What difference would it have made?'

A faint smile curved the edges of his mouth, and there was a faint twinkle in his eye. 'I would have acted differently. Been more gentle.'

That remark, plus the look in his eye, deepened her colour again. 'You were gentle,' she assured him, quite unable to lie about that. 'You didn't hurt me.'

'Really? I thought I must have done, after your cold reaction this morning.'

'You mean that's never happened before?' she asked sceptically, and his smile was rueful.

'Once or twice. I just never expected it from you.'

Her chin came up. 'Why? Because I made it so easy for you?' she couldn't help snapping back at him, and he frowned yet again.

'Is that what you think? That you were easy?' Jonas asked in surprise and she looked away, her jaw working madly, feeling as if the situation was getting away from her.

'It doesn't matter. Last night was a mistake,' she declared flatly, for the truth was she knew she had made it easy for him by forgetting the principle by which she now lived her life.

'Do you regret what happened?' he challenged immediately, and just a little sharply, which surprised her.

She cast him a quick glance before concentrating on the view of the garden. 'It shouldn't have happened. It wouldn't have done if...' Aimi caught herself up swiftly, but Jonas latched on to the words.

'What would have stopped it, Aimi?'

Aimi was still smarting from her own self-castigation and his question roused her anger. She spun round, jabbing a finger at her chest. 'I should have stopped it. It isn't as if I didn't know better! I just wanted...but that was wrong. I know that now.'

Jonas shook his head, clearly bemused by the way

she was behaving. 'What's going on in that head of yours?' he queried, taking her by the shoulders. 'All we did was make love.'

Aimi shrugged him off. 'We didn't make love; we had sex.'

Jonas took a step back, something dark flickering in his eyes. 'If I just wanted sex, there are any number of places I could go,' he declared tautly.

Aimi had the strangest feeling that she had hurt him, and yet she couldn't think how. Besides, she couldn't allow herself to weaken. She had already said far too much. 'Then I suggest you go there next time. I won't be available.'

Jonas stared at her in silence. 'You don't think very highly of me, do you?'

She drew in a ragged breath, knowing the truth was she didn't think very highly of herself right now. 'Your reputation speaks for itself.'

He laughed bitterly. 'Does it, indeed? Would it interest you to know that I'm not quite the love 'em and leave 'em bastard the press insists on painting me as?'

'It doesn't matter. Whatever you think there is between us, I'm ending it right now,' she declared firmly. There, she couldn't have made herself any clearer.

'Why? Scared you might enjoy it too much? And, before you open those delicious lips and hit me with a bunch of lies, you did enjoy last night. I have the scratches on my back to prove it!'

That stopped her in her tracks and she stared at him, absolutely mortified. 'You're lying,' she gasped, shaking her head in swift denial.

Quick as a flash, Jonas had pulled his shirt from his

trousers and turned, raising the back to show her the red welts. 'Does that look like a lie?' he demanded, swinging to face her again and tucking his shirt back in. 'You were a tigress, sweetheart. And I know that all I would have to do is take you in my arms and kiss you, and you would get that love-drugged look back in your eyes. It wasn't just sex. We made love, whether you care to call it that or not.'

His words were a pointed reminder of what she had been trying to forget. Uttering a strangled sob, she bit her lip and looked away. 'So help me, Jonas, if you don't shut up, I'll scream!'

'Do it,' he taunted softly. 'I like the way you scream.'

'Damn you!' Pushed to the end of her tether, Aimi swung round, hand raised to strike him. Jonas stopped her easily, catching both wrists and securing them behind her back, an action which brought her body up against his. Chest heaving, she stared up at him.

'That's better. Now you remind me of the woman I know. There's fire in your eyes and heat in your blood. That's the true Aimi Carteret, not the woman with ice in her veins you want to project!' he declared with grim satisfaction.

Aimi paled, feeling sick as she realised she had fallen for his tricks and displayed yet again the side of herself she had tried to keep locked up. Steadying the raft became imperative, and she called on all her experience in order to restore calm. 'Let me go, please,' she commanded in a more reserved tone and, when he complied, she moved away from him. 'Thank you,' she added, still with the same cool control, and Jonas shook his head.

'You should have been an actress, with that command over your emotions,' he remarked ironically, and Aimi laughed.

'I discovered a long time ago that I had no real talent for it,' she corrected him, seeing again her mother's wry acceptance that her young daughter would not follow in her footsteps.

'You were wrong. You have an amazing ability to cover what you're really feeling. It's an act I suspect you've honed to perfection over the years.'

Aimi shot him a frosty look. 'This is not an act. This is who I am.' She had not pretended to change herself; she had actually done it!

He smiled faintly. 'It's who you would like to be. I've seen the other you, and I like her better.'

'Because she slept with you?' Aimi retorted with a curl of her lip. 'Well, she won't be doing it again.' Now she knew the old Aimi could resurface at any time, she would be taking more care.

His smile broadened. 'Don't be so sure of that. I can be very persuasive. I'm not ready to say goodbye yet, Aimi. Last night has only made me want more.'

'That's too bad, because last night made me realise I had had more than enough!'

Jonas laughed and it was whilst Aimi was battling the urge to slap him, because he wasn't taking her seriously, that Paula emerged from the house.

'Goodness me, you two are up early!' she exclaimed with her customary jaunty good humour. 'Lord, what a night! I feel like a wrung out dish rag!'

'It was hot,' Aimi agreed, inordinately grateful for the change of subject. Moving along the wall, she put more distance between herself and Jonas.

'Very hot,' he agreed, and the glint in his eye told Aimi the heatwave he was talking about had nothing to do with mother nature.

'What time were you thinking of driving back, Jonas? We're going early, trying to beat the crowds,' his sister interrogated him as she flopped into a chair at the table.

'After lunch. Aimi probably needs to spend a few more hours in the library, doing Nick's research,' Jonas responded, quirking a questioning eyebrow at her.

Now that Paula was here, Aimi found it easier to keep her composure. 'I do have some work to finish up,' she confirmed.

'You can always come back any time to do more. Mum and Dad would be glad to see you,' Paula said, smiling warmly at Aimi. 'Listen, I've been thinking. We all live in town, so why don't we get together for dinner one evening? Me and James, Nick, Jonas and you. Wouldn't that be great?' She beamed from one to the other, seeking support.

Right then, Aimi couldn't think of anything less great. 'I'm not family, Paula. You shouldn't include me.'

Paula swiftly knocked that idea on the head. 'Nonsense! I know we haven't known each other long, but I like you, Aimi. Please say you'll come,' she urged, her eyes as huge and wistful as a spaniel's.

Aimi knew when she had been backed into a corner, and gave the only answer she could under the circumstances. 'All right, I'll come,' she agreed, knowing she could always beg off at the last minute, and Paula clapped her hands.

'Marvellous! I'll do all the arranging, so you just wait for my call.' Having arranged matters to her satisfaction, Paula immediately jumped up and went in search of her other half to tell him the news.

Jonas pulled a wry face. 'Paula is something of a runaway train at times, but she means well.'

She looked at him for the first time since his sister had joined them. 'I can see that. I like Paula, but I doubt very much if I will be free that night.'

'Running away won't change anything,' Jonas remarked sardonically, and she didn't pretend not to know what he was talking about. 'This isn't over, Aimi.'

'It is if I say so. And there's no need to trouble yourself about giving me a lift. I'll take the train,' Aimi added for good measure.

'You won't,' Jonas corrected at once. 'Unless you're prepared to tell my parents why you don't want to go with me. You're stuck with me, so get used to the idea,' he enlarged with a mocking smile. 'Look, if anyone wants me, tell them I've gone for a run around the lake. Unless you want to join me?' he invited.

Aimi shook her head quickly, still smarting over the fact that she couldn't refuse to go with Jonas without causing a fuss. 'You go. I have work to do.'

'Think of me while I'm gone,' Jonas said with a laugh, then turned and trotted down the steps to the lawn. Moments later he was jogging over the grass.

Aimi watched him go, unable to stop herself admiring his rear view. He was, without doubt, a near perfect specimen of manhood, but he was not for her. It ended here. The sooner she was safely back in the real world, in her own life, the better. Then she would forget all about Jonas Berkeley and those heated hours down by the lake.

* * *

The remainder of the morning Aimi spent with her nose buried in books, but there was no avoiding having lunch with the family. Naturally, Jonas was there, but he kept his distance from her and never gave even the slightest hint that his interest in her was more than casual.

In fact, he paid so little attention to her that she began to hope that he might have had a change of heart—until she caught him looking at her, and the heat in his gaze was enough to burn her up on the spot. Her reaction was beyond her control. She gasped faintly, heat rising into her cheeks, and there was a taunting twist to his lips as he glanced away again. The same thing happened once or twice more during the course of the meal, and she realised that he was being deliberately provocative in a situation where she could do nothing to stop him. All she could do was grit her teeth and bear it.

In the early afternoon, Aimi packed her things ready for the return journey. She was not looking forward to it, but she had faced worse situations. Calling on all her powers of self-control, she carried her bag downstairs to take her leave of the family for the last time. Whilst Jonas stowed her case in the boot of his car, she said goodbye to his parents, who had been so welcoming and made her short stay so enjoyable. Then it was time to be off.

It was a roomy car and Aimi was able to make herself comfortable without brushing shoulders with him. She had brought her notebook with her and, as soon as they were under way, she flipped it open and gave it all her attention. Her intended aim was to keep busy the whole journey, but she glanced up in surprise when, after they had gone less than half a mile, Jonas suddenly steered the car off the road into a lay-by.

'Is something wrong?' she queried automatically, watching him unfasten his seatbelt.

'No. I've merely forgotten something,' he responded blandly, and she frowned.

'Is it important?'

'Absolutely,' he confirmed, moving towards her. 'I've forgotten exactly how those luscious lips of yours taste,' he added, slipping a hand around her neck before she knew what he was about, and pulling her towards him.

Too late, she realised she had been neatly tricked by a master. Though she raised a hand to hold him off, her seatbelt held her trapped as his lips found hers, taking them in a powerful kiss. Aimi tried not to respond, but her wilful senses rebelled. They would not obey her silent command and in an instant she was floundering, her lips parting to allow him to plunder her mouth in a deeply satisfying way that sent *frissons* of pleasure winging through her entire system. She was quivering when he eased away to look down at her and the wicked glint of triumph in his eyes made her bite her lip and look away.

'Ah, now I remember!' he exclaimed softly, running a finger over her lower lip until she had to draw in a ragged breath.

She looked at him then, eyes dark with anger directed as much at herself as to him. 'Damn you!' The words were a croak, and ultimately telling.

'Stop fighting it, Aimi. You know you don't want to.'

'I do! Leave me alone!'

'I couldn't even if I wished to. I want you too damned much,' he replied, brushing her lip with his finger once more, before righting himself, locking on his seatbelt and setting the car in motion again.

Aimi turned her gaze to the window, but she saw very little of the passing countryside. Her thoughts were a mess. Why couldn't she be stronger? Why was it that every time he touched her, she simply melted? Why didn't she have the backbone needed to keep her word to her friend? *I'm so sorry, Lori.*

She sighed wistfully, closing her eyes, unaware that the small sound caused Jonas to look round with a frown. Maybe it was a trick of the light, but he saw a vulnerability in the curve of her cheek that gave him pause. There was more to Aimi Carteret than met the eye, and he realised he wanted to unravel the mystery of her. Without quite knowing why, he knew it was important. Not one to question his instincts, he switched on some soothing background music and sat back to mull over just how he would do it.

Unaware of all this, and bone-weary from all the emotional ups and downs of the past few days, Aimi's thoughts began to drift. Before she even realised it, she was asleep.

When she eventually awoke, the music was still playing softly but, instead of being upright in her seat, she was angled to one side, her head resting on Jonas's shoulder. Aimi knew she ought to move, but couldn't quite bring herself to do so right away. Being close to him like this meant every breath she took brought with it the scent of him and, though she knew it was a mistake, she couldn't help indulging herself for a moment. There was the subtle fragrance of his cologne and, beneath it, another that was the pure male scent she recalled so very vividly from last night.

They took a bend and she was fascinated by the way Jonas's hands moved on the steering-wheel. They were long-fingered, capable, and it didn't take much effort to recall them moving over her body, arousing her to a fever-pitch of need. The sensual thought sent heat racing through her veins, increasing her heartbeat and shortening her breath in a flash.

Finally alarm bells went off in her head, reminding her that she was flirting with danger through her indulgent thoughts. She was supposed to be dampening down her desire for the man, not stoking the flames! It was the spur she needed to move and she sat up abruptly, putting as much space between them as she could.

Jonas took his eyes off the road long enough to glance at her quizzically. 'Bad dream?' he asked as he returned his gaze to the road ahead.

She almost laughed, for the whole situation between them was like a bad dream. 'You shouldn't have let me fall asleep on you. You should have given me a nudge,' she returned, hoping he hadn't guessed what had been going through her mind.

'You looked too comfortable,' Jonas observed with a shrug of the shoulders.

She had been comfortable—very! 'I never would have done it had I known,' she explained, needing to make sure he knew she hadn't changed her mind.

'I know, which is why I left you,' he said lightly, then flashed her a rakish grin. 'I was indulging myself. I liked having you so close to me,' he confessed flirtatiously.

'Well, I hope you made the most of it, it's the last

time it will happen,' she told him firmly, only to hear amusement in his voice when he answered.

'So you keep telling me. Who are you trying to convince—me or yourself?'

Aimi didn't answer, for the truth was she supposed she was trying to convince both of them. Everything was going wrong. Part of her didn't want to want him, whilst the other wanted to revel in it. To experience everything. To know some joy for however long it lasted. She did know that the more she was with him, the harder it was going to be to walk away. Yet that wanton side kept asking why she had to walk away at all. Her conscience told her why she should but, as more time went by, she didn't know if she could. Last night, everything had seemed so simple, yet it was anything but.

She looked at him, wondering just what it was that made him so different from all the other men she had met. Why was it she couldn't seem to say no and mean it when it meant so very much to her to do that very thing?

'Figured it out yet?' Jonas asked, without taking his eyes from the road.

She jumped, having been lost in her thoughts. 'What do you mean?'

'Whether it's safe to go with your instincts or not.'

'That would rather depend on which instinct you're talking about,' she answered with a wry touch of humour. She had two, and they were pulling her in opposite directions. Right now, she didn't know which would win, and that was something she wasn't used to. Her path had been so clear, but now it was like looking through frosted glass.

'You're too intelligent to make the wrong decision,'

he informed her lightly, and she pulled a face he couldn't see.

'I don't think intelligence has anything to do with it,' she replied dryly.

'There's nothing wrong in wanting someone, Aimi. It's the most natural thing in the world. Take a risk. What's the worst that can happen?'

A chill ran through her as his words brought back the memory of Lori on the last fateful day they had been together and the full horror of what she was fighting against. Lori had said pretty much the same thing. Taking risks had been part of their lives then, and she had found out the hard way that the worst that could happen was that somebody died.

The skiing holiday had started out so well, too. They had planned it for months. Lori Ashurst had been her best friend since boarding school. They had spent holidays together every year. Their families were wealthy and had indulged their offspring, so that both girls had learned to ride horses, scuba-dive and ski, amongst other things. They had been taking a gap year, having worked hard to get places at university. Young and oblivious to everything but what they wanted, they had partied hard and done outrageous things, and generally had a good time. Neither had known that the good times were soon to come to an end.

It had been Aimi's idea to ski off-piste, and Lori had agreed it was a great idea. They had known it was risky, but taking risks was the only way to go—then. So they had set off, and it had been great fun. They had whooped with the thrill of it as they'd traversed the slopes…and then it had happened. An overhang had fallen off higher up the mountain, setting in motion a devastating avalanche. Both of them had felt its advance at the same time and had stopped to look behind. They had been right in its path, and fear had galvanised them into action. Signalling Lori to head to the side, Aimi had set off, expecting her friend to follow her, but Lori had decided to go another way. It hadn't been until Aimi had reached the relative safety of the trees that she had dared to stop and look back. She had been horrified to realise Lori wasn't behind her, and then terrified when she'd seen her friend still in danger. She had cried out, but the thunder of the crashing snow had taken her voice away. Then it was too late. She had seen the avalanche swallow Lori up. For one moment she had caught sight of her crashing downhill and then she had gone from sight. Gone for ever.

The avalanche of guilt which had crashed down on Aimi then had been every bit as devastating as the one that had killed her best friend. Another skier had seen what had happened and had called for help, but it had been too late for Lori. The experienced rescue team had found her body after hours of searching, and seeing her taken away on a stretcher had underlined for Aimi that it was she, and not the avalanche, that had really killed her friend. It had been her idea that they should do it, and she had known that Lori always followed where she led. If she hadn't wanted to experience the thrill of off-piste skiing, Lori would still have been alive. It had been her fault. All her fault.

Drowning in a sea of guilt, Aimi had remembered all the times Lori had tried to persuade her not to do things, but she would not be swayed. She had ignored Lori's fears and gone on selfishly to do whatever it was, and now Lori was dead and there had been nowhere else to look for blame than to herself.

Aimi had accompanied her friend's body back to England and during that awful plane journey she had sworn to change. To turn herself into somebody that people could admire. Someone who was a responsible member of society, and who could be relied upon. There would be no more shopping and partying. No more meaningless romances with handsome young men. She would be the antithesis of the old Aimi in every way, for how could she let herself have fun when Lori could not?

Guilt was a terrible thing to live with, and the most awful thing was that Lori's death had been put down to misadventure. At the inquest she had been confronted by Lori's parents. They, too, blamed Aimi, and the things her mother had said in her grief only added to Aimi's burden. She had barely been able to bring herself to face them at the funeral, and they had simply ignored her. Aimi's mother had tried to console her, telling her it had been an accident, but Aimi had known it wasn't true. It had been her fault and she had to atone for it. It was the only way she could live with herself.

To her mother's alarm and horror, she had cut herself off from her old life completely. Had thrown herself into her studies, then into her work, and over time had slowly come to find a kind of peace with herself. She had learned to laugh again, to take some pleasure from the world around her, but she had never been able to forgive herself. Because of that, she could not allow herself to have the things that Lori would never have.

Nothing had happened to alter the course of her

life—until she had met Jonas. He had made her feel things she had thought she never would again. He had invited her to re-enter the world she had sworn to forsake, because it was the one she had inhabited with Lori. The dilemma Aimi faced was that she wanted to go there but, if she did, she would be betraying her friend. How could she do that?

It ought to have been easy to say no, and last night she had been determined to turn her back on it, but with every second that passed, and despite everything she said, she could feel her resolve weakening. Would it hurt, just once, a small voice asked, to drop her guard and allow herself to know some joy again? Would it be so very wrong? Dared she, as Jonas wanted, take the risk?

CHAPTER SIX

IT WAS several hours before Jonas finally drew the car up before the apartment block in which Aimi lived. Holiday traffic had clogged the roads, turning a simple journey into a nightmare. Aimi felt like a limp rag, for the temperature in the city was higher than the country-side. She knew her apartment was going to feel like an oven, and wasn't looking forward to entering it after the better part of four days.

All through the remaining part of the journey she had been plagued by her memories, reliving that awful time over and over again in her mind. For some years she had been haunted by nightmares, but that had slowly faded, so that she rarely had one now. It wouldn't surprise her, though, if she had one tonight.

When Jonas switched off the engine the sudden silence was deafening. She still did not know what she was going to do. She knew that she ought to walk away, and yet no sooner had the thought entered her head than a voice cried out inside her, *No, I'm not ready to give this up! I don't want to be put back in the cold and the dark yet! I want to live! I want to have this!*

Staggered by the strength of the feeling, Aimi felt dazed, but at the same time she knew she had just been given her answer. The resurgent Aimi had won, drowning out the small voice of her conscience. She simply could not walk away from this right now. She had tried, but it was just too strong to fight. As soon as she accepted that, her inner battle came to an end. Like magic, she could sense the restraints which had held her back falling away, and deep inside it felt as if a small bird had woken from a long sleep and was flapping its wings as it prepared to fly free.

Almost light-headed, she turned to Jonas with a cool smile that hid a certain amount of inner turmoil. Even though she knew the path she was going to take, she felt nervous. She knew she was stepping out on a limb that was far from secure. It wouldn't take much to knock it down. 'Thank you for bringing me home. It must have been out of your way,' she said politely.

One eyebrow rose at her tone, and his lips twitched momentarily. 'I gave Nick my word that I would get you home safely,' he returned ironically and, because her anxiety level was heightened, that answer stung.

'Yes, well, you've done that,' she responded, gathering up the notes she had barely looked at for hours and slipping them into her bag. 'I'll be sure to tell him you did a marvellous job.' She couldn't stop herself giving him the pithy reply because it dawned on her that she didn't know how to tell him she had changed her mind.

Fortunately it bounced off Jonas the way everything else she had ever said had done. 'OK, let's get you inside,' he declared, opening the door and climbing out.

Aimi scrambled out, too, whilst Jonas retrieved her

case from the boot. 'There's no need for you to come all the way upstairs,' she told him, feeling edgy and not a little ridiculous as she headed for the door to the building in his wake.

'Trust me, Aimi. Need is the reason there is every need,' he retorted dryly, and her heart took a sudden wild lurch. 'I've just spent a tortuous number of hours locked in a car with you, unable to so much as lay a finger on you for fear of having an accident!'

Her senses reacted wildly as she heard those words, and her pulse took up a faster rhythm as she looked at him. 'Did you want to touch me?' The provocative question slipped out before she even knew she was going to say it. Once said, though, she knew it was the perfect solution to her dilemma, so she held her breath for his answer.

When he looked round, the fire in his eyes was enough to singe her. 'What do you think?'

Jonas studied her carefully for a moment, as if he had at last seen the subtle change that had taken place in her. He took a deep breath and laughed wryly. 'It's a wonder I'm not insane!' He held the door open for her to precede him inside the building.

The lift was on the ground floor, so they stepped in and Jonas pressed the button for her floor. Leaning against the back wall, Aimi looked at him, wondering at the sea change this man had wrought in her in so short a space of time. Such was the power of him that for the moment her demons were totally vanquished.

Jonas couldn't have made it any clearer that he wanted to kiss her, and she wished the lift would go faster. Desire was a flickering ember deep inside her, and it was growing stronger with every passing second.

His head turned, blue eyes blazing hot. 'If you keep looking at me like that, we'll never make it to your apartment,' he growled seductively, and she shivered in anticipation.

'I don't think we should rush into this. Maybe you should see me to the door, and then go,' she said, suddenly feeling slightly nervous.

His laugh was taut with emotion. 'Don't freeze up on me, Aimi.'

Her eyes were huge as she looked at him. 'You want me that much?'

'I've never wanted a woman more. Does that surprise you? Why? You're a beautiful, intelligent, extremely sensual woman.'

It was instinctive for Aimi to shake her head. 'I'm not,' she denied, and he laughed.

'Don't argue with me or I might just have to come over there and prove it to you. Which would be highly dangerous; I only have so much control left.'

Her nerves leapt as their gazes clashed and became locked in a heated exchange that pulsed in the air between them. By the time the lift door opened, Aimi was finding it hard to breathe and her legs barely had the power to carry her. She didn't care what was wrong or right any more—all she knew was she wasn't going to think about it now, she would think about it tomorrow. She fumbled for her key in her bag as they approached her front door and Jonas took it from her, unlocking the door with impatient movements. Then they were inside with the door shut, and he turned to her, almost tossing her case aside.

Aimi dropped her bag to the floor just as Jonas took

her into his arms and kissed her with a searing depth of passion. She was swept up in it, returning each kiss only to discover that their mutual hunger increased, becoming ever more powerful. Her hands went around his neck, needing to explore the strong male shape of him, but only came in contact with his shirt. It had to go, and her hands fumbled to push it from his shoulders. Realising what she was doing, Jonas took his arms from around her and helped her to undo the buttons and push the shirt down his arms, then he urged her back against the wall, holding her there with the weight of his body as he pulled her blouse from her skirt and slipped his hands under it, exploring the silken skin beneath.

Aimi lost her breath and dragged her mouth from his, whereupon Jonas swiftly dealt with the buttons of her blouse and tugged it off her arms, tossing it aside as he pressed his lips to the valley between her breasts. She could feel her body responding, her nipples tightening into aching points that yearned to be touched by the lips mere inches away. At the same time she longed to explore the firm male body pressed so intimately close to hers. Her fumbling fingers tugged his shirt free of his trousers, and then she could experience the heady pleasure of running her palms over the undulating planes of his back.

Nothing could describe the delight she felt when Jonas arched into her touch, and she caught the low moan of pleasure he gave. Then it was her turn to gasp as his hands glided up her spine, released the catch of her bra and pushed it upwards, releasing the swollen globes to the mercy of his seeking lips. When he took her engorged flesh into his mouth, she thought she would die, then his tongue flickered over one tight nub and she cried out with the intense pleasure of it.

Of course, that was not enough for either of them, and in short order shoes, skirt and bra were all tossed aside in passionate abandon. In the next instant Jonas had lifted her up and settled her on his hips, pressing her back against the wall as his lips and tongue once more plundered her breasts. Aimi folded her legs around him, hands tangling in the dark silk of his hair, neck arching back as she savoured the pleasure he was administering.

When he raised his head and looked up at her, she could see the need in his eyes despite the gloom of the unlit hallway. 'Where's your bedroom?' he asked in a voice made gravelly by passion.

'The first door,' she could only gasp back as her heart thundered inside her.

Pushing them away from the wall, Jonas carried her down the hall and into her bedroom. In three strides he was at the foot of the bed, knelt on it and lowered them both on to the covers. Swiftly, the remainder of their clothes were discarded by impatient fingers and finally they were free to explore each other without any barriers.

Jonas came up on one elbow and explored the velvety slopes of her body with eyes and hands, and it was highly erotic to Aimi to watch him concentrate on learning the shape and feel of her. His touch was so gentle it was almost reverent, and aroused her to a pitch of need she had never experienced before. Because of it, she was not afraid to let him see what he was making her feel, arching her body into his touch, uttering helpless little sighs and moans as he stoked the flames of her desire with sensual mastery. When, eventually, his lips followed the path laid down by his hand, seeking out the hidden core of her femininity and laving it with exquisite strokes of his tongue, she closed her eyes and let herself drown in the sea of pleasure.

Yet she was not inclined to take a passive role for long. She had to give as well as receive, and when his ministrations threatened to plunge her over the edge of reason, she took control by trailing her nails down the sensitive skin of his spine, making him catch his breath and straighten up. With her body still pulsing from the pitch of desire he had aroused, she set about working her own magic on him. To her infinite delight, he was as sensitive to her touch as she had been to his. His flat male nipples responded as hers had to the brush of her tongue and the nip of her teeth, and when she heard him gasp in pleasure it brought a cat-like smile to her lips.

She wanted him to feel what she had, and used all her ingenuity to arouse him. His body was perfect—firm to her touch yet as smooth as hot silk. She explored every inch of him and he abandoned himself to whatever she cared to do. Slowly, and with infinite care, she trailed her hands and lips down his body, over his taut flat stomach until her fingers found and closed around his hard male shaft. Jonas's whole body jerked as his breath hissed in sharply between his teeth. He muttered something that sounded like a prayer and Aimi glanced up, fascinated to see the man she thought of as unflappable gritting his teeth in a superhuman effort to retain control.

She took pity on him, taking pleasure instead in exploring her way back up his body until she could look down into his eyes. Jonas brought his hands up and framed her face, his thumbs brushing across her lips.

'You have the ability to drive a man mad,' he murmured scratchily.

'That's only fair, because you're driving me insane, too,' she whispered back.

At that he rolled them over until he was resting over her, his hips cradled on hers. 'I have a cure, but if I use it there will be no going back. If you want me to stop, this is your last chance.'

Aimi had no intention of asking him to stop, so she smiled a sultry smile and moved against him. 'You're talking too much. Don't you know actions speak louder than words?'

Jonas caught his breath as her movements sent a wave of heat rushing through his veins. 'OK, OK, I get the message,' he responded with a growl, and stopped talking to start some interesting moves of his own.

From that point on the only sounds were their sighs and moans of pleasure. It was hard to know where one body ended and the other began as tanned limbs tangled in a timelessly sensual dance that stoked the already incandescent fires of need. When Jonas finally entered her, Aimi experienced a moment of intense joy that had nothing to do with passion. Nothing in her life had ever been so right as this moment of joining with him. She felt complete in a way she had never known before and knew that without him she would never again feel whole.

The moment was lost when he began to move, his thrusts controlled to give the maximum amount of pleasure to them both. Yet that very pleasure fed on itself, creating a need for more that was a tight coil inside her. Every move she made to meet and deepen his thrusts increased the tension, and when she heard

Jonas groan achingly she knew he had lost the power to control his actions. There was only their mutual driving towards a goal that seemed just beyond their reach. Then Jonas gave one final desperate thrust which pushed them both over the edge in a white-hot climax that had them both crying out.

Aimi held on as they floated through a kaleidoscopic world of the most intense pleasure. It seemed an age before they came back down to earth, and the reality of the two of them wrapped around each other on her bed. With a sigh, Jonas moved on to his back, taking her with him so that she was tucked into his side, her head resting over his heart.

'What did I tell you? Extremely sensual,' he murmured into her hair, and Aimi gave a barely audible sigh.

Tonight with Jonas had felt like discovering herself all over again. Yet it wasn't the same as before, because Jonas had made it different. It was totally new, totally incredible. She wanted to savour it, because she knew it couldn't last. Eventually Jonas would start to drift away, as he always had, and she would have to let him go. But not yet. Not yet.

Aimi was roused before dawn next morning by the soft brush of lips on hers. Blinking to focus her eyes, she smiled groggily when she saw it was Jonas leaning over her.

'Good morning,' she greeted gruffly, still full of sleep, running her eyes over the face and body of the man she had spent last night making incredible love with. A frown darkened her brow as she noted the clothes he was wearing. 'You're dressed.' Her heart sank, though she didn't know why.

Jonas smiled regretfully. 'I know. It's early still, but I have to get back to my place to get ready for work. I have several important meetings today. I made you some tea.' He picked up the mug he had set on her bedside table.

Aimi wriggled into a sitting position and took the mug from him. 'Why didn't you just go? You could have left me a note,' she pointed out, taking a sip of the hot liquid.

'Because that way I wouldn't be able to kiss you goodbye, now would I?' he explained simply, and Aimi stared at him solemnly, whilst inside a long-buried imp of mischief rose to the surface.

'You don't have to. I know what to expect,' she declared with a sigh of resignation, then fought down a smile as Jonas immediately frowned back at her.

'Just what is it exactly that you expect, Aimi?'

She shrugged diffidently, whilst acknowledging that he was remarkably easy to tease. 'That you'll pretty much come and go as you please, for as long as it suits you. When you find someone else, you'll be gone. Don't worry, I'm not going to make a fuss,' she assured him resignedly, taking another sip of tea. To her amusement, he looked quite grim.

'Let me get this straight. You think I'll turn up for a quick roll in the hay, then be off about my business again? A wham-bam-thank-you-ma'am kind of thing?'

His tone was so steely, she knew he was really taking her seriously. Which was why she decided to string him along for just a little longer. 'What else?'

After looking at her long and hard for several minutes, making her think for a moment that he had seen through her ruse, Jonas took the mug from her and set it down on the bedside table again. 'And just where did you get that idea?'

Aimi bit down hard on her lip, lest she start to giggle. 'That's how it is with men like you, isn't it?' she managed to challenge in a small voice, and his reaction was anything but small.

He snorted in disgust. 'No, that isn't how it is with me. You have a lot to learn about me, Aimi Carteret, and we'll start with this. I do not want every woman I meet. Those I am attracted to, it is for more than sex. I want to know her. I want to enjoy her company. I like giving her presents and making her happy. Sex is just a part of it, not the whole.'

She blinked at him, taken by surprise. 'Oh!'

Now he smiled again, that roguish twist of the lips that made her feel warm inside. 'Is that all you can say? You were eloquent enough a moment ago?' he taunted softly, and she realised she had, indeed, been found out.

'You knew,' she accused, and he laughed.

'Not right away, but then I remembered just what a good actress you are.'

'You're not such a bad actor yourself,' she shot back, for he had fooled her.

'It wouldn't do my business any good if everyone could read what I was thinking,' he informed her dryly. 'I had no idea you could be a tease. Is it any wonder I find you endlessly fascinating? I've never met anyone like you, and that intrigues me.'

Aimi made herself comfortable against the pillows and smiled winsomely. 'Really? Tell me more.'

'What would you like to hear? That I know there's a warm, lovely woman under the cool exterior you adopt, and I want to see more of her?' he charged in a soft voice that shivered over her nerve-endings like a warm summer breeze.

Her throat closed over, making her voice husky when she responded. 'You've seen pretty much all of me already.'

Jonas's smile faded whilst the heat in his eyes grew. 'I have, and it takes my breath away. I'm glad you changed your mind and decided to take a chance on me.'

A tiny voice tried to make itself heard, but she forced it back down. 'So am I.'

He studied her for a moment in silence, then uttered a heartfelt sigh. 'Damn, but you're beautiful. Do you take after your mother? Is she beautiful, too?'

Aimi smiled fondly as a picture of her mother formed in her mind. 'I think she's the most beautiful woman in the world. I have her eyes.'

'Just her eyes?'

'Uh-huh. And I've heard people say I have my father's chin,' she added, touching the gentle cleft there.

'Heard?' Jonas queried, one eyebrow raised.

She shrugged fatalistically. 'He died when I was small. I never knew him.'

'That's a shame. I'm sure he would have loved you.'

Surprise shot through her at such a statement coming from him. 'How can you know that?'

Jonas grinned and tapped the tip of her nose with a finger. 'Because fathers always dote on their daughters. It's a prerequisite for the job.'

All of a sudden Aimi could feel tears burning the back of her eyes at the notion that the man she had never met would have loved her just because she existed. 'I'd like to think that's true,' she admitted huskily, and Jonas frowned as he noted the way her eyes glittered like diamonds.

'I didn't mean to make you cry,' he apologised gruffly, and Aimi gave him a watery smile.

'They're happy tears. I'm feeling a bit emotional today. Thank you for saying what you did.'

'You're welcome,' he replied, and bent forward to press a soft kiss to her lips. 'Now I really must go.'

With his departure imminent, Aimi found herself wanting to throw her arms around him and keep him there. She didn't, though she was tempted. Neither did she ask the other burning question: when will I see you again? 'Don't work too hard,' she advised instead.

'I'll try not to,' he promised, leaning across to kiss her deeply, and when he broke away she could see the banked fires in his eyes. 'That will have to see me through the day, unless you're free for lunch?'

Aimi shook her head regretfully. 'I won't have time. I'm working on a draft of a lecture your brother is due to give.'

Jonas was amused. 'So I have to make way for my brother, do I? Ah, well, at least I won't have to worry about who might be flirting with you. Nick never thinks of anything but work,' he said brightly.

With that he rose, pressed another swift kiss to her lips and left the bedroom. Moments later, she heard the front door open then close behind him. Immediately, Aimi sank back against the pillows and hugged herself. She looked back over the last few days and the amazing changes that had happened. It was almost too much to take in, yet she wouldn't change a thing. She had made her bed and was content to lie in it.

With a sigh she slipped down beneath the single sheet, intent on getting a few more hours sleep. She wasn't going to worry about the future or what might happen. Better to live in the now and enjoy these moments whilst she could.

Aimi was late that morning, for the first time since she had started to work for Nick. She had quite forgotten to set her alarm and consequently had overslept. As she let herself into his house, she felt oddly unsettled for having had to rush.

'Sorry I'm late,' she apologised breathlessly when she entered the study to find Nick already writing at his desk. He looked up at her, did a double take, then his jaw dropped. Aimi blinked back at him in surprise. 'What is it? What's wrong?'

Gathering himself, Nick waved a hand in her general direction. 'Your hair,' he said simply, and she raised a hand to it, shocked to find it hanging down around her face.

'Oh, my goodness! I forgot!' she exclaimed, feeling oddly vulnerable. Sitting down at her desk, she pulled a container of pins from a drawer and quickly pinned her hair up in its pleat with fingers that actually shook. How on earth could she have forgotten? It was one of the first things she did every day—putting on her armour against the world. Except this morning she had been thinking about Jonas, and fixing her hair had quite slipped her mind. 'There!' she exclaimed with a final pat to make sure all was secure.

'How do you do that without looking?' he asked in some awe, and Aimi laughed.

'Practice. How did the operation go?' Sliding her

chair forward, she picked up the large desk diary that ordered his daily workload.

'It was touch and go for a while, but I think we're over the hump now. I had to wait in case we needed to go back into surgery, but that didn't happen.'

Aimi looked up with a relieved smile. 'Oh, that is good news. At least we won't have to bump anything today.' Very quickly she ran over his timetable with him. There were one or two things to swap around, but the rest was fine.

Nick sat back in his seat and watched her as she turned on her computer and quickly typed in the new information. 'So tell me, did Jonas behave himself when he brought you home yesterday?'

The unexpected question made her nerves leap out of her skin, and she felt warmth enter her cheeks. 'Of course he did,' she confirmed swiftly. 'What made you ask?'

'Because you're not acting like you this morning,' he observed, and she very nearly groaned, for she knew that already.

'It's this heat,' she explained without making eye contact, praying he would drop the subject. 'It's making us all out of sorts. It's got to break soon.'

'Amen to that,' Nick responded, diverted, and the subject was soon forgotten.

They worked together in harmony for the next hour, then Nick left to go upstairs and get ready for his first appointment at the hospital. No sooner had he gone through the door than the telephone on her desk rang demandingly.

Caught in the middle of rephrasing a particularly knotty paragraph, she picked up the receiver with a sigh. 'Berkeley residence, Aimi Carteret speaking,' she responded in her usual fashion, then felt the hairs on the back of her neck rise just as the caller spoke.

'Hello, Aimi Carteret.'

A thrill travelled the length and breadth of her body as she recognised the voice, even though she had known who it would be in that split-second of silence. Her heart seemed to skip a million beats and her senses leapt to attention.

'Jonas?' Her voice sounded low and breathless to her own ears, as if she hadn't used it in an age.

'Were you expecting someone else?' Jonas asked, his tone low and mellifluous, sending a shiver down her spine.

Stunned all over again by her reaction to him, she leaned back in her chair and spun it so she was facing the window and the garden beyond. 'I wasn't expecting you to call. Is something wrong?'

'Nothing's wrong—unless you count my state of mind. I'm actually in the middle of an important business meeting,' he revealed wryly.

That made her frown. 'Oh, I don't think so. I don't think anything would stop you doing business.'

He laughed. 'Up until five minutes ago I would have agreed with you.'

Aimi felt a smile start to curve her lips. 'So what happened five minutes ago?'

'I suddenly experienced an urgent desire to hear the sound of your voice.' The confession stole her breath away, and her heart seemed to expand in her chest.

'What?' Aimi could barely get the word out.

This time when he laughed, there was the strangest edge to it. 'I know. Who would have thought it, but I love the way you talk to me in that sharp way when you're irritated, and in that soft breathless tone you have when we make love.'

If she hadn't been sitting down, her legs would never have held her up. 'You're crazy!' It had been a long time since she had had this kind of telephone conversation with a man, and she had forgotten how much fun it could be.

Jonas chuckled. 'The men in the other room probably think so. I don't usually walk out in the middle of a discussion.'

'But you did, just to talk to me?' Aimi felt a deep sense of warmth invade her system, filling her from top to toe. It even felt as if her heart swelled a little. Another heavy sigh came down the line.

'The need to hear your voice was stronger than my desire to buy the damn business we were discussing. I thought it would help to ring you, but I think it's backfired.'

Aimi closed her eyes and bit her lip. 'Backfired?'

'Now I want to see you, and touch you, too,' he admitted with a sexy growl that swept its way through her body like wildfire, setting her nerves tingling and her blood pulsing thickly through her veins.

Whatever her voice was doing to him, his was a sensual caress to her ears. 'Stop! Don't do this!' she commanded, but there was no real conviction in her voice.

'What am I doing, Aimi?' The urgency in his voice tightened the muscles in her stomach. 'Is it anything like what you are doing to me? Is your pulse racing and the blood zinging through your veins?'

'Jonas, I have work to do! How am I supposed to concentrate?'

'Tell Nick you're not well, and take the day off. I'll do the same.'

Her eyebrows rose. 'Can I be hearing correctly? You're suggesting missing out on a business deal just to see me? It could cost you millions!'

'Aimi, darling, you would be worth every penny!'

'I bet you say that to all your women!' she taunted, whilst experiencing two different emotions. She liked to think what he said was true and hated the sound of all these nameless, faceless women.

A short silence followed before he answered. 'On the contrary, you're the first.'

Aimi didn't quite know what to say, or how to feel. 'If that's true, then I'm flattered,' she responded simply. 'Unfortunately, I can't take your advice because I have work to do, and you need to help this company that is in trouble. You do that, and I'll make you dinner tonight.'

'And if I can't save it?' he questioned wryly.

'Then I'm sure you will have done your best.'

'So I still get dinner?'

'Of course.'

'You have a deal. Now I'd better go before they think I've changed my mind. I'll be looking forward to tonight.'

'Goodbye, Jonas,' she said with a sigh, and heard the phone go down at his end.

She was smiling as she spun her chair round and returned the receiver to its rest. It had been such a long time since she'd enjoyed a flirtatious conversation over the phone. But then, she hadn't wanted to flirt with anyone until Jonas had come into her life. He had changed so many things in the last few days, and they were still changing. Where it would all end? She had no idea, and wasn't about to think about it.

Humming softly to herself, Aimi turned to her computer and did her best to concentrate on her work, despite the fact that Jonas's wicked smile constantly invaded her thoughts for a long, long while.

CHAPTER SEVEN

BY THE time Aimi arrived home that evening, she was excited yet nervous. It was so long since she had cooked for anyone but herself, and she had no idea what Jonas liked. Deciding it was still too hot to eat anything heavy, she planned to make a vegetable risotto, to be served with a fine wine and fresh bread.

It wasn't a difficult meal to make, which was just as well given her state of nervous anticipation. She prepared all the ingredients in advance, which gave her ample time to take a leisurely bath and wash her hair. Then, after drying her hair and slipping into burgundy silk underwear, she went to examine her wardrobe.

It was, to put it mildly, less than inspiring. She didn't even possess a posh frock.

Her work clothes were all functional, designed to tell everyone she was serious about what she did, and her casual clothes were too casual for dinner. She ought to have gone shopping, but it was too late now. In the end she chose a pair of lightweight grey trousers and topped them with a sleeveless cream silk blouse.

Looking at herself in the mirror, for the first time in

a long time, she regretted that she had nothing more feminine to wear. Oh, her lingerie was silky and sensual, but nobody was ever meant to see it. However, there was nothing she could do now, so she sighed and put her hair up again. She could have left it loose, but it was hard to let go of all her old habits at once. One day, perhaps, but not now.

Returning to the living room, Aimi carefully set the table with her best linen and china. She liked fine things, and the crystal glasses she took from the cabinet were truly elegant pieces of craftsmanship. When she was satisfied with how it looked, she went back to the kitchen, put on an apron to protect her clothes and started preparing the cheesecake she planned to have for dessert.

When the front doorbell rang some fifteen minutes later she glanced at her watch, surprised to see it was only a quarter past seven. Too early for Jonas, she imagined it was her neighbour, Ruth, who was always running out of milk or sugar. Wiping her hands on a tea towel, she went to answer the summons and was startled to discover it was Jonas after all.

'You're early!' she exclaimed stupidly, and he pulled a wry face.

'I know. I waited as long as I could, but the need to see you got the better of me, so here I am,' he confessed with a boyish grin.

Aimi got that bubbly feeling inside again, and couldn't help but smile back. 'So you are. You'd better come in.' She stepped back as he entered, shutting the door behind him, and was about to turn when he took her by the shoulders and drew her towards him.

Pulling her into his arms, he lowered his mouth to hers

and kissed her with long slow, deliberation. Aimi melted against him with a sigh of pleasure, knowing she had starved for this all day. When Jonas raised his head again, she looked up at him mistily and he smiled down at her.

'When you look at me like that, all I want to do is pick you up and carry you off,' he confessed huskily.

'But you can't. I'm cooking dinner,' she pointed out just a little breathlessly, and he uttered a resigned sigh.

'I guess I'll have to wait, then. But there is one thing…' Before she could stop him, Jonas neatly whipped the pins from her hair, letting it fall freely about her shoulders. 'There, that's better. Now you look like the woman who fell asleep in my arms last night.'

Aimi's smile slipped a little. She hadn't been prepared for him to do that, and her nerves jolted. Half shorn of her image, she felt more than a little uncomfortable. Yet the way he was looking at her stilled her automatic move to restore order. 'It will get in the way,' she protested half-heartedly as he ran a smoothing hand over the silky blonde mass.

'But you'll leave it anyway?'

'Yes,' she agreed, knowing that to do otherwise would make him wonder what all the fuss was about. He probably thought it was just something she did for work, but it was more than that. She might have taken a giant step in order to have him, but there were still many things she could not talk about.

He grinned roguishly. 'Then lead me to the kitchen and I'll help you with dinner.'

'Can you cook?' she asked over her shoulder, leading the way.

'We'll soon find out.'

As it turned out, Jonas was quite comfortable in the kitchen and clearly cooked for himself when the mood took him. Taking off his jacket, he hung it over the back of a chair and rolled up his sleeves. Amused, Aimi gave him some tasks to do, and they chatted whilst she whipped up the cheesecake and set it in the dish.

The domestic atmosphere was enlightening to Aimi and the same companionable mood spread into the living room when they carried their meal through and sat down to eat it in the slight breeze from the window beside them. Aimi couldn't remember ever being so relaxed and, as the evening wore on, her guard lowered until it was virtually non-existent. She felt almost… euphoric, as if she had been released from an immense burden. She knew she was happy, and it was a good feeling.

Jonas insisted on making the coffee and when he returned with it she looked up, smiling, tossing her hair back as she did so. He went still in the act of setting her cup down, and her smile turned to a frown as she watched him.

'Do that again,' he directed, which only puzzled her more.

'Do what again?'

'Toss your hair back like you just did,' he enlarged, and her frown deepened.

'Why?'

'Because it reminded me of someone, and I can't place her,' he mused. He studied her frozen features for a moment or two, then shook his head. 'No. It's not coming. Has anyone told you before that you look like someone else?'

Aimi's heart sank and she got a sick feeling in her stomach. If she told him she looked like her mother, then there was every chance he might recall the stories that had been spread across the world's newspapers about the famous actress's daughter. She did not want that. Did not want him probing her past. Did not want him to know what kind of person she had been. She had to steer him away from the dangerous rocks.

'No,' she denied as evenly as she could. 'Nobody has. I don't think I'm the kind of woman who looks like anybody else,' she added with an uneasy laugh.

Unaware of the turmoil he had unleashed inside her, Jonas smiled as he finally sat down. 'They say we all have a double somewhere in the world.'

'I think one of me is quite enough,' she responded with an atavistic shiver.

'Have you always worn you hair up?' Jonas asked next, and Aimi groaned as he refused to let the subject drop.

'When I was younger, I used to leave it down,' she admitted, trying to be casual when memories were surfacing that made her uncomfortable. Yet she realised that if she made her answers too secretive, he would start to wonder why. She had to tell the truth, so far as it went. 'I...began to pin it up when I went to university.'

'I would have thought that was the time you would start letting your hair down!' Jonas teased gently and, though Aimi smiled, those same memories made her feel cold inside. She had already let her hair down far too much by then.

Sighing, she shrugged. 'You'd think so, but I was serious about my studies. I...needed to work hard. The last thing I wanted was distractions.' Only by burying herself in work had she been able to survive.

Jonas rested his chin on his hand and watched the play of emotions cross her face. 'You mean male distractions. I can see why you would get a lot of interest.'

Aimi winced, picking up her spoon to idly stir her cup of coffee. 'Yes, well, I wasn't interested. I just wanted to work.' To forget—only that had never been possible.

'So you started putting your hair up,' he mused, only to frown faintly. 'From my point of view, that wouldn't work. You had your hair up when I met you, and I wasn't deterred,' he reminded her with a grin, and she had to smile.

'I wore glasses, too.'

His brows rose. 'Do you need them?'

Aimi shook her head. 'No, but it's true what they say. Men don't make passes at women in glasses.' They had stayed away, and she had been free to go about her studies.

'You could have had fun, too,' Jonas remarked softly, and she looked at him sharply.

'I told you—I was there to work. Besides, I had made someone a promise, and I wasn't about to forget it,' she added solemnly. Then, because she could feel the weight of that promise still, she made an effort to raise her spirits. 'Blondes have a bad time of it, you know. If we're not thought of as dumb…'

'Then it's as some kind of sex object,' Jonas filled in the blank for her. 'I can understand your position. Beautiful women sometimes have a hard time being taken seriously.'

There was no way Aimi could agree with his placing her in that category. 'I'm not beautiful.' Once, with the vanity of youth, she might have thought so, but that Aimi was long gone.

Jonas, however, was not about to be gainsaid. 'You are to me, even with your hair tied back.'

Aimi smiled, as she was supposed to do, yet shook her head. 'Maybe I don't want to be seen as beautiful.'

He laughed softly. 'Beauty is in the eye of the beholder. I took one look at you, and you reached parts of me I had forgotten about. You could wear a sack and my response would be the same.'

She sighed as his words touched her heart. He was a good man, in a world where good men were hard to find. No matter what, she could never regret knowing him. 'You don't have to say things like that. I'm content to be here,' she told him simply. A choice, once made, had to be lived with, whatever the eventual outcome. Yet she knew she dared not look at this moment too closely, for fear of what she might see.

Jonas reached across the table and took her hand. 'I'm just telling you the truth, Aimi. There's no ulterior motive.' Turning her hand over, he rubbed his thumb over her palm. 'Except, perhaps, to reassure you that you can trust me.'

Her brow furrowed. 'Trust you? I do trust you.' Why else would she be here?

Sighing, he enfolded her hand in both of his and looked at her steadily. 'I'm trying to say you can trust me with your demons, too.'

Her nerves crashed against each other in sudden alarm. 'My demons?' The question stuttered out of her suddenly dry mouth. Oh, Lord, what was he implying? What did he know? 'W-why do you say that?'

'Because you were muttering and crying in your sleep last night,' he informed her, and her throat closed over.

'Th-that's ridiculous!' she denied faintly, yet knowing it was possible. She had woken up crying many times in the past. She had been afraid the bad dreams might resume. Now it seemed her worst fears had been realised.

Jonas raised his eyebrows questioningly, resisting her attempts to pull her hand free. 'Is it? It didn't seem ridiculous when I soothed you until you quietened and fell back asleep.'

Aimi stared at him, not knowing he had done that for her. 'I'm sorry if I disturbed you,' she apologised diffidently, and Jonas sat forward.

'You didn't disturb me. I was concerned for you. You sounded desperately unhappy.' The sound of her quiet sobbing had chilled his heart. 'I know how painful inner demons can be.'

The confession took her by surprise. 'You?'

'Me,' he concurred with a wry smile. 'I once gave a man my word that I would save the factory that was his pride and joy. I thought I could do it, but unfortunately things turned bad and I couldn't keep my word. That gave me bad dreams for a very long time, but eventually I beat the demons by doing better for others.'

She stared into his eyes for a moment, then dropped her gaze to their joined hands, for his words had struck a chord with her. 'Some demons are harder to fight than others. Some acts can never be forgiven,' she declared quietly. Caught on the raw, she was speaking from the heart.

'True. But some things are not for us to forgive. That is for a higher authority. Do you want to talk about it?'

he asked softly, and she looked up quickly, only then realising she had said far too much.

'There's nothing to talk about,' she denied with a
swift shake of her head, managing to free her hand at last.

'Aimi…' Jonas began, only to stop when she shot
him a fierce look.

'Don't!' she commanded with authority. 'I get bad
dreams from time to time. They're nothing for you to
worry about. Please leave it alone.' He looked as if he
wanted to argue but, after a moment's thought, shrugged
fatalistically.

'Very well,' he agreed calmly. 'Just remember, if
there is anything you want to talk about, I'll be here.'

Aimi took a steadying breath, very much aware that
she had almost lost her vaunted calm. Though she hadn't
really revealed anything, Jonas would have to be quite
dense not to realise she had secrets. She would have to
be more careful in future.

'Thank you for the offer, but I doubt that I shall need
it.'

'It stands, anyway,' Jonas countered, then adroitly
changed the subject.

The conversation became more general after that,
and Aimi was slowly able to relax again whilst she
listened to him talking about his meeting with wicked
humour. However, even that couldn't stop her yawning
as tiredness slowly settled over her.

'Sorry,' she apologised the third time, and Jonas
laughed ruefully.

'I'd better be off, so you can get to bed,' he declared
as he stood up.

Aimi stared at him in surprise as she got up, too.

'You're leaving?' she queried, completely astounded. She had assumed he would want to stay the night.

Jonas read the look on her face with ease. 'I know what you were thinking, but I came to be with you and share a meal. It was never my intention to leap into bed with you. Don't get me wrong. There's no place else I would rather be, but I wanted to prove to you that this relationship is not just about sex.'

Aimi couldn't stop her heart doing a crazy flip-flop in her chest. 'What is it about?'

Jonas pulled her unresisting form into his arms and kissed her deeply. When he raised his head, she could see the banked fire in his eyes. 'This is about you and me getting to know each other. I already know what makes your body respond to mine and mine to yours. Now I want to know what makes you tick.'

'Why?'

'The why comes later,' he said, releasing her. 'Now, see me to the door,' he urged, holding out his hand, which she took and they walked to the door, where he held her by the shoulders and stared down at her broodingly. 'Thanks for the dinner. It was delicious.'

Bemused, Aimi smiled up at him. 'Are you sure I can't tempt you to stay?'

Jonas closed his eyes with a groan. 'Darling, you could tempt me to do anything, but I promised myself I would do this. Goodnight, Aimi. I'll call you tomorrow.'

Aimi watched him walk past the lift to the door to the stairs. He paused briefly to glance back and raise a hand, then he vanished through the door and was gone. Shutting her front door, she leant back against it, pondering the unexpected turn of events.

She had had a terrible shock when Jonas had told her about the way she had cried in her sleep. It had been a tense time, and she was amazed that he had let the subject go. She knew he only wanted to help, but she could not talk about what had happened in the past because she wasn't going to think about it. Couldn't allow herself to, if she wanted to cling on to the happiness she had.

Thinking of Jonas reminded her that this was not how she had envisioned the evening turning out, but at the same time she was undeniably pleased. She wasn't exactly sure why it should be important, she just knew it was. It was as if he understood her better than she understood herself.

She shivered and pushed herself upright with a brisk shake of her head. Determinedly she walked back into the living room and set about clearing the table. She did possess a dishwasher, but found there was something quite satisfying in cleaning up a meal she had prepared and cooked, so the crocks went into the bowl and she hummed to herself as she carefully washed and wiped.

It was getting late by the time she had finished, and she took herself off to her lonely bed. Changing into her nightdress, she lay down and pulled the spare pillow into her arms, hugging it tight. Closing her eyes, she hoped the nightmares would stay away and her dreams would all be of Jonas.

Next morning, Aimi made sure her hair was securely pinned before she left for work. Nick was operating today and would already be at the hospital, so Aimi let herself into his house and ensconced herself at her desk, determined to get through a small mountain of paperwork.

However, no sooner had she started than her thoughts drifted to Jonas. Last night he had been different, and she really didn't know what to make of it. Pushing her chair back, she rose to her feet and crossed to the window, staring out at the immaculately well-kept garden.

He was a mystery—far from being the Lothario she had once thought him. He had managed to soothe her night fears without her even knowing he was doing it. Why had he done that? And, having done it, why had he stuck around? A lot of men would not have been interested in…what did Jonas call them…her demons. Yet he had wanted to help if he could. It was as strange as his comment that he wanted to get to know her better. Why would he want to do that, and why did it make her feel warm inside to know that he felt that way?

Sighing, Aimi abandoned her introspection and went back to her desk, knowing she had more questions than answers and not enough time to think them through. She had barely settled in her seat, though, when the front doorbell rang. She listened, heard Nick's housekeeper go to answer it, and was studying the pages she was going to transcribe when there was a quick knock on the door and the housekeeper walked in.

'This just came for you, Aimi,' she declared with a bright smile, holding out a long narrow box to Aimi, who took it with a look of surprise.

'For me?'

The other woman laughed. 'It has your name on it,' she insisted and went out again, closing the door softly behind her.

Aimi had a good idea what was in the box, so she was smiling when she lifted the lid. Lying in a bed of pure white tissue paper sat a single deep pink rosebud. It was perfect, and all of a sudden she felt moisture enter her eyes. Reaching inside, she lifted the rose and breathed in deeply, her senses instantly flooded with a heady, creamy scent. Only then did she notice the card which was tucked in at one side.

Her heart missed a beat when she read the simple message, written in a strong male hand: *I missed being with you, Jonas.*

Aimi's throat closed over, for she had missed him, too. The rose made her feel better, though, and she went off to the kitchen in search of a vase to put it in. Then she set it on her desk where the warm breeze wafted the scent over to her. For some reason she found it much easier to settle down to work after that, and was concentrating hard some fifteen minutes later when the telephone rang.

'Did you miss me?' Jonas asked in a lazy tone when she took the call.

As ever, the sound of his voice set her nerves tingling expectantly. 'Yes,' she replied honestly. 'Thank you for the rose. It's beautiful.'

'The florist said it was called Amy, so I knew it was the one for you.'

She smiled to herself at his words. 'The scent is heavenly.'

'As are you,' Jonas returned smoothly.

Aimi shook her head, even though he couldn't see her. 'You don't have to shower me with compliments, you know.'

'I know,' he confirmed, 'but I happen to like doing it. I don't think you've had enough of them lately.'

She frowned. 'What makes you say that?'

'Because it makes you uncomfortable to receive one. However, I intend to change all that by lavishing compliments on you left, right and centre,' he told her teasingly.

'Don't be silly!' Aimi protested, feeling rather odd inside. 'I haven't done anything.'

Jonas's voice became low and intimate, 'Darling, you exist, and you're beautiful. You have a fine mind and a good heart, all of which are worth complimenting. They are also worthy of…' He broke off for a split second, before adding, '…more than that.'

Aimi had no idea what he had meant to say, only that he had stopped himself at the last minute. Not that she minded, for what he had said was more than enough for a spirit that had been bruised for many years.

'So, is that why you rang, to pay me compliments?' she asked and could sense him smiling.

'Partly. The other was to tell you I've booked a table for dinner tonight. Hold on a moment.' The line went quiet for a few seconds, then Jonas came back. 'Sorry about that, but I have an important call on the other line. I'll pick you up at seven, if that's OK with you?'

'It's fine,' she assured him. 'Take your call. Bye, Jonas.' He rang off, and she put the receiver down again, her thoughts in a whirl.

It would, she realised, be very easy to fall in love with a man like Jonas, but she wasn't going to do that. She was far too sensible to mistake a powerful sexual attraction for love. Having come this far, admittedly further than she had ever intended, she was going to enjoy what they had for as long as it lasted.

For the first time in a very long time, Aimi skipped

lunch to go shopping. She could not go to dinner in one of her working suits, however smart they were. Fortunately there were some good shops nearby and she easily found what she wanted. In fact, the choice was so hard to make that she bought a small selection of items and carried them back to the house with a sense of excitement and a floaty feeling in her stomach.

Midway through the afternoon, Nick returned from the hospital and the first thing he noticed when he walked into the study was the rose sitting in its vase on her desk.

'You have an admirer, I see,' he remarked teasingly.

Aimi felt her cheeks grow pink as she glanced from the rose to her employer. Nick had been quite clear that he didn't want her to get involved with his brother, which left her in an awkward situation. 'It's nothing,' she demurred, hoping he would move on, but Nick was clearly intrigued.

'Who is he? Anyone I know?'

The heat in Aimi's cheeks doubled in strength, and she found she couldn't look him in the eye for more than a second or two. 'Oh, no!' she refuted hastily. 'I…um…don't think so.'

The smile vanished from Nick's face as he studied her scarlet one. 'Oh, no, Aimi, you didn't fall for Jonas's line!' he exclaimed in disbelief. 'It is him, isn't it? After all I said!' He paced away from her, then turned back abruptly. 'I could see it coming. I saw him looking at you, but I thought you had more sense. I could kill him!'

Aimi rose to her feet, her heart thumping madly at seeing him so upset by what he thought his brother had done. 'I'm a big girl, Nick. Jonas did nothing that I didn't want him to. It was my choice.'

He looked at her, dragging a hand through his hair in a helpless gesture. 'Don't you see, Aimi? He's very good at making a woman think it's all her own idea. My God, I thought that with you at least he would keep his hands to himself! When I see him, I'll…'

'Do nothing,' Aimi declared firmly, and that brought him to a halt. 'Thank you for worrying about me, Nick, but this really has nothing to do with you. Getting involved with Jonas was my choice, and I'm happy with it. Please don't be angry with him.'

Nick heaved a huge sigh. 'I just don't want to see you hurt.'

She smiled reassuringly. 'I won't be. My eyes are wide open.'

He didn't look happy, but he had to follow her wishes. 'All right. As you say, it's your business. Just be careful. Promise me that.'

Aimi nodded, relieved that he had calmed down. 'I will be, and I'm sorry if I've disappointed you.'

Immediately Nick looked contrite. 'You haven't. I'm just over-protective where you're concerned. It's a big wide world out there, and it's not always a safe place.'

She wondered what he would think if he knew just how much of the big wide world she had already experienced. She knew just how unsafe it was, but with Jonas it wasn't the same. For all that their relationship would be a fleeting one, he made her feel quite safe and secure.

It was a strange feeling for her to have, given Jonas's reputation, yet she trusted him instinctively. When she had time, she would have to ponder just why that should be.

CHAPTER EIGHT

THE next few weeks were a magical time for Aimi, who didn't allow herself to question what she was doing but simply lived for the moment. Whenever her conscience attempted to raise its head above the parapet, she forced it back down again, not wanting to listen. Yet, even whilst she enjoyed the blossoming relationship, she couldn't throw off a feeling that she was living in a house of cards that would soon come crashing down around her.

She had imagined Jonas would want to dine out every night, and be seen in all the smart places, but discovered the opposite was actually true. Sometimes they did dine out but, more often than not, they would eat at her apartment or his house, simply enjoying each other's company. At weekends he drove them out into the country, finding lovely little hotels to stay in, from where they could take long, leisurely walks.

At times Aimi felt as if she must be dreaming, for she was having much too much fun. Yet how could she help it, when Jonas was such fun to be with? She found that with him she could relax. It was a monumental relief to

just be herself, and she would always be grateful to
Jonas for giving her that.

Sometimes, though, she would catch sight of herself
in the mirror when she was getting ready to go out, and
be unable to look herself in the eye. Those nights her
dreams would be troubled, and she would wake in the
morning and know from her heavy eyes that the nightmares had visited her. It would take a concerted effort
to act as if nothing had happened. Jonas never asked, but
she knew he knew. He was waiting for her to make the
first move, but she never would. Eventually the mood
would pass, and she would be all right until the next
time. What troubled her was that the next time was
always sooner than the last.

She wasn't thinking about that now, as she lay with
her head cradled on Jonas's shoulder, listening to him
breathe as she waited for him to wake up. It was hot
already, but the heatwave that had almost melted the
country just weeks ago had broken eventually, to the
tune of spectacular thunderstorms, returning them to a
more normal heat of summer. They were in Jonas's bed,
and through the open window she could see birds flying
in and out of the trees.

Her pillow took a deep breath and she glanced round
and up, her green eyes meeting sleepy blue ones. 'Good
morning,' she greeted softly, liking his dishevelled look.

Jonas combed a hand through his hair and sighed.
'What time is it?'

'A little after half past nine,' she told him, taking a
quick look at the clock on the bedside table.

'That late? You should have woken me,' he chided,
but Aimi shook her head.

'I enjoy watching you sleep,' she confessed, and one eyebrow quirked as his lips twitched.

'Do you now? And how often does this happen?' he asked, shifting slightly so that he could run his hand caressingly over the lissome curve of her back and hip.

Her body stirred at his touch and she made a tiny purring sound in her throat. 'Only now and again.'

'Well, next time it happens, wake me. That way we can both enjoy the moment,' he suggested, lowering his lips to hers and taking them in a long, slow, deeply erotic kiss.

One thing led to another and it was quite some time before they were both capable of rational thought again. Later they shared the bathroom, Aimi showering whilst Jonas shaved. She was humming to herself, rinsing off the soap, when she thought she heard him speak. Turning off the tap, she opened the door a crack.

'Did you say something?'

Jonas looked at her in the shaving mirror. 'Uh-huh. Paula rang me yesterday to invite us out to dinner. I meant to tell you last night, but we got a little distracted,' he added with a wicked grin.

For once the look didn't register with Aimi; she was concentrating on what he had said. 'Did you say "us"?' she queried, reaching out for the fluffy bath sheet and quickly wrapping it around herself.

His eyebrows rose at her tone. 'What's wrong? Apparently she tried to contact you at home and, when she couldn't, rang Nick. He told her to talk to me.'

Aimi's heart sank and she stepped out of the shower. 'Oh, no,' she exclaimed in dismay. 'Why did he have to say that?'

Jonas went still, the hand holding the razor dropping as he slowly turned to face her. 'Why shouldn't he?'

'Because Paula isn't a fool. She'll realise that you and I are seeing each other!' Aimi explained in frustration, failing to see the odd look that flickered in his eyes for a moment. She had wanted to keep their affair from the other members of his family. Once it was public, it became real, and she could no longer ignore that reality.

'Are you ashamed to be connected with me, Aimi?' he asked her in a strangely level tone, and she belatedly realised how her remark must sound to him.

'No, no! That wasn't it at all!' she insisted, crossing to his side and touching his arm. How could she explain that their relationship was something she had entered into at great personal cost? She had broken faith with Lori to have this, and she knew it was that which troubled her sleep. She was being torn, and going public would not make things easier. 'I just wanted to keep it our secret.'

He shot her a dubious look. 'Well, Nick knows, and that didn't surprise you, so I assume you must have told him,' he pointed out reasonably, and she sighed.

'I didn't tell him; he guessed. He warned me against getting involved with you right from the beginning, and I made a mess of trying to pretend it wasn't you who sent me the rose,' Aimi explained quickly.

Jonas dropped his razor into the water and drew her into his arms. 'Well, you're right about Paula; she will have made the connection, which means the cat is very much out of the bag. So you're left with two options. Either you sit at home squirming, or you face her head on. What's it to be?'

Aimi might not have wanted to make their affair public knowledge, but if Paula knew the truth there was no point in hiding it. The damage was already done. 'What time do we have to be there, and should I wear a posh frock?' she asked by way of an answer, and Jonas's rakish grin reappeared like magic.

'Saturday, eight-thirty. I've not been to the place but, knowing Paula, it's bound to be expensive, where they do dinner and dancing. A posh frock is definitely required.'

Aimi smiled up at him, then, going on tiptoe, dropped a kiss on his nose. 'I'll go shopping for one during my lunch hour,' she promised and wriggled out of his hold before he could stop her. Laughing, she hurried into the bedroom, hearing him chuckling behind her.

Her smile faded, though, as she sat on the bed to dry off her hair. Suddenly she felt as if a shadow had fallen on the happy cocoon she had been living in, and she shivered as if a chill had passed over her. Immediately she told herself not to be so fanciful. Though she would much rather Jonas's family didn't know about them, there was nothing she could do about it now. There might be a few moments of embarrassment, but that would pass. Really, thinking about it, she was amazed that they had been able to keep the secret this long.

Yet, in the deep recesses of her mind, she couldn't shake off the feeling that something bad was going to happen.

When Saturday finally came around, Aimi paid a great deal of attention to dressing herself in the new dress she had bought for the occasion. She had treated herself to a pair of strappy sandals and matching evening purse, too. The deep blue of the dress complemented the soft blonde of her hair. After much thought she had decided to leave her hair down tonight, too.

Examining her reflection in the wardrobe mirror, she was almost amazed by what she saw. The woman who looked back was a stranger. An alluring, attractive stranger who didn't remind her of herself at all. Aimi was more used to seeing the cool, controlled person she had been these last nine years. This woman looked so much different from the young woman she had been before that. Of course she was older, but it was more to do with the way she held herself, with the confidence that only came with maturity.

Aimi couldn't help smiling a little, for she realised that she had been so busy she had failed to see she had grown up. More than that, she looked how she felt—happy—and that was all down to Jonas. At least, she was happy most of the time. She always felt that way when she was with him, but the bad dreams were getting her down, weighing on her mind when he was not there to distract her.

A glance at her watch told her that he would be here any minute. Even as she was thinking it, the doorbell rang and she smoothed her palms nervously over her thighs before going to open the door. However, any nervousness she was feeling vanished the instant she saw Jonas in his dinner suit. He was…breathtakingly handsome in the silk suit and all at once her heart was bombarded with all sorts of emotions, none of which allowed her to utter a word.

Jonas, on the other hand, had no such trouble.

'Stunning!' he declared when he saw her. 'I'll be the envy of every man in the room.'

'And I'll be the envy of every woman,' Aimi responded, finally managing to get her voice to work.

'I'm glad you left your hair down,' Jonas observed as he stepped inside. Carefully taking her into his arms, he kissed her and, like magic, Aimi forgot about her fears. When he drew back, he smiled gently. 'Nervous?'

'A little.' Whilst Aimi got on well with Paula and Nick, she couldn't help feeling neither would be happy that she was involved with their brother.

'Well, don't be; you're with me, so you can relax and enjoy yourself.'

Aimi stared up at him solemnly, then nodded. 'I'll do my best. You must think I'm ridiculous, worrying about what they will think,' she added with a wry laugh.

'Not at all. I've had my own worries,' he confessed, and she looked sceptical.

'You?'

Jonas shrugged. 'It's not easy to think seriously about a woman when you know that most of those who go out with you do so only because you're rich. After a while you start to wonder if they see you or your wallet.'

'I never thought of that. It must be unpleasant,' she responded sympathetically.

'It was, until you came along, and I realised here was a woman who saw my wealth as a turn-off. Naturally, I was intrigued,' he told her, eyes full of gentle humour.

'I've met a lot of rich men, and it didn't take me long to realise it's no measure of decency,' Aimi confirmed, thinking back to the world of the rich and famous she had once inhabited.

'And just where did you meet this horde of rich men?' he asked her teasingly.

Aimi dropped her gaze and moved away from him, ostensibly to collect her evening purse which lay on the coffee table. 'In another life,' she responded uncomfortably, not wanting to go there. Finally she turned back to Jonas and smiled. 'Shall we go? We don't want to be late.'

Jonas remained where he was, studying her broodingly. 'You'll tell me one day,' he said gently and her heart leapt, for it had been a while since he had mentioned her demons.

'There's nothing to tell and, even if there was, it's none of your business,' she told him firmly, which only made him smile grimly.

'I'm hoping that one day you'll trust me enough to make it my business,' he responded, stepping away from the door so that she could precede him out of it.

'Why would I do that?' she asked with a frown, watching him pull the door closed, then take her arm.

'Darling, the answer to that will be obvious when the time is right,' he told her lightly, hardly making things clearer so far as Aimi was concerned.

Aimi was puzzling over that very odd remark when they walked out of her building and she discovered Jonas had a taxi waiting for them.

Immediately Aimi started thinking ahead to the moment they entered the nightclub. She realised she was going to be making quite an entrance, and that set the butterflies fluttering around in her stomach. All eyes would be upon her, because she was with Jonas, and being the centre of attention was something she had become unused to. After all this time, she wasn't looking forward to it.

Strangely enough, though, when she did walk into the nightclub on Jonas's arm, she felt quite amazingly calm. Yes, people looked at them, some even seemed to recognise Jonas, but after that the attention faded away, leaving Aimi feeling a little bemused.

As if he felt something of what she was experiencing, Jonas glanced round, placing his free hand over hers. 'OK?' he asked, and her smile blossomed naturally.

'Yes…yes, I am!' she responded, and he grinned back at her before giving his attention to the waiter who was leading them through the crowded tables.

Paula was already smiling when Aimi and Jonas reached the table, and it was so warm and welcoming that Aimi forgot to be embarrassed.

'My goodness, Aimi, how lovely you look!' Paula exclaimed, rising and rounding the table to give her a friendly kiss on the cheek. 'Oh, dear, that didn't come out right, but you know what I mean!'

Aimi laughed. 'I do, and thank you, Paula. I love your dress.'

There followed a swift round of greetings and, in the midst of it, nobody but Aimi appeared to notice that Nick's response to Jonas was brusque at best. She had thought Nick was coming to terms with their relationship, but she could see that he was still angry with his brother, and that saddened her.

When they were all seated again, Paula leaned forward, her expression even more animated than usual. 'Isn't this a marvellous place? We've been sitting here name-spotting, and it's enough to make your head spin! Who have we seen? Let me see.' She began to relate a list, ticking them off on her fingers as she went.

'Did you get any autographs?' Jonas teased her, and she pulled a face.

'No. I was thinking about it, but James wouldn't let me,' she responded, shooting her husband a mock glare, then something caught her eye and she sat up straighter. 'Oh, my goodness, you'll never guess who just walked in!'

'Don't tell me, it's the Pope,' James quipped indulgently and received a kick for his pains.

'Don't be silly, he's in Rome. No, it's that fantastic actress. Ooh, you know!'

'I haven't the foggiest idea,' James told her, and Paula tutted.

'It's on the tip of my tongue. She gets all those fabulous meaty roles that make me weep buckets! I've got it. Marsha. Marsha Delmont!' Delighted at having made the connection, she beamed at everyone around the table.

Aimi looked round quickly, attempting to spot her mother, but the room was buzzing with people, making it difficult to see. 'Where?'

'She's gone,' Paula answered disappointedly. 'No, there she is, over the other side of the room.'

They all turned to look, and this time Aimi caught sight of the familiar figure of her mother. She smiled as a wave of pleasure swept over her. Her mother had been filming in New Zealand for the past three months, and she had missed her. She could see other heads turning, for Marsha Delmont was something of a national treasure. It was always the same wherever she went, and her mother responded with a small, friendly wave before she sat down.

It was then that Jonas, who had been looking across the room, turned to study Aimi intently. Almost at once she saw a look of comprehension enter those fascinating blue eyes and knew that he had discovered the answer to the mystery of who she reminded him of. Before he could say anything, though, the waiter, who had been hovering to one side, took their order for drinks and departed.

Opening her menu, Aimi knew it was only a matter of time before Jonas brought up the subject of her mother. She knew she should have told him, but she hadn't wanted him to make the connection, because then he could have remembered how her mother had rushed to be with her after the tragedy. She knew now that she didn't want him to think badly of her, although she knew he must. Who could think anything else?

The words of the menu blurred before her eyes as a profound question occurred to her in that moment. Why should she worry so very much about what he thought? The answer came shockingly loud and clear. Because a woman wanted the man she had fallen in love with to think only the best of her.

Aimi's lips parted on a tiny gasp as her true feelings were emblazoned in her heart and mind. She was in love with him. How could she not have known it before now? Because she hadn't been expecting to feel anything like this. Her affair with Jonas was just supposed to be a light thing, nothing so deep and momentous as falling in love. And yet she might have guessed it, because nothing about her relationship with him had been ordinary.

At that moment she suddenly became aware that Paula was laughing and looked up to find everyone at the table was looking at her. Having been miles away, she had totally lost the plot.

'What is it?' she asked and, across the table, Paula grinned.

'The waiter wants to know what you would like to eat,' she prompted and colour stormed into Aimi's cheeks.

'Oh, sorry,' she apologised and looked back at the menu, choosing the first thing her eye lit upon. The waiter made a note, smiled in a friendly fashion, then departed with the menus. Wondering what to say, she discovered she didn't have to when Jonas took her hand.

'Dance with me,' he urged her and, taking her agreement for granted, he stood up. She went with him for the simple reason that, if he was going to say anything, she didn't want everyone else to hear.

The dance floor was already crowded with couples and there was no chance of Aimi keeping some sort of distance from Jonas, even had she been inclined to, which, having discovered her feelings for him, she wasn't. He turned her into his arms, one hand settling in the small of her back, the other holding her hand close to his chest. Aimi placed her free hand on his shoulder, which brought her head close to his. Slowly, they began to move.

They had never danced together before tonight, and it was, quite simply, the most sensual dance she had ever experienced with a man. Their bodies touched from shoulder to thigh, and every gliding step she took brought with it the tantalising brush of his toned, muscular body. She was in love with this man was the thought going through her head, and consequently she made no attempt to stop her senses coming alive, registering every subtle nuance and sensation. Her body seemed to turn molten, softening, moulding itself to his in a way that stole her breath and started an ache way down deep inside her.

'It's crazy, isn't it?' Jonas murmured in a low voice next to her ear. 'That two supposedly intelligent people can't control the attraction they feel for the other, even in the middle of a dance floor.'

The provocative statement caused her to smile faintly and tip her head up so she could see him. 'You must be speaking for yourself. I have no trouble with my self-control!' she claimed flirtatiously.

Blue eyes danced. 'Liar,' came back his answer on a sighing breath.

Aimi stifled a moan as she felt the heat of his hand branding the small of her back. Dancing with him like this, knowing how she felt about him, was the most agonisingly sweet torture.

'You might not know me as well as you think you do!' she teased breathlessly, letting her fingers explore his neck and shoulders.

Jonas moved his head so that his cheek touched hers. 'I know you lied about not knowing who it was you look like,' he murmured for her ears only, and Aimi caught her breath, tensing a little. 'Why didn't you want me to know your mother is Marsha Delmont?'

Aimi closed her eyes momentarily, then bit the bullet. 'It isn't a connection I brag about, simply because my mother always wanted me to live out of the goldfish bowl she has to live in.' Although that hadn't worked, because Aimi had simply created her own notoriety. She crossed her fingers, hoping he knew nothing about her past.

To her relief, Jonas merely nodded. 'I can appreciate that. Now that I know, I realise where you get your acting ability from,' he declared, and Aimi laughed.

'I can't act my way out of a paper bag. It's my father

I take after. He was an academic. I get my love of history from him.'

'Beauty and brains. An irresistible combination,' he said with his devilish charm, and neatly turned her out of the way of a collision. 'Are you going to go and say hello?'

'A little later,' she confirmed, preferring to do it with a bit more privacy.

'Good, I'm looking forward to meeting her. There are some things I want to ask her about you,' he added, and her heart lurched anxiously.

'What sort of things?' she asked, her voice sounding unnaturally sharp, and felt the laughter in him.

'Don't worry; I only want to ask how she managed to produce such a beautiful, talented daughter,' he told her and, raising their joined hands to his lips, he pressed a kiss to her fingers.

Even so gentle a touch played havoc with her senses and brought a catch to her breath. 'Stop that!' she ordered huskily, though her attempt to pull her hand away was half-hearted at best.

'I can't help myself,' he admitted huskily, steering them over to the far side of the room. 'Whenever I'm with you, I have this urge to touch you. You haunt me, Aimi. My every waking moment is filled with thoughts of you, and my dreams...' He let the declaration tail off, knowing she would understand.

Aimi bit her lip hard, stifling a groan. 'Devil!' she berated him, but her eyes when she looked up at him were smoky with hidden passion.

'I've warned you about looking at me like that,' Jonas growled, and she smiled seductively.

'What are you going to do about it?' Aimi challenged, and he immediately stopped dancing.

'Nothing in front of all these people.' Casting a hasty look around, he found what he was searching for. 'Come with me,' he commanded, and took her by the arm to urge her through the tables to where French windows opened on to the night air. Her heart started to beat just that little bit faster.

However, they had only gone a few paces on to the terrace when a voice halted them.

'Aimi?' The soft question was comprised of hope and uncertainty.

At the sound of it, Aimi came to a halt and turned back to face her mother, who blinked rapidly, then sent out a beaming smile.

'I thought it was you!' she exclaimed, closing the distance in no time and sweeping her daughter into a tight hug. Aimi hugged her back, as ever inordinately glad to see her.

'I thought you were still away on location. When did you get back?'

Marsha Delmont laughed. 'Actually, darling, I'm not really back. Adrian broke a leg and is out of the production, so I've come home for a few days whilst a replacement is found. It's all too frustrating, but at least it gives me the opportunity to see you. Let me have a good look at you,' she said, and stepped back to put Aimi at arm's length. What she saw had her eyes widening in astonishment. 'Oh, my goodness!' She had to let go of her daughter's hands in order to bring them to her face. Tears spilled out down her cheeks. 'You don't know how long I've waited to see you like this! Oh, darling, thank God! I've been so very worried, but look at you. Your hair…your clothes… It's…absolutely wonderful!' More tears fell until Marsha was virtually sobbing.

Stricken to realise from this reaction just how concerned about her her mother had been, Aimi quickly gave her another hug. 'Don't cry. Please don't cry,' she urged, feeling wretched.

Marsha eased herself away and sniffed. 'I'm OK, darling. You know how emotional I get. Now I'm sure I had a tissue in here,' she declared, searching through her evening purse.

'Use this,' Jonas suggested, holding out a pristine handkerchief.

Taking it, Marsha used it to dab at her eyes, then took a good look at the man who had come to her rescue. Her eyebrows rose, and then she smiled. 'Now I understand,' she said knowingly, looking from Jonas to her daughter. 'Whoever you are, I am so very, very pleased to meet you!'

'Jonas Berkeley, Miss Delmont, and I'm honoured to meet you,' Jonas introduced himself with a smile, giving Aimi's mother a taste of his rakish charm.

'Marsha, please,' the older woman invited. 'And let's not stand upon ceremony. When I'm with my daughter I'm her mother, not an actress. If you're responsible for this transformation, then I'm in your debt.'

'Mum!' Aimi exclaimed in dismay, but her mother merely turned and smiled at her with so much love it brought a lump to her throat.

'Darling, I've waited so long for this day, don't try to stop me enjoying it.'

Aimi bit her lip. She knew what her mother was thinking, and she had to put her right. For, whilst she might have fallen for Jonas, she very much doubted he felt the same way. 'Mum, Jonas and I...we're not...'

Marsha laughed delightedly and cupped her daughter's cheeks. 'Darling, I don't care what you are or aren't, just be happy. Now, much as I would love to stay and chat with you for hours, I must go. Come and see me. I'm here until the end of next week. Bring Jonas. I absolutely insist upon it!' she added with another tinkling laugh, then kissed her daughter, smiled at Jonas and went back inside.

'Your mother is a truly lovely person,' Jonas remarked as he came to join Aimi, who looked up and smiled.

'I think so.'

'She's right about you, too. You look amazing, but that has nothing to do with me.'

Aimi knew better. He had a lot to do with how she was today. 'You're wrong. I would never have gone out and bought a dress like this but for you, and she knows it.'

Jonas turned her into his arms and brought her up against him. 'And are you happy?'

Aimi hesitated a moment, not because she wasn't happy but because it was such a difficult thing for her to say. To admit it would be a further renunciation of her friend. And yet...how could she not say it when, for the first time in so very long, she actually was deeply happy. 'Yes,' she admitted huskily, 'I am.'

He smiled. 'Good. That makes two of us,' he told her softly, and kissed her with exquisite gentleness.

Aimi rested her head on his shoulder, unable to stop

herself experiencing a new wave of guilt. Yet no sooner had the thought come, than she forced it back, not wanting to think about it now. She would only think of this moment, and no further.

They stood like that for an age, until another couple came from inside, breaking the mood.

'We'd better go and join the others. They'll be wondering where we've got to,' Jonas proposed as he released her, and immediately she missed the warmth of his closeness and its ability to fend off unwanted thoughts. He did hold her hand as they made their way back inside, but Aimi felt the cold winds of her past following in her wake.

No sooner had they reached their table than Nick jumped to his feet. 'Can I have a word with you?' he asked his brother in a surprisingly stern voice. Jonas's brows rose as he settled Aimi in her seat. Squeezing her shoulders encouragingly, he nodded.

'Of course, Nick. We won't be long,' he said to Aimi and the others, then turned to follow a rigid-backed Nick to the side of the room.

Not surprisingly, the others were intrigued by this turn of events and watched the distant conversation with as much interest as Aimi. It was clear to see that Nick was furiously angry, gesticulating wildly as he harangued his brother. Jonas simply stood and listened to it all. However, when Nick stopped for breath, he held up his hand and started to speak. Whatever he said, the change in Nick was profound. His posture softened and, as he listened, he dragged a hand through his hair. Then he had a question or two to ask and, when Jonas nodded, he hesitated for a moment, then held out his hand. Jonas took it, and they hugged. Seconds later, both men walked off in the direction of the bar.

'Well!' exclaimed Paula, looking from her husband to Aimi. 'That was interesting. What on earth do you think was going on?'

Aimi was frowning, wondering the same herself. 'I have no idea.'

'I know Nick didn't like you and Jonas being gone so long. Would it be too indelicate to ask what you were doing?' Paula's expression was part grimace and part wheedling as she looked at Aimi.

Aimi couldn't help laughing, whilst Paula's husband groaned aloud. 'Honestly, Paula!'

'It's OK,' Aimi responded. 'Actually, we were talking to my mother.'

Of all the things Paula had been expecting to hear, that wasn't one of them. 'Your mother!'

There was nothing else Aimi could do than come clean. 'Marsha Delmont is my mother,' she confessed, and Paula's face was a picture.

'Oh, my goodness! Really? Oh, Lord, did I say anything nasty about her? I did, didn't I? Oh, I just want to curl up and die!' she exclaimed, covering her face with her hands.

Aimi smiled understandingly. 'It's OK, Paula. You were very polite. My mother will be glad to hear she has another fan.'

'And I do like her. I really do!' the young woman declared earnestly. 'Now, spill the beans—tell us what it's like, growing up the daughter of a screen goddess.'

Amused and diverted, Aimi spent the few minutes until the men returned relating a few of the funnier episodes in her life. When Jonas finally took his seat beside her, she looked at him curiously.

'What were you and Nick talking about?' she asked immediately.

'He wanted to tell me what he would do to me if I harmed a hair on your head,' Jonas enlightened her with a wry smile, and Aimi caught her breath.

'I hope you told him to mind his own business,' she returned sharply. Employer or not, he had no right to interfere in her private life.

'Actually, I told him that if I ever did, then I would save him the trouble and do it myself.'

Aimi stared at him in a state of bemusement. 'Really?'

Jonas nodded. 'Really. I've come to realise that if there is one person in all the world I would never want to hurt, it's you. The simple truth of the matter is, I've fallen in love with you, Aimi Carteret.'

CHAPTER NINE

IT STARTED as it always did, with her whole body feeling the vibration. Then came the awful moment when she turned and saw the huge cloud of snow billowing its way downhill towards her. She couldn't move, no matter how much she struggled. Her heart was thundering sickeningly fast and, just when she thought it must burst, the picture changed and she was in the trees, watching. Watching Lori going the wrong way, trying to get out of the path of destruction. She tried to call out to her to hurry. *Hurry!* But the dreadful noise took her voice away, and she could only watch. Watch as Lori was swept up and tossed around like a rag doll, until she vanished from sight. Then the noise was gone and, where Lori had once been, there was only metre upon metre of uneven snow and debris. Horror gripped her as she realised her friend was gone, and she cried out against it. *No. No.*

'No!'

Now Aimi was trying to battle her way over the snow, but it was stopping her, fighting to keep her where she was, and she flung out wildly with her arms and legs until slowly a voice began to intrude.

'Wake up. Aimi, wake up. Don't fight me. Hush now. Hush.'

Slowly the snow that held her transformed into strong male arms and the voice she could hear was known to her, too. She subsided, trembling, looking up into familiar features.

'Jonas?'

He nodded and held her tighter, soothing her with the gentle stroking of his hand over her back. 'I'm here. I've got you.'

As reality impinged, Aimi realised she was sitting up in the bed and Jonas was beside her, his strong arms comforting her. 'What happened?' Her voice sounded odd, croaky and her throat hurt.

Jonas's heartbeat began to return to normal, too. 'You woke up screaming. When I tried to hold you, you started thrashing about. You must have had a bad dream.'

Bad dream? Aimi closed her eyes, knowing what had happened. She had had the nightmare again. These days she only had it around the time of the anniversary of Lori's death, but that was months away. She thought she knew the reason why it had come early, but then remembered something Jonas had said.

'Did I hurt you? When I was thrashing about?' she asked remorsefully, studying his face for signs of damage.

His lips twitched into a faint smile. 'No. I managed to get you in a rugby tackle. I thought you might hurt yourself.'

Aimi sighed and rested her weight against him. 'I'm OK,' she told him, though she wasn't really. She was still shaking. The nightmare never went away easily, but stayed with her for hours afterwards. 'I'm sorry I woke you.'

Jonas pressed a kiss to her temple. 'I'm more concerned about you than of losing sleep. What was the dream about?'

'I can't really remember. It's hazy and jumbled.' Again she lied, but she had never told anyone about her nightmares. They were too raw. Too private.

'You seem to be having quite a few bad dreams lately. Is something bothering you?' The concerned question set the nerves in her stomach jangling.

'No, it was just a random event. I have to use the bathroom,' she told him, wriggling out of his arms and scrambling off the bed. 'I won't be a moment.'

Once inside the bathroom, Aimi switched on the light and stared at herself in the mirror over the basin. There were dark shadows in her eyes, and she knew why. Two things had happened at dinner tonight. She had realised she was in love with Jonas, and he had told her he had fallen in love with her. It should have made her happy, and it had, yet the nightmare had come again.

Groaning softly, she ran some cold water into the basin and bent to splash it over her face. The cold felt good on her heated skin. Yet it couldn't take away the knowledge that she had been having more and more restless nights and uncomfortable dreams. It was as if the happier she had become, the more severe the dreams grew. Until, tonight, the nightmare had returned with a vengeance.

After weeks of being ignored, Aimi's conscience was raising its head over the barricade. It was no longer prepared to take a back seat. The moment she'd realised she was in love, it had risen up and tried to tell her something. But what? That she had taken too much for granted? That she had presumed too much? What? she asked herself, and her reflection in the mirror returned the taunting answer. *You know.*

Abruptly Aimi looked away, drying her face on a fluffy towel. She didn't want to think about it. Didn't want to acknowledge what her conscience was trying to tell her. She wanted to be with Jonas. Wanted to feel his warmth and know she was alive.

Without looking at herself again, she drained the water and switched off the light. Hurrying back into the bedroom, she slipped into the bed beside Jonas, who was resting back against the pillows, and held on to him tightly. Slightly surprised, he instinctively wrapped his arms around her.

'Are you OK?' he asked cautiously, and she squeezed her eyes shut.

'I will be. Just hold me, please,' she asked in a small voice, which for some reason made his heart turn over.

'Always,' he promised. 'Always.'

Aimi sighed heavily, praying his words would dispel the chilly sense of time running out that was growing inside her. Very slowly she began to relax and her breathing became more regular. To the man holding her, it was a sign that he, too, could relax. Then he heard the words he had been hoping to hear.

'I love you, Jonas,' Aimi murmured, very close to sleep, so that her words were slurred.

Jonas smoothed his hand over her silky hair. 'I love you, too, Aimi. Sleep now.'

At his words she uttered a faint sigh and slipped over the edge into forgetfulness.

* * *

The following morning Aimi woke before Jonas and from the second she opened her eyes she had instant recall of everything that had happened. She wanted to feel happy about Jonas telling her he loved her but, even as she thought it, she shivered. She couldn't help feeling that it wasn't right. That it was wrong to be this happy when her best friend had been denied the possibility of happiness.

Creeping from the bed, Aimi left Jonas asleep whilst she showered. She felt torn. On the one hand wanting what she could have with Jonas, yet on the other having this almost overwhelming feeling that she did not deserve to be given such a gift. The guilt over her best friend's death reasserted itself, weighing on her heart, turning the warm sunny day into something cold and dark.

Shivering, Aimi turned off the water and stepped out of the cubicle, drying herself on a large fluffy towel. Padding back into the bedroom, she quickly slipped into a pair of jeans and a long-sleeved lightweight top, then went to the kitchen and made herself some coffee. Whilst she sipped the steaming liquid, she noticed the small pile of mail she had tossed on to the counter the day before. A couple were bills, but one was handwritten, and Aimi recognised the writing. Setting the mug down, she picked up the envelope with trembling fingers and opened it.

Inside was a birthday card, and the sentiment in it was a stark and pointed reminder to Aimi. It said: *To our darling Lori. Happy birthday, with all our love, Mum and Dad.*

Aimi drew in a ragged breath, realising she had forgotten what day it was. Every year, Lori's mother sent

Aimi the birthday card she could not send her daughter, and it was as devastating to the recipient as it had ever been.

'Oh, God!' Aimi pressed a hand to her stomach, fighting back a wave of nausea. The timing was awesome, combining as it did with Aimi's own conscience reasserting itself. She was being assailed from all sides, and she knew she needed to get out into the open air where she could think.

Tossing the card on the counter, she headed for the front door. Yet she hesitated at the bedroom, staring down at Jonas's sleeping form. He had soothed her in the night, and she had felt safe from the ghosts of her past, but they had come back to haunt her anyway. Whilst part of her wanted him to hold her now, the other knew he could not help. She had to do this by herself.

So she turned away, collecting her bag on her way out of the door. At first her route had no purpose, except to take her away from the source of her present dilemma, but having done that, she slowed down, eventually finding a bench in a nearby park where she could sit and collect her thoughts.

Aimi knew what she needed to hear. She needed to be told that it was OK for her to have Jonas. But Lori was the only one who could give her that permission, and it was beyond her. Maybe she wasn't being rational, but she never could be. Not about what she had done. If Lori were here… But she wasn't—only her parents were.

Aimi sat up straighter, drawing in a ragged breath. Lori's parents. Mrs Ashurst had blamed Aimi as much as Aimi had blamed herself. Obviously she still did, from the card she had sent. But if she could just talk to her, try to explain what had happened, maybe she would be able to move forward. Find the true peace which was just beyond her reach.

Knowing now what she had to do, Aimi set off in search of a taxi to take her to the Ashursts' house. Her heart was thundering in her chest as she walked up to the front door. She had been here so often in the past, it had almost been a second home. Surely the friendly woman she remembered from her childhood would at least listen now.

Lori's mother opened the door herself and when she saw Aimi standing on her doorstep her expression froze, becoming tight and remote. 'Oh, it's you,' she said coldly, and Aimi's heart lurched. Still, she pressed on.

'Could I speak with you for a moment, Mrs Ashurst?' she asked the older woman, her voice gruff through a dry throat.

Mrs Ashurst's brows rose superciliously. 'What can we possibly have to say to each other?' she challenged, making no move to invite Aimi inside.

'Please, Mrs Ashurst. I need to talk to you about Lori. If we could just...' That was as far as she was allowed to get.

'Don't you dare let me hear you say her name! Lori's gone. You killed her!' The anger and bitterness were as strong as they had ever been, and Aimi felt herself begin to shake inside.

She swallowed hard and her voice faltered as she responded. 'I know I was at fault, and I'm sorry for it, but it's been nine years now, and I thought perhaps we could talk about that day.'

Lori's mother laughed scathingly. 'I know what you

thought, Aimi Carteret! You thought you could come back here and say you were sorry and then I would forgive you! Well, I don't forgive you! I shall never forgive you! You killed my daughter. She followed you like a slave and did everything you demanded of her! It sickens me to see you walking about free as a bird whilst she…' The woman faltered, dragging air into her lungs as she found she could not say where Lori was.

The older woman's face took on a vicious look. 'I don't care how sorry you are. It won't bring my daughter back to me. Go away. Get out. I never want to see you again!' And with that she slammed the door in Aimi's face.

Dazed and distraught, Aimi turned away and staggered down the steps. The other woman's venom was an awful thing to feel, and Aimi felt it slice into her heart, draining the warmth out of her along with the faint hope of being forgiven. Totally unaware of where she was going, she turned left out of the gate and simply walked. Her own sense of guilt expanded to encompass that which had just been levelled on her by Lori's mother. It weighed her down, almost as much as it had in the beginning.

There was no way out of it, and there shouldn't be. She *was* guilty. Nothing she had done could ever take that away. She had changed her life, become a better person, but that couldn't wipe away the blame. How could she even think of making a future for herself, with Lori's death on her conscience? Nothing could make that right. Lori's mother had proved that to her today. She didn't deserve the things that Lori could never have.

Lost in the labyrinth of her guilt-driven thoughts,

Aimi was unaware of anything around her. Not the people, nor the traffic. She just walked, and not even the sudden blaring of a horn could penetrate her numbed mind. Even the pain of the contact with the car which tried to avoid her but caught her a glancing blow that sent her spinning into a parked car barely registered. There was a scream which finally made it through the mist but, seconds later, all was blackness.

She seemed to be walking through a mist, on a surface she could not see. She knew she was looking for something, but it was beyond her sight, out of reach. She moaned softly, and almost immediately felt a hand holding hers. It was strong, yet gentle. It was instantly comforting and she relaxed, allowing the darkness to swallow her up again.

The next time Aimi stirred, the mists were gone, and she blinked her eyes open to the real world. It was night. She could tell that from the muted lighting that allowed her to open her eyes without discomfort. She had no idea where she was, or why, and when she tried to lift her left arm a dull pain shot through her wrist, so she quickly put it back down.

Somewhat alarmed, she tried moving her head, but she moved too fast and that set a dull pain throbbing inside it. Realising that she must have been hurt, Aimi tried all her limbs one by one, discovering she could move her legs and right arm, though not without pain. When she tried to sit up, the whole of her body protested, and she fell back against the pillows, gasping for breath.

She had to be in hospital, she realised, and a careful check to either side of her confirmed the suspicion. The big question, then, was how had she got here? What on earth had she done?

The question was silent but the answer was audible.

'You had a collision with a moving vehicle,' a familiar voice told her, and Aimi looked round to see her mother was standing just inside the room.

'I did?' Her voice sounded scratchy, for her throat was as dry as a desert. She couldn't remember having an accident, though right at the back of her mind she had the vaguest memory of a piercing scream.

'Yes,' Marsha Delmont declared wryly, coming to take the chair she had been sitting in for goodness knew how many hours. 'Apparently you stepped off the kerb almost into the path of a car. You were lucky. You got away with bruised ribs and a fractured wrist.'

That explained why her left wrist hurt. She tried to probe further, but that only increased the throbbing ache in her head, so she desisted. 'Is the driver OK?'

Leaning on the edge of the bed, Marsha took her daughter's hand. 'She's suffering from shock. As am I. You really must stop putting me through this, Aimi. My heart can't take it.'

'I'm sorry, Mum. I wish I could remember. Where did it happen?'

'In Chelsea, near the river,' Marsha revealed, and held her breath, but Aimi only frowned.

'What was I doing there?'

Her mother took a deep breath. 'Well, darling, it was rather close to where Lori used to live,' she said cautiously, and saw comprehension finally dawn on her daughter's bruised face.

The mention of Lori's name cleared the fog for

Aimi. She recalled where she had been, and why. 'I went to see her parents, but only her mother was there,' she said starkly.

Marsha's heart contracted. 'Why, darling?'

Aimi gave her mother a tired smile. 'I wanted to talk to them about her. It was…important to me. I thought… I hoped…that, after all this time, they would forgive me. I ought to have known they never will.'

Tears glistened in her mother's eyes. 'Oh, Aimi, Aimi, I'm so sorry you had to go through all that again. I tried to approach her several times in those first years, but she refused to see me. Maybe I would be the same, if I lost you. You have to try and understand how she feels, and not judge her too harshly.'

Aimi squeezed her mother's hand. 'I don't. I know she's right in everything she said.'

'What did she say?' Marsha enquired, not liking the sound of that at all.

'Only what I've always known, that it was my fault Lori died.'

'But Aimi, nobody blamed you.'

Aimi smiled wanly, not wanting to upset her mother any more. 'I blamed me. But don't worry, everything's all right now.'

Marsha was relieved to hear it. 'That's good, darling. Put it all behind you. You've been so much more like your old self lately, so I knew something had changed. It's Jonas, isn't it? He's a good man, and he's been so worried about you he refused to go home.'

Aimi froze. 'He's here?' She didn't know why she hadn't thought of that earlier, but her brain wasn't functioning properly yet.

'Of course. He's gone to get us some coffee. He'll be so relieved to find you've woken up at last.'

'Tell him to go away. I don't want to see him,' Aimi ordered bluntly. She knew why she had gone to Lori's parents, and that encounter had reminded her of what she had forgotten in the heat of passion. Jonas, and everything he represented, was out of bounds to her. She could not have the happiness she had denied her friend.

Not surprisingly, her mother was confused. 'But why? I don't understand. Has something happened?'

Yes, something had happened. She had stopped living an impossible dream. 'We haven't had a fight, or anything like that. I simply don't want to see him. Please, tell him to go home.'

'All right, if that's what you want,' Marsha agreed unhappily.

'It's OK, Marsha, Aimi can tell me herself,' Jonas declared evenly, and they both looked round to see him standing in the doorway, two steaming cups of coffee in his hands. These he set on a counter inside the door, then came further into the room. 'Would you give us a moment?' he said to her mother, who rose gracefully to her feet.

'Ten minutes,' she agreed, then, looking from one stony face to the other, sighed and left the room.

Jonas didn't take the seat Marsha had vacated, but stood beside the bed and slipped his hands into the pockets of his jeans. 'You gave me one hell of a fright. First I wake up to find you gone, then I get a call from your mother telling me you're in hospital. What were you thinking, stepping off the kerb without looking?'

Looking up at him, Aimi could see he was dreadfully tired and in need of a shave. Her heart ached, until she hardened it. 'I…had a lot on my mind. I just didn't realise the road was there. How long were you standing there? What did you hear?'

'Long enough to hear you say you didn't want to see me,' he enlightened her. 'How do you feel?'

'I seem to ache everywhere,' she responded, wincing as she tried to make herself more comfortable.

'That's because you're one huge bruise at the moment,' he returned with studied calm. 'So, why don't you want to see me, Aimi? What did I do to make you leave your apartment without a word?'

'I went out because I needed to think,' she told him curtly. 'And I don't want to see you because there would be no point. There's no future in our relationship, so the best thing to do is end it.'

That unexpected statement had his eyes narrowing. 'What do you mean, we have no future? Just last night you told me you loved me!' Jonas declared with justifiable disbelief.

Aimi swallowed hard. 'I lied,' she said gruffly, and he simply stared at her, patiently trying to understand what was going on.

'You lied?' Shaking his head, he dragged a hand through his hair. 'Oh, no, darling. I don't think so. If you've lied at all, it's now.'

Her heart lurched at the accurate claim. 'Why would I do that?'

Jonas uttered a derogatory bark of laughter. 'I don't know, but I sure as hell intend to find out!'

Aimi turned away from him, staring blindly at the wall. 'I'm tired. I want you to leave now. Please don't come back.' Although she couldn't see him, she could hear him take a deep breath.

'OK, I'll go, but this is not over. I'm not walking away from you, Aimi,' he promised, and she closed her eyes.

'You should. There's nothing for you to stay for. I can't give you what you want.'

'Then I'm doomed, darling because, so far as I'm concerned, you're the only one who can,' he responded, and turned and walked out of the room.

Aimi looked around, eyes fixed on the doorway he had just gone through. She knew she had done the right thing, but she hadn't thought it would hurt so much. It was as if someone had taken her heart and ripped it to shreds.

A movement in the doorway drew her from her painful reverie. It was her mother. Marsha crossed quickly to her daughter's side and sat down. Her eyes were full of concern.

'I met Jonas outside. He didn't look happy. Why did you send him away, Aimi? The man loves you. I can see it. Surely you must, too. Why are you doing this?'

Sighing, Aimi smiled sadly. 'Because I forgot about a promise I made, but I've remembered it now, so everything will be all right.' Her lashes fluttered down, and she heaved another sigh. 'I'm tired. I think I'll sleep now.'

Sitting back in the chair, Marsha shivered as if someone had walked over her grave. She had an awful feeling that she knew what her daughter was talking about, and it appalled her. She had been so overjoyed to see Aimi last night, looking radiant and happy, and she was determined that it would not be lost if she could help it. As soon as she could, she had phone calls to make and people to see. She was going to fight for her daughter as she had never fought before.

CHAPTER TEN

AIMI was not kept in hospital long, for her injuries had been blessedly minor—something of a miracle, given the circumstances. Jonas had not attempted to visit her again and she had been relieved, for she hadn't wanted to fight with him. He had stayed away, and she had done her best not to think about him. Through him, she had lost her way for a while, but she was back on track now.

Though she was allowed home, there was no way she could return to work. Nick had been extremely concerned about her accident and had insisted she take as much time off as she needed. She was grateful, yet at the same time had to wonder if she could still work for him. He was Jonas's brother, after all, and that was bound to create complications. Still, she wasn't going to think about it until she had to.

Her mother, who had delayed her return to work to be with her daughter, had come up with the perfect plan for her recuperation. She had been given the use of a cottage on an island in one of the Scottish lochs, and Aimi was going to stay there until she was fully recovered.

By the time she left hospital, she was longing for the

peace and quiet of the Highlands. Her thoughts had been anything but pleasant for, though she knew she was doing the only thing she could, her dreams were plagued with memories of what she had shared with Jonas and the possibility of what might have been. She had never been this troubled by a decision before and needed some quiet time to get her mind in order.

Marsha's driver took them to the station, where her mother waited to see her off, waving from the platform until a bend in the line took Aimi from sight. Aimi sat back in her seat then, knowing she had a long journey ahead of her.

Hours later, she discovered her mother had made arrangements for a car to take her from the nearest station to the loch, where a local man was on hand to ferry her over to the island. The same man helped to carry her cases up to the cottage.

'How will I contact you if I want to get off the island?' she asked him before he left.

'By phone. You'll find a number on the board in the kitchen. Enjoy your stay,' he added with a friendly smile, then walked back down the path. A little while later Aimi caught sight of him rowing back across the calm water of the loch.

Looking around her, Aimi breathed in a shaky sigh of relief. It was an idyllic spot, quiet except for the sound of birds and sheep in the distance. Though not big, the island was studded with trees and bushes, and there was a cottage garden all around it. Someone had put a lot of care and attention into it, and it was the perfect place to get away from her troubles.

She discovered, as she slowly unpacked her things,

that the cottage had all the usual appliances required for modern living—not that she would need them. She intended to live quite simply. By the time she had taken a walk around the garden, finding a shed with a generator in it, obviously for use if the electricity failed, it was late and she was getting hungry.

Back in the cottage, she made herself a sandwich and a cup of tea, and by the time she had finished both exhaustion was taking its toll. So, turning out the light, she locked up and took herself up to bed. She fell asleep almost the instant her head hit the pillow and knew no more until morning.

The next day was beautifully sunny and lifted Aimi's spirits immeasurably. After breakfast she decided to do a bit more exploring and, taking an apple with her in case she should get hungry, set off to walk to the southern end of the island. She was almost there when she thought she heard an outboard motor but, when no boat sped by, gave it no more thought.

Sitting on a rock in the sunshine, she ate her apple and watched the ducks go about their daily lives, hunting for food and chasing off rivals. Eventually, though, her stomach began to growl in earnest and she slowly made her way back to the cottage to make herself some lunch.

It wasn't until she approached the back door that her steps faltered. She had left it closed, but now it was open and she caught the waft of something delicious cooking. Noises followed, of pans being moved on the cooker. Her anxiety that somebody had broken into the cottage deepened to confusion at the idea that the same somebody was actually cooking.

'You might as well come in and wash up, the fish will be ready soon,' Jonas's voice called out to her from inside and anxiety gave way to shock.

'Jonas?' What was Jonas doing here?

Stepping inside, Aimi stared at the man standing at the cooker. He turned and smiled at her, and her heart leapt at the sight of him before she could stop it. She hadn't seen him since she had told him to go away at the hospital, and she hadn't realised just how very much she had missed him until this moment. Of course, as soon as she thought that, she forced herself to squash the emotion, to remain firm in her resolve.

'How did you get here?'

Jonas turned back to his cooking. 'I keep a boat at the dock. Jock looks after it for me. He also caught these fish. There's nothing like freshly cooked fish when you've been out in the fresh air.'

Aimi listened to the explanation in a state of disbelief. He kept a boat? 'How could you keep a boat here?'

'Because this is my cottage. My island, too, come to that. Look, make yourself useful and set the table. You'll find cutlery in the drawer over there.'

She was staggered, and knew her expression showed it. 'Your cottage? But I thought...' She never actually finished what she thought, for it dawned on her then that her mother and Jonas had planned this between them. 'I don't believe it! How could she do this to me?' she exclaimed, hurt by her mother's action.

Jonas took the frying-pan off the heat and turned off the gas. 'Because she loves you,' he answered simply, moving round and setting the table. Next he dished up the fish and vegetables on to two plates and set them on the table.

Aimi watched all this in silence. 'She had no right to interfere. I know what I'm doing,' she said stolidly, and Jonas shot her a questioning look as he came to hold out a chair.

'Do you? We'll talk about that later. In the meantime, the fish is getting cold, and it would be a shame to spoil it. Sit and eat, Aimi. You look like you could do with some food in you.'

She sat because she was too stunned to do anything else. The fish smelt wonderful, and her stomach rumbled. Telling herself it would be a crime to waste good food, she started to eat. Across the table, Jonas watched her for a moment, then started on his own food.

They ate in silence. Aimi couldn't have spoken anyway; her thoughts were too jumbled. Besides, she was still learning to cope doing things one-handed, and had to concentrate on cutting up her food.

'Does your wrist give you much pain?' Jonas asked after a while, and she had to look up.

'Some. I have painkillers but I try not to use them.' What with that and her bruised ribs, she sometimes felt like one big ache, but it was getting better, slowly.

'You've left your hair down, I see,' he remarked next, and automatically she raised a hand to her neck.

'I can't put it up with one hand,' she admitted, and it had left her feeling far too open. She couldn't even tie it back, so it had to fall to her shoulders in a blonde swathe.

'Now I'm here, I can help you,' he stated matter-of-factly, and Aimi stared at him.

'You won't be staying,' she stated as firmly as she could, but Jonas merely looked faintly amused.

'It's my cottage, remember?'

Her jaw tensed. 'Then I shall leave.'

Jonas pulled a face and rubbed his hand around his jaw. 'That might be a problem.'

Her heart lurched. 'Why? All I have to do is phone across.'

'The phone's been disconnected and, before you ask, there's no reception here for a mobile phone. You're going nowhere, Aimi. Not until we've talked this thing out.' He was no longer smiling. Looking into his eyes, she could see the steely purpose there.

'We have nothing to talk about. And I will get off this island, even if I have to swim for it!' she informed him, feeling anger coiling inside her at the trap she had walked into.

'How far do you think you would get with that wrist? We are going to talk—sooner or later.'

Aimi pushed her plate away, her appetite vanishing. 'Then it will have to be later!' she exclaimed, and attempted to push her chair away by bracing her hands against the table. Pain shot through her wrist and she gasped, clutching it to her chest. 'Damn! Damn, damn, damn!'

Jonas had shot to his feet in an instant, rounding the table to squat down beside her. 'Have you done any damage? Let me see.' He tried to take her arm, but she twisted away.

'Don't touch me!' she gritted out angrily. 'This is all your fault! Why did you have to come here?'

'Because I love you, Aimi Carteret, and I don't intend to lose you without a fight,' he told her with simple honesty, causing invisible fingers to tighten about her heart.

Aimi glared at him, unaware that her chin was trembling as she fought with her emotions. 'Don't say that! I don't want to hear it!'

'You think you don't, but I know better,' he contradicted, rising to his feet again, and Aimi stared at him helplessly.

'Why won't you listen to me?'

Jonas uttered a wry laugh. 'Because you haven't said anything I want to hear yet.' He collected up the plates, put the scraps in the waste bin, then piled them in the sink. 'Why don't you go and sit in the other room, whilst I make a cup of tea?' he suggested, setting Aimi's teeth on edge.

'Why don't you stop telling me what to do?' she retorted and, whilst she did get up, she stomped out of the cottage instead of into the sitting room.

She had no real idea of where she was going, just so long as it was away from Jonas. How dared he do this? It was her life, and she could choose to live it her way. *Even if it's not the way you really want...?* an insidious voice asked, and she hated herself for thinking it.

Pursued by her inner thoughts, if not Jonas, she walked on, going towards the other end of the small island. It was as she walked that she recalled what Jonas had said. He had a boat which he'd used to get here. Which meant it had to be moored somewhere close by. If she could find it, then she could use it to leave.

Spurred on by the idea, she followed what appeared to be a path that took her down to the rocky shoreline. From there she picked her way round the rocks and pebbles, until she saw what she was looking for. A boat-house had been built over a small inlet, and it was this she made her way over to. As she approached, she could see a padlock on the front, but guessed there had to be another way in. Rounding the corner in search of it, she stopped short at the sight of Jonas sitting on a large boulder, soaking up the sun.

'What kept you?' he asked blithely, and Aimi ground her teeth together in annoyance.

'I didn't know this was here,' she replied shortly.

'But you worked out that I had to have a boat some-where,' Jonas added, smiling. 'It's locked, but you can try it for yourself.'

She didn't even attempt to, for she knew he was telling the truth. Instead, she turned her back on him and stared out over the sparkling water. 'I'm tired of playing games. I want to get off this island.'

'I'll take you anywhere you want to go, providing you talk to me first,' he bargained with her, and she did look over her shoulder at him then.

'What do you expect me to talk about?'

Blue eyes bored into hers, the power in them apparent even at a distance. 'Lori. You can start by telling me about her.'

Shock tore through her at the sound of her friend's name on his lips. Her gasp was audible, and she knew she paled. 'Who told you about Lori?' she asked faintly, her voice sounding stiff and unnatural.

'Your mother. When you wouldn't see me, I paid a call on her. We had a long talk. A very interesting talk,' Jonas said in a firm yet gentle voice.

Aimi could feel her heart knocking against her ribs

as her anxiety level rose higher. 'I'm surprised you were interested.'

'Darling, everything about you interests me. The reason you do some things. The reason why you won't do others.' His choice of words had her throat closing over.

'What do you mean?'

Jonas got to his feet and crossed the uneven ground to stand before her. 'Simply this. It isn't that you don't love me. It isn't that you can't love me. The fact is, you won't allow yourself to love me. Why? You were prepared to, until the day of the accident. What happened? What did Lori's mother say to you that made you change your mind?'

Aimi was finding it difficult to breathe, she was so tense. 'It doesn't matter what she said,' she bit out tersely, but Jonas shook his head.

'Oh, no, darling, that's wrong. It does matter. Whatever she said turned you from the warm, loving woman I know you to be, into someone I barely recognised. Don't let her do it.'

She laughed, a harsh sound that made his blood run cold. 'Don't you get it? It isn't her, it's me!'

'What did *you* do?'

Aimi shook her head, closing her eyes against the remembered pain. 'I forgot.'

Jonas took her by the shoulders, expecting her to try and shrug him off, but she didn't. 'What did you forget, Aimi?' he asked softly, with all the precision of a skilled surgeon. 'That Lori was dead, or that you weren't supposed to be glad you were alive?'

To Aimi, hearing her secret thoughts voiced aloud,

it was as if a huge wave of cold water had washed over her, taking away all the oxygen. In the next instant, she took in a deep, rasping breath as if coming up for air.

'Why should I be glad?' she gasped faintly, shaking her head to try and clear it. 'Why should I be happy, when Lori's dead?'

'Why shouldn't you be?' he countered instantly, and she stared at him helplessly. 'How long is this penance going to go on?' Jonas asked next, taking the strength out of her knees, so they barely held her up.

'What penance?'

Jonas looked quite grim. 'Aimi, you've been living your life as if two people died on that mountain nine years ago, but only one did. I'm sorry your friend died, but you're alive, Aimi, and it's time you started really living again.'

'Don't say that!' she cried out, pounding her fist against his chest. 'Don't you understand? I killed Lori! I killed my best friend!'

'The avalanche killed her, not you,' he corrected in a flash.

Her eyes were wild with a mixture of anger and pain. 'She wouldn't have been there but for me! She always did what I said!'

Jonas's gaze bored into her. 'Then why didn't she follow you that day?'

The question confused her. 'What do you mean?'

'There was another witness to what happened, remember? You got to safety in plenty of time. If she had followed you, she would have been safe. Why didn't she?' He gave her a firm shake. 'Why, Aimi?'

Aimi blinked, trying to think. 'I...I don't know,' she said hoarsely, but Jonas wasn't having that.

'You do know. Lori didn't always do what you said, did she? Your mother told me she was a little spoilt and wilful. Why didn't she follow you?'

A picture flashed into her mind of Lori, not trying to ski to the other side of the avalanche as Aimi always saw her, but skiing down at an angle ahead of the boiling snow. 'She was trying to outrun it!' she gasped out at last. 'Oh, my God! Lori, you fool!'

The strength did go out of her then and she collapsed against Jonas, who gathered her up as if she weighed nothing at all. He said nothing more, but carried her back through the trees to the cottage, where he deposited her on the couch and wrapped a blanket around her.

'I'll make a cup of tea,' he said gently, running his hand over her hair before going into the other room.

Aimi could hear him moving about as she sat there in a state of shock. All these years she had lived with the knowledge of her guilt, and yet now she realised that Lori had been as much at fault as she had been. Neither of them should have been on those slopes but, when danger had come, Lori should have run for cover. She had had time. Instead, she had chosen to fly in the face of it, and had paid the price.

Jonas returned with two mugs of tea. He handed her one and she clasped her chilly fingers around it, needing the warmth. 'How do you feel?' he asked her as he sat at the other end of the couch, watching her carefully.

'Shaky,' she admitted. 'I'd forgotten what she did. I thought I was to blame.'

'That's what guilt does. You knew you were in the wrong, so you took on all the blame. Lori took a risk that day, and paid for it. But you've been paying for it ever since. It's time to let go.'

Aimi looked at him, tears welling up and running down her cheeks. 'How can I, when the original fault was mine? I should never have suggested we do it.'

'No, you shouldn't,' Jonas agreed softly. 'You were young and foolish, and the outcome was tragic. It may be the hardest thing you will ever have to do, my love, but you have to learn to forgive yourself. Until you do that, it really won't matter if anyone else does.'

A sob escaped her and more tears spilt over, tracking their paths down to her chin. 'How do I do that?'

'By being easier on yourself. By accepting that you're human and capable of making mistakes. By knowing that those people who love you will never abandon you, no matter what you do. I'm here for you, Aimi. There's nothing you can tell me that will make me love you less. It's OK to be alive, darling.'

Aimi cried then. Deep, racking sobs that shook her body. Jonas took her mug and set it down with his, then moved so that he could take her in his arms and hold her close whilst she let out all the sadness within her. Finally the tears subsided, and she sighed wistfully.

'I miss her,' she confided in a small voice, and Jonas smoothed his hand up and down her arm.

'Of course you do. She was your best friend,' he responded gently. 'Your mother said you never cried like this.'

'I couldn't. The tears just wouldn't come.'

'So you cried in your sleep, when your defences were down, instead.' He made the logical jump easily.

Aimi sighed again, feeling all the accumulated tension of nine years falling away from her. 'Probably. I don't really remember. All I knew was that I had to change. I wanted to be a better person. Someone I wouldn't be ashamed of.'

Jonas put a finger beneath her chin and tipped her head up so that he could see her face. 'You are a good person, Aimi. Never let anyone tell you differently.'

She caught his hand and brought it up to cup her cheek. 'I wasn't always. That's why I couldn't allow myself to have anything Lori couldn't. I didn't think I deserved to be happy.'

'No one deserves it more. You've done more than was ever required of you, darling. Nobody would deny you the right to happiness.'

She shivered as a shadow passed over her. 'Mrs Ashurst would,' she argued and saw a grim look set about his eyes and mouth.

'Lori's mother? I found a birthday card in your kitchen which must have come from her. How long has she been sending them?'

'Every year.'

Jonas looked as if he would like to do murder. 'My God, no wonder you were never able to deal with your guilt—she never let you forget, even for a moment!'

'Don't be angry with her. I never let myself forget. I just knew I had to make up for what I did,' Aimi soothed, touching his lips to stop the flow of words.

His expression softened as he looked at her, and finally he smiled and let out a deep breath. 'I'm angry because I almost lost you. You've more than made up for the past, Aimi. Now you have to look to the future. To us. Our happiness. Can you do that?'

She smiled back at him, at last allowing the love she felt for him to shine from her eyes. 'Yes. I've wanted to—so much. It was when I knew I had fallen in love with you that my conscience resurrected itself and stopped me in my tracks. Then the card came, and I was torn. I didn't want to lose you, but there was still my promise to Lori. I went to see her mother, hoping she would finally forgive me, but I guess she never will.'

Jonas shook his head. 'No, she won't, and she wants you to live in purgatory, too. But ask yourself this, Aimi. Would Lori want you to do that, or would she tell you to get on with your life?'

Aimi considered that, seeing in her mind's eye her friend's laughing face. Lori had always loved life, had been eager for the future. She would have urged Aimi to grasp it, too. 'She would have wanted me to be happy. To follow my heart.'

'Then that is what you should do, don't you think?' Jonas urged her to agree, and she nodded.

'Yes, it is.'

'In which case, I have to ask you a very important question. Will you marry me, Aimi Carteret?'

Looking deeply into his eyes, Aimi could see the hope and the fear he was feeling. He hoped she would say yes, but feared she might still say no. For her part, Aimi at last had no doubts. She might have moments of sadness over her friend but, with Jonas's help, she knew she would never again feel weighed down by blame. So her answer was simple.

'Yes, I will marry you, Jonas. How could I do anything else, when you've given me my life back, and I love you so much?'

Jonas closed his eyes for a moment and let out a heartfelt sigh. When he looked at her next, his blue eyes were ablaze with a quite stunning depth of emotion. 'Thank you. I'll make sure you never regret it.'

Aimi slipped her arms around his neck and hugged him tightly. She hadn't known this man long, but it felt as if she had always known him. He was the missing half that made everything right. 'I'm sorry I hurt you when I said I wouldn't see you,' she whispered in his ear, and one of the hands he had used to hold her rose to cup the back of her head.

'I think my brother and sister would tell you it was a lesson I needed to learn,' he returned wryly. 'The thought of losing you was…terrifying.'

'Well, you haven't lost me. I'm here for good,' she told him, easing back so that he could see just how much she meant it. 'I didn't intend to fall in love with you, but I'm so glad I did.'

His smile was half wicked, half sensual. 'Amen to that,' he agreed, and kissed her.

THE BRITISH
BILLIONAIRE'S
INNOCENT BRIDE

BY
SUSANNE JAMES

Susanne James has enjoyed creative writing since childhood, completing her first—sadly unpublished—novel by the age of twelve. She has three grown-up children who were, and are, her pride and joy, and who all live happily in Oxfordshire with their families. She was always happy to put the needs of her family before her ambition to write seriously, although along the way some published articles for magazines and newspapers helped to keep the dream alive!

Susanne's big regret is that her beloved husband is no longer here to share the pleasure of her recent success. She now shares her life with Toffee, her young Cavalier King Charles spaniel, who decides when it's time to get up (early) and when a walk in the park is overdue!

For all my friends and their lovely dogs
who walk with Toffee and me each day in Alice Park

CHAPTER ONE

On a fine July morning Lily got out of the taxi at Heathrow and, after paying the driver, trundled her overnight case towards the entrance.

Her emotions were a strange mix of regret and relief that her contract with Bella and Rosie's family had ended. She'd only been nanny to the eight-year-old twins for a year, but it had been long enough for her to know that she'd made a mistake at trying her hand at this particular occupation. Child-minding was not for her—even though, towards the end, she'd begun to establish a much better relationship with the over-indulged children. Had begun to like them and feel sorry for them—their mother, a single parent, had very little time for them, which was hard on the children. But it was not what she wanted to do with her life. She was honest in admitting that her own background was probably responsible for her sense of inadequacy, and sometimes feeling out of her depth.

Fortunately she'd saved up enough money so that she could afford to be unemployed for a short time while she took stock of her situation. She would easily be able to afford the mortgage on her tiny one-bedroom flat in an unremarkable Berkshire town, and knew that with her cookery diploma she could walk into another job within the hour at any of the countless hotels and restaurants in London if she wanted to. But she was restless, feeling the need for a change but not knowing how to bring it about, so she'd decided to have a couple of days in Rome and visit her brother Sam, who part-owned a small hotel there.

She checked in and was delighted at being upgraded to business class as the flight was overbooked. In the queue waiting to board the aircraft, she glanced at her ticket. She'd booked a seat next to the window—not because she enjoyed watching take-off and landing, but because it seemed to offer a greater chance of not being disturbed on the journey by people who were intent on relaying their life story to anyone who would listen.

As they all waited to board, Lily noted that almost everyone—as usual—was casually dressed, mostly in jeans and holiday wear. For some reason she'd chosen her fine grey suit and a white shirt, together with sheer black tights and high heels, for the journey. Perhaps that was why she had been lucky enough to get bumped up to business class.

At last they all filed on board, and Lily edged her way along the aisle, glancing upwards until she located her seat number. The row was still unoccupied, so she didn't have to ask anyone to get up, and she took her place, glancing idly out of the window at all the activity outside.

After a moment she was suddenly aware of the arrival of the person who would be sitting next to her and, turning her head quickly, found herself gazing up— very far up—into the dark eyes of the most handsome man she'd ever come across in her twenty-six years. He pushed his hand luggage into the overhead compartment and slammed it shut, then sat down and glanced across at her. 'Morning,' he said, non-committally.

Lily coloured up to the roots of her hair, and was conscious of her usual feeling of anxiousness. Her heart was gathering pace rapidly, and the feeling of being trapped was threatening to overwhelm her.

'Oh—hi—' she said, trying to match his lazy attitude and failing miserably. Why should it matter that she was going to be sitting this close to someone like him for a couple of hours? He didn't look the sort who would want to make small talk all the way. His powerfully authoritative manner was obvious at once, and his strong profile and determined chin sent a shiver down her spine. He was formally dressed, in a dark well-cut suit, gleaming shirt and plain blue tie, his black hair was immaculately styled. Why couldn't he have been a portly, elderly, kindly type, instead of this undeniably sexy individual who, Lily was aware, was attracting covetous glances from adjacent females?

He shifted his long legs slightly, trying to make himself more comfortable in the restricted space, then turned to glance at her, noting her stylish appearance, the rather sweet heart-shaped face, the wavy fair hair piled elegantly on top, giving her a brisk, businesslike air. Then he stared past her out of the window, feeling momentarily disturbed inside. And after a second or two, he knew why. It was the first time he had noticed a woman since Elspeth had died.

It had been over a year now—quite long enough for anyone to adjust. But immediately the mental picture of his wife made him think of his three children—his two sons and Freya—who, at nine years old, was so like

Elspeth, with her glossy brown hair and hazel eyes. He frowned slightly as he thought of his daughter. She was the difficult one—the one he didn't seem to have the same rapport with as he had with the boys, he realised. And because of that he'd reluctantly agreed to Freya's request that she should be a weekly boarder at her school, to be with her best friends. He'd been determined to try and keep them all together, a close family, and this move had seemed to dent that somewhat. But he'd finally agreed, and he had to admit that life had become a bit easier without his daughter's occasional difficult temperament to deal with. And the weekends, when the family was complete, were usually trouble-free.

Thankfully, soon they were loaded and ready for take-off, and as the aircraft began bumping rapidly along the runway, Lily caught her breath, her knuckles white as she gripped the arms of her seat.

Feeling her tense, he looked across at her. 'Does this bit bother you?' he asked mildly, and she was surprised at the question, because it indicated a concern for her. Why should a complete stranger care how she felt? About anything? But those few words sent an unexpected rush of warmth through her, and she smiled up at him quickly.

'No, of course not,' she lied. 'I'm fine.'

He raised one eyebrow briefly, clearly not believing her, but said no more, and in a few minutes they were airborne. People began undoing their seat belts, and Lily's companion immediately got up to retrieve his briefcase from the locker above them. Good. He was obviously going to be deep in paperwork. There'd be no need for pointless conversation. He took out a folder, then shut the case firmly—giving Lily a brief glimpse of the name on the identity panel.

'Theodore Montague', she read. That was all, but it fitted the man exactly. He couldn't have been called anything else! But what a handle! Would anyone ever dare shorten it? Did his nearest and dearest call him 'Theo' or 'Ted'? Somehow she doubted it.

Leaning forward, she pulled out a magazine from her holdall, flicking the pages idly She was seldom able to read anything worthwhile on journeys. She couldn't believe how some people could get stuck into a novel, much less concentrate on important matters—as the man next to her was obviously doing…

Presently the chink of cups and spoons announced the arrival of the refreshment trolley, and Lily thought that a cup of coffee would be more than welcome— she'd not eaten any breakfast before she'd left home. A flight attendant came alongside them and gazed down at Theodore Montague, clearly captivated, flickering her false eyelashes at him coquettishly before asking him what he wanted. He turned to Lily.

'What would you like?' he asked, his deeply intense eyes looking straight into her smoky-blue ones, and once again she was touched by his consideration. No one had ever bothered to put her first in these circumstances, she thought.

'Oh—just a black coffee, please,' she replied quickly. 'No sugar…thank you.'

'Snap,' he said easily, and for the first time she saw the uncompromising lips part in a brief smile, giving a glimpse of strong white teeth. He looked up at the attendant. 'Then that's two black coffees, please,' he said casually.

As they sipped the scalding liquid, he looked across at her. 'You don't like in-flight food, either?' he asked.

'Oh, I expect it's quite nice,' Lily replied, 'but in these

cramped conditions, and with everything shrink-wrapped in plastic, I find my appetite disappears straight away.'

'My own thinking exactly,' he said. 'Anyway, on short flights food is hardly an imperative, is it?'

So…they *were* beginning to make conversation—and for once Lily felt totally at ease. With no trouble at all he seemed to have completely disarmed her, and she relaxed in her seat.

'I can't think that either of us are on holiday,' he murmured. His eyes ran the length of her body and back again to meet her gaze. 'We seem to be the only passengers not wearing jeans and T-shirts.'

'Actually, I'm going to visit my brother in Rome for a few days. He part-owns a hotel there,' Lily said. 'And I've got some thinking to do,' she added. Now, why had she said that? she asked herself crossly. It was the sort of thing that would invite him to question her. But he didn't. He gave her a long, slow look, and she had the awful suspicion that he could read her mind and knew all about her already! Which was silly.

'And you—you're not on holiday?' she asked tentatively.

'Grief, no—I've a seminar to attend. I managed to avoid it last year, but I'm due to give a paper this time, so there's no getting out of it I'm afraid. Still…' He smiled that devastating half-smile again. 'I'm sure I'll survive. Rome is a good place to spend a few days—for whatever reason.'

There was a companionable silence between them for a while as the aircraft droned on.

'What's the seminar about?' Lily asked curiously, suddenly wanting to know more about the man, what he did. Would it be marketing? Public relations? Something important in the City? She was surprised at his reply.

'I spend my life thinking about children,' he said casually. 'I lecture in paediatrics, which is all very well, but it means that I don't get to spend much time on the shop floor, so to speak.' He shrugged. 'Still, you can't do everything, and I'm apparently deemed more use on the lecture circuit at the moment.' He paused. 'I expect that will change in due course. Life never stays the same for long, I find.' He pressed his lips together tightly.

Who could ever have imagined the nightmarish situation that had taken his beautiful wife from him so tragically? That an unidentifiable virus would end her life so dramatically, so unexpectedly? It had taught him not to look too far ahead, or to take life for granted.

Lily sensed his change of mood at once, and it made her want to tell him about herself, about things… 'Well, *I'm* hoping to change my life in some way,' she said, 'but I don't really know how to.' She paused. 'I did a cookery course after I left school, which was OK—but I got sick of cooking for other people all the time, even though it was good experience in London hotels and clubs… Last year I thought I'd have a go at nannying…' She shuddered. 'It was not a good move. I think I was unlucky with the family who employed me—very spoiled eight-year-old twin girls. They were awful. But so was I,' she added truthfully. 'They ran rings round me, and I just didn't know how to handle the difficult situations that seemed to crop up on a daily basis. I was beginning to get more switched on by the end of the contract, but not enough for me to contemplate pursuing that particular career any further.' She sighed. 'You have to live in order to learn, don't you?' she said wistfully. 'I'd have loved to love Bella and Rosie, and I did try. But I don't think they wanted to love me.'

He had not taken his eyes from her face as she'd been speaking, and he nodded slowly. 'Everyone hits the buffers at some time in their lives,' he said. 'And all experience—even hurtful experience—teaches us something, I suppose.' He opened the folder on his knees again. 'I do hope you find what you're looking for,' he added quietly.

'It's brilliant to see you again, Lily!'

Lily smiled across the table at her brother, feeling a glow of sisterly affection sweep over her. They were sitting in Agata & Romeo, a bottle-lined restaurant near the main station in Rome, and had just dined on delicious broccoli and pasta in skate soup—one of the many delicacies on the menu. As she spooned up the last mouthful, Lily knew that it certainly wouldn't be the last time she tasted it.

'That—was—divine—' she said, sitting back. 'I was really hungry.'

'Talking of things divine,' Sam said, as he topped up Lily's glass with the rest of the wine. 'Who was the bloke you came off the plane with? Drop-dead gorgeous, or what? He seemed very…attentive as he helped you with your stuff,' he added.

Lily looked away, forcing herself to keep the ever-ready blush from her cheeks.

'Just the man who happened to be sitting in the adjoining seat on the plane,' she said casually.

'Really? There was something…something that suggested a certain familiarity, I thought,' Sam said, looking at Lily curiously. 'I really thought there was something going on there.'

'Don't be silly,' Lily said, picking up the menu to see

what else she'd like. 'I've never met him before. He was just someone…interesting to talk to, that's all.'

Sam said no more—he knew from his short acquaintance with his sister that when she decided a subject was closed, it was closed.

Thinking about it, Lily admitted to being surprised at how short the flight had seemed. She and her neighbor had managed to make light, undemanding conversation for much of the way—during which he'd mentioned that he had three children. He'd also spent some time absorbed in his papers, and she'd been careful not to interrupt him. She'd been genuinely surprised when their approaching landing had been announced.

After a minute, Sam said, 'Is there anything else you'd like, Lily? A cappuccino will do me, but choose away. I want to spoil you.' He paused, thinking how beautiful Lily was. 'I don't get the chance to do that very often, do I?' he went on. 'We really must make an effort to get together more—twice a year is nothing, and now that we've found each other we mustn't waste it.' He leaned across and covered her hand with his briefly. 'Promise that we will manage it somehow, Lily.'

Lily looked back at him, her large eyes warm and moist with almost-tears. Putting down the menu, she turned her palm to hold his fingers tightly. 'You're right, Sam,' she said quietly. 'We must make some dates and stick to them. It's not good enough to let work come first all the time—and, speaking of which, how's the hotel going?' she asked. 'You look very affluent.' She smiled, noting his well-cut trousers and designer open-neck shirt, exhibiting his tanned skin.

'Work's good,' he said. 'A bit too good. That's why

Federico and I don't have time to go chasing girls—or sisters,' he added.

Sitting there with her long-lost brother—two years older than her, attractively open-faced, with his brown hair bleached golden by the Italian sunshine—Lily felt her heart soar, and she felt so ridiculously light-headed she wanted to laugh out loud, to jump up and tell everyone how happy she was. Of course it had to be the wine—or was it simply Rome, with its perfect weather, its magical fountains and warm-hearted people, and the scent of jasmine in the air which had filled her nostrils as they'd wandered along the streets earlier? Or was it because at last she belonged to someone—really belonged to the good-looking man who was holding her hand?

'Do you realise that two years ago neither of us knew of each other's existence?' Sam said. 'All that wasted time when we could have been together,' he added quietly.

Of course Lily realised it. And it was thanks to her seeking out her past—with help from the Salvation Army—that she'd eventually discovered she had a sibling. Their now-deceased mother had borne them both before she herself was seventeen years old.

Lily was honest enough to admit that her ignorance of her early life was probably her own fault... She'd been a rebellious, difficult child, passed from one home to another, one foster family to another—and she'd run away twice. It was no wonder everyone had got confused, including the agencies responsible for her welfare. Her personal details had seemed permanently lost somewhere in the system, and by the time she'd reached sixteen and gone on to train at catering college everyone had been glad to be shot of her. But Lily had an instinctive sense of survival, and had worked hard at the course, and at the jobs she'd subsequently got, finally revelling in the purchase of her tiny flat, her first very own private space, where no one could tell her what to do. At last she was in charge of her own life, her own destiny. And that was how it was going to stay. Always.

Sam, apparently, had been different. He'd told Lily how happy he'd been growing up, behaving himself and always doing as he was told by his foster carers. But he hadn't known, either, that he had any family. When he and Lily had come face to face at last their blood tie had swallowed up those lost years and they'd fallen into each other's arms with hardly any self-consciousness.

'I think a coffee is all I can manage, too, Sam,' Lily said now. 'I don't think I'll be able to eat another thing for the rest of the day.'

'Oh, you'll make room for supper later,' Sam assured her. 'No one eats here until nine or ten o'clock in any case. There'll be plenty of time for you to work up an appetite.'

After lunch they sauntered back along the sun-hot pavements, searching out the cool shade of buildings to walk beneath whenever they could.

'I think I'll pamper myself and have a siesta this afternoon,' Lily said.

'Good idea. And I've some paperwork to go through with Federico, so that'll suit us both,' Sam replied easily.

The small hotel—with a mere four bedrooms—was situated in a narrow lane just off Piazza Navona, and Lily had been allocated a chic room at the front. It was well-appointed and comfortable, and she flopped down on the bed, kicking off her sandals and laying back languidly. She'd changed out of her suit as soon as she'd arrived, and was wondering whether the small amount of clothes she'd brought was going to see her through her three-night stay. She shrugged happily. If she ran out of clothes she'd buy some more! She'd never been an extravagant shopper—she'd never had the money—but, hey, she was on holiday, and she was in Rome! There were no frontiers, nothing to hold back her glorious sense of freedom.

To her amazement, when she woke up Lily realized that she'd been asleep for nearly three hours! She hadn't come here to sleep, she thought. She'd come here to enjoy herself, to explore Rome—as well, of course, as meeting up with her brother.

Sliding off the bed, she went into the bathroom to shower. Although Sam's hotel was air-conditioned, there was a distinct sense of the pervading sultry heat outside, so choosing what to wear would be easy. She'd put on the cream cotton sleeveless sundress with the low neck, she decided. It wouldn't matter if it was still a bit creased—although she'd hung it up as soon as she'd arrived—because who was going to notice her, anyway?

She dressed and brushed out her hair, tying it back in a ponytail. Then she moisturised her face, adding sunblock but no make-up. She knew she was lucky with her complexion which, although fair-skinned, seemed to have an olive under-layer which saved her from burning or freckling. She added just a touch of blusher and lipstick and went downstairs.

There was no sign of her brother, but Federico was on duty, and he came over at once to greet her with the typical approach of the Italian male when meeting a woman. He took her hand and kissed it gently, looking down at her appreciatively with his dusky, bedroom eyes.

'Ah…Lileeeee,' he murmured in his heavily accented English. 'What a charming pleasure to 'ave you to stay here. You are so…beautiful.' He paused. 'You look—wonderful.'

'Thank you, Federico,' Lily said lightly. How could you take these people seriously? she thought. He'd be saying the same to every one of his female guests. Yet she automatically smiled back, responding to his compliments. At least *he* wasn't pretending to be someone he wasn't. What you saw was what you got—a red-blooded Latin male, with no nasty surprises in his temperament and a straightforward, lusty appreciation of the female sex. He made Lily feel feminine, and desirable. And because of his openness, he was totally unthreatening.

Still holding her hand to his lips, Federico said, 'I'm so sorry…Sam is—unwell. He is lying down. Head,' he added, touching his forehead. 'He asks you to see him later tonight.'

'Oh, poor Sam,' Lily said, remembering that her brother was prone to migraines—as she herself was. 'Tell him not to worry, Federico. I'm going off to explore, and I'm quite happy being by myself,' she added, as he went to object. 'Tell Sam I'll see him in the morning.'

People were starting to mill about again in the evening sunshine as Lily wandered around. She'd only been here twice before, but it felt surprisingly familiar as she drank in the atmosphere. She stopped idly from time to time, to watch some artists at work, before buying herself a large vanilla ice-cream. She licked at it appreciatively as she sauntered along. It had to be the most delicious confection known to man, she thought, as the creamy substance coated her tongue and slid down, cooling her throat. The Italians certainly knew how to make the stuff.

Presently she came to the Trevi Fountain, and sat down on a nearby seat to watch the huge gush of water stream from its natural spring. The evening sun shone on the spectacle, lighting up the whole picture like an elaborate stage set, and Lily found herself daydreaming as she sat there, her hands clasped in her lap.

Suddenly a light tap on her arm made her turn quickly.

'Hello, there. What are you doing here all by yourself?'

Theodore Montague was standing there, looking down at her, and Lily felt her throat constrict as she gazed up at him.

'Oh—hello—' she said uncertainly. Well, was it really any surprise that they should meet? she asked herself. Rome wasn't that big a place. She moved over to make room for him to sit down.

He was wearing white trousers and a dark open-neck shirt, his bare feet thrust into strong brown sandals, and Lily felt her heart fluttering anxiously in the usual way. Yet it wasn't exactly anxiety that she was feeling, she thought. It was something else—something she'd never actually felt before—and she wanted to push it away. But somehow she couldn't, so she let the sensation wash over her until, hopefully, it would melt away.

They sat there for several moments without saying anything until he murmured, 'Magical, isn't it?' He turned to look at her briefly. 'Why is moving water so mesmerising?'

'I think that everything here is just magical,' Lily said. 'The weather plays a part, though, of course. Why can't we have some of this in England?'

'It's certainly perfect tonight,' he agreed. 'Though next month might be just a tad too hot.' He paused. 'You could presumably come here to live, if you wanted to?' he suggested. 'Maybe it's the change you're looking for. You said that your brother already lives here, so…'

'No, I have no plans to live abroad,' Lily said at once. 'Perhaps one day I will change my mind, but not yet. I feel that my…fate—whatever it is—lies in England.' She smiled as she looked up at him. 'That doesn't sound very enterprising or ambitious, does it?'

He hesitated for a moment before turning to her properly, holding out his hand. 'Look—this is silly. Why don't we introduce ourselves? I'm Theo Montague— and you know why I'm here…'

'And I'm Lily Patterson,' Lily said quickly, taking his hand briefly. 'And you know why *I'm* here.'

He nodded. 'That's better. I don't care for nameless faces,' he said. 'So…go on telling me about yourself, Lily. You mentioned ambitions. *Are* you ambitious?'

'I think I am,' she said slowly. 'But, as I said before, I don't really know where my ambitions lie. Do I want to go on in catering? Maybe secure an appointment with a wealthy family in a lovely house somewhere in the country, so that I can sit in the garden in the afternoons and paint…?'

'So—you like to paint?'

'Yes, though I don't do it very well—yet. But I'm practising. And I'd love to learn to play the piano. I had some lessons once, when I was a child, but they sort of…stopped…and I never took it up again.'

They'd stopped because at the time, she had been living in one of the homes she'd run away from, she reminded herself.

'I think most children are guilty of that,' he said. 'Starting things and not wanting to go on with them.' He was thinking of Freya as he spoke, who seemed to have lost interest in most things since her mother had died.

There was quite a long silence after that, but Lily realised that she hadn't felt so comfortable, or secure, or so plain contented for a long time. She was painfully aware of Theo's elegant legs stretched out in front of him—the strong, masculine thighs evident beneath the fine cotton of his trousers, the well-kept, unblemished brown toes protruding from his sandals—and she checked herself hurriedly. These thoughts weren't part of her life plan. They weren't part of anything to do with her at all. Suddenly she wanted to go back and see how Sam was feeling.

'I ought to go and see how my brother is,' she said, standing up. 'He crashed out with a migraine after we'd had lunch. He was going to take me somewhere for supper, but…'

As soon as she'd said the words Lily could have kicked herself. She'd fed him the line—and he took it.

'Well—why don't you let me buy you supper instead?' he said. 'Your first night in Rome shouldn't be spent alone.'

'Oh—I don't really think—' Lily began, but he cut in.

'Look, why don't you ring to find out how your brother is—whether he's well enough to take you out? If he isn't, I'm sure he'd be happy to think you were being taken care of. Besides,' Theo added, 'I don't much like eating by myself.'

That would have been the perfect pick-up line, Lily thought, had it been said by anyone other than the man sitting next to her. But she knew it wasn't.

Doing as he said, she rang the hotel from her mobile, to be told by Federico that Sam was still in bed and unlikely to surface before morning. She ended the call and looked at Theo.

'Sam is still out of it, I'm afraid,' she said. 'But wouldn't you rather…? I mean, wouldn't some of your colleagues be more interesting company than me?'

'They certainly would not,' he said lightly. 'We'll have quite enough of each other during the day. The evenings are free, thank goodness, to do what we like with. So—' he grinned down at her '—let me show you some of the places I've been to before, and you can choose which one you like the look of.'

His teeth were almost blindingly white as he smiled, and the face which on first impression had seemed serious and somewhat formidable to Lily now exhibited a heart-throbbingly purposeful expression, indicating someone strong, reliable…and utterly captivating. The sort of man she might one day paint riding on a white charger to rescue damsels in distress.

Lily choked back her disbelief at her own thoughts. Rome was a mad place! It was making *her* mad! That, or she had a bad touch of the sun…

CHAPTER TWO

THEY left the piazza, walking side by side with plenty of space between them as they strolled along. The jostling crowds were an eclectic bunch—families, middle-aged couples wandering hand in hand, and lovers oblivious to anyone but themselves, who stopped at regular intervals to indulge in passionate kissing. At first Lily felt acutely embarrassed when they had to side-step an amorous couple, though it wouldn't have mattered if she'd been on her own, she thought. But witnessing it with Theodore Montague there as well seemed to put a different aspect on everything. He, however, appeared not to notice or care what was going on around them.

He looked down at her. 'I expect your brother has already introduced you to most of the sights, the tourist must-sees?' he enquired.

'Some,' Lily replied. 'But there's plenty I haven't seen—and lots I'd like to visit again.' She stopped to let a small child dash between them as he ran to keep up with his parents. 'Sam never seems to have a great deal of time to spend with me when I visit—he and Federico, his business partner, work so hard, and I understand that he must fit me in when he can.' She looked up and smiled. 'I don't mind. I'm used to sorting myself out alone. It's just lovely to be here with him now and again—to catch up.'

Would they ever manage to catch up? Lily thought. There were so many years to talk about—so many things to explain and discuss. Would one lifetime be enough?

After a few minutes, Theo said, 'It's a bit later than I thought—and I'm getting hungry. Perhaps you'd let me decide where we're going to eat? I promise you won't be disappointed.'

Lily didn't need convincing about that. 'Wherever we go will be fine by me,' she said casually.

'The place I have in mind boasts a panoramic vista of the city—so we'll have two for the price of one,' Theo said. 'Excellent food, and a view as well.'

He was right. And presently, sitting opposite him at a candlelit table, Lily wondered if she was dreaming. This was the stuff of fairy tales, she thought—to be here in this timeless city, on an evening so balmy that there was no need for a shawl to cover her bare neck and shoulders, even if she'd brought one with her that night, and to be sharing delicious food with the handsome Mr Theodore Montague… Not that his appearance made the slightest difference to her, of course, but it was impossible to ignore the glances he attracted from any woman who spotted him. He was after all the quintessential human male that artists and sculptors liked to fashion. He could have been the model for Bernini's *Apollo* himself, Lily thought, smiling briefly at the thought.

While Theo chose swordfish for his meal, Lily selected equally delicious veal wrapped in ham and dressed with sage. For a few minutes they said nothing as they ate.

'You don't drink, then?' he asked, as he refilled Lily's glass with sparkling water, before drinking some of the red wine he'd chosen.

'Not often,' Lily said carefully, privately adding to herself, Not with anyone she didn't really know. And, after all, she *didn't* know him—not in any real sense. Of course it was different drinking with Sam…he was the only man she'd ever been able to feel completely at ease with—and she'd had to wait a long time to experience that, she thought ruefully.

Theo had been watching her covertly as she finished the last of the food on her plate, finding himself really liking his dining companion. The cream dress she was wearing showed off her light suntan to perfection, and her fair hair shone with health. Her eyes were cast down as she ate, and he observed how long her lashes were, unusually dark and moist as they rested on her cheeks. He swallowed, picking up his glass, searching for a word that might describe her—but he couldn't readily find one. She had a sort of diffident air, yet there was an undeniable strength apparent just below the surface. The way she occasionally raised her chin as she spoke indicated a force to be reckoned with at times, he thought. Was she a trustworthy type? Almost certainly. Shy? Not exactly—but not very forthcoming, either. Loyal? From some of the things she'd said her brother obviously meant an enormous amount to her. There was an almost child-like love and regard for him. Theo liked that.

He cleared his throat. 'So—let's talk about your plans for the future,' he said briefly, in a way that he hoped wouldn't appear intrusive. 'In spite of what you've said, I feel sure you've got some good ideas floating around.'

Lily looked across at him, the soft candlelight en-

hancing the delicate shape of her face. 'No, I haven't—
not yet,' she replied honestly. 'I'm waiting for some inspiration—but so far nothing.' She smiled. 'I can't wait
for ever, of course,' she admitted. 'My funds will keep
me going for a month or two, but not for much longer.'
She stopped what she was saying abruptly. This man
was a stranger, she reminded herself again. Or nearly. Be
careful. Don't get close. Don't let him get close.

She sat back, steeling herself not to become enrap-
tured with the situation she was in—the atmosphere, the
company…and the penetrating blackness of those eyes
which seemed to enter her very soul. 'Tell me about your
children,' she said firmly. 'You said you've got three?'

He paused for a moment before replying. 'Yes. Tom
is three, Alexander is five, and Freya is nine.'

'Your wife must have her hands full,' Lily said lightly.

'My wife—Elspeth—is dead,' he said flatly, not
looking at her as he spoke, his gaze fixed somewhere
over her shoulder into the far distance. 'Fourteen months
ago she succumbed to a virus and was gone in three
days.' His expression was impassive as he spoke, but
those dark windows of his soul said it all, becoming
blacker and even more intense as he relived the ordeal.

Lily felt a huge wave of compassion sweep over her.
What a shock—what a tragedy for anyone to have to
suffer, she thought. She let a moment pass before saying
anything. Then, 'I am…so…sorry,' she said quietly.

He shrugged. 'We're surviving it together, the four
of us,' he remarked briefly. 'Tom and Alex are just
young enough to weather the storm fairly easily—but
Freya…' He sighed and looked at Lily, noting that her
eyes were swimming with unshed tears. 'Freya has
taken it very badly, I'm afraid. There was never any

problem with her when Elspeth was alive—she was a bright, easygoing child—but my daughter seems to have a huge, resentful chip on her shoulder all the time now.'

'That's understandable…' Lily murmured.

'Of course,' he replied quickly. 'And, because of that, when she asked I allowed her to be a weekly boarder at her school, to be with her friends. I must say she seems easier now when she's back home—which she is full-time now, naturally, because it's the school holidays. I know she misses her mother, but I can't take her place, and—well…I'm not sure I understand women,' he added, looking thoughtful for a second.

'Are there grandparents around?' Lily asked.

'No—'fraid not. My parents are dead,' he said slowly. 'They were both well into middle age when I came along…' His lip curled. 'I was probably a very unpleasant surprise.' He shrugged. 'They were both practising doctors with busy lives—I never actually saw too much of them during my childhood.'

So, Lily thought, he might have known his parents, but in essence he'd been almost as alone as she had.

'And Elspeth's parents…?' she ventured hesitantly.

'Her father is alive, but he lives in South Africa. We seldom see him.'

'So—who takes care of the children?' Lily asked. 'When you're at work?'

'Well, of course I've had to employ nannies…though they've seldom been asked to stay overnight.' The strong mouth tightened as he spoke. 'As soon as I come home, I'm the one in charge.'

And how, Lily thought.

'But luckily for me I have Beatrice—or Bea—and her husband,' he went on. 'They live nearby. Bea used to help my wife in the house, and then with the babies as they came along. But she's over seventy, and I don't want to take advantage of her good nature, even though she says she loves helping out. Which she's doing while I'm here,' he added. 'She and Joe move in and sleep over until I come back—the kids adore them. But—as I said—I don't want to wear them out.' He leaned back in his chair, crossing his legs. 'It was a good job we hadn't any more offspring, because three are about as many as I can handle… We'd intended having a much larger family, but—well—fate had other ideas,' he said.

'Well—you may yet have more one day…' Lily began.

'Oh, that won't happen,' Theo replied at once. 'I shan't marry again. That's not on the cards.' He paused for a second. 'I have no plans for myself. The children and their welfare, their future—that's all I care about, all that keeps me going.' Who could ever take the place of his beloved Elspeth? Who would he ever *want* to take her place?

Lily shrugged to herself. He was still young, and a very marriageable prospect for any deserving female, she thought. But it was obvious that his mind was made up, and she somehow knew that he wasn't likely to change it.

Thinking that he'd divulged far more of himself than he ever had before to anyone—certainly not to a random female—Theo leaned forward.

'And you?' he asked. 'D'you have any other siblings?'

'No. It's just Sam and me,' Lily replied. 'Though it would have been nice if there'd been more of us.'

'I'm sure you'll make up for that one day,' he said easily. 'Have lots of kids of your own, and—'

'No. I don't want children,' Lily said bluntly. She paused. 'If you'd seen me with those twins…I just don't think I'm a natural mother, that's all. It wouldn't be fair—to any of us.' And I'm never going to be a natural wife, either, she added silently to herself, recoiling at the thought, remembering her past with something approaching revulsion.

'And your parents—they're obviously still alive…?' he went on, making the presumption as Lily could only be in her early twenties.

Lily's spine began to tingle, and she tore her gaze away from his. She didn't want to discuss any more of her life with anyone—certainly not with him. Yet he had been surprisingly honest about his own position, so she found it difficult to be evasive.

'Our parents are no longer living,' she said. Well, who knew where their father was? 'So, you see, we're both orphans, you and I.' She smiled. 'I can't even remember them.'

'Who brought you up?'

'Oh, an assortment of aunties and uncles,' Lily said, looking away. There was no need to say that she'd been a human reject, despaired of by foster carers. Because it hurt her to think it—even to herself.

Theo looked at her for a long moment, sensing an undercurrent of something he couldn't explain passing between them. She was bright, obviously articulate and intelligent—yet there was something about her that reminded him of Freya. She was sad, too, he thought. Not just about being an orphan, as she'd said, but for other, deeper reasons.

The meal ended rather soberly after all that, and, foregoing dessert, they left the restaurant and walked towards St Peter's. Late as it was, there was still plenty of activity everywhere, and Lily realised that she didn't feel at all tired, but relaxed and happy. And she couldn't put that down to the wine, because she hadn't drunk any since lunchtime… It had to be Rome, she thought. With just a little credit going to the man walking along beside her. Theo had been personal, and personable, all evening, but he had not once stepped over that line of familiarity which was unacceptable. She realised that no man had ever made her feel so…protected…so appreciated. He seemed to enjoy being with her, with not a hint of wanting anything more. She breathed in deeply, silently. It was a relief to feel this secure.

Presently Theo said, 'Perhaps it's time I got you back to your hotel.' He looked down at her. 'If your brother has recovered, he's sure to be wondering where you are by now.'

'Oh, he won't be worried about me,' Lily said at once. 'He knows I'm perfectly capable of taking care of myself.' She hesitated, thinking how smug and self-sufficient that must sound. 'It's just that I've had to stand on my own feet for so long I never expect anyone to feel responsible for me in any way,' she explained. 'And—that's the way I like it,' she added.

He nodded slightly. 'Yes—I can understand that,' he said, thinking that he was in much the same position himself. Ever since he'd become a lone parent he'd had to almost fight off the well-intentioned efforts of various women wanting to help shoulder some of the responsibility. But he'd been determined from the outset that that would not happen. This was his problem, and he was going to solve it himself. And he'd done all right so far, he thought—even if Freya was a continual source of worry to him. But he felt sure that it would all come right one day.

'Your brother's hotel is very well situated,' he re-marked. 'You said it's off Piazza Navona? Couldn't be better.'

'I know,' Lily said. 'So I don't have to look far for entertainment. The hotel is just far enough away from the beaten track to be surprisingly peaceful. I've never lost a night's sleep there yet.'

It didn't take long to get back, and Theo realised, rather disturbingly, that he didn't want the evening to come to an end. He'd enjoyed himself—really enjoyed himself. Since Elspeth had gone, he'd hated eating alone in foreign countries, and he'd been glad of the chance to invite someone other than a professional colleague to have supper with him. It had been a bit of luck that he'd spotted Lily sitting alone by the fountain, and even more lucky that her brother hadn't been well enough to ac-company her. For some reason he felt…lighter—lighter in spirit than he had for fourteen months. But of course the reason for that was quite clear. He'd been on a mission—even if he hadn't been aware of that at first. A project had presented itself, and projects were what kept him going these days. The fact was that he liked Lily— liked the woman's company. She didn't grate on his nerves, which was often the case now, when he was with a member of the opposite sex. And subconsciously a plan had been forming in his mind, without him knowing it. Why else had he quite shamelessly been assessing her all the evening—assessing her character, sizing her up?

Just as they approached the lighted entrance to her hotel, he stopped, forcing Lily to halt her steps. She looked up at him, smiling quickly.

'Well, thank you, thanks a lot for that lovely meal, Theo,' she began.

'No—thank you—for agreeing to come with me tonight,' he said seriously, waiting for the right words, the right moment to continue. 'Actually, Lily, I've been wondering whether you'd…' he began.

Lily presumed that he was going to suggest they meet up again while they were in Rome. But she was here to be with her brother—they only had another two days, after all. She'd have to think of a diplomatic refusal, she thought.

'No—I'm sorry…I really must be entirely free for Sam. We have such a short time here together,' she said, 'and we've not seen each other since last year.'

He smiled down into her upturned face. 'No—no, of course. I wouldn't dream of intruding upon any more of your holiday,' he said. 'It's not that.'

'Oh?' Lily said, immediately feeling foolish and frowning slightly. 'Well…what is it, then?'

Unusually for him, Theo had difficulty finding words, but then he managed to come out with what he had to say in his normal forthright manner.

'Would you… Would you step in and look after the boys for me—just for a few weeks?' he asked. 'I did notice from the address on your luggage earlier that we live in the same town… I'm between nannies at the moment, and I'm in a bit of a fix. I loathe the thought of interviewing yet more girls who seldom turn out as I'd hoped. It would just be for a short time,' he added quickly. 'Not a long-term commitment, but it would give me time to—well, to regroup…while you make up your mind about *your* future. It would be just a temporary thing, I assure you. The children will be back at school in a month or so, so you'd have plenty of time for yourself to make plans, write off for interviews, make telephone calls and stuff… And I pay well over the going rate for the job,' he added, almost afraid to hear her reaction to his request.

Lily sank down on to the low stone wall skirting the entrance of the hotel and looked up at him, amazed at what he'd asked. 'Do you honestly believe that I could be up to the task?' she said. 'I've told you—I don't think I'm any good with children. If you're looking for Mary Poppins, you've come to the wrong person.'

'I'm sure you'd be better than some of the girls I've employed so far,' he said flatly. He hesitated. 'I expect it's my own fault—I must be rubbish at the selection process,' he said. 'They all seem OK at interview—but it never quite works out.' He held her gaze for a moment. 'And—by the way—I'm not asking you to be Mary Poppins. I'm just asking you to be a stand-in until I find her.'

'Well—how many nannies have you employed so far?' Lily asked curiously, still utterly taken aback by the unexpectedness of his proposal. What on earth was she going to say? What on earth did she *want* to say?

'Three in just over a year,' he said. 'I had to sack two of them because they turned out to be totally unsuitable, and the third left because she'd suddenly decided to take off and go backpacking for a year. So then I had to use the temporary services of an agency, and that wasn't ideal at all. The poor kids never knew who was going to be there when they got home.'

Lily swallowed, not sure how to respond. She'd made up her mind that being with children all day was definitely not for her, but deep down she felt that it might not be such a bad idea to fall in with Theo's wishes. It could be a timely stop-gap while she reviewed her future—as he'd suggested.

He broke in on her thoughts. 'If you did agree, Lily,' he said, 'it would mean turning up in time to take Tom and Alex to school in the mornings—though of course they're on holiday for the next six weeks or so—and to pick them up at three. Then giving them their tea and waiting with them until I get back at about seven. I always put them to bed,' he added. 'And of course you'd need to be available all day at the end of the phone to deal with any problems when they're at school. Although I'm obviously contactable in a dire emergency, I cannot leave my post for minor things.' He ran a hand through his hair. 'I suppose what I'm really trying to do—what my subconscious hope is—is to find a replacement for my wife... Which is unreasonable of me, of course. How could that ever happen? How could any staff member fill that sort of gap?'

He sat down next to Lily, the lighting from the hotel throwing strange shadows across his face, and, staring across at him, Lily thought how tired he looked—and a bit lost. She sighed inwardly. Despite all her misgivings, something was dragging her towards accepting his offer. From what he'd said, it shouldn't be too onerous a commission, and his boys weren't likely to be such little horrors as the twins. They wouldn't dare—not with Theodore Montague for a father!

She smiled suddenly. 'Let me sleep on it,' she said. 'I need a little time to make important decisions.'

'Quite right—I'd go along with that,' he said earnestly, sensing victory. Somehow he'd read her mind, and in that brief instant he knew that she was going to say yes to his request. But he also knew that she would make him wait a while for his answer.

The frown on the handsome brow cleared, and he stood up, taking a business card from his pocket.

'My mobile number's on this,' he said briefly, handing it to Lily. 'Give me a ring—any time—with your decision.'

Lily studied the card. 'What if I interrupt something important?' she asked, not looking up at him.

'Oh, don't worry about that,' he said at once. 'Bea also has my number, and she knows she can contact me at any time if necessary. My children come first in my life.'

They eventually said goodnight, and Lily watched for a moment as he strode away to return to his own hotel on the other side of the city. When she went inside, Sam was at the reception desk.

'Oh—Lily!' he exclaimed, coming over to give her a hug. 'I'm terribly sorry about this evening. I'll make up for it tomorrow, I promise. Is everything OK—where have you been?'

'Out to a wonderful supper—and walking about, soaking up the atmosphere,' Lily said happily.

And she *was* happy. She'd had a great evening, and she'd enjoyed a man's company more than she could have believed possible. But most of all bubbling up in her consciousness was the fact that not once had he attempted to touch her, to take her hand or even to brush against her. They had not made physical contact all evening. And that was the best thing of all. No wonder she'd been able to completely relax.

As she got ready for bed, she glanced at the business card again. She'd ring him later on tomorrow, with her acceptance. After all, she'd be daft to turn down the opportunity of marking time—and being paid for it— while she reassessed her future.

CHAPTER THREE

A WEEK later, Lily caught the bus which would take her to the opposite end of the town—the posh end—where Theodore Montague lived. She was too ashamed to drive over in her battered old car, preferring to leave it where it was outside her flat.

It was Saturday, and she'd been invited over to tea to meet the children, and to see where she'd be spending much of the next three months of her life.

Gazing out of the window, Lily remembered again how appreciative Theo had been that she'd fallen in with his request, and he'd accepted the fact that she would give it until the end of October before moving on to pastures new.

'By that time I ought to be able to find someone else,' he'd said. 'Especially if you're around to sit in on the interviews.' He'd paused. 'I do think that a woman is better at assessing another woman in these special circumstances. You'll probably spot the warning signs that seem to have gone over my head so far,' he'd added.

Lily hadn't made any comment, still surprised that he considered her, or her opinion, to be of any value. But it had made her feel good inside—had even made her look forward to the challenge of taking up this unlooked-for post. She would try her best to succeed where others had failed—maybe prove to herself that she wasn't as bad at handling children as she'd thought. After all, it was only going to be for twelve weeks.

The house turned out to be one of a terrace of Georgian dwellings, opening out onto the street, with no front garden. The imposing shiny black front door was flanked on either side by two bay trees, and looked solid enough to keep out the most determined intruder.

Lily took a deep breath as she raised her hand to grasp the large knocker—but before she could make her presence known the door was flung open, and a tall, elderly grey-haired woman stood there, with two small boys jockeying for position in front of her.

'Hello…you must be Lily!' the woman exclaimed. 'Do come in. We've been watching at the window, waiting for you.' She smiled, standing aside for Lily to enter, and almost at once her heart lifted at the genuine welcome she was receiving.

'Yes, I'm Lily,' she said hesitantly. She looked down into the upturned faces of the children, whose interested eyes and ready smiles demonstrated their obvious well-being. 'And you're…Tom? And…Alexander?' she asked.

'No. I'm Alex,' Alexander said promptly. 'I hate people calling me Alexander.'

'And I'm not Thomas. I'm Tom-Tom,' the smaller child lisped.

'I'll remember.' Lily smiled. She turned to the woman. 'And you're…Bea?' she asked shyly.

'That's right, dear—Jill-of-all-trades and mistress of none!' She looked down at the children. 'Aren't you going to say hello to Lily properly, boys?'

'Hi, Lily,' they chorused obediently.

'That's right. Now, Freya is out playing tennis at the moment,' Bea explained, 'but she'll be back in an hour. Do come on through, Lily. Theodore is busy in his private study at the moment, but he'll be finished shortly.'

Lily tried to take in her surroundings all at once—something she was very good at—and she was aware straight away of the luxury which surrounded her. The huge oak-floored entrance hall was enhanced at one end by a massive antique dresser on which stood two golden-shaded lamps, some expensive-looking objets d'art, and in the centre a silver-framed photograph of a beautiful dark-haired young woman. Lily glanced away quickly, not wanting to appear inquisitive—she didn't need telling who that was. It could only be Elspeth, whose picture there—to be met by the gaze of every visitor—told its own story. She was still mistress here. Still the most important woman in the house.

Lily was ushered into a spacious, sunny, high-ceilinged room, with three large patterned sofas facing each other, and various footstools and small occasional tables. There was a mirror over the ornate fireplace, and on the mantelpiece were family photos—the one in the centre being of Elspeth, surrounded by her three children. The full-length windows were curtained to the floor in ivory and red striped material, and although opulence screamed at her from every angle, Lily immediately felt this to be a homely room—a room to be enjoyed rather than admired. To prove the point, the two boys immediately leapt on to one of the sofas and started having a friendly fight.

Lily wandered across to look at the garden, which was not only full of fruit trees and flowering bushes, but also the usual trappings of childhood—a climbing frame and a slide, a sandpit, and several footballs lying in corners.

She looked back at Bea, smiling. 'Everything's lovely,' she said, and the older woman nodded.

'Yes,' she said, 'it is.' She sighed. 'I understand that you've been told of the circumstances here? So sudden…so sad,' she added.

'Yes,' Lily said quickly, glancing across at the boys.

Bea followed her gaze. 'It is beginning to get easier,' she said quietly, 'and we still talk about Mummy, of course.' She raised her voice. 'Now then, boys—who's going to help me in with the tea things?'

The children immediately scrambled off the sofa and followed Bea out of the room, and Lily sank down on to one of the upholstered stools for a moment. She had never set foot in such a place in her life. Bella and Rosie's home didn't even come close, she thought. For a moment, she panicked. What was she doing here? Had she had a sudden rush of blood to the head in agreeing to do this? Theodore Montague might have seemed a pleasant person away from England, but she was in no doubt that he could be very different in a work situation. And that was what she was here for. To work.

She could hear the children's raised voices in the distance—obviously coming from the kitchen—and Lily dropped her head into her hands for a second. Here she was, having to prove herself once more, she thought. Somewhere new, with different people—whose true expectations were unknown.

'Is everything all right?' The well-remembered dark tones cut into her reverie, and Lily raised her head quickly, standing up. Her new employer stood just inside the door, looking across at her with that whimsical expression on his face she'd come to recognise. He was wearing chinos and a dark rugby shirt and his hair was tousled, as if he'd been running his hands through it.

'Of course—yes—everything's fine,' Lily said, not bothering to add that all day yesterday she'd been fighting off a migraine—which would probably account for her light-headedness today, she realised. 'I was just thinking what a beautiful home this is,' she said, smiling briefly.

He nodded, then came over to stand next to her. She seemed even smaller today than he remembered her. Younger, and rather vulnerable... He wondered whether she'd be robust enough to deal with his sometimes obstreperous children. Then he shrugged inwardly. She'd only be here for a few months, and at least once she was back at school his daughter would only be present for two days out of every seven.

'You had no difficulty finding us?' he enquired, glancing down at her. She was dressed in blue jeans and a white T-shirt, her hair tied up in one long plait at the back.

'No, it's an easy address,' she said, in answer to his question. 'And it's actually on my bus route. It only took half an hour.'

'I did offer to fetch you...' he reminded her.

'There was no need for that,' Lily said quickly. 'At least I know what to do if my car refuses to start.'

Just then the tea trolley made its entrance, pushed enthusiastically by Tom and Alex, with Bea coming behind, holding the teapot and hot water.

'Careful, boys,' Theo said. 'We'd like those cakes on the plate rather than on the floor, thank you.'

Everyone sat down, while Bea handed out plates and paper napkins, and Lily glanced around, struck by the easygoing atmosphere. There were dainty little sandwiches, and buttered scones with jam and cream, and some small squares of iced cake. The children, sitting side by side on one of the sofas, tucked in to everything they were offered. Even the three-year-old seemed to have no difficulty in eating food from a plate balanced on his small knees, though he was given a plastic mug to drink his tea from. Lily noticed that there was not a crisp or a sausage or a soft drink in sight—the children were enjoying afternoon tea, and she sensed their mother's hand in that.

Lily automatically glanced up at Elspeth's photograph, captivated by the woman's warm, engaging expression—somehow she felt that she, Lily, was being appraised by someone no longer here, yet whose presence was tangible. *I'll do my best,* she promised. *I will try to do my best.*

Although all the food looked delicious, Lily could only manage one sandwich and a small cake. As usual, when she was on edge, her appetite disappeared. But she was glad of the strong, unsweetened tea, and she allowed Bea to refill her cup. She noticed that Theo was not eating anything at all, but sat beside his sons, a half-drunk cup of tea on the small table beside him.

Conversation was dominated by Bea, telling everyone to help themselves, and the chattering of the boys, who were not in the least shy. Well, they'd become used to countless strangers passing through their lives, Lily thought, so one more was no big deal. In fact, after the first few moments of their initial meeting, she'd been more or less ignored by Tom and Alex. They were beautiful children, with naturally wavy fair hair, but their dark eyes—even at this early stage—exactly matched their father's. Glancing at Theo, she realised that he had been watching her, and she wondered what he was thinking. Well…the fact that she was here at all was his idea, not hers. And it had not been just an idea, either—it had been a plea. A plea she'd found irresistible.

She met his gaze unblinkingly. She'd try to fill this temporary gap to his satisfaction, she thought. They'd all survive her efforts—and it wasn't going to be for long.

When everyone had finished their tea, Theo stood up. 'I think we ought to show Lily the rest of the house, don't you? So that she knows her way around,' he said, and the boys jumped down from the sofa while Bea began clearing things away.

Tom came immediately over to Lily and caught hold of her hand. 'I'll show you,' he said importantly.

'We both will!' Alex said.

'Let's all do it,' Theo placated, tilting a smile down at Lily, and for the next twenty minutes she was given a guided tour.

A beautiful dining room was dominated by a huge mahogany table—obviously used for entertaining, Lily thought instinctively—and there was another smaller, television room with a conservatory attached. There was a study area and, best of all in Lily's opinion, the kitchen, where Bea was putting the tea things away. The room seemed to disappear into the far distance, with cupboards and fitments and cooking facilities at one end, and at the other a long refectory table and benches, with two or three easy chairs alongside. One wall was taken up with shelves that held books and toys, haphazardly placed.

Lily took a deep breath. This wasn't only the engine room of the house, she thought, it was comfortable and homely and where the family obviously liked spending time. It was where she would like to be, too, she decided. Quite apart from the gleaming Aga there was a double oven, and her professional eye had taken in all the details—a marble slab perfect for rolling pastry, huge wooden chopping boards, and what looked like acres of space to put things down. She wasn't going to mind preparing the children's teas here. It was a kitchen to die for.

Upstairs, she was shown Theo's master bedroom, with private study attached. Each of the boys had a room, and there was a spare room as well.

'Freya's room is up on the next floor, where there's another guest room,' Theo said. 'She prefers to be by herself, apparently.' He paused. 'It's the untidy one, I'm afraid. The boys are far better at putting their things away.'

'Thanks for that, Dad,' a voice from behind said suddenly, and they all turned to look at the speaker. Freya had arrived, unnoticed, dressed in tennis whites, and she moved to push past them. She was tall and slight, her long hair hanging untidily around her shoulders.

'Freya—this is Lily, who I've told you about,' Theo said firmly, barring her way. The child stopped just long enough to say, off-handedly, 'Hi—Lily,' before running upstairs to her room.

She hadn't attempted to make eye contact, Lily noticed, but had managed to be just polite enough for her father to do no more than raise his eyebrows helplessly as he glanced at Lily. Lily smiled up at him. Why should the girl show any interest in yet another carer who'd be gone in no time, to be replaced by some other stranger?

'You missed Bea's super tea, Freya,' Theo called up.

'I had tea at the club,' the girl replied.

'I thought you were going to come home for tea today?'

Freya's face appeared over the banisters above them. 'Well, everyone else was staying, so I thought I would as well,' she said.

No more was said, but the dark expression on Theo's face didn't go unnoticed by Lily. Suddenly she remembered something, and, slipping her pretty holdall from her shoulder, she opened it, taking out a large paper bag.

'Are you allowed chocolates and sweets?' she asked the boys, and before she could go on Tom had come to her side to peer at what she was holding.

'Yes—but I don't like chocolate. I only like jellies,' he said.

'Well, what a good thing I brought some, then.' Lily smiled, taking out a packet and handing it over.

'I *love* chocolate!' Alex said, and as Lily gave him a large bar his eyes lit up. 'This is my favourite! How did you know that, Lily?'

'Ah, that's a secret,' Lily said. 'I know a fairy who tells me things sometimes.' She suddenly felt a surge of pleasure run through her. She was being accepted—even if it *was* because of the sweets she'd brought with her.

They all went back downstairs then, and Alex said, 'When are you coming to look after us, Lily? Is it soon?'

'Lily will be here again on Monday morning,' Theo said, answering for her. 'But I'm sure she wants to go home now, because she's probably going out somewhere with her friends tonight. We mustn't keep her to ourselves.'

'Oh, I'm not going anywhere,' Lily said quickly— then wished she hadn't. Didn't every young, single woman go out on Saturday nights? She'd made herself sound pathetic!

'Well, if you're not going out, you can stay and help

Daddy put us to bed,' Alex announced hopefully. 'Can she, Daddy?'

'I'm sure Lily has better things to do…' Theo said. 'Even if she isn't going out.'

'Of course I'll stay—if I can be of any use,' Lily said simply.

The fact was, she already loved being here—enjoyed the atmosphere of this lovely home.

Theo shrugged. 'You've won, then, Alex. Lily can do the honours.' He turned to look down at her. 'Thanks,' he said briefly.

The next hour passed rapidly as Lily took control of a bathing session. There was a lot of splashing, and mucking about with toys, but Lily let them get on with it, not caring too much that she was getting soaked as well.

She spotted their toothbrushes on the shelf, and handed them down to the children. 'Scrub until I've finished counting up to one hundred and twenty,' she said firmly.

Finally, she decided that enough was enough. 'Time's up, boys,' she said, taking one of the big white fluffy towels and holding it up. 'Come on—you first, Tom-Tom.' She lifted him out and held him to her, wrapping the towel around him snugly.

'I can dry *myself,*' Alex said, jumping out as well, and Lily thought what sturdy little bodies they had, and what lucky children they were—to be born into a family like this one—even if their mother *had* died. How could anyone go wrong, literally enveloped in all the luxury and love that was evident here?

They scampered out of the bathroom ahead of her, and once they'd put on their pyjamas were ready to be tucked in for the night. Going into Tom's room, Alex said cheerfully, 'Tom-Tom and me have been sleeping in here together since Mummy went.' He jumped into one of the single beds, and pulled the duvet up around him. 'Because it helps him to go to sleep,' he added. 'And we always have milk to drink before we go to sleep.'

Lily sat down on one of the low chairs beside the bed.

'I have mine cold, and Tom-Tom has his warm,' Alex went on helpfully.

'Well, thank you for telling me that,' Lily said, glancing at the younger child, who was already curled up in his bed, sucking his thumb. She paused. 'Would you like a story before milk or afterwards?'

There was a brief silence. 'We don't usually have stories,' Alex said.

'Ahh—would you like one?'

'Yes, please!' both children chorused.

'Then I'll go and get your drinks, and then you can cuddle down and listen while I tell you a story.'

In the kitchen, Lily had no difficulty locating where everything was, and it took her only a few moments to heat some milk. There was no sign of Theo, and she was glad. She didn't want him standing there, watching her. She'd known almost from the first moment that she was going to get on OK here—as long as she was left to do it her own way, with no one interfering. Alex and Tom were good kids—though she wasn't too sure about Freya, who seemed to have done a disappearing act.

Back upstairs, she gave the boys their milk, then started on the storytelling, deliberately keeping her voice low to encourage them to sleep. She wasn't going to tell them that she couldn't remember ever having had a story told to *her* at bedtime, because what did it matter now? she thought.

It wasn't long before Tom had dropped off to sleep, and Alex was having difficulty keeping his eyes open.

'Tell Daddy to come up and say goodnight,' Alex said sleepily, and Lily nodded.

'Of course I will,' she said. 'And I'll tell you the rest of the story on Monday,' she whispered, getting up. As she turned, she just caught sight of Freya, running up the stairs. Lily called up softly, 'Freya—you haven't had any of the sweets I brought for you.'

The girl turned and stared down. 'I don't usually eat sweets,' she said.

'What—never?'

'Well, only sometimes.'

'There are jellies, and some chocolate—oh, yes—and some mints as well.'

'I do eat mints,' Freya said, coming down the stairs slowly.

'Good. Mints are my favourite, too,' Lily said non-committally. She paused. 'They're in my bag.'

She led the way downstairs, and Freya followed her into the sitting room, where Theo was sitting, reading a newspaper.

He looked up. 'Ah—how did bathing go?' he enquired. 'It sounded fairly dramatic.'

'It was fine,' Lily said, handing the bag of sweets to Freya. 'They're waiting for you to tuck them in.'

He got up straight away, and as he went past Freya ruffled her hair affectionately. 'Did you win your game today?' he asked.

'Naturally,' the child replied, unwrapping a butter mint and putting it into her mouth. 'But we lost the doubles. Gemma and me have worked out a strategy for next time.'

'Sounds ominous,' Theo said casually as he left the room.

It was already gone seven o'clock, and although Lily didn't want to go home, she felt that there wasn't any point in staying any longer. She'd achieved what she'd come for—meeting the children and finding her way around the house—so, standing up, she glanced across at Freya, who'd kicked off her sandals and was stretched languidly out on one of the sofas.

'I'm going home now,' she said briefly.

'D'you have to?' was the unexpected reply, and Lily was genuinely surprised.

'I'll be back on Monday,' she said.

'Yes, but why d'you have to go *now?*' the child persisted. 'It's early.' She paused. 'And I'm hungry.'

Just then Theo came back in, and Freya looked up at him. 'Lily doesn't have to go home yet, does she, Daddy? Could she stay and make my supper? Please?'

Theo glanced down at Lily. 'Perhaps you'd better ask her, Freya.'

'Please, Lily, would you make me some scrambled eggs?' Freya began, and Theo interrupted.

'What's wrong with *my* scrambled eggs?' he said.

'Well—nothing, really, Dad. But I just thought that…'

'Of course I'll stay and make your supper.' Lily smiled. 'And I'll show you how I've learned to scramble eggs so that they don't stick to the pan.'

'In that case, make it scrambled eggs for three,' Theo said easily. 'You'll stay and have some with us, won't you, Lily?'

Lily smiled warmly, ridiculously pleased that she wasn't going home just yet. 'All right,' she said. 'Thanks.'

Freya jumped up. 'Great!' she said. 'And while you're doing it, will you finish that story? I promise not to tell the boys the end.'

CHAPTER FOUR

ON MONDAY morning Lily was up even earlier than usual. She'd never been a late riser, so it was no hardship to be ready for the day by six-thirty. As the children had already broken up from school for the long summer break, Theo had told Lily that there was no need for her to arrive before nine.

After the three of them had eaten the scrambled egg supper at the kitchen table, Theo had insisted on driving Lily home on Saturday night. Bea only lived four doors away, and had been only too happy to sit with the children for the short time it took him to make the journey. Sitting beside him in the sleek, silver Mercedes, Lily had felt like a queen. The soft, cream leather upholstery had given her the impression of being enfolded in pure luxury, and, glancing across at him briefly as they'd moved effortlessly through the traffic, she'd felt almost overwhelmed at being there at all. A chance encounter on an aeroplane had deposited her in the company of this rich, influential man, and it filled her with a pleasurable feeling of security. He was strong, purposeful—perhaps even masterful—she thought, but he'd given no hint of being attracted to her, or whatever it was that usually made her feel so uncomfortable when she was in male company. She breathed in deeply. Live for the now, she had told herself. Don't look forward. Don't look back.

Today she decided that she would drive herself over to Theo's house rather than take the bus—but she wouldn't lower the tone of the neighbourhood by parking right outside! She'd find a space somewhere out of sight, she thought.

Theo came to the door himself in answer to her knock. He was casually dressed, Lily noticed—immediately jumping to the conclusion that he wasn't going anywhere on official business today. Echoing her thoughts, he said, 'I'll be working at home, Lily… I thought it only fair to be on hand—as moral support for you, if nothing else—on your first day.' He smiled, as if guessing what she was thinking, and Lily smiled back, knowing that he was noting every little thing about her.

And why not? Why shouldn't he? She was being given charge of his most precious possessions—his three children—and he would expect high standards in every way. But he needn't bother himself, Lily thought. Despite her fractured background, she was a perfectionist in her own way. She was wearing neatly pressed grey trousers today, and a short-sleeved honey-coloured top that seemed to reflect her freshly shampooed hair, which she'd tied back in a ponytail.

Hearing voices, the boys appeared from nowhere, still in their pyjamas, and Alex said, 'We've been waiting for you. You've been a long time.'

'Have I? I'm sorry,' Lily said, wrinkling her nose briefly. There was an undeniable smell of burning coming from the kitchen.

Theo shrugged mildly. 'Freya is cooking breakfast,' he murmured.

Freya popped her head around the door, her small face flushed. 'Lily—I'm doing you some sausages,' she greeted her, before going back to the stove.

As the boys raced on ahead into the kitchen, Theo explained, 'We're not usually this disorganised in the mornings, but it is holiday time. For them, if not for me. Routine tends to go out of the window, I'm afraid. And the boys wouldn't let me help them get dressed. They insisted that they wanted you to do it.' He paused. 'You seem to be something of a hit already, Lily,' he said casually.

She shook her head. 'They're hoping I've brought some more sweets, no doubt,' she said, smiling.

'Well—come on through,' he said easily. 'Coffee's made.'

The glorious smell of it percolating was even more overpowering than the aroma of charring sausages, and Lily had to admit that, if pressed, she could probably eat something. And certainly enjoy a freshly made coffee.

On the long table, she saw that bowls of cereal had been put out for the children, and the boys immediately sat down and began to eat. Lily was touched to see that they had set a place for her, too. She looked around quickly, wondering where their father usually sat, but he was busy pouring coffee and making drinks for the children, and she realised straight away that he'd either had his breakfast or never bothered with the meal at all.

He came over and filled her cup to the brim. 'Sit down, Lily,' he said. 'Uh…I think the sausages are on their way.' He gave her the merest suggestion of a wink as Freya approached, and the child set the plate down in front of Lily, looking at her expectantly.

'Freya—these look absolutely yummy!' Lily exclaimed. 'But, goodness me—I never eat three at a time!'

'There are more over there,' Freya said, waiting for Lily to start eating. 'D'you like mustard with them, or tomato ketchup? I've put both out for you—see?' She paused. 'Daddy never eats breakfast,' she added offhandedly, 'so I haven't made any for him.'

Lily made a great fuss of enjoying the food, and although the sausages were rather blackened, the centres were cooked well enough, and were surprisingly appetizing. She was able to finish them without any trouble. Though, because Freya was being so sweet, and had cooked them specially for her, she'd have eaten them whatever they tasted like.

Theo drank his coffee and turned to go. 'I'll be upstairs in my study today,' he said briefly, looking down at Lily. 'Bea will be doing the lunches—but please help yourself to anything in the house. The children know how everything ticks—feel free to give me a shout if you need me. And you three,' he said, glancing at the children, 'be *good*.'

Lily smiled, looking up quickly. 'I'm sure we shan't be disturbing you,' she murmured. 'Besides, I know there's a big play park nearby, so we'll probably be going down there later, when everyone's dressed.'

He nodded and left the room, feeling quite pleased with how things were going as he went up the stairs. He'd never seen his children react like this with any of the other women he'd employed. The boys were always quite wary of newcomers, and Freya was always only just on the right side of being rude, her negative attitude permanently on parade. But Lily seemed to have cast a spell on his daughter, who'd got up early to prepare breakfast. And as for cooking sausages—the mind boggled! Long may it last, he thought. And as he went into his study and shut the door he admitted to a very unusual, comforting sensation of…what? Optimism? Or relief? He'd found someone suitable for the kids—even if she wasn't going to be here long. Whatever it was, he knew that he felt slightly less screwed-up about his situation than he had for months. He glanced down at the picture of his wife on the desk, smiling back at her for a second.

Later, Lily and the children trooped down to the park, arriving back in time to sit and enjoy Bea's delicious salad and jacket potato lunch.

'Aren't you having anything, Bea?' Lily asked, looking up at the woman who was busying herself with adding ice cream to the fresh fruit salad she'd prepared.

'No, dear. I'll be going home in a few minutes to have my lunch with Joe… We always eat a bit later than they do here—not that Theo ever has much at all during the day when he's home. I've taken him up a sandwich and a coffee, but once he's shut himself in that study that's usually the last we see of him until suppertime.' She paused. 'He works so hard—he's tireless, really. I worry that he overdoes it, but…' She lowered her voice so that the children, who were chattering loudly, wouldn't hear her, adding, 'We think it's his way of coping with his loss, you know. Burying himself in his work to forget.' She sighed. 'We do our best to lighten the load, but there's only so much anyone *can* do, and Joe doesn't enjoy the best of health now, so we're limited in that way.'

'I know Theo is immensely grateful to you both,' Lily said at once. 'You've been a tower of strength to him…' She paused. 'Bea—what usually happens about the evening meal?' she asked. 'You don't do that as well, do you?'

'Well, holiday times are different—we sort of take it in turns,' Bea replied as she handed out the little dishes of fruit. 'Theo isn't much of a cook, but he can produce simple meals, and I make sure they have a roast or a meat pie now and then as well. We sort of mix and match.' She smiled.

'Well, as long as he doesn't think I'm trying to interfere and take over,' Lily said firmly, 'you can leave supper to me for as long as I'm here.' She looked up at the older woman. 'I'm a trained cook, Bea,' she said, 'so I'm not likely to poison the family.'

Bea looked surprised—and pleased. 'Really, dear? Theo never mentioned that you were a cook—he merely said he'd found someone he knew would be good with the children.' She paused. 'But if you really feel you could do some of the cooking it would be a tremendous help. It's not that I mind at all, you understand, Lily— I enjoy being in the kitchen, especially this one—it's just that I get really tired in the evenings, and by the time I've cleared up I'm pretty exhausted. I know that Theo worries that I'm doing too much,' she added.

'Yes, he mentioned that,' Lily agreed. 'So…I'll square it with him, of course, but from now on leave the suppers to me, Bea. And surely you don't need to come in every single day to do lunches?'

'Well, we'd better discuss all this with Theo and see what he says,' the older woman suggested.

After Freya had been collected to go to her daily tennis session the boys went outside to play in the garden. Lily had a good look in the fridge and freezer.

There was enough food there to feed an army, and if Theo agreed with her suggestion she'd have a great time preparing meals in his fantastic kitchen. She smiled to herself as she thought what a simple task it would be to cater for a family compared with the hectic atmosphere that had prevailed in some of the hotel kitchens she'd worked in, where there had been a constant flow of requests for different dishes. Here she would be her own boss—up to a point—and as soon as she'd discovered the kind of food that the children and their father liked it would be a doddle!

The boys passed the afternoon happily in the garden—especially after Lily agreed to fill their paddling pool for them to splash about in. She was in the kitchen, making a jug of squash to take outside, when Theo appeared.

'How are you surviving your first day here?' he asked, leaning casually against the doorframe and watching as she took down mugs from a shelf. 'Any problems?' He paused. 'Did Freya behave herself this morning?'

'Freya was a model child,' Lily said, 'and happy to push Tom on the swings. She seemed to enjoy mothering him, I thought.'

'Oh, she's fine with the boys,' Theo said slowly. 'It's me who seems to be the problem. When I'm around everything is an issue.'

Lily finished putting the drinks on a tray and glanced up. 'Will you join us for a glass of this? It's so warm today and…you've been shut away for hours.' As soon as she'd said that, Lily shuddered inwardly. What he did was none of her business—and she felt that he was quite capable of telling her so!

But he gave a slightly crooked smile at her words.

'I'm working on a particularly difficult lecture at the moment,' he said, 'and it's giving me some grief.' He shrugged. 'The time simply disappears, I'm afraid. But—yes, thanks, I'll take a glass of that.' He opened the freezer door and took out a tray of ice-cubes, adding them to the jug. 'Perhaps I'll come outside for ten minutes to drink it. Give myself a breather,' he added.

Carrying his glass, he followed Lily out into the garden. The boys immediately dashed up to him.

'We've been making sandcastles—look, Dad,' Alex said.

Theo nodded in the direction the child was pointing. 'Yes,' he said mildly, 'and you've certainly altered the appearance of the lawn, too, Alex. But those castles look good, I must say.'

'They're for me to jump on in a minute,' Tom said, 'when Alex says I can.'

Lily sank down on to a cushioned hammock and handed the boys their drinks, sipping at hers gratefully while Theo perched on the edge of a low, ornamental stone wall. Soon the children resumed their activities.

Lily glanced across at Theo, wondering how best to make her suggestion of taking over in the kitchen. Even though he was apparently watching what the boys were doing, she knew his thoughts were miles away. The handsome face was serious, the black eyes mirroring his thoughts in their intensity, and she cleared her throat nervously. Perhaps this *wasn't* a good moment? But would there ever be one?

'I was wondering…' she began, and he turned quickly to face her, his eyebrows raised. 'It's just that…I was speaking to Bea at lunchtime, and—well…I don't think her husband is too well at the moment—'

'What is it? She didn't say anything to me,' he cut in.

'Nothing specific—I don't think. But she is anxious. So, I…' Lily swallowed. She didn't want to assume anything, or to be officious in any way. 'If you've no objection, I'd be happy to see to all the meals while I'm here,' she said quickly, her words coming out in a rush. 'To save Bea having to come in all the time. Just as a temporary thing, of course,' she added hurriedly. 'I did make the offer to Bea, and she said that as long as you were agreeable she'd be happy to hand over the reins.' There—she'd said it. She hoped he didn't think she expected a raised salary.

'Well, I don't know—' he began, so Lily went on.

'I did explain—when we were in Rome—that I've been trained in cooking.' She paused. 'I can bring over my diploma to show you, if you like…'

He gave a short laugh. 'Don't be an idiot,' he said. 'I don't want to see formal evidence of your achievements. My only doubt is that it might be too much for you. Handling three children is quite enough, heaven alone knows.' He hesitated. 'I don't want to take advantage of you,' he said slowly, 'of your willing nature. I would feel bad asking it of you.'

'But you haven't asked it of me,' Lily said simply. 'I've offered. It's my idea. Anyway,' she went on, 'let's give it a try for a couple of weeks, and see if you all approve of the meals I put in front of you. If you don't, you can sack me and reinstate Bea.'

He grinned down at her. 'That sounds good to me,' he said easily, clearly happy at what Lily had suggested. 'The boys and I are easy enough to please, but Freya can be picky. Or she is at times. Recently she decided to go vegetarian—until she smelt Bea's roasting chicken one Sunday lunchtime, and quickly changed her mind.'

Lily felt relieved that Theo had taken her suggestion on board so easily. 'What time do you eat supper?' she asked.

Theo stood up. 'About six—for the kids, I mean. I have mine after they're in bed—about eight, I suppose.' He looked down at her. 'But feel free to make up some of the rules for yourself, Lily. We're in your hands now. I only hope you don't regret it!'

Much later, after Freya had come back from tennis and the boys had been cleaned up, Lily sat them all down at the kitchen table.

'Now, then,' she said, taking a notebook and pen from her bag, 'I'm going to be the kitchen queen for a couple of weeks, and what I want from you is a list of what you all like to eat—just so that I get it right. Fire away. You first, Tom-Tom.'

For the next half an hour the children argued about everything they wanted put in front of them, and before long it turned into a hilarious game of thinking up horrible suggestions like roasted worms and steamed slugs. But Lily had learned enough to satisfy herself that, as she'd expected, the family ate all the usual dishes—with one or two exceptions.

'Does Daddy like all that as well?' Lily asked, glancing at Freya.

The child shrugged. 'S'pose so. He doesn't have supper with us. We're in bed by the time he has his, so we don't know what he eats.'

Lily frowned slightly at the rather dismissive remarks. Theo was right, she thought. His daughter's attitude was undeniably cool where he was concerned. Lily bit her lip. He was such an obviously devoted parent…the sort any child should be grateful for. She, herself, had never had much reason to be grateful to anyone—but what did children know about gratitude? she asked herself, being honest for a second. Perhaps those bad things in her life, which were so unforgettable, had clouded over and hidden other, happier times which she had chosen to deny.

After Lily had given the children their supper, they all went in to watch television.

'I don't want to watch any of this,' Alex said suddenly. 'Lily—can you tell us the rest of that story you were in the middle of on Saturday?' He came over to her and flopped down on the floor.

Lily was surprised. 'Wouldn't you prefer to see this programme?' she asked. 'You said it was your favourite.'

Tom jumped up and switched off the TV. 'No…come on—let's have the story *instead!*' he shouted cheerfully, at the top of his voice.

Presently, when at last the boys seemed ready for sleep and, worn out, Freya, too, had got herself ready for bed, Lily felt as if she'd lived two days instead of one! The non-stop chatter, the continual questions from the children about everything under the sun—including about her own life—made Lily realise what a challenging job she'd taken on. Yet she'd amazed herself at how much she'd enjoyed the day—at how well she'd coped with it all. Perhaps she wasn't such a hopeless case with children, after all. Anyway, if today was anything to go by, she'd at least manage to live through the rest of her time here. And when school began again, she'd have the opportunity to consider her long-term future.

For now, she'd do her utmost to help Theodore Montague with his offspring—and maybe free up his mind to concentrate on his work. She frowned slightly, remembering the faraway look in his eyes when he'd sat outside with them earlier. He was obviously engaged in something which was giving him food for deep thought… She shrugged. She couldn't help him with any of that, but at least she could take the pressure off him where the family was concerned.

With a sudden rush of warmth she knew, without anyone having to spell it out, that Alex and Tom-Tom and Freya *liked* her. And she *loved* them! From the very first moment she'd felt a distinct kinship with the children—something she hadn't experienced with Bella and Rosie. She couldn't explain it, even to herself, but why bother to try? Enjoy the *now,* enjoy the *now,* she repeated silently. The now would all too soon be the past.

'Can you ask Daddy to come and say goodnight?' Alex said, as he snuggled up in his duvet.

'I was just going to do that,' Lily replied.

She waited a few seconds by the closed door to Theo's room, then tapped gently. 'The children want you to tuck them in,' she said softly.

There was no reply, but in a few moments he emerged, giving her a brief smile. 'I'm finished for today. I'll be down in ten,' he said.

In the kitchen, Lily looked around her thoughtfully. Was she expected to eat with Theo? Or should she just lay a place for him and then make herself scarce? She'd earlier made her own quick-recipe fish pie for the children, and a separate one for their father. It only needed to be heated through, and served with some green vegetables taken from the freezer. Deciding to err on the side of caution, she laid a single place, with a wine glass alongside—she'd noticed an opened bottle of white in the fridge, so Theo probably had some with his evening meal.

She was just putting the steaming vegetables into a dish when he came into the kitchen. He glanced across at the table, then stared down at her for a second.

'Aren't you staying? D'you have to go now?' he asked abruptly, and the way he said it, with his expressive eyebrows lifted just slightly, reminded Lily of the way Alex had looked at her countless times that day.

She hesitated before answering him. 'I wasn't sure whether...' she began uncertainly, and he came right over to stand beside her, his perceptive mind knowing exactly where she was coming from.

'Lily,' he said patiently, 'you are already stepping into a massive breach for me in taking on my children—temporarily, of course—not to mention letting Bea off the hook in here... I want you to consider this your home. In so far as you feel able.' He paused. 'Please have your evening meal with me,' he said. 'I'd like you to...unless you've got other plans?' he added quickly.

Lily smiled up at him, grateful that the point had been cleared up and she knew where she stood. 'I'd be happy to, Theo,' she said. 'I... I did make enough for two,' she added shyly.

Before she could do it, he had set another place at the table, and before she knew it they were sitting opposite each other, enjoying the fish pie.

'This tastes wonderful,' he said. He raised the bottle of wine and glanced at her. 'Will you join me?' he asked. She shook her head.

'I usually only drink water, and I have to drive home, remember?'

He nodded at that, but said no more, remembering

her comment about not drinking alcohol often when they were in Rome. He grimaced inwardly as he remembered one of the nannies he'd employed emptying the gin bottle which she'd discovered in his drinks cabinet. He glanced at Lily covertly as she finished her meal. He liked this woman, he thought. He liked everything about her. He liked her appearance—well, she had a figure that any discerning male would approve of—she was beautiful, well turned-out, and, although she had a reasonably confident manner, there was an underlying vulnerability about her that he found attractive. He was almost thinking *desirable*—but stopped himself just in time. Desire had nothing to do with it—with anything.

They cleared up together, then Theo put coffee on to percolate.

'I really will have to go soon,' Lily said. 'But I'll be back by nine in the morning.'

He smiled without looking at her. 'Go and sit down in the other room,' he said. 'I'll bring this through in a few minutes.'

Now Lily *was* beginning to feel tired—and warm and relaxed after the food, which had proved to be even more delicious than usual. She sat down thankfully on one of the sofas, resting her head back. For a first day it had all gone pretty well, she thought sleepily. There had not been one cross word from the children, and she'd only teasingly had to tell the boys that she was 'counting up to three or else' to get them out of the paddling pool. And Freya—Freya was a sweet child who loved fairy stories. And she had shown such a touching affection for Lily that it made her want to put her arms around the child and hug her. But she wasn't going to do that. Didn't want to get into too close a relationship with any of them. Because it wasn't going to last. By Christmas they'd have forgotten what she looked like.

A call on his mobile had kept Theo in the kitchen for a while, and when he went into the sitting room he saw that Lily was fast asleep, her head drooping gently onto one shoulder, her long eyelashes lying restfully on her cheeks, her hands clasped loosely in her lap. Silently he put the tray down and stood watching her for a few moments. His instinct was to try and make her more comfortable, to put a cushion under her head. But he didn't touch her. Didn't want to disturb her. The poor girl was worn out, he thought. Let her sleep for as long as she wanted to—he'd order a taxi to take her home if it got too late for her to drive herself.

And in the vivid images of early sleep Lily didn't see the children she'd been minding all day. All she saw were the strong, enigmatic features of Theodore Montague as he stared down at her in that rather special way he had. But he was standing at a safe distance away from her, so that it was only his dark, mesmeric eyes that could touch her. Lily shifted just slightly in her sleep, wishing that he would come nearer, just for a second, so that she could lace her fingers with his...

CHAPTER FIVE

By THE time ten days had passed, Lily felt as if she'd been living with the family all her life. She had quickly established a routine that seemed to suit everyone, and was quite glad to be told that a cleaning person came in three times a week to sort out the laundry, dusting and polishing. For everything else, Theo seemed only too pleased to leave it all to Lily. Anyway, by her third day, he was leaving for work as soon as she arrived at nine, was seldom home again before seven—sometimes later. But Lily made sure that there was always a nutritious meal waiting—which she made a point of having with him, as he'd asked her to on that first day.

One evening after supper, as they were clearing up their dishes, Lily said, 'Would it be OK, Theo, for me to drive the children to the moors tomorrow? This lovely weather isn't going to last—so the forecast says—and we'd like to go for a picnic.' She shot him a quick glance, wondering whether he thought she might not be safe behind the wheel—or whether her car was reliable.

'Why not?' he said briefly. 'They'll love that—and there's nothing like eating food in the open air.'

'It's just… I mean…my vehicle is hardly the sort

they're used to being driven in,' she went on, spreading a teatowel to dry in front of the still-warm oven.

He raised an eyebrow, feeling that he knew Lily well enough by now to be reassured that his children were in safe hands, whether in a car or not.

'Oh, that won't matter to them,' he said easily. 'Go and have a great time.' He paused. 'They'll need booster seats, though.'

'Yes. I've got two—which I used when I was looking after Bella and Rosie,' Lily said. 'But I'll need a third one.'

'I'll make sure I take it out of my car in the morning,' he said, following her into the sitting room.

It had become the norm for Lily to stay for a while after supper—just long enough for her to recount the day's happenings. Theo always wanted to hear what had gone on, and she couldn't help observing that Freya was the one most on his mind. He wanted to know how Freya had acted, how Freya had behaved, whether Freya had enjoyed herself. Lily was always quick to defend the little girl, to reassure Theo that the child was perfectly amenable, and in fact was surprisingly mature for her age.

'She loves to help with the boys—and with everything else,' Lily had said, more than once, and Theo had nodded, clearly perplexed at the barrier his daughter seemed to have erected between them.

Now, they sat for a while in silence, and then Theo got up and went across to the window. He turned to glance across at Lily. 'I need to ask another favour, Lily—' he began.

'Ask away. I like doing favours,' she said quickly. She realised, happily, just what a comfortable relationship had developed between herself and her employer. She no longer felt that she had to watch what she said all the time, or to treat him with undue deference. It seemed to her now like a kind of friendship…unhassled and undemanding.

'I have to be away for three nights for a conference. Would you mind staying over?' He paused. 'I would normally ask Bea to step in, but I spoke to her this morning, and she was telling me that Joe is due to have a series of tests this week at the hospital…'

'Of course I'll stay,' Lily said quickly—privately thinking that not going home each night would be much more convenient anyway.' She smiled. 'It's obviously not going to be another trip to Rome?'

'Sadly not. The north of England this time,' he said, looking at her thoughtfully for a moment. The memory of that short stay in Italy had remained with him for a surprisingly long time—and he knew why. This woman was the reason. He still couldn't believe his good luck in finding her. She was the perfect solution to his nanny problem, and she'd come—literally—out of the blue. If he had the guts he'd try and persuade her to stay…to prolong her contract for at least six months or a year. But he knew he couldn't be that selfish. Lily was searching for something far deeper than a job to get by on. She was searching for her future—trying to unwrap some deep-seated ambition, find something that would give her fulfilment. His expression darkened. He liked Lily enough to hope, to *really* hope, that she'd find what she was looking for.

'That's great,' he said, coming back to sit down on the sofa opposite her. 'I leave on Friday and I'll be home Monday.' He leaned his head back and stared up at the ceiling for a second. 'And the other thing which I completely forgot to mention was our holiday plans.' He glanced across at Lily. 'I've booked a couple of weeks at a hotel on the south coast—we've been there before, and it's very child-friendly and supremely comfortable.' He paused. 'I feel it's time you were spoiled for a change—you're spoiling us all the time. I don't want to wear you out!'

She looked across at him blankly. 'You mean…you want me to come as well?' she asked.

'Of course!' he exclaimed. 'I don't know what the children would say if we left you behind. But only if you want to come, Lily. Maybe you'd rather be back home at your place—do your own thing and catch up on your own life for a bit?'

Would she rather be back at *her* place? Not in a million years! She smiled across at him. 'What girl in her right mind would turn down the chance to have a holiday by the seaside?' she said. She bit her lip, already feeling excited at the prospect. 'It'll be a lovely… treat,' she added, not caring if she sounded too willing to fall in with his wishes all the time. The fact was she loved agreeing with everything he wanted. She was living in his beautiful home, looking after his super children—and now she was going to be taken away on holiday for two whole weeks! And being paid to do it! Someone pinch me, she thought. I'm dreaming. I'm dreaming…

The following day, after she'd got the children ready and put the booster seats in the car, they began to put the picnic together. Lily filled some small rolls with ham and cheese, and put Freya in charge of sorting out the orange squash they'd decided to take with them, while the boys were busy choosing crisps and snacks, and putting apples and bananas into one of the baskets.

'Can we take chocolate biscuits as well, Lily?' Alex

asked, already opening the large tin which held all their special favourites.

She turned to glance down at him. 'I'm afraid they might melt in this heat, Alex,' she said. 'My car doesn't have air-conditioning, like Daddy's does.'

'We don't care about that,' Freya said, screwing the top firmly onto one of the bottles. 'We can have the windows open, can't we, Lily? And anyway,' she added, 'we can take some sweets instead, and have the chocolate biscuits when we come home.'

'Good thinking,' Lily said, looking down at the three little heads, intent on their individual tasks. Looking after them wasn't work, she thought, admitting that she'd not felt this happy in years.

Presently, they set off for the moors, with the children sitting comfortably on the back seat. 'I like *this* car,' Freya announced. 'I like it much better than Daddy's.'

Lily glanced at them in the rearview mirror. 'One quick question,' she said mildly. 'Does anyone suffer from car-sickness?' That was something which hadn't crossed her mind—she hoped the answer would be in the negative! The small pouch of wipes she'd brought wouldn't much help in a major crisis.

'Tom-Tom does—' Alex said cheerfully.

'Not all the time,' Freya cut in. 'Only when we've been a long time in Daddy's car.' She paused. 'Mummy used to say that it was a bit too comfortable.'

'Well, that's OK, then. It's not likely to happen in *my* car,' Lily said firmly. 'Mine doesn't have posh springing, and you can hardly call it too comfortable, can you?'

'I like it when you jerk us about,' Tom-Tom said, as the car hit a particularly bumpy bit of the road. 'It's fun.'

Lily knew exactly where she was taking them,

because it was a favourite spot she'd found as soon as she'd started living in the area. She pulled off the road and drove slowly along a little track to where she knew she could park, and the children could play safely.

'Here we are. Go and explore,' Lily said, and they all jumped out of the car. Well, they'd arrived OK, she thought, with no one complaining of feeling sick, hot, tired or bored. Spreading some rugs out on the dry, soft turf, she sat down and leaned back on her elbows, watching them. Freya was already in charge of proceedings, she noted, organising a game of hide and seek among the low bushes, and Lily thought again what a grown-up child she was. She knew exactly how to handle her brothers, and they responded with no argument at all to everything she was saying.

It was a fantastically hot day, but the heaviness Lily was starting to feel across her temples made her realise—with sickening apprehension—that the thundery storms which had been forecast would mean she'd probably have a migraine before the end of the day. But she was fine at the moment, she reassured herself, and if her normal pattern was anything to go by she'd be able to get through most of the day without any problem—especially if she swallowed a couple of her preventative pills now.

Opening her holdall, she searched for the precious bottle among all the stuff she'd brought with her—and with a lurch of horror realised that it was still in her other bag. The bag which at the last minute she'd decided she wouldn't need... There had been so many other things she'd been thinking about! But that she could have forgotten her tablets...that was a first!

Zipping up the bag firmly, Lily pushed all thoughts

of herself well into the background—she'd brought Theo's family here to enjoy themselves, and she was not going to waste time worrying about a headache which she didn't have—yet. Getting up, she called out, 'Shall we play with the ball for a bit before we have lunch?'

There was no reply, and frowning, she looked around her quickly, pulling back some branches to see where the children were hiding. Even though she knew that they were somewhere very close, a tremor of panic ran through her. She'd only taken her eyes off them for a minute or two…

She called out—louder this time. 'Freya—Alex—Tom-Tom…'

Suddenly, from right behind her, they all flung themselves at her so that she almost fell over. Screaming with laughter Freya hugged Lily around the waist.

'We were hiding from you, Lily!' Alex said.

'We made you jump!' Tom-Tom added.

'You *did* make me jump, you little horrors,' she teased, breathing a sigh of relief. What if she'd lost Theo's precious children on their first outing?

Everyone decided that it was too hot to play ball—and also that they were all getting hungry. So they set out the picnic and began eating. Watching them demolish everything put in front of them, Lily thought, Theo was right. There was nothing like enjoying food in the open air. She wondered what he was doing at this precise moment, whether his day was going well, and her mind automatically flicked to thoughts of the supper she'd prepared for that evening. She'd slow-cooked some braising steak in a wine-enriched gravy…all it needed was a crusty lid of pastry on the top and some nice vegetables… The children would have theirs at six, and the rest would be cooked and served for Theo and her to enjoy later. Last night, at home, she'd made a large jar of creamy fudge sauce. She knew the children would enjoy with ice-cream…

When they'd eaten nearly everything they'd brought with them, Alex said, 'What are we going to do now, Lily? Can we go for a walk?'

'After you've had a little rest,' Lily said, starting to put everything back into the baskets. 'I've brought some books for us to look at…'

'Please, Lily—tell us a story,' Freya said, and Lily groaned inwardly. By now she was definitely not feeling good. Her own lunch had consisted of half a roll, a cherry tomato, and almost a full bottle of water. The last thing she needed was to start inventing stories.

'I will later, Freya,' she said.

Tidying everything up, she stacked their belongings into the boot of the car, then sat back down beside the children. Reaching for her holdall, she pulled out her make-up and glanced at her reflection in her mirror—and shuddered. All the tell-tale signs were there… Her face had taken on an ashen shade, and her eyes seemed huge, with dark circles underneath.

As he watched her touch her nose and mouth with a tissue, Alex said suddenly, 'I like your face, Lily. You're pretty.'

Lily couldn't help smiling. That was the last thing she'd have called herself just at this moment!

'Well, thank you for that, Alex,' she said. 'And I like *your* face. I like all your faces.'

They watched her solemnly as she brushed the lightest touch of blusher on to her cheeks in an effort not to look as bad as she was feeling. Glancing at her watch, she saw that it was only two-thirty. They couldn't leave to go home just yet, she thought. She'd have to stick it out for another hour or so.

Somehow Lily managed to keep the children entertained, and to take them for quite a long walk before they all returned to the car, hot and thirsty. By which time the familiar bright zig-zag lights over one eye made Lily realise that she just couldn't go on.

Freya, ever-perceptive, was the first to notice. 'Lily—what's the matter? You look funny.'

The boys stared up at her, and Lily thought that the time for keeping quiet was over.

'I—I shall have to lie down for a bit…I've got a headache coming on, and I can't see very well. I shan't be able to drive us home just yet…'

Just then, her mobile rang, and Lily's heart sank as she took it from her bag. It could only be Theo, ringing to make sure they were all enjoying themselves. But before she could answer it Freya had almost snatched the phone from her.

'Daddy? Lily's got a headache and she can't drive us, and…' There was a pause as Theo spoke to his daughter, and then the child handed the phone to Lily. As soon as she heard his voice, her heart started to race. She couldn't even be trusted to bring his children back home from a picnic—that was what he'd be thinking.

The strong voice made her head ache even more when he spoke. 'Lily—what is it? What's the matter?'

Her reply was faint and feeble as she answered him. 'I'm—terribly sorry, Theo,' she said tremulously. 'I'm afraid I've started a migraine, and I…I forgot to bring my tablets with me…' How pathetic did *that* sound? she asked herself. 'We'll be a bit later home than I thought—I'll have to wait until my vision improves before I risk driving.'

'Stay exactly where you are,' he said at once—and it was a command, not a request. 'Tell me how to find you. I'm coming to fetch you.'

Lily's hand went to her mouth. This was dreadful! He was disgusted with her. That was obvious. Not because she had a headache, but because she was thoughtless enough to forget the all-important tablets. What did that say about her? And why did she care so much, anyway? She cared because she wanted to please Theo, to convince him that she was a suitable person to be in charge of his family—even though her appointment had been his idea and not of her seeking.

Fortunately her mind was clear enough to give him precise instructions as to where they were, and once the call ended she sank back down on the rug they'd left on the grass, the children gathered around her protectively. Even Tom, only three years old, wanted to hold her hand, telling her that she'd be better soon.

Thankful to close her eyes against the mid-afternoon sun, Lily tried to ride out the pulsating throbbing in her temples. She could just imagine how irritated Theo would be feeling—not to say angry. Thanks to her, he'd have to leave his post and rescue them all, probably in the middle of something vitally important at the hospital where he'd told her he'd be working that day.

Lily cringed as she dwelt on it, but must have drifted off in to a kind of semi-doze for a while. It seemed no time before Alex shouted, 'Daddy's here!'

Struggling to sit up, Lily watched him stride along the track towards them, and her mouth dried as he approached. He'd obviously left his car the half-mile away on the road, rather than negotiate the narrow dusty path which Lily had taken.

The children jumped up and scampered towards him, all clamouring to give the news. But he barely looked at them, coming over to Lily and offering a hand to bring her to her feet. She had no idea what he was thinking, because his sunglasses hid any expression, but his voice was kind enough.

'Lily—poor you,' was all he said, and she looked up at him.

'Theo—I'm so…sorry…' she began.

'What for? For getting a migraine?' The question was almost rough.

'No—I mean, I cannot believe that I forgot my tablets. They don't exactly stop a headache, but they delay the worst of it. I should have been able to get us home without having to bother you.' She looked away, feeling unsteady on her feet for a second, and he immediately put a strong hand under her elbow, helping her balance. 'Did I interrupt something terribly important?' she asked.

'No. We'd finished what we had to do—that's why I rang. To say that I'd be home early today.' He looked down at her, conscious that she had leaned into him for support. 'Come on, everyone. Let's get poor Lily home to bed,' he instructed.

Such a huge feeling of thankfulness swept over Lily that she could have cried. He wasn't angry—or if he was he wasn't going to show it in front of the children.

'Everyone help to transfer the picnic stuff to my car,' he said. 'Give me your keys, Lily, and I'll lock yours up for now. I'll arrange for my garage people to come along later and drive it back. It won't come to any harm here for a few hours.'

Overwhelmed now, with thick, steady pain, Lily walked slowly along beside the children, who were all helping Theo carry their belongings towards his car. What an awful end to the day, she thought miserably. And it was all her silly fault that Theo had become involved.

As soon as they got into the house he turned to look down at her. 'Choose your room, Lily,' he said. 'Because you're not going home. You need an early night.' As she looked up to protest, he added quickly, 'Look, you've agreed to stay for a few nights in any case—what does it matter if it's a day early? Tomorrow you can drive back home to fetch your stuff.'

'Is Lily sleeping over?' the boys chorused. 'Yeah! Great!'

And Freya said, 'Please sleep in the room next to mine, Lily! *Please!*'

Theo smiled faintly. 'Do I need to say anything more?' he murmured. 'And don't you dare think about our supper—Freya and I will cope alone, I promise you.'

Lily had got past the point of arguing about anything at all, and she let Freya take her to the guest room she'd be sleeping in. It had an *en suite* bathroom, and was perfectly equipped—apart from night clothes, which didn't matter because as soon as she was alone all Lily had to do was slip off her cotton jeans and shirt and sleep.

Much later—after Theo, with a bit of help from the children, had rustled up cheese omelettes, to be eaten with oven chips taken from the freezer—everyone got ready for bed.

'Can we go in and see Lily?' Alex said, making for the stairs to the second floor.

'No, we cannot,' Theo said firmly. 'No one is to interrupt her or make a noise. She's got to get well enough to look after you three for a few days all by herself, because I shan't be around.'

'That's OK, Dad, we'll manage without you,' Freya said cheerfully, and Theo looked at her sideways.

The remark his daughter had just made hadn't held the normal dismissive tone he'd become used to hearing. It had been more of a reassurance that they would help look after each other, and the hint of a smile tugged at his strong, uncompromising mouth. For a brief second that had sounded just like something Elspeth might have said.

Deep into her drugged sleep, Lily tossed and turned on the pillow, her hair damp with perspiration on her forehead, her dreams vivid and nightmarish. Theo was furious, staring down at her, his anger white-hot as he berated her over and over for her incompetence.

Much, much later, when everyone was asleep and Theo had locked up for the night, he went slowly up the stairs, pausing to look in on the boys before going up to the second floor to check on Freya. He stood for several moments outside the guest room, listening for any sound from Lily. There was complete silence, and he pushed the door open tentatively. She had looked so ill during the afternoon—almost ghost-like. He opened the door wider and stepped inside, going over to the bed and gazing down on her inert form. She was so still lying there, clad only in her bra and panties, her tanned, slender legs slightly bent beneath her, one arm stretched above her head, her hair as pale as a cold winter sky, tumbling around her face. But she was breathing normally.

He took a step backwards, momentarily disturbed at his own emotions. Of course she was an overpoweringly delectable sight—but what was that to him? he thought angrily. She was the young woman he'd engaged to look after his offspring—nothing more, nothing less. He'd only truly desired one woman—had only had one meaningful relationship in his life, with the mother of his children. To whom he'd committed himself for ever. And that was the way it was going to stay. No one could ever, *would* ever, replace Elspeth. Why, then, was his body sending out all these disturbing, persuasive messages, threatening to unbalance his frame of mind?

CHAPTER SIX

WHEN she woke up the following morning, Lily couldn't think where she was. This wasn't *her* room… She'd never set foot in here before! Then memory rushed in and she sat up quickly, recalling everything that had happened yesterday. She cringed again. Theo had been very kind and considerate, she couldn't deny that, but she knew she must have gone down in his estimation. If she was too careless to look after herself, how could she be expected to look after his children?

It was early, and there was no sound in the house. She washed and dressed quickly, before treading lightly down the stairs and passing the children's rooms without going in. If Theo needed to leave soon to go to his conference she'd better get her act together as quickly as possible and check up on a few things, she thought. The smell of percolating coffee drifting up towards her made Lily realise that his day had already begun. She knew that he would have arranged for her car to be brought back here, so she'd drive home now, without delay.

When she went into the kitchen, he had his back towards her as he stood by the stove. Hearing her footsteps, he turned to look down at her.

'Ah—how are you this morning?' he asked, and to her it sounded like the kind of impersonal, polite enquiry he would have made to anyone. He was immaculately dressed in a dark business suit, his black hair gleaming in the sunlight that shafted in through the window, and Lily swallowed, looking away quickly.

'I'm better…thank you,' she replied, matching his coolness of tone. 'I had a very good, long sleep. I'll be fine now,' she added. 'I don't get those attacks very often, so it'll be a while before I get another one.'

'I'm glad to hear it,' he said, and Lily looked at him sharply.

Go on, say it, she thought. Tell me that if I'm going to take to my bed while I'm supposed to be doing my job, we'd better call it a day now. But he didn't say that. He just looked at her closely for a moment.

Even though obviously she was wearing what she had had on the day before, she still managed to look fresh and dainty—and desirable, he thought. With a decisive movement, he turned to pick up the coffee.

'Can I pour you a cup of this?' he asked quietly, feeling annoyed that he was still painfully aware of the sensuous vibes which had troubled him last night. He needed to get away soon—get away from her and concentrate on his work. Work had been his salvation for the last fourteen months, and it would be again.

'No, I'll have tea instead, thank you.' She picked up the kettle and poured some boiling water into a mug, adding a tea bag and swirling it around for a moment.

'Is my car back?' she asked.

'Yes, it is,' Theo said, going over to the table. 'It's outside. When you're ready, perhaps you'd go and fetch what you need from home? I must leave here at eleven.'

'I'll go straight away,' Lily said at once. 'As soon as I've drunk this. There's no sound from the children— they're obviously sleeping in this morning,' she added.

'Yes. They're usually tired after a day in the open air,' he remarked. He had opened his morning paper, spreading it on the table in front of him, and without looking up he said, 'By the way, I think I ought to get in touch with the agency again—about acquiring someone permanent here, I mean. The weeks are going to fly by, and I don't want to be caught out with you expecting to finish up and there being no one to replace you. I'll ring them this morning,' he added. Still not looking up, he said, 'That *is* what you want, isn't it? To be free to change your life?'

'Yes. It is,' Lily said faintly.

Standing by the stove, her mug of tea in her hand, Lily felt as if she'd been punched in the stomach. Her fears had been well-grounded, she thought. After yesterday he couldn't wait to get rid of her—couldn't wait to replace her with a professional. She fought back her tears, sipping at the steaming tea to take control of herself. It was only a couple of days ago that he'd spoken so warmly of the holiday they were all going on together, and she'd felt so wanted, so special…as if she belonged with his family. But today he was different—cruelly different. She hadn't seen Theodore Montague in this kind of mood before. He seemed distant and detached, and for the first time she was being made to feel like the employee that she was. Why had she let herself think that she was liked any more than any of the others had been?

Defiance took over, and saved Lily from letting herself down. She went over to the table and sat down beside him calmly.

'I'll do it,' she said coldly. 'I'll ring this morning, as soon as you've gone. Why don't you leave the number of the agency you like to deal with, and I'll arrange some interviews for the week after next? The week before you go on holiday. Shall I do that?'

'That'll be perfect,' he said obliquely.

Almost immediately Lily drove herself home to collect some clean clothes and other personal belongings. Glancing around at her little flat, she couldn't help comparing it with Theo's place… Chalk and cheese just about summed it up, she thought. Then she straightened her shoulders. It might be a humble dwelling, but it was cosy and private, and always clean and tidy…the way she liked to keep it. She shrugged as she left, locking her front door securely. She'd be back here full-time sooner than she'd thought. Just as soon as a permanent and much more suitable nanny could be found for the Montague family. And that was fine by her!

When she got back the children were up and dressed and running around. Theo stayed just long enough to say goodbye and to tell them all to be good.

'Remember, there are three of you and only one of Lily,' he said. 'So be kind children and do as she asks.'

He turned to Lily for a second. She'd changed into a flowery sundress with a halter neckline which showed off her slender neck and shoulders, and she'd pulled her hair right back in a high ponytail, making her look pure and innocent…and lovely.

His features darkened. He'd better be going, or he'd be late. 'Are you quite sure you're OK today, Lily?' he asked as he went towards the door—knowing full well that she was. There was not a hint of the stress she'd endured yesterday.

'I've told you—I'm quite well, thank you,' Lily replied swiftly, only just managing not to sound as aggressive as she was feeling. 'The children will be perfectly safe with me, I assure you, and I won't drive them anywhere. So please don't worry about them. There's no need.'

He didn't look at her, but shrugged briefly. At that moment he hadn't been thinking about his children, he'd been thinking about her—but she was obviously feeling defensive this morning, guilty because she'd forgotten those wretched tablets, he thought. 'You've got my mobile number,' he said. 'Ring me—any time—if you need to.'

Although there were times when she felt utterly exhausted, the following day passed amazingly quickly for Lily. The children seemed to treat her as a contemporary, rather than someone older, and there was never a shortage of things to do.

On the second day, Bea looked in on them while they were all sitting at the kitchen table doing some colouring.

'Well, well,' she said, leaning over to admire what they were doing. 'What beautiful pictures!'

'We went to the shop this morning, and Lily bought us all new pens,' Alex said, not even bothering to stop what he was doing.

'Yes, and we're making pancakes for tea,' Freya said. 'Lily's going to show us how to toss them.'

'They're going to go right up to the ceiling!' Tom-Tom exclaimed, not wanting to be left out.

Bea smiled down at Lily. 'You've certainly got everything all sussed,' she said kindly. 'I know it's such a relief to Theo that you're here.'

Lily smiled faintly. 'I hope so,' she said slowly. 'But

he's asked me to arrange some interviews…to find someone more permanent to replace me,' she added. As Bea raised her eyebrows, she said quickly, 'And how is your husband, Bea? I'm sorry he's got to have tests.'

The older woman shrugged. 'Oh, well, it happens to all of us from time to time. But he'll be OK, I'm sure. His dad lived to be ninety-nine!'

Bea waited a few more minutes before departing. 'Don't forget to give me a shout if you're desperate, Lily,' she said. 'You know where I live.'

Leaving the children to finish their colouring, Lily went into the sitting room to ring the agency again—and wasn't surprised to learn that there was a shortage of possible candidates at this time of year. There were only two on offer at the moment, she was told, so she made an arrangement for them to come on two consecutive mornings during the week she'd agreed with Theo.

With an undeniably sinking heart, Lily replaced the receiver. Doing this was like sealing her own fate—signing her own death warrant. Yet she knew that was silly. She'd known all along that her contract with Theo was only temporary—her own wish, because she didn't want to be tied down. She'd told him so again the morning he'd left. That she wanted time to make her own plans. But the problem was that she loved her three charges more than she'd ever have thought possible—really loved them. And it was the prospect of saying goodbye to them that was getting to her.

She allowed her thoughts to pause for a moment before continuing with her soul-searching. It was right that she should go, that she should not stay here any longer than necessary, because she admitted to undergoing a sea change in her personality. She admitted to wanting to be near—physically near—to the children's father, and that must never happen. It flew in the face of her determination never to let a man touch her ever again. Up until very recently, the thought had been repellent, disgusting! But, unbelievably, that was beginning to change. And she must not let it. Because she could never again trust a man. Theo was right to take steps for someone else to replace her. For Lily's own sake and sanity she must be prepared to draw a line beneath her present situation and retreat once more into the protective shell she'd formed around herself since childhood.

On Monday there was a call from Theo to say he'd be home later, hopefully in time to see the children before they went to bed. 'I haven't heard from you,' he said to Lily, 'so I assume everything's been OK?'

'We've got on well, thank you,' Lily replied. 'We've had a great time in the park and the garden, and we all went to the local swimming baths yesterday.' She paused. 'They're brilliant swimmers, aren't they? I was impressed—even Tom keeps himself afloat with no difficulty.'

'Yes. My wife took them swimming almost as soon as they were born,' Theo said. 'But I'm quite surprised that Tom agreed to go—he seems to have become rather afraid of it since his mother's not been here.'

'He wasn't afraid at all,' Lily said. 'Of course I stayed close to him all the time—the other two just splashed around by themselves, and Freya can do several lengths without stopping.'

There was a pause, then, 'And you, Lily? They haven't run you off your feet, have they? No more migraines?'

Lily sighed inwardly. He wasn't going to let her forget that in a hurry. 'No,' she said shortly. 'I've been perfectly well, thank you. I told you—I don't expect to get another like that for quite a while.'

He cleared his throat. 'Have you had the torrential rain that we've been enjoying up here?'

Lily was faintly surprised. He didn't seem to want to ring off, she thought. But wasting his time talking about the weather didn't fit the man's persona at all. 'No rain here,' she said. 'Sunshine all the time.'

'Oh, that's good.' Another pause. 'Did—did you contact the agency?'

Lily's throat contracted. Of course! That was what he'd been leading up to. He just hadn't liked to mention it straight away. 'I did,' she replied. 'You'll be seeing two candidates next week—a Mrs Evershot, who's in her fifties, and a Miss Green, who's just qualified. She'd be in her early twenties, I guess.'

'Oh, right. Well, then, we'll have to see what we make of them.' He hesitated. 'I shall rely utterly on your opinion—I don't have much faith in my own where this is concerned.'

Lily swallowed, not trusting herself to speak for a moment. The thought of Freya and Alex and gorgeous little Tom-Tom having to get used to yet another stand-in for their adored mother was as painful to her as it would surely be for them.

Eventually he rang off, and Lily sat where she was, the receiver in her hand. She could still hear his deep, mesmerising, reassuring voice. How was she going to restart her life without them all? she thought, with a feeling of despair touching her.

Theo, standing by the window in his hotel room, was having difficulty understanding himself…having difficulty understanding the rush of tenderness which had swept over him as soon as he'd heard Lily's voice. He breathed in slowly, then exhaled—a long, slow sigh, part-revelation and part-shame that this young woman could reawaken such emotions in him.

Presently, Lily stood up and went out into the garden, where the children were playing. 'Daddy's just been on the phone,' she said, 'and he'll be home at bedtime.' He had not asked to speak to any of them, she noted.

Freya came over to her. 'But you'll be able to finish that next story, though, won't you, Lily? I love it when you leave us halfway through like that, because I try to make up my own ending. I think I know how the fairy is going to sort everything out this time,' she said eagerly.

'Oh, well—if you know, there's no need for me to tell you,' Lily teased.

'Yes, there is!' the child said at once. 'Your endings are always lovely, Lily. The best bit! I just want to know whether this one is the same as mine.'

Lily had to smile. Even the boys liked listening to her fairy stories—she only hoped they realised that that was all they were: stories. She'd hate to be accused of filling their heads with nonsense.

Theo arrived home in time to see the children have their supper—Lily had prepared roasted cod with fresh garden peas, which they'd all helped to pod earlier in the day. When he came into the kitchen, the children jumped down to greet him—though Freya merely held her face up for a perfunctory kiss before moving away. Lily bit her lip. The child showed very little real affection for her father, and Lily knew how deeply hurt he must be.

Much later, when it was bedtime, Theo came too, joining in the bathtime antics as the boys splashed about.

Afterwards he went downstairs, with a request from Lily that he switch on the oven for their own supper. 'I shan't be long,' she told him.

'Lily's got to finish the story before you can have your supper, Daddy,' Freya said.

He grinned, clearly pleased to be back home, and Lily, glancing up at him, thought how young and boyish he looked, his hair damp on his forehead after all the splashing in the bathroom. 'I just hope the story doesn't take too long,' he said over his shoulder, 'because I'm hungry.'

After the children were asleep, and Theo and Lily had eaten their supper, they went into the sitting room with their coffee, each taking their normal places on opposite sofas.

'Have you been comfortable enough here—in your own room, I mean?' Theo said, as he filled their cups from the percolator.

'You don't need to ask,' Lily replied. 'I feel perfectly at home—thank you.' She looked up at him quickly. He'd only asked her to stay for the three nights while he was away—perhaps this was his way of saying that it wasn't necessary for her to stay overnight any longer. But he cut in on her thoughts.

'Well, then, why don't you stay with the arrangement?' he said easily, handing her the jug of cream. 'I can't help thinking that it would be more convenient from your point of view—not having to make the trip across town twice a day.' He drank from his cup. 'It's not that I would expect any more from you—we'd get our own breakfasts—just that for the relatively short time you'll be here with us I should think it would be less irritating, more convenient than having to go home each night.' He paused. 'The children clearly love having you here.'

Now he looked across at her, his searching gaze searing into her. She might have had the total care of his children for the last three days, listening to their endless chatter and cooking for them, but she still managed to look attractive and relaxed, he thought, her complexion clear, her eyes bright as she looked back at him.

Lily, aware of his perceptive scrutiny, was conscious that her colour had risen at his words. Yes, she thought, it would certainly be *very* convenient—for *him!* To have her around twenty-four hours a day would give him complete freedom to come and go as he pleased! But even as she thought that she was ready to give him the benefit of the doubt. He had not taken advantage of her in any way at all since she'd been here, she acknowledged. He was impeccably polite and considerate—especially when they were here alone, she thought gratefully. He was totally unoppressive, leaving her room to breath, and to be herself.

And why shouldn't he be? She was merely his employee, filling an inconvenient gap in his personal affairs.

'Whatever you think best, Theo,' she said coolly, in answer to his suggestion. 'If it suits your purpose then I'll stay. I agree that in some ways it will be more straightforward for me not to have to go home each evening. Though I'll naturally have to return now and again to see to things at the flat…'

'Of course,' he said at once, getting up. 'You can have what time off you like, Lily—so long as you liaise with Bea about covering for the children. That is the arrangement I made with her when you took over—that she'd be on hand if necessary.'

Lily got up then too, and looked up at him. 'Goodnight…I think I'm ready for bed,' she said, and he nodded.

'I'm not surprised.' He hesitated. 'You work hard, Lily—and I— I very much appreciate all you do for us here.'

Well, that was a nice little formal pat on the back for her, Lily thought.

Just then the doorbell rang, and they looked at each other in surprise. It was almost ten o'clock.

'I'm not expecting visitors,' Theo said briefly, moving past Lily and going into the hall. 'And it can't be Bea, because she has her own key.'

He opened the door wide and took a step backward. 'Oliver!' he exclaimed. 'What in heaven's name brings you here? Come in!'

The visitor—tall, fair-haired, and clearly having had a lot to drink—entered the house, clasping Theo's outstretched hand of greeting and looking past him at Lily.

'So sorry to burst in on you uninvited, Theo,' Oliver said thickly. 'I should have rung to warn you, but you know me.'

'Yes, I do, Oliver,' Theo replied cheerfully. 'You were never one for life's little details…but it's great to see you. Come and tell all!' He turned to Lily. 'This disreputable creature is Oliver Crowe, Lily—we've known each other since university. It must be at least three years since we had a get-together.' He paused, turning to Oliver. 'Lily is my children's nanny…'

The man lost no time in advancing towards Lily, towering above her as he took her hand. 'Well, you certainly know how to pick 'em, old man—but then, that is but one of your many gifts, I seem to remember.' He gazed down at Lily, taking in her appearance with a long, salacious stare. Then he turned to Theo. 'I'm in the middle of a mate's stag night—in the town at the

Royal Hotel. There are going to be some antics laid on for later, I believe… I suddenly remembered that this is where you live and thought I'd get a cab and pay you a flying visit.'

He lurched slightly on his feet, and Theo's lip curled slightly. He turned to Lily.

'D'you mind rustling up some coffee for my inebriated friend, Lily? I think we'd better bring him down to earth if he's going to enjoy the rest of the celebrations.'

'Of course,' Lily said, going at once to retrieve their own coffee things from the sitting room, then moving quickly past the men into the kitchen.

As she prepared the drinks she could hear them chatting—Oliver's voice strident and excitable. And as she reached for the cream from the fridge her hands were trembling and colour had risen in her cheeks. Oliver's podgy hand had been clammy in hers, and his fingers had curled suggestively into her palm. His breath, hot and beery, had been overwhelming…she could still smell it. She shuddered, her body trembling right down to her toes.

She stood impatiently by the kettle, which was taking ages to boil. She'd give them their coffee, then disappear rapidly into the sanctuary of her room, she thought.

But before she could do that Oliver had come in to stand beside her, his admiration unrestrained. 'Theo's just gone upstairs to dig out some photos we've been talking about,' he said. He continued staring down at her, and Lily felt herself cringing, her heart doing a mad dance in her chest. 'You're a pretty little thing,' he said, his voice slurring slightly. 'I wonder where Theo found *you*.' He came even closer, nudging his hip against Lily's, and she could feel the soft roll of excess fat around his middle wallow against her thinly clad body.

Suddenly she knew she couldn't stand this a second longer, and wrenched away from him.

'No. *No!*' she cried out. 'Go away—get off!'

With the force of her movement he staggered back, and held on to a chair for support.

'What the…? What did I do?' he said, clearly amazed at her reaction.

Lily was shaking all over, her hands hardly able to continue what she'd been doing. Just then Theo came in. He strode towards her, his dark eyebrows raised.

'What's the matter?' he demanded roughly. He stared down at Lily's flaming cheeks and immediately took the kettle of boiling water from her. 'Here—let me,' he said. 'Did you scald yourself, Lily? When I heard you call out I thought something awful had happened.'

'It's all right…nothing's happened,' Lily said shakily. 'I was just—I was afraid…' She knew she was stuttering incoherently. 'I was afraid that Oliver was going to jog my arm as I was pouring the boiling water. I'm sorry—I'm sorry…'

There was silence for a moment as Theo turned to make the coffee, and Lily was aware that her cheeks were wet with the tears which had formed unstoppably in her eyes. She was aware that Theo had seen them too.

He had realized straight away that something more had gone on, and that whatever it was had upset Lily, who was clearly agitated. Had upset her a lot. And that upset *him*.

He loaded the tray. 'Come on, Oliver. Let's get some of this down you,' he said, in a surprisingly curt tone. He'd known his friend for many years—knew his reputation with women—and although he had only been absent for a couple of minutes it had obviously been long enough for Oliver to try it on with Lily. He glanced down at her. 'You go on to bed, Lily,' he murmured. 'And thanks for doing this.'

The two men left the kitchen and Lily stayed where she was for a few moments, waiting for her heart-rate to lessen, for her breathing to become steady. She knew that tomorrow, when they were alone together, Theo would question her about what had really happened. He would have known straight away that it had been nothing at all to do with boiling water.

And then Lily's tears really did begin to flow, offering her some relief. Because what would be her explanation? How could she tell Theo of the revulsion which had gripped her when she'd felt the heat of his friend's body close in on hers? How could she tell him of the fear which had dogged her nearly all her life…that men spelt danger and disgust and disquiet? Of her conviction that their main function was to control and to seduce until women agreed to their demands?

She took a tissue from the box on the table, dabbing at her eyes. How could she say all that to one of the most handsome, magnetic, mesmerising, totally unmenacing men she had ever met, whose interest in her was solely out of practical necessity? How could she tell him that he was the only man she'd known in all her years she felt she could trust with her very life?

With a shock of realisation Lily knew that, unimaginably, Theo Montague was the first man whose body she longed to feel hard against her own.

CHAPTER SEVEN

To Lily's immense relief, Theo didn't refer to the incident in the kitchen, and the following week passed in the normal way, with him seemingly totally wrapped up in his work. He left very early most mornings, and on three occasions didn't come home for his supper, apparently having evening meetings which ended in a meal somewhere.

When he was at home, although he treated Lily in much the same way as usual, she couldn't help being aware of a slightly different attitude towards her. At the end of each day, alone in her room, she found herself going over and over everything—every word which had passed between them—trying to define the reason for what she saw as his strange coolness towards her. It was not what he said, it was the way she caught him looking at her now and then. And once or twice, when their eyes had met, his gaze had seemed to lock onto hers—which had sent Lily's colour flooding her cheeks, as usual.

Perhaps Oliver had complained to him about her rather irrational behaviour that night? Lily thought. And it might have upset Theo that his friend had felt insulted. Perhaps that was what it was.

But, thankfully, the children were as delightful as ever, and the days passed happily for Lily, making her realise just how much she was going to miss them.

On the Tuesday of the following week Mrs Evershot was due to make an appearance, and although nothing much had been said about it, Lily wondered whether her own presence was still required at the interview. She turned to Theo as she finished clearing their supper things the evening before.

'You haven't forgotten that you're seeing a possible nanny tomorrow?' she asked, not looking at him. 'She'll be here at ten.'

'No, I haven't forgotten,' he said shortly. 'I've made arrangements for someone to cover for me until mid-day…it shouldn't take too long, should it?'

He looked down at her with that expression in his eyes again, and Lily thought, Why ask me? You've done this sort of thing before—I haven't! But she replied, 'I should think an hour would be plenty… I imagine that one knows almost immediately whether a person is going to be suitable or not…and of course the children's reaction is important too, isn't it?'

He thrust a hand through his hair. 'Yes, of course.' He hesitated. 'It's always tricky,' he added slowly.

'And then Miss Green will be here on Wednesday,' Lily said, trying to lighten the atmosphere by brightening her tone. 'Also at ten o'clock.'

'That'll be OK,' Theo said. 'I've taken that day off, so there's no pressure.' He paused. 'I thought we'd all go out together somewhere afterwards—as a sort of treat.' He stared out of the window moodily. 'This business is hard for them.'

Lily let his words sink in as she stared up at him. *Tell*

me about it, she thought. *I know all about meeting strangers who are going to look after me. I know all about different faces, different personalities, different expectations, different rules.*

'You *will* sit in on the interview with me, won't you, Lily?' he said earnestly, and for the first time since she'd known him Lily detected a sudden lack of his usual self-assurance. This strong, dynamic, highly intellectual man looked a bit lost—bewildered, even—and she dragged her gaze away from him, feeling such an unexpected rush of warmth towards him that she moved right away, out of his orbit, busying herself with rearranging some mugs on the shelf.

'If you think I can be of any practical use, Theo,' she said over her shoulder, 'then of course I'll be happy to meet the women…and give you my opinion. For what it's worth.'

'I'm sure it's worth a lot more than mine,' he replied at once. 'I haven't done too well so far where this matter is concerned—apart from the present incumbent,' he added, smiling. 'You seem to know exactly how to handle my kids, Lily—they've not been this happy, relaxed and contented since—' He broke off before finishing the sentence.

Lily said slowly, 'Maybe that's because I, too, had a succession of different people trying to bring me up,' she said. 'I know how it feels.'

He shrugged. 'Well, whatever the reason, I'm grateful for it. Even Freya seems to have lost that permanently injured expression on her face—except when she looks at me, that is,' he added.

No more was said, and instead of going into the sitting room to have coffee with him, Lily excused herself, saying that she wanted to go to bed, and that she also wanted to make a call to her brother.

Upstairs, Lily went over to the window and stared out across the garden. She felt empty and dispirited—and she knew the reason why. The thought of helping to select another person to have charge of the Montague children was giving her actual physical pain, and she pressed her hands into her sides to try and quell the sensation. She knew the procedure had to be gone through, yet how could she bear it?

Then common sense took over. It had been wrong, all wrong, to let herself get this close to the family, because it was going to end in tears. She knew that the children would hate saying goodbye to her, and when the time came her own heart would be at breaking point, she thought. But her agreement with Theo had only been a very short-term one. She had never seen herself as a full-time carer for other people's children—or any children, for that matter. Definitely none of her own, that was for sure. She shuddered at the thought of the physical obligations which must be endured in creating a new life.

She smiled suddenly as she spotted a tiny field mouse scampering through the grass in the garden. That little creature's plans were far less complicated than her own, Lily thought. All it required was finding enough to eat and to stay alive. Simple, really. She turned away from the window. No, staying here was muddying the waters of her ambition… Surely there was something, somewhere, waiting for her, beckoning to her? Something she hadn't even thought of yet to give her fulfilment? And if she was to discover what it was she needed to break away from this house—and its occupants.

Picking up her mobile, she rang Sam's number. Almost straight away his lovely familiar voice answered.

'Lily! Great to hear you! Tell me all. It's nice and quiet here now, so fire away. How's the job going?'

Lily had told him what she was doing until October.

'The job's fine,' she replied.

There was a chuckle. 'And how's Mr Wonderful?'

'Mr who?'

'Come off it, Lily. We both know who I'm talking about… Mr Drop-Dead Gorgeous who you met on the plane…that *is* who you're working for, isn't it?' Sam persisted.

'Oh, yes, I'm looking after his children,' she said airily. 'But it's work, Sam—work. And it's all coming to an end in no time at all. He's interviewing for my replacement tomorrow, as a matter of fact, and at the end of the summer I shall be footloose and fancy-free once again.' Despite her best endeavours, a stifled sob left Lily's lips as she spoke the words, and she swallowed hard to control herself.

There was a short silence.

'Lily—are you OK? What's the matter?' Sam hesitated. 'He's not giving you grief, is he? Not trying it on…?'

'No, of course not, silly!' Lily blew her nose. 'I was trying not to sneeze just then, that's all,' she lied.

'Well, then, just so long as you take care of yourself, Lily…'

'I'm used to doing that, Sam,' she said. 'I've been doing it all my life, remember?'

'Well, don't forget you're welcome here any time,' he said. 'Come for an extended holiday while you work out your next step—you may even find something here that interests you.'

They chatted on for a while. Sam was still excited about his prosperity, and anxious to share it all with his sister.

Lily smiled briefly as she snapped her phone shut. She still found it hard to believe that she actually had a blood relation who cared about her. Even though they didn't see very much of each other, it was lovely just knowing that he existed. That he was there.

The next morning at breakfast, Theo casually told the children that someone was arriving who might be coming to help look after them. All three looked up at him as he spoke.

'What's she called?' Freya asked flatly.

'Mrs Evershot,' Theo said.

'Is she coming to shoot us, then?' Alex asked.

'I don't like her,' Tom piped up. 'I don't like her name.' He looked across at Lily. 'You won't let her shoot us, will you, Lily?'

Lily had her back to the children while she was making their milk drinks, and she said, without turning around, 'Of course she's not going to shoot you—or anyone else,' she added. 'And anyway, she's only coming for a visit today.'

There was an uncomfortable silence after that, while the children finished their toast, and Theo threw a quick glance at Lily, raising his eyebrows briefly.

She sat down at her place at the table. 'I've organised a very difficult set of tasks for you three today,' she said brightly. She sipped from her mug of tea. 'First of all, you have to search for some of your toys that I've hidden in the garden. There are twelve out there altogether. And then when you've found them you must colour the pictures I've chosen for you to do… If they're good enough, we'll mount them on some sugar paper and hang them up here in the kitchen. And then,' she said, her eyes twinkling across at them, 'there's a very, very, *very* difficult quiz you've got to do.'

'I love quizzes,' Freya said eagerly, drinking in every word that Lily was saying. 'And I'll help Tom-Tom with the answers, because he's only little.'

'That's kind of you, Freya,' Lily said, 'but I've made Tom's a bit easier than yours—and Alex's a bit harder than Tom's. So it's all going to be fair.'

All this information had completely taken over from the thought of Mrs Evershot's arrival, and Theo looked across at Lily as she nibbled at her slice of toast. Her opinion of herself as being rubbish at looking after children was completely unjustified, he thought. She knew exactly how to deal with them—seemed to understand what made them tick, how they were feeling. And she'd obviously spent some time devising the morning's activities in order to take their minds off having to meet another stranger. His expression darkened, and he breathed a long sigh of regret that Lily was going to leave them—that her weeks here were numbered. But he knew that it just had to be… She wanted to spread her wings and fly to some unknown destination, and he would never try to stand in her way.

He knew with painful certainty that it was right she should go…soon. Because he readily admitted to himself that his feelings for her were developing rapidly, with every moment she was around. And that disturbed and even shocked him. The mere thought that anyone should so soon take Elspeth's place in his heart was unacceptable. He had closed his mind to that part of his life—not only because he had made that silent promise to his wife as she died, but also because he would never, ever expect his children to have to try to accept and love a step-mother. Too much had been spoken and written about the enormous emotional difficulties of such a situation—even though there were many happy exceptions to the rule. His children would never have to witness their father loving another woman, sleeping with another woman, speaking in the affectionate terms which had been purely the privilege and right of their mother to another woman. They had suffered enough already.

He shook his head as his thoughts tossed and tumbled in his mind... Why had he ever met Lily? What fateful hand had touched his shoulder and made him ask her to look after his family, to move in with them so that he was forced to be near her, admire her, smell her delight-ful presence, even seated as she was now, a foot or two away from him? The faint drift of her now familiar perfume tormented him, and he was filled with such a longing to drag her into his arms that he had to stand up quickly, pushing his chair back.

'I'll be up in my study until...for an hour or so,' he said, and Lily nodded.

'As soon as we've cleared up here the children have a lot to do!' She looked down at them. 'I'll give you half an hour to find those toys that I've hidden—and they're not in easy places,' she warned them. 'If something's too easy, it's no fun.'

At precisely ten a.m. Mrs Evershot arrived, and as she opened the door Lily's heart sank. Could this be her re-placement? Was this the person who was going to be looking after her charges? The woman was middle-aged, with a straight, no-nonsense kind of face, her grey hair was swept up in a bun at the back of her head, and she was neatly dressed in a suitable grey straight skirt, mid-calf-length, with a matching jacket over a plain blouse.

Lily ushered her into the sitting room, and for the next half an hour or so Lily sat quietly listening to the conversation between Theo and the woman. He was polite and businesslike as he asked her about her previous experience and what she expected if she came to work here. Mrs Evershot didn't leave him in any doubt about that.

'I take it that I shall be living in?' she said flatly. 'But I expect my days to end at eight, after the children are in bed, and to have a day and a half off each week.' She paused. 'I am prepared to organise light meals, but no spectacular cooking. I'm afraid that's not my line. But they won't starve while I'm here.' She flicked at some-thing invisible on her skirt and sat back. 'Also, if I'm required to be with the children during the evenings— say if you have a late function to attend, Mr Montague— then that would be an additional extra to my agreed salary.' She gave him a tight little smile. 'I find it's much better to get all these little details sorted at the outset.'

Lily stared blankly ahead of her, not wanting to catch Theo's eye. This was obviously just a job to Mrs Evershot, she thought. Vocation didn't come into it. She was undoubtedly a supremely efficient woman—but with something other than blood running through her veins. Old memories piled into Lily's consciousness, making her throat dry and her palms clammy. The woman had barely mentioned the children, other than to confirm their names and ages.

Theo stood up—and to Lily's perceptive gaze he looked weary. 'I'm sure you'd like to meet my off-spring,' he said casually. 'They're in the kitchen.'

He brought the children in, and with a painful stab to her heart Lily saw that Freya was holding both the boys' hands protectively. They looked so small and defenceless standing there, with not a smile on their faces. Lily wanted to rush and gather them all to her and run out of the room, run away with them…

After the introductions were made—with Mrs Evershot taking a long, hard look at them all, saying that she was sure they would get on well together once certain rules were established—she stood up decisively.

'Well, there we are, then.' She glanced at her watch. 'I must go—I've two more of these to get through this morning.' She turned to Theo. 'If you consider me suitable, Mr Montague,' she said primly, 'I'll have a tour of the house to see where everything is at that point. The agency informed me that I won't be needed for some time?'

'Yes, that's right,' Theo replied shortly. 'Well into October…'

'Wonderful! That gives me some time to relax before battle commences!' the woman said, with an awkward attempt at jocularity.

As soon as she'd gone, the children flung themselves at Lily.

'I don't like her,' Freya said, without preamble. 'You didn't like her, either, did you, Lily? I could see by your face.'

'And she *is* going to shoot us,' Alex said. 'She said there would be a battle!'

Theo put his arms around his sons, glancing at Freya, who had climbed onto Lily's lap. 'Don't worry,' he said, 'that's the last we'll be seeing of Mrs Evershot.'

Lily eased Freya from her lap and stood up. Theo glanced down at her, a rueful half-smile on his lips.

'Well?' he asked quietly.

'Thanks—but no, thanks, I should think,' Lily said briefly, and suddenly, without stopping to think what he was doing, Theo wrapped his arms around them all—including Lily—in one big circle, so that they formed a close family unit, clutching at each other for support. And being pulled this close to him, feeling his firm muscles tensing against her body, Lily experienced an almost overwhelming need to touch him…to be touched by him.

Just as suddenly he released them all, and walked briskly towards the door to go to his afternoon clinic.

Lily, followed by the children, went into the kitchen to inspect the colouring.

'These are all going to be fantastic!' she exclaimed. 'This afternoon we'll get the paddling pool out, if you like.'

Getting ready for bed that night, Lily could hardly bear the thought of seeing tomorrow's candidate. Trying to be objective about deciding who was to be taking care of the children was almost impossible, she thought. No one would ever be good enough. No one would ever be worthy of the care of Freya and Alex and Tom-Tom. They needed a mother, not a job-seeker—someone who'd be here today and gone tomorrow… They needed consistency and stability—something Lily herself had felt deprived of all the time she was growing up. And while she admitted that she'd often been difficult—had often perversely not *wanted* the latest family to succeed where everyone else had failed—the children living here were blameless. They had done nothing to deserve their present situation.

Sitting late at his desk in his private office at the hospital, Theo stared at the bundle of files in front of him—stared at the computer waiting to receive yet more information about his little patients. All these children had problems—physical problems, some worse than others—which he was doing his best to sort out. He never failed to be thankful that his three were so healthy, only suffering from the normal childish things from time to time. But their pain was a different pain. Their life was not straightforward, either, he thought. Their problem was one which he didn't seem able to relieve. There was no remedy for sadness and acute loss, however hard he tried to think of one.

He'd failed utterly...until he'd met Lily, that was, who seemed to have stepped into the children's hearts as if it had been pre-ordained. If only he could feel, deep inside himself, that it was the right thing to do, he'd beg her to stay with them. For ever. He'd triple her salary—anything to persuade her to have the long-term care of his children until they were old enough to function alone, as young adults. But although she clearly adored them, he was certain she wouldn't agree. Despite her transparently sweet nature, there was a band of steel running through Lily, which he'd detected from the outset, and she wasn't likely to change her mind about anything important—anything she'd set her heart on.

But what about his own needs? he mused, opening the next folder and smoothing the pages down carefully. He knew his children's needs, and he thought he knew Lily's, but what of his own? What about those? He stared blankly at the typewritten information in front of him, only just beginning to accept the undeniable truth that he needed her—not just any woman, but the woman living in his house, nurturing his family. He needed to hold her in his arms, to cover her mouth with his, to actually feel her heart beating in tandem with his own.

This self-revelation made him exultant and despairing at the same time. Exultant because he had admitted, at last, that he was not dead inside after all…and despairing because he knew that this unexpectedly passionate masculine desire would never be satisfied. Not with the woman who seldom left his thoughts.

The following day—ten minutes late for the appointment—Miss Green arrived. She was dressed in a sexy, thigh-skimming multi-coloured sundress, with her long, auburn hair hanging loosely around her bare shoulders, her slender legs tanned, and her feet, with toenails varnished bright red, encased in sparkling strappy sandals.

Lily was faintly amazed at the girl's appearance, which didn't seem quite right for an interview, she thought.

But as if she knew what Lily was thinking, Miss Green said, 'It's such a *super* day—I decided to come in mufti! After all, I'm not on duty yet, am I?' She giggled as she followed Lily into the sitting room.

Theo was already there, and as he'd taken the day off he, too, was dressed casually in light cotton trousers and an open-neck sports shirt. He stood up immediately to greet the visitor, taking her outstretched hand and looking down at her with what Lily saw as typical male admiration. And Miss Green was clearly bowled over by the sight of her prospective employer, who towered above her, his dark eyes glinting, the cut of his jaw pronouncing his total strength and masculinity.

Lily stood well back by the window and watched Theo conduct his second interview.

For the next few minutes she hardly heard a word of

what the two were saying to each other. She was trans-fixed by Miss Green's uninhibited attitude towards Theo. Refusing the seat opposite, she sat down next to him on the sofa, her bare leg resting lightly against his thigh, looking up at him with a longing expression on her face, letting her eyes and her long lashes speak volumes. Theo's richly dark voice resonated domi-nantly, mingling with the high-pitched little giggle emerging regularly from Miss Green's fulsome lips. He stared down, seeming to take in everything about her, considering her answers to his questions, and as his elegant head bent slightly to the side, Lily suddenly felt anonymous—and pointless.

She wasn't needed here at all, she thought. Theo Montague was quite capable of sizing people up without any input from her! And sizing her up he certainly was! He couldn't take his eyes off her! Surely he wasn't being taken in by the girl's unashamed flirting?

Presently, the boys came in, and Lily noted that this time they did show slightly more interest than before—though they still kept their distance.

'Where's Freya?' Theo demanded.

'She says she's not coming down,' Alex said. 'She doesn't want to meet anyone today.'

Lily moved swiftly. 'I'll fetch her,' she said, and soon all three children stood waiting to be looked at.

'Oh, aren't they *sweet?*' Miss Green gushed, going over at once and kneeling down by Tom. 'I love little boys…*all* little boys,' she added mischievously, looking up at Theo as she spoke, and then adding as an after-thought, 'And little girls too, of course!' Then she sat down again, obviously in no hurry to go.

But Lily couldn't stand being in the room a moment

longer, and went quickly towards the door. 'You must excuse me,' she said briskly. 'I've things to do...'

'Yes, we mustn't keep you any longer, Miss Green,' Theo said smoothly. 'Thank you so much for coming... I'll be in touch with the agency this week.'

Miss Green stood up reluctantly. 'Oh...OK, then...' she said. Barely glancing at Lily, she treated Theo to another of her seductive looks before following him to the door. Finally he closed it, and she was gone.

'Ye gods,' he said, running his hand through his hair. He moved across to stand by Lily, and put both hands on her shoulders. 'Thanks for prising her out of the house,' he said. 'I thought we were never going to get rid of her.'

'We don't like *her,* either,' Freya said cheerfully.

'No, we don't,' Tom said. 'Do we, Alex?'

'Her toes were bleeding,' Alex said. 'There was blood all over her nails.'

As they stood there for a few seconds, Lily let the warmth of Theo's hands seep through her, and when he slid them gently over the tops of her shoulders and down across the length of her arms, it was the nearest thing she had ever experienced to the truly sensual touch of a man— the closest thing to being caressed in the significant way in which a male caressed a female. And she loved it.

Lily felt herself start to tremble. A little bit at first, and then more so. Not with the fear and distaste she knew so well, but with a desire she'd never known she was capable of. And this time she wasn't going to pull herself away and run away and hide. She would stay perfectly still and wish that this moment could be frozen in time for ever.

CHAPTER EIGHT

IN SPITE of having had to meet the two prospective nannies, the children cheered up very quickly—especially as their father was going to be with them for the rest of the day.

'What are we going to do, then, Daddy?' Alex asked, looking up at Theo.

'I thought we'd go to the fair this afternoon,' Theo replied. 'It's only here until the weekend, so we'd better make the most of it.'

'Yes, and Lily is going to sit with *me* in the dodgems,' Freya said. 'You always go with the boys.'

Theo shot her a quick glance. 'If I remember rightly, Freya, last year you refused to go on anything at all.'

'Well…I didn't *feel* like it then, did I?' Freya answered petulantly. 'Anyway, I don't like it when people bang into each other on purpose.'

Lily got them all ready for the trip, letting them choose what they wanted to wear, and presently they came jostling and pushing down the stairs, just as Bea looked in to say hello to everyone. She beamed at the sight of them looking so obviously happy and excited.

'Well—what's on the menu today?' she asked.

'We're all going to the fair!' Alex exclaimed. 'D'you want to come, Bea?'

The woman laughed. 'I've given up on those things, Alex.' She glanced at Lily. 'You're certainly giving them a good time while you're here, Lily,' she said.

'Oh, this was Theo's idea,' Lily said. She paused. 'And it's a good thing that he *is* coming, because I'm not very brave on fast roundabouts and rollercoasters. I shall probably be standing at the side, watching.'

Just then Theo came down, and Bea, looking up at him, was struck by how relaxed he seemed. Her shrewd mind sensed that Lily probably had something to do with that. Her eyes narrowed briefly. It was not right that this highly eligible man should shut himself away emotionally, as he'd undoubtedly done since his wife had died. She and Joe had discussed it privately, many times... Theo was far too young not to have a woman in his life, and, glancing at him now, it seemed to her that the present nanny for his children seemed to be filling several gaps at once.

Bea crouched down for a moment to secure one of Tom's sandals. Wouldn't it be wonderful if Lily could stay on indefinitely? For Theo's sake as well as for the children—who clearly adored the girl. Bea checked her thoughts. She knew she was inclined to be romantic at times—but what if she was? Lily was pretty, intelligent, and so warm-hearted—a man could do worse. And even if her presence did turn out to be the expected temporary arrangement, she might kick-start Theo into realising that permanent mourning was not right. That one day soon he should make a life for himself that wasn't entirely wrapped up in children—his own and other people's.

Bea stood up and pulled Freya towards her, to re-tie her hair ribbon which had come loose. 'Well, now, you all go and enjoy yourselves,' she said, and, giving Theo a sidelong glance she added, 'I think it's time that Lily had a bit of a treat all to herself.' She hesitated. 'Why don't you take her to that special restaurant, Theo—the one you've taken Joe and me to a few times? She'd love it, I'm sure—and with all the cooking she has to do here I think she deserves an evening off, don't you?'

Bea showed not a trace of embarrassment at making the suggestion. She'd been enmeshed in this family's life for so long, in good times and bad, she'd become more like a member of the clan rather than a neighbour of long standing.

Lily coloured up, opening her mouth to protest, but Theo responded at once. 'What a good idea, Bea. Can you do the honours later, then—give the children their supper and put them to bed?'

'You don't need to ask!' Bea's face was wreathed in smiles—her little ploy had worked first time! 'Anyway, I *should* take over now and then,' she said, 'or I shall forget how everything's done.' She turned to Lily. 'What's for supper, Lily?'

'It's cold roast chicken and salad tonight,' Lily said, and Tom broke in.

'Can we have some more of that fudge sauce with our pudding as well?' He looked up at Bea. 'Lily has made fudge sauce again, and it's yummy, yummy, *yummy!*'

'Chicken salad and fudge sauce it is!' Bea said happily. 'I think I can manage that.'

'And before we go to sleep, Bea, can you tell us a story?' Alex asked eagerly. 'Lily does—every night. It's always about a little girl called Eve and a fairy who's her friend, and this fairy makes nice things happen to everyone, and—'

Bea put up her hands in mock horror. 'I'm no good at telling stories,' she said. 'But I'll certainly read to you. Will that do?'

Sitting opposite Theo in the exclusive restaurant, Lily felt all her diffidence melting away. When Bea had put him in such an awkward position earlier, making it impossible for him to disagree with her suggestion, Lily had thought she was going to die of embarrassment. But she had to admit that he'd jumped at the idea. Perhaps he needed to be away from his kids for an hour or two occasionally, for his own sake?

Bea had whispered to Lily that 'smart' was the dress code for the place they were going to, and luckily she'd brought a sleeveless cotton sundress with her when she'd packed to come and live at Theo's home, which flattered her smooth shoulders and suntanned skin. Earlier, Freya had watched Lily get dressed, and gold, rather long and dangly earrings—a present from Sam—had been the child's selection from Lily's modest jewellery case. Lily had to admit that, with her hair coiled up in a simple chignon, the overall effect was good enough.

Freya had sat on the edge of her bed to watch proceedings, and had given her approval.

'You look really, really, *really* pretty,' she'd said. 'I'm going to have a dress like that one day.' She'd paused. 'I wish I was coming with you.'

'Maybe you'll be coming next time,' Lily had said. 'And anyway, Bea is looking forward to being with you... I'm sure she misses you since I've taken over.'

'I think the afternoon was a great success,' Theo said now. 'We've never missed this annual treat yet.'

He stared across at Lily, unable to hide his admiration. She was wearing the dress she'd worn when they were in Rome, and he remembered thinking then how well it suited her. But she seemed to become lovelier every time he looked at her, he thought. Maybe he was wearing the proverbial rose-tinted spectacles where she was concerned, because of the profound effect she was having on his children. They had not been this contented since before Elspeth had died, and that fact alone filled him with a rush of gratitude that he feared he might mistake for something more emotionally significant.

He shrugged inwardly. Stop going on about things, he told himself. He was happy to be here, alone with her, just for an hour or two. His preoccupation at work with children who needed him, and with the constant demands of his own offspring when he was off duty, sometimes made him feel completely submerged—as if he would never function again as a human being in his own right.

Lily smiled across at him, conscious that the flickering candlelight between them made his eyes look mysterious and enticing. She looked away quickly. 'Yes—I think all children like to be terrified of certain things now and then—so long as they're with people they trust,' she said. 'I was surprised how little Tom took it all in his stride, too. He's totally fearless, isn't he?'

Theo nodded. 'Yes—Freya's usually the squeamish one.' He hesitated. 'Although *you* don't seem to be a lover of fairgrounds, Lily. Do the rides upset you?'

'It's not that,' Lily said quickly. 'It's…' How was she going to put this without sounding pathetic? 'It's just that once you're strapped in, and the music starts, and then the ride begins to get faster and faster…well, you can't get off, can you? I always feel trapped. Entirely at the whim of the man working it—until *he* decides when it's all over.'

'You're right, of course. Though that's never crossed my mind,' Theo replied, thinking seriously about what Lily had just told him.

Just then the waiter—a young, attractive man— appeared at their side. 'May I bring you something to drink, Mr Montague?' he asked, throwing an appreciative glance at Lily.

Theo looked across at Lily. 'Will you have some wine this evening, Lily—or would you prefer something else?'

Lily smiled. This didn't seem like an occasion for her usual glass of water. She'd push the boat out! 'I'd love some wine, Theo,' she said. 'But please don't expect me to choose—I don't have much of a clue, I'm afraid.'

He grinned back at her, and Lily's heart gave a small but undeniable leap. His well-cut dark jacket, worn over an open-neck casual shirt, gave the merest glimpse of black body hair, visible against his strong, tanned skin. And his hands as they held the wine list were strong and capable, the fingers long and sensitive.

He pointed out his choice of wine to the waiter, adding a request for some sparkling water, and Lily felt herself relaxing more and more with every moment that passed. As usual, she felt totally unpressurised when she was with Theo, sensing that he understood her, that he could read her mind. And she liked the feeling it gave her.

Leaving them with a copy each of the dinner menu, the waiter departed. Theo leaned back in his chair for a moment.

'You might have declined the opportunity of going on the rollercoasters,' he said, 'but I was impressed at the way you handled that dodgem car. You managed to stop everyone—including the boys and me—from bumping into you. That certainly went down well with Freya—and you seemed to enjoy it, too, Lily.'

'The dodgems are the only things I'll go on,' Lily said, looking down at the selection of food on the list. 'Because I know I can get off if I really want to. Steer to the side and hop out.'

Theo was watching her as she spoke, his analytical mind attempting to penetrate this woman's complex nature. He could see that for some reason she was intrinsically insecure, despite the tangible, feisty undercurrent of strength in her nature.

'Have you ever done that—hopped out of the car while the ride was still going on?' he asked casually, looking down at his own copy of the menu.

'Yes—once,' Lily admitted.

There was silence for a few moments, then, 'You see, I can't bear not to be in control of a situation…' she said simply. 'I have a fear of being…trapped.'

She looked up to see him gazing at her thoughtfully with a look that almost made her melt, and she found herself saying things—unburdening her soul in a way she'd never done before to anyone. 'Do you know, it has taken me a long time to even be able to lock the door in the ladies' loo?' she said matter-of-factly. 'And as for public lifts…' She shuddered. 'But I am improving. I'm not nearly as bad as I used to be. Probably beginning to grow up at last,' she added, somewhat shamefacedly.

He gave a slightly crooked smile as he resumed his examination of the menu. 'Most people have a hang-up about something,' he said. 'The first step is to face it and admit it. Which you've already done.'

Lily chose a lobster-and-prawn terrine to start her meal, followed by braised calves' liver, and she looked across at Theo gratefully. 'It really will be nice to have dinner cooked for me,' she said. 'Thanks for bringing me, Theo.'

'Not at all. Bea was quite right—as she always is,' he said easily. 'It's high time that you sat back and were served for a change. I should have thought of it myself.' He paused. 'To tell the truth, you seem to understand exactly what we all like to eat, so it's very tempting to stay at home and enjoy it—especially as the average place I eat when I'm away isn't a patch on what you do.'

Lily couldn't help feeling gratified by his remarks— and she knew that he meant every word he said. Theodore Montague never used unnecessary pleasantries, whatever he was talking about.

The wine arrived, followed almost immediately by the food. Theo had decided to have the same as Lily and they ate in companionable silence for a while. It wasn't until they'd almost finished the bottle of wine, and were waiting for their desserts to arrive, that Theo said casually, 'Tell me all about yourself, Lily.' He paused. 'I know quite a lot already, of course—not only from what you've told me, but from what the children say about you. But...for example...where were you born?'

Lily looked down, twisting the corner of her crumpled napkin before considering her answer. She never discussed her past with anyone—not that many had ever bothered to enquire in any case. In her opinion, her past was so inglorious it was better hidden.

'I was born in Hampshire,' she said shortly. 'But we...we moved about the country quite a bit—never in one place for long. Our parents died when Sam and I were very young.' She bit her lip. She was trying to tell the truth without giving away too much.

'Yes, I remember you telling me that you were brought up by other family members,' Theo said, twirling the stem of his wine glass slowly. 'Do you see any of them now?'

'No. I'm afraid we've all lost touch,' Lily muttered, conscious that her tongue was beginning to dry at all this questioning. 'Sam and I are the only ones in close touch now.'

How awful did that make her sound? she thought. He'd be bound to think her very ungrateful to abandon the relatives who'd looked after her.

Theo emptied the last of the wine into their glasses and looked at her steadily. His next question hit Lily like a bolt from the blue.

'Have you ever been married, Lily?' he asked bluntly.

Her reply was just as blunt. 'No. I have not,' she said shortly, picking up her glass and taking a large gulp. 'I don't want to be married. I don't want to be tied down in any way. Ever.'

He raised one eyebrow, but let the matter drop, and soon the subject of the two interviewees arose.

'I thought both those women were appalling, didn't you?' he asked casually.

'Yes, I did.' Lily paused. 'I think we should try another agency. There must be more suitable people around than them.'

He waited a moment before answering. 'Yes. That's a good idea,' he said slowly. 'But it'll have to wait until after the holiday now—there's no time left this week, is there?'

His mood had changed in an instant, and, sensing it, Lily wanted to cry out, Don't employ anyone else…the children have had enough to put up with already. But how could she say that when she couldn't offer a suitable alternative? She'd told him enough times that she was seeking pastures new…but what he *didn't* know, and never could, was that—incredibly—she had discovered what being 'in love' was… Had allowed herself to fall for a man who had told her from the start that his children were the only thing that mattered to him and that that would never change.

They, the children, had become just as important to her, too, she thought. But if she *were* to extend the agreement she had with Theo for longer—say for a year or two—how could she stay on and be close to him without one day betraying her feelings? And what if he ever found out about her background? So different from his own privileged one? How could she ever bring herself to tell him that she had lived so much of her life on the human scrapheap, passed from pillar to post? The situation was quite useless, she thought miserably. Staying on here with this family that she'd come to really love could never work out.

Lily was a realist. She knew she must accept her time with them as being one of life's experiences and learn from it. And move on.

Tearing herself away from all this introspection, she said steadily, 'Yes, we might as well put the nanny subject on the back burner until after the holiday.' She was realising that being away with the family—with him—for two whole weeks wasn't going to help, either. It would just make things worse for her emotional turmoil—make her even more aware of what she was having to give up and forget.

With that minor decision made, Theo seemed to cheer up again. 'I've booked the family suite for the children and me,' he said. 'The one we've had before. Luckily the hotel had a vacant room for you next door to us. Though I can't promise that you won't have one or two—or three—small intruders from time to time during our stay…'

'The children are always welcome—wherever I am,' Lily said coolly.

Theo looked at her sharply. She suddenly looked very tired, he thought. He hoped the wine hadn't gone to her head—he knew that she rarely drank. She had been so relaxed and chatty earlier, but now there was a distinct change, a wistfulness about her.

It was almost eleven o'clock when they left the restaurant, and Lily turned to look at Theo as they drove rapidly through the lessening traffic. They had not said much to each other for the last few minutes, and she thought that he was probably glad that the evening was over. He'd done his duty, given her a little treat, and now he was anxious to get back.

'Thank you very much for this evening. It was lovely food,' she said formally.

'My pleasure,' he said, without taking his eyes from the road. 'You obviously couldn't find fault with the cuisine?'

'Certainly not,' she replied, staring out of her side window.

They arrived home, but before Theo could put his key in the lock Bea had opened the front door, her face ashen. 'Oh—Theo—Lily—I—I—'

They came inside quickly, shutting the door behind them, and Theo said, 'What is it, Bea?' His voice was commanding, but controlled. There was clearly something wrong.

'I cannot find Freya!' Bea practically gasped out the words, putting her hand to her mouth. 'I've searched the whole house—I haven't left the place, obviously, since you've been gone, so I know she must be here somewhere, but she's just disappeared!' They could see that the older woman was shaking, and Theo immediately put a reassuring hand on her shoulder.

'Now, Bea…it's all right. We'll find her—she's probably hiding somewhere…'

'Well, yes, that's what I thought. But I don't know where else to look…'

Lily squeezed Bea's arm. 'Come on,' she said calmly, 'one of us will be sure to discover where the little minx is…' But she frowned. Freya was quite a deep sleeper, and it wasn't like the child to leave her bed once she'd been tucked in.

'I've checked on all of them three times since you've been gone,' Bea said. 'About fifteen minutes ago I looked in on them again, and Freya's bed was empty. I can't understand it…'

'We'll do a systematic search, Bea,' Theo said. 'Don't worry—she can't be far.'

For the next twenty minutes the house was gone through room by room—under beds, behind cupboard doors. Although Lily wasn't really worried, a little prickle of something cold ran down her spine. This was silly. The child had to be somewhere near, safe in her own home…but where *was* she?

She looked up at Theo. 'Has Freya done this sort of thing before?' she asked, and his reply was immediate.

'Never—not to my knowledge.' He frowned, and Lily sensed that he was becoming irritated. His daughter had proved to be a difficult child to understand since his wife had gone—but she'd apparently never given them the runaround like this before.

'I wonder if she's gone outside—' Lily began, but Bea cut in.

'Oh, she wouldn't do that!' she said. 'Not at this time of night.' She hesitated. 'Although I *have* been engrossed in watching something on the box… I suppose she just might have slipped out without my knowing…'

Almost before she'd finished speaking, both Theo and Lily had reached the door together, going outside into the darkness. It had been a wonderfully warm day, and the heat still persisted as they peered around them.

Then, quietly, Lily said, 'There she is.'

Freya was curled up comfortably on the hammock, fast asleep. Theo went across straight away and looked down at his daughter, shaking his head in disbelief.

'Well, I'd have put money on her not leaving the house,' he said softly, 'but you never can tell with kids.' He was clearly relieved. They had all known that the child couldn't possibly be far away, but as each minute had passed without knowing where she was it had begun to trouble them.

By now Bea had joined them, making no bones about her relief.

'Oh, Freya,' she whispered, 'please don't ever give me a fright like that again, darling.'

Theo bent to pick Freya up, cradling her in his arms and brushing the top of her sleepy head with his lips. The child woke up with a start.

'Oh…where am I?' She yawned, looking from one to the other unconcernedly. 'Oh…I remember now…' She didn't go on, and they all went back into the house, Theo still holding her tightly.

When they got inside, he said gently, 'Now then, perhaps you'll tell us what you think you're doing outside in the garden at this time of night?' He looked down at her. 'You gave Bea a bad fright, Freya—that's not kind, is it? Were you too hot to stay in bed?'

Freya looked rueful for a moment, then turned to Lily. 'I…I went on the swing, Lily… To see if the fairy would come.'

Lily's heart gave a jolt. This was her fault! she thought.

'I was in bed for ages and ages, and I couldn't get to sleep,' Freya said. 'And then I thought if I crept downstairs I wouldn't disturb Bea, and if I went and started to swing—ever so gently, like you said—I might make the fairy come and grant me my wish…' The words tumbled out of Freya's mouth, her gaze fixed on Lily. 'But she didn't come, Lily.'

'Well, it doesn't matter now, Freya,' Theo said. 'It's high time you were back in bed.' He snuggled her into him again. 'Would you like a drink before we take you upstairs.'

'Yes, please—can I have some cold milk?'

Bea made for the kitchen. 'I'll get it,' she said at once, and Lily moved over to Freya and looked down at her fondly.

'I'm sorry if you didn't see a fairy, Freya,' she said quietly. 'But my stories are just that, sweetheart— they're stories. I make them up in my head. I told you that, didn't I?'

'Yes—but *sometimes* wishes can come true, can't they, Lily? You said that sometimes they can.'

Lily smiled. 'Yes. I believe that they can. Sometimes,' she said.

'So what were you wishing for, Freya? What were you hoping the fairy would make come true?' Theo enquired.

Freya turned her head and looked straight into his eyes. 'I was wishing what we all want...Alex and Tom-Tom and me. That Lily will never go away. That she will live with us for ever and ever and ever.'

CHAPTER NINE

THE holiday hotel was as impressive—and as welcoming—as Lily had known it would be. On their arrival they were greeted by the manager, and Theo introduced him to Lily.

'You know all of us, Barry—only too well,' he remarked. 'But this is Lily Patterson, the children's present nanny.' He glanced down at Lily. 'Barry has been looking after us for—what is it? Four years, I think—isn't it, Barry?'

The man smiled, taking in Lily's appearance. 'Yes, it must be, Mr Montague.' He paused. 'And you children are growing up so fast I hardly recognise you!' He looked down at Lily. 'I do hope you'll find your room suitable, Miss Patterson. Please let me know if there's anything else you might need.'

Lily smiled back at him. 'I'm sure it will be fine, thank you,' she murmured, thinking that although she'd spent a lot of time working in hotels, and had stayed with Sam in Rome, she'd certainly never stayed as a guest anywhere as grand as this.

Although the children wanted to rush in and inspect Lily's room, Theo was adamant that she should be given some time to herself first. 'You can all come and have a wash and tidy up,' he said firmly, pushing them in front of him into the family suite.

Alone for a few minutes, Lily went to open her window wide. Their rooms looked right over the sea, and the glorious drift of salty air filled her lungs as she breathed in deeply. Even though her emotions were so mixed up, she was determined to try and enjoy this holiday.

As she leaned pensively against the windowframe for a moment, her mind kept going back to the other evening, when Freya had slipped out of the house. Theo had not referred to it again, but Lily couldn't help feeling that the little girl's unusual behaviour had been all *her* fault. That she'd been filling the children's heads with too much make-believe. But she'd always invented stories—stories with happy endings. Which was probably something to do with the emptiness she'd felt in other ways, she mused. But was it wrong to let children think for just a little while that the impossible could happen? That wishes could come true? Surely that was what all stories were—fantasy, meant to entertain, which they had been doing for generations of children?

But she had been totally unprepared when Freya had announced what *her* wish was…that Lily could stay with them for ever. She remembered again the rush of colour that had flooded her cheeks. She hadn't looked at Theo, hadn't wanted to catch his eye or to see his expression. But he had totally ignored what Freya had said, as if he hadn't even heard it, merely taking the milk from Bea before carrying his daughter back to bed.

Now it was late afternoon, and Theo had told her that the children's supper was always served at five-thirty—obviously much later for the adults. Lily knew they must be ready for something to eat by now, so she had a quick wash, and was just brushing out her hair when an excited knocking on the door made her smile. Straight away they all burst in.

'Where are you going to sleep, Lily?' Alex asked, going across to the two single beds.

'Oh, probably the bed nearest the window,' Lily said.

'If I get fed up with the boys, can I come in and sleep in this other one sometimes?' Freya asked, sitting down and bouncing on it gently.

'If you like. Whatever Daddy says,' Lily replied. 'Come on—you must all be hungry.'

Theo was just locking their door as they all left Lily's room, and as the children scampered towards the lift he called out, 'No—let's use the stairs tonight. We all need some exercise after that long drive.'

Lily glanced up at him quickly. He'd clearly recalled her fear of lifts. 'It's quite OK, Theo—really…' she said. 'I'll be fine if I'm with all of you.'

'No, we'll go down the stairs tonight,' he repeated.

'But I wanted to work the lift!' Freya protested.

'Tomorrow,' Theo replied firmly. 'You can do it tomorrow.'

Their reserved family table was one of the large round ones near a window, and Freya plonked herself down beside Lily. 'We always sit here,' she said happily.

Soon the children were tucking into the ham-and-cheese omelettes the waitress brought, while Lily and Theo were served a pot of tea. The gentle hubbub of childish voices in the room made Lily's senses swim with pleasure at being here. Theo had described the place as child-friendly, and it was certainly that. Glancing across at him as he lounged back in his chair, she could imagine that he, too, must benefit from a time of complete relaxation in such surroundings. She watched him helping Tom butter a crust of bread, watched him lean forward to hear something Alex was saying—and wondered for the hundredth time what it must be like to have someone like him for a parent. She remembered what he'd said to her many times—that the children were the only thing that mattered in his life. He was totally engrossed in their welfare, she thought, and in the welfare of his patients. There was nothing else that mattered, or would ever matter, to him.

The days that followed had to be some of the happiest Lily had ever known. A simple routine seemed to establish itself at once. Freya would join the other slightly older children to have a tennis lesson on the hotel's courts straight after breakfast, and Lily and Theo would take the boys for a walk, or go down to the beach.

On the Thursday of the first week Lily overslept—an almost unique experience for her. Sitting up quickly, she saw that it was already eight-thirty, and, slipping off the bed, she went across to the window and out onto her tiny balcony. The hotel had its own swimming pool—which was situated almost immediately in front of their bedroom windows—to see the children were already splashing about.

They saw her standing there almost at once, and Freya called out, 'Lily, come down...we've been waiting ages for you!'

Lily waved back, and stayed to watch them for a few seconds. Theo was crouching down to encourage Tom with his strokes, then he gave a thumbs-up to Freya as she swam past him rapidly, to show off her expertise in the water… But Lily found herself drawn helplessly to the sight of Theo Montague…to his robust, athletic body. The white shorts he was wearing emphasised his strong, tanned thighs, which tensed and flexed with every movement. His dark glossy hair, shining as usual, was beginning to show the merest suggestion of greying at the temples, she noticed, but it only added to his distinguished, desirable appearance.

He knew she was watching them, and he looked up and waved briefly, his throat tightening as he saw her clad in her scanty T-shirt nightdress, her hair still in sleepy tumbles around her slender shoulders. He cursed himself inwardly for ever having introduced her into their lives. He had done it for his children's sake, yet the sight and nearness of Lily never failed to arouse him, threatening to take him off course.

He turned back to concentrate on his offspring. Soon Lily would be gone. Another line in his world would be indelibly drawn.

By the time the children were dressed for the day, and they'd all had breakfast, it was time for Freya's tennis lesson. She looked up at her father as they went outside.

'I don't want to go to my lesson today,' she said. 'I'd rather stay with you instead.'

'Sorry, Freya,' Theo said firmly. 'You said you wanted me to book you in, and it was your own idea. We just can't come and go when we like, can we? Not after we've made a promise. They'll be expecting you to turn up—they're probably waiting for you now.'

'But what if I was ill?' Freya grumbled.

'That would be different. But you're not ill, are you? So come on—no more arguments.'

Lily looked at Freya. 'Tell you what, Freya,' she said.

'I'd love to see how well you play—why don't I come and watch while Daddy takes the boys somewhere?'

That put a very different aspect on the matter. 'Brilliant!' Freya cried, then, 'Cheerio, Daddy…see you later!'

Theo smiled quickly at Lily. She seemed to know just what was needed at any given moment. 'I'll take the boys to the car museum in town,' he said. 'See you back here at eleven-thirty?'

As she turned to go with Freya, Lily spoke. 'Theo…if you would like me to stay with the children for the rest of the day I'd be only too happy,' she said tentatively. 'I mean, you've not had any time to yourself…to do what *you* want to do…and this is meant to be your holiday as well, isn't it?'

He looked at her thoughtfully for a second. 'Isn't it meant to be yours, too?' he said.

'Well…perhaps… But I am being paid to take care of your children,' she said. 'You are with them night and day, no time for yourself at all. I am their nanny, aren't I? Which should mean that you can go off and do your own thing whenever you want to…' She trailed off awkwardly. She hoped that didn't sound churlish, or as if she wanted to be rid of him!

But he smiled down at her. 'Thanks for the offer,' he said easily. 'If I get desperate you'll be the first to know.'

Later, after they'd had a light lunch on the terrace, they packed up to go down to the beach, and after a while Lily decided that she should sample the water. The children had been nagging her to join them ever since they'd arrived, but she'd felt slightly embarrassed to be undressed in front of Theo. It was true that her black tankini was not quite so revealing as her one bikini was, but it didn't leave much to the imagination. Still, she had to go along with it, so gritting her teeth and using a large beach towel, she slipped out of her underwear, cotton trousers and sun top, and was soon racing towards the water's edge, both boys holding her hands.

Theo and Freya were leading the way. Watching him as they ran ahead, Lily was struck by the slight lessening of the atmosphere between father and daughter lately. They made such an appealing sight, she thought, the dainty, long-haired little girl, with such perfect limbs and skin, and the handsome, virile man holding her hand so protectively.

The sea was so calm and warm they stayed in much longer than they'd meant to, and soon it was a mad scramble for everyone to go back and get dressed. Just as they picked their way across the shingle, Freya suddenly screamed, falling onto one knee dramatically and calling to Lily.

'Oh! Lily…look…I've hurt myself! I'm bleeding… Look! *Look!*'

Both Lily and Theo turned quickly, and were by her side in a second. Theo stooped at once to examine the damage. 'It's OK, Freya,' he said. 'It's just a little scratch from a sharp pebble, I expect.' He looked around to see if there was any glass, but there wasn't. He put an arm around her shoulder. 'Come on, get up. You'll be right as rain in a minute.'

But Freya was not going to be so easily pacified. 'Ow, *ow!*' she yelled. 'It's hurting… Lily, *you* look! See? See there?'

Now Lily stooped as well, carefully wiping some sand away from the affected area with her finger. As Theo had said, it was a small scratch, but the blood continued to trickle down Freya's big toe, and by this time Alex and Tom were also bending to have a look—both very interested in taking part in the crisis.

'Does it hurt very much, Freya?' Tom asked sympathetically.

'That's nothing, Freya,' Alex chipped in. 'Remember when I cut my finger on a piece of paper that time? Everyone said that a paper cut is *really* painful—you'll be OK.'

Lily never went anywhere without her modest first-aid kit—not since she'd been in charge of children—and she'd soon cleaned the wound and put antiseptic gel on it, before fixing a plaster in place. 'There,' she said kindly. 'Does that feel more comfy, Freya?'

Freya sniffed, not looking up at Theo, who had already changed out of his swimming trunks and was towelling the boys dry with a huge beach towel. 'A bit,' she admitted, still not wanting the occasion to pass quite so lightly. 'But it *does* hurt. Anyway, Daddy, I don't think I can put my sandals back on…not until it stops.' She paused. 'You'll have to carry me back to the hotel.'

Theo looked down at Lily, one eyebrow raised quizzically, and she glanced back at him. They both understood that Freya's dramatic injury might be a way for her to get out of her tennis commitment.

'We'll sort you out between us, Freya,' Lily said. 'But first I've brought all sorts of snacks to keep you going before suppertime. Just let me get dressed, and then you can choose from my bag.'

With Freya limping badly, they eventually made their way back to the hotel. As they entered the building, two elderly ladies gently pulled Lily to one side.

'We just *have* to tell you what a beautiful family you are,' one said quietly. 'We cannot take our eyes off you!'

'Oh—but—' Lily began, and the other woman cut in.

'As soon as we saw you come into the dining room we were enchanted. Your little girl is exactly like you, dear, and aren't the boys the living image of their daddy?'

'Well, actually…' Lily tried again. 'I really ought to explain…'

'Oh, it's natural to feel a bit embarrassed when someone like me accosts you with compliments,' one of the women said. 'But I'm not one for saying what I don't mean. And to see a delightful family like yours…so happy together…with such a pretty mother and handsome daddy. Well…'

By then the children were calling from the lift, and, making suitable pleasantries to the women, Lily escaped and rejoined them.

'What did those ladies want, Lily?' Freya asked curiously, and Lily fumbled in her handbag for a tissue to recover herself.

She'd never been good at accepting praise—not that she'd ever had much practice, and certainly not while she'd been growing up—but what had just been said to her had filled her with huge pleasure. Even if the ladies *had* got entirely the wrong idea. She liked it that she'd been thought of as an integral part of Theo's family— and more importantly that she might have been his wife…and that he might have been her lover. How strange was *that?* she thought.

'Oh—nothing,' she said vaguely. 'Something about the hairdressing facility here, that's all.' She wasn't going to tell them the truth—and she certainly wasn't going to tell Theo that they thought she was his wife! Lily knew that there was only one woman in the world who would ever have that title—and it certainly wasn't her.

Apart from the minor injury to Freya's toe, the day was deemed to have been another happy and successful one as Lily and Theo took their places in the dining room later. The children had been almost too tired to get ready for bed, so bathing had been completed in record time, and now, with the resident child-minder on duty upstairs while they enjoyed their evening meal, they, too, felt ready for a rest.

'I cannot believe the summer we're having,' Lily said, looking down at the menu. 'I think I probably got a bit sunburnt today.'

'Well, I did wonder whether you were neglecting yourself,' Theo replied, glancing across at her. 'You've been plastering the kids with protective cream ever since we arrived, but I haven't seen you putting any on your own skin.'

He studied her as he spoke, thinking how utterly ravishing she was, lightly tanned and with hardly any need for make-up—and always groomed to perfection. In spite of all she did, he'd never seen her with a broken nail or unkempt hair. He sighed inwardly and returned his attention to the menu.

After their meal they returned to their rooms, deciding to have an early night, and Theo paused outside Lily's door for a moment. 'Come in for a nightcap, Lily,' he said. 'It's only just gone ten o'clock.' He paused. 'Our balcony sports a table and chairs—and it's blissfully cool now…'

Lily hesitated. 'Won't we disturb the children?'

'No—they won't surface until morning. Not after the amount of sun and sea air they've had today,' he replied. He was looking down at her as he spoke, suddenly longing to have her to himself just for a while. Without any interruptions. Without anyone there to see them, to notice them.

'All right,' Lily said. 'As long as my nightcap can be a cup of tea.'

They let themselves into the room quietly, and Lily immediately went over to the three single beds to see the sleeping children. She half turned to Theo. 'Aren't they just...delicious, Theo?' she whispered, and he came alongside her to look down as well.

'Yes, when they're asleep,' he joked, adding, 'And most other times, too.' He paused. 'I'm so lucky to have them,' he said quietly. 'I never forget that—ever.'

Out on the balcony it was still warm. The gentle air from the sea fanned their faces, the subdued lighting in the hotel grounds adding its own magic as the water in the swimming pool shifted and glinted in the reflections.

'I shall never forget this holiday,' Lily said slowly, picking up the teapot which Theo had earlier brought to the table and filling her cup. 'It's the sort that you just wish would never end.'

Theo added a chunk of ice to his glass of whisky, swirling it around for a moment. He wanted to say that he wished so many things would never end, but now was not the time. He knew that the time would never come when he could ask Lily to forget her own ambitions and come and stay permanently. For the children she would be the perfect solution—a solution made in heaven, he thought wryly. They adored her, they trusted her, they never wanted her out of their sight... And he knew that he was beginning to feel that way, too.

He took a gulp from his glass, not looking at her, and

suddenly her closeness became too much. Without thinking, he put his glass down and leaned over to her, covering her hand with his own.

'Lily…' he began, and she looked up at him, her eyes wide, moist. 'I…I want to tell you how much… how grateful I am to you for entering our lives,' he began, not quite knowing how to go on. 'When I asked you—you know, when we were in Rome—if you would fill a temporary gap for me, just for a few months, I had no idea how indispensable you would become.'

His hand tightened on hers, and she turned her palm so that her fingers coiled into his. That simple gesture aroused him as much as if he could see her naked in front of him. But she didn't say anything. Her lips just parted, inviting…

He went on quickly. 'So…if the opportunity doesn't occur again…I just want you to know how much we've…all…loved having you in the family.' He let his hand slip away from hers and sat back, a mild exhaustion seeping through his limbs. He wanted to say so much more…but there wasn't anything else *to* say. In a few short weeks the curtain would finally come down on this part of his life. She would be gone, and they would never meet again.

She had not uttered a single word after he'd spoken, and now he looked across at her—to see that her cup was rattling in its saucer as her hands shook. He frowned and half-stood.

'Lily…are you OK? What is it? Are you ill?'

She must have caught the sun, he thought instinctively, because she was suddenly acting strangely. He took the cup and saucer from her and set it down on the table, then came around to stand beside her. Lily looked up at him, an expression on her face that he'd never seen before.

'I'm sorry,' she whispered through dry lips. 'I feel rather faint... I must lie down... I must go to my room...' She got up quickly, knocking against the table, and Theo put out his arm to steady her.

'Let me help you, Lily—I'll fetch a glass of water. Just a minute...'

'No! It's all right. I'll be all right in a minute,' she repeated. 'I just need to lie down.' She didn't stop to give even a passing glance at the sleeping children, but pulled herself away from him and made for the door. Before he could say another word she'd gone into her own room, without a backward glance.

Lily stood there, her back against the door, for maybe five, six minutes, waiting for the shaking to stop, before she slipped down to the floor and crouched, her head in her hands. She was in utter torment—worse than she'd ever experienced in her life... The touch of Theo's hand on hers had sent such a fierce passion racing through her that she had almost completely lost her senses. And it had terrified her. All the secret evils locked up in her past were coming back to taunt her.

For a few moments she allowed herself to weep silently, then she dragged herself up from the floor and went into the bathroom to get ready for bed. It had been such a perfect day, she thought, staring at her reflection in the mirror for a second, recognising the frightened, confused person looking back at her. Life should not be like this for anyone, she thought. Not for *anyone*. But she was trapped—always would be—in the fears and anxieties that pervaded her life. There was no escape. Not for her.

After an hour of tossing and turning, Lily finally lapsed into a deep sleep where dreams filtered in and out at random. There was Theo… They were swimming together, their bodies embracing, writhing in the deep warm water. His strong legs entwined around hers, wrapping themselves around her, shielding her, holding her. It was so strange, so blissful… They were in ever deeper water, yet she could breathe without difficulty, and there was no danger, no threat of drowning or suffocation.

They floated together effortlessly, swirling, drifting, and as she reached up to put her arms around his neck she could feel the tensing of his glistening muscular shoulders beneath her touch. With one swift movement he lifted her high above him, and she gazed down into those black enticing eyes that were smiling at her, beckoning to her. Then he came into her bed and drew her towards him, and their still-drenched bodies became locked together. He was whispering to her softly…and those gentle, sensitive hands began to slide over her, to caress her naked limbs. His fingers were touching her, exciting her, his mouth was on hers, their parted lips were united in mutual seduction. His hardened body became tense against her, and then, in slow motion, he moved across and over her, and entered her with such exquisite tenderness that Lily felt herself soaring with excitement and pleasure—and relief. Relief at the impossible made possible. And in total wonderment she heard every bird that had ever been caged singing in exultation at the ecstasy of freedom.

CHAPTER TEN

AT BREAKFAST the following morning the usual childish chatter dominated the meal around the table, but for once Lily found it hard to join in. When she had woken up she'd felt at peace with the world, but it hadn't taken her long to remember the hopeless fantasies which had filled her dreams. It had unsettled her, made her wish that her contract with the Montague family could end sooner than after the few weeks that still lay ahead.

She didn't want to look at Theo, but was even more acutely aware of his overpowering presence. Every movement he made seemed to have special significance today, she thought as she observed him, saw his strong hands reach for the jug to pour more milk into Tom's glass, lift the percolator to fill her cup with coffee.

And was it her imagination that he, too, seemed somehow different this morning? she wondered. She had seen him glance at her oddly once or twice, then look away quickly—but was that a surprise? She had left his room so suddenly last night, clearly in some sort of distress, yet had offered no explanation or excuse for it. He must be wondering what on earth was going on, but he hadn't mentioned it this morning.

And what about everything he'd said to her as they'd sat out there on the balcony…about how much he appreciated her and how perfectly she had fitted in? Praise indeed, she thought—praise for someone who received a handsome cheque each week for her trouble.

But she knew that his perceptive gaze had taken in her appearance as they'd left their rooms this morning—had felt his eyes boring into her, forming his own conclusions. And she was glad that she'd gone out of her way to look as good as usual, had showered and shampooed and perfumed, chosen a simple denim dress to wear and brushed her hair into a ponytail.

Freya touched Lily's arm briefly. 'My boiled egg wasn't as nice as the ones you do for us at home, Lily,' she said. 'The yolky bit was quite hard—yours are always dippy.'

'Well, that's because I usually only have your three to do,' Lily replied, smiling. 'The poor chef in this kitchen probably has dozens to think about—as well as all the fried ones and the poached ones…and the sausages and the bacon.'

'And they've got to cook Daddy's fish as well,' Alex chipped in. 'Daddy likes fish—don't you, Daddy?'

'I certainly do,' Theo replied. 'But I agree with Freya—Lily always manages to get it exactly right when we're at home.' He raised his eyes and held Lily's gaze for a fraction of a second. 'I would rate my breakfast today at ninety-nine per cent—while Lily's is always well past that.' He put down his knife and fork, and Lily, feeling slightly embarrassed at his words, took a slice of toast from the rack and started to butter it.

'All these compliments,' she said lightly. 'I hope I can maintain the standard when we get home…' That last word had barely left her lips when she caught her breath. She had meant to say when we get *back*. She had made the remark sound so personal, so over-familiar… It was their home, not hers. She must not allow herself such possessive thoughts and instincts. It was silly. She twisted the cap from a tiny pot of marmalade and began to spread some on her toast.

'It isn't time to go home yet, is it?' Alex asked. 'How many more sleeps have we got, Daddy?'

'Oh—about eight,' Theo replied vaguely.

He remembered Lily's words last night, when she'd said that she wished their holiday would never end, and he found himself wishing the same thing. He leaned back in his chair, folding his napkin carefully. What a situation they were in, he thought—and how on earth would the children ever accept Lily's departure? They would be heartbroken; he knew that. And there was nothing he could do about it.

One morning in the middle of the following week Lily was woken up by urgent knocking on her door, and Alex calling her name. Rubbing her eyes, she jumped out of bed and went quickly over to see what was wrong.

'It's Freya's toe!' the child exclaimed. 'It's been bleeding all over the sheets. Daddy says can you come…?'

Frowning, Lily turned to grab her white cotton housecoat from the back of the door and, shrugging it on, stopped just long enough to fetch her first-aid box before following Alex into the family suite.

Freya was sitting on the bathroom stool, holding her leg in the air as fresh blood coursed down…and crying hysterically. Theo was wringing out a flannel at the sink, and he looked up quickly as Lily came in.

'She won't let me near her. She wants you to look at it,' he said over the noise. He was bare-footed and wearing a dark green dressing gown—and was obviously still unshaven because Lily could see the dark stubble on his jaw.

She crouched down and looked up into the child's reddened face. 'Stop crying for a minute, Freya,' she said firmly. 'And let me see what's going on here.'

Almost immediately Freya's yells became more of a whimper, and with the aid of the flannel which Theo had handed her, Lily wiped firmly over the foot and examined it closely. 'I can see what's happened,' she said. She smiled reassuringly at Freya. 'While you count up to ten—you two can count as well—' she addressed the boys, who were there in the doorway like fascinated bystanders '—I shall perform one of my magic tricks.'

Bending, she took something from the first-aid kit. 'Right—start counting!' she commanded.

The three children began chanting slowly, and Lily bent her head so that Freya couldn't see what she was doing. Then carefully, deftly, with one gentle movement using a small pair of tweezers, she extracted a tiny shard of glass. She held it up triumphantly.

'Ta-da!' she said. 'You've been hiding this in your toe ever since you cut it on the beach last week, Freya—and today it was determined to escape! See?'

Theo had been standing a little way apart, and now came over to look. 'D'you think there's any more in there?' he said.

'I doubt it,' Lily said. 'This'll be a one-off. I saw the same thing happen to someone else once, and eventually these little foreign bodies do work themselves out.'

She paused. 'But we'll give this a good clean and put on a plaster.'

Now that the panic was over, Freya cheered up at once as Lily washed and dried her foot. 'It hardly hurts at all now,' she said with studied bravery. 'Not like it did before…when it really, *really* did.'

'Yes, you were a poor wounded soldier,' Lily said, 'but never mind. You're OK now, Freya.'

'I'll have to explain to Barry,' Theo said, 'about the sheets…'

'I'll do that,' Lily said. 'This sort of thing is hardly unknown in hotels.'

Theo looked down at Freya, who was leaning into Lily's side. 'If your foot is too uncomfortable to play tennis this morning, Freya,' he said, 'we can tell them when we go downstairs to breakfast.'

'Oh—no, that's OK,' Freya said airily. 'There are only two more sessions in any case. I might as well carry on.'

He smiled. 'Good for you,' he said, ruffling her hair.

Much later in the afternoon, when the children had been whisked off to watch a puppet show which had been laid on for all the youngsters in the hotel, Theo and Lily found themselves alone together by the pool. They were lying, side by side, on two sunloungers, and Theo turned his head to look at her as she relaxed, her eyes shut against the sun.

She was wearing brief navy blue shorts, which exposed her slender, tanned limbs, her small feet were thrust into white sparkly sandals, and the flimsy sun top she had on revealed her curvaceous figure just enough to excite interest… Well, it excited *his* interest, he thought honestly. He had met many women in his life, but Lily stood out as one of the most understated yet intensely desirable members of the female sex he'd ever encountered. And the funny thing was she didn't seem aware of it… She never flaunted herself in any way, either by look or gesture. He frowned slightly. He couldn't understand it—found it strange that a woman with such obvious female charms never seemed to worry one way or the other about the picture she presented to the world. She obviously took great care of her appearance at all times, no one could deny that, but it never seemed for personal publicity purposes. The way she was turned out was purely for her own benefit and satisfaction.

He turned his head away from her for a moment, wondering how she'd managed to remain single for so long. There had never been any mention of a boyfriend, and she'd been emphatic about not wanting to be tied down by marriage, or by having children of her own. And yet there was something odd about that, too, he thought. Lily Patterson wasn't only good with children, she was fantastic with them. She understood how they ticked, how to entertain them, how to deal with them— and his three had responded to her like no one else before—apart from Elspeth, of course. Even dear old Bea didn't fit in like Lily had done since she'd been with them. His three offspring seemed to consider Lily more of their own generation than as the person who was in charge of them.

She opened her eyes then, and turned to see him watching her, immediately drawing her knees up to her chin. 'I thought you were asleep,' she said softly.

He didn't answer for a moment, then, 'No—I was…' He'd been going to say, *I was watching you,* but instead said, 'I don't know what I'd have done without you this morning. Freya was determined that I was not going to have anything to do with it, or even to look at her foot. Only one person was to have that privilege—you, Lily.'

Lily shrugged. 'That's kids,' she said casually. 'If I hadn't been around she'd have *had* to let you help her.' She paused. 'Poor Freya—all that blood was quite frightening, wasn't it? But because I'd seen something like it before I guessed almost at once what the problem was.'

'Well—I was…grateful…for your assistance…' he said slowly.

Lily smiled in response, and turned her head away just as Theo's mobile rang. He reached into the pocket of his shorts to answer it. 'This is the first call I've had since we've been away,' he said, 'and I hope it isn't going to be a record-breaker. They know they can contact me from work only if it's absolutely essential,' he added, hoping fervently that their precious last few days were not going to be interrupted by any sort of crisis.

As soon as he heard the voice at the other end, his expression cleared. 'Olly!' he exclaimed. 'How're you doing?'

When Lily heard who was calling she froze for a moment. Even though the man was obviously nowhere near, the memory of his unexpected visit came back to her in a flash. Listening to Theo's one-sided conversation did nothing to give her any comfort.

'Of course you can… You know you're always welcome,' Theo said, in answer to an obvious request from Oliver. Lily turned her head away, as if to shut out the possibility that *she* might be involved in any way. 'Two weeks on Saturday, did you say?' Then, 'No, we shall be home by then.' He paused. 'I'm actually speaking to you from our holiday hotel, but we're due back on Saturday. Yes, we're having a great time…superb weather non-stop.' Another pause. 'No, really? Of course—bring her as well. It'll be good to see her again, Oliver. Now, look, you don't need to take us out to lunch on the Sunday—the amazing Lily will rustle up something for us all, I'm sure. Yes… Yes… Of course I don't mind…there's no problem. Look forward to it. Bye, Olly.' Theo snapped his phone shut and glanced across at Lily. 'That was Oliver,' he said. 'You remember he dropped by before?'

Lily nodded, her eyes closed. 'I remember,' she said briefly.

'He's asked if he and the present lady-friend can stay over—a fortnight on Saturday. There's a big party they're going to, apparently, and both our local hotels are already fully booked.' He turned away for a second. 'They don't expect to be with us until the early hours—but we'll have Sunday morning to catch up with all their news. You probably heard me say that we could offer them lunch.' He paused and glanced across at her, but Lily didn't turn her head to look at him.

'Of course I'll prepare lunch for you all,' she said simply—not bothering to add, *You're the boss, after all*.

'He's with Alice Thorpe at the moment, so he told me,' Theo went on. 'We all go back quite a long way… I wonder what she looks like now.'

Lily didn't bother to respond to that, only experiencing a sinking feeling that she was obviously going to have to be polite to Theo's boorish friend. Then she comforted herself—she'd be in bed by the time the couple returned from their party, and she'd be busy the next morning with the children, and providing lunch for

Theo's guests. She'd have no difficulty in keeping herself well occupied and out of the way. Besides, she thought reasonably, Oliver had been very drunk that last time… Surely no friend of Theo's would be an actual creep? Her over-sensitive memory had probably exaggerated the smell of the man, his overbearing closeness, she argued to herself.

After that they lapsed into the normal, easy silence that they'd both become accustomed to enjoying when they were alone together, before Theo said, 'By the way, on the last Friday evening of the season, Barry usually makes a point of providing a sort of farewell event. Dinner is served at nine—later than usual—and there's always some sort of entertainment.' He paused to wipe his sunglasses with the hem of his T-shirt and smiled across. 'We seem to be part of a pretty youngish crowd this time, who might appreciate something a bit different… Anyway, he'll warn us what to expect.'

Lily looked back at him. 'Does that mean dressing up?'

'Well, I've brought my dinner jacket just in case,' he said briefly. He paused. 'As far as you're concerned, most of what I've seen you in will do, Lily… That, um, that lemon-colour sundress would be perfect.'

Lily leaned back and closed her eyes again. She quite liked the idea of a special evening… She'd not had many of those in her life—certainly not in the company of someone like Theodore Montague—and luckily she'd packed her one and only 'occasion' number, a draped, three-quarter-length dress in shades of blue: the palest cornflower colour at the low-cut neckline, changing and floating down in varying degrees to a midnight-blue shade at the hem. It was dressy, yet casual in a summery way. Lily had taken it with her to Rome—

thinking that she and Sam might go somewhere appropriate—but if this coming Friday was to be a special one, she knew that she would feel perfectly comfortable wearing it for the first time.

Presently, the scampering of feet and energetic, childish voices announced the return of the children, and they all ran up, throwing themselves onto the sunbeds.

'Did you enjoy that?' Theo asked.

'It was great!' they chorused.

Then Freya said suddenly, obviously having waited for the right moment, 'Daddy, because of my toe and everything, can I sleep in Lily's room tonight?'

Theo looked at her sharply for a second. 'Well, I don't know,' he said. 'Aren't you happy in with the rest of us?'

'Yes…of course,' Freya said guardedly. 'It's just that—well, when we first arrived I asked Lily if I could sleep in the other bed in her room, and she said it was up to you.' She hesitated. 'I was thinking just now that—what if my toe starts bleeding again in the night? You'd have to call Lily, and disturb everyone, but if I was there with her in the first place it might save everyone a lot of trouble.'

Theo smiled his crooked smile. 'If Lily doesn't mind—' he began.

'Of course I don't mind,' Lily said. She smiled at Freya. 'It'll be just us girls—and I hope you don't snore!'

As they were leaving the dining room later on—after the children had eaten their supper—Barry met them in the hall.

'Hello again, everyone,' he said jovially. 'My goodness—what weather you brought with you! You're all beginning to look like polished conkers!' He turned to Theo.

'Supper will be late on Friday night,' he said. 'It'll be served at nine, and I've booked a local band—they're excellent—to entertain us for a few hours afterwards.'

'Sounds wonderful,' Theo said, glancing at Lily. He realised that he knew very little about her likes and dislikes, what branch of the arts, or of the musical world in general, that she preferred. He bit his lip. It didn't matter one way or the other what she liked, he thought. Soon it would be nothing to do with him.

'I'm going to sleep in Lily's room tonight,' Freya told the manager. 'Because of my toe.'

'Yes—I heard about your poor toe,' Barry said sympathetically. 'Is it OK now, Freya?'

'Well—it *nearly* is… But I'm sleeping in with Lily just to make sure.'

The man grinned. Lily had spoken to him about the soiled sheets, and he'd assured her that that kind of thing was all in a day's work for his staff. 'Well, don't go stepping on glass again, will you?' he said. 'You're much too beautiful to go spoiling your looks—even if it was only your toe that was damaged.'

It wasn't long until bedtime, and the children seemed extra tired tonight, Lily thought. Tom had almost fallen asleep over his warm milk at the table, and even Alex seemed quiet.

'I think we should do some colouring or play a game now,' she said lightly. 'We've all had enough exercise for today. I could show you some card tricks, or—'

'Yes! Let's play cards!' Alex said. 'I know a trick, Lily. I'll show you…'

Lily looked up at Theo quickly, realising how natural it had become for her to make decisions for the family. She hadn't bothered to see what Theo wanted them to do. Over the long holiday it had become the norm for them to automatically share the responsibility. She had not once been made to feel like the employed nanny, or as if she should check with him as to what his opinion was. They seemed to have slipped unconsciously into the smooth running of everything they did with neither of them querying the other.

She had to admit that the routine seemed to suit Theo well enough. He was relaxed, unhurried, and appeared to be totally content. And the almost uninterrupted sunshine had served him well—his handsome face was devoid of the occasional brooding appearance she'd been aware of once or twice at home, and the frown line across the broad forehead was almost invisible. It had obviously been time for him to have a complete rest from his work and to recharge his batteries.

When it was time for bed Lily went into the family suite, as usual, to get them all bathed, with Theo agreeing to sit out on the balcony and let her do it alone.

'I don't think this is going to take long.' She smiled. 'Everyone seems exhausted tonight.'

Later, after they had had their own meal, and had spent some time in the lounge with a drink, Lily excused herself.

'I think I'll go up,' she said, getting up from her chair and looking down at Theo. 'I feel as tired as the children today.'

He half stood, his whisky glass in his hand. 'Yes—go and have a good rest, Lily.' He paused. 'I hope my daughter doesn't keep you awake—on any pretext. She can be a little madam at times...and seems to have acquired a talent for twisting people around her little finger. Don't let her take advantage of you.'

Lily shook her head quickly at the suggestion. 'Goodnight, then.'

'Goodnight, Lily.'

He watched her go, conscious of the glances of other men in the room. She must be used to turning heads, he thought, yet she seemed totally unaware of it.

Lily let herself quietly into her bedroom. Freya was curled up on the other single bed, her long fair hair tumbling over the pillow, and Lily moved across to look down at her. Soon this whole episode, her time with the Montagues, would be a distant memory, and the thought brought a terrible lump to her throat. She wished that she'd never met Theo on that journey to Rome. All he had done was disrupt her life, cause her to question her own feelings, her own ambitions, and remind her that the sort of life she was enjoying—no, *revelling* in—would never be hers in her own right. The happiness she was experiencing was second-hand, lent to her for a fleeting few weeks. And then it would be back to normal…to treading her way cautiously, to protecting herself, protecting her emotions. To living her life outside the accepted parameters of other human beings.

Suddenly Freya leapt up and flung her arms around Lily's neck. 'Boo!' she cried. 'I haven't been asleep… I've been waiting for you!'

Lily stepped back in surprise. 'You little monkey! I thought you were fast asleep.' She uncoiled herself from the child's hold and stepped back, sitting on the side of the bed for a moment. 'It's late, Freya—you're going to be very tired in the morning…'

Freya sat up, hugging her knees and looking at Lily

with her large, sensitive eyes. 'I hate Daddy,' she said. 'I was waiting up to tell you that. I hate him.'

The statement was matter-of-fact, and came as an unpleasant surprise to Lily. But her face remained expressionless, and she let a few moments elapse before replying—equally matter-of-factly. 'I hate my mother,' she said coolly.

Now it was Freya's turn to be caught unawares. 'You…hate your *mother*, Lily?' she said. 'Why…? Why on earth would you hate your mother?' The thought was preposterous to Freya. 'No one hates their mother… do they?'

'I do,' Lily said, still sitting where she was, sensing that there was much more to come in this conversation.

'But—*why?* What…what did she do?' Lily's revelation was much more interesting to Freya than her own statement had been.

'Because she gave me away,' Lily said simply—and even after all this time tears sprang to her eyes. 'She didn't want me, Freya, so she gave me away to someone else.'

Freya sat forward and hugged Lily to her desperately. 'Oh, Lily…why would your mother do that?' She paused, gulping. 'My mother would never, never have given *me* away!'

Lily shrugged. 'I don't know, really,' she said slowly. 'I think she was very young. And—and she wasn't married to my father. Perhaps she didn't have any money of her own to buy me food and look after me.'

Freya pulled away slightly and gazed up into Lily's face. 'I don't know why anyone would want to give *you* away, Lily,' she said slowly. 'You're lovely. We all love you—and Daddy loves you, too.' She paused. 'Do you like Daddy, Lily?'

'I do like him,' Lily replied carefully, then, 'But why do you hate Daddy, Freya? You did say that, didn't you?'

Freya's expression changed in an instant. 'Because he let Mummy die,' she said flatly.

The bald statement took Lily's breath away, and she had to wait a moment before going on. 'What do you mean?'

Freya shrugged. 'Well, he's a doctor, isn't he? Doctors make people better—they don't let them die.'

'Freya—don't you think that Daddy *wanted* your mother to get better? Don't you think that he tried every way he knew to make her better?'

Freya shrugged. 'Well, he didn't try hard enough, did he? And anyway—' she paused '—he's not sad. Not like Alex and Tom-Tom and me are.'

Lily felt helplessness sweep over her. This was difficult ground that she was being asked to cover. She realised that the little girl—with all her common sense and grown-up ways—was confused and unhappy. No wonder there had been tension between her and her father if the children really thought Theo could have saved his wife if he'd tried harder. It beggared belief. Yet how understandable it would be to their innocent minds. Doctors were there to make people better.

She leaned over and took Freya in her arms, holding her close. 'How do you know that Daddy isn't sad?' she asked softly.

'Because he never cries,' Freya said at once. 'We've never, never seen him cry. Not once. Not even on the day Mummy died. He just stood there looking cross, with a funny look on his face. Everyone cries if they're sad, don't they?'

Lily hugged her even closer. 'Freya, listen to me,' she said, trying to keep the urgency from her tone. 'I can promise you, with my hand on my heart, that Daddy would have done everything in the whole wide world to make Mummy better… But even doctors—even the very best of them—can't always succeed. That's just the way it is.' She rocked Freya gently for a moment. 'I know that Daddy loved Mummy very, very much. I can tell when I see him looking at her photograph sometimes. And…' She paused. 'And I'm also sure that Daddy does cry sometimes, when he's by himself. Not when he's with you…because he doesn't want you all to be made even sadder. Would… Would you have felt any happier if you *had* seen him cry?'

'No-ooo…' Freya said slowly. 'I don't *want* to see Daddy cry… I just thought it strange that he never did, that's all. But I don't want him to cry.' She paused. 'We wish that he could make you stay, Lily… But he's told us that it wouldn't be fair because you've got lots of other things you want to do.' She looked into Lily's eyes again. 'He said he didn't think you particularly wanted to work with children…that you were going travelling and stuff…but I said that if he tried really hard he could *make* you stay.'

Lily lifted back the duvet and laid Freya down gently. 'Let's not talk about that now, Freya,' she said. 'You really must get to sleep. But…' She paused. 'But maybe I could stay on for a bit longer—we'll see, shall we?' She dropped a kiss on Freya's forehead. 'One thing I must make you promise me, Freya—never, never say that you hate Daddy. Because he loves you all so much—all he wants is for you to be together, nice and cosy, even without Mummy. So—promise?'

Freya snuggled down. 'I promise—and *you* must promise not to say you hate your mummy, either, Lily…'

Lily smiled. 'Yes, I promise not to say that ever again,' she said truthfully. Because who could ever know just what it had cost her mother to part with her two small babies? Her life must have been full of contradictions and problems—things that, still only in her teens, she had been unable to deal with. 'So—we don't hate anyone, do we, Freya?' she said.

Freya was getting drowsy, a slight smile on her cherubic lips. 'No. We don't hate anyone, Lily,' she said. 'Not our daddies and mummies, anyway.'

CHAPTER ELEVEN

As LILY stepped into her dress on the final Friday evening of their holiday, she found it hard to believe that they had only been away for two weeks. To her, it seemed so much longer than that... She and Theo and the children had covered so much ground, being together for practically the whole time, with each day providing yet more insight into their lives. It had been a wonderful time for all of them, with only two damp mornings to contend with. And apart from a few minor quarrels between the children, not to mention the toe incident, there had been nothing to spoil what had been, for Lily, the best two weeks of her life.

She sighed briefly, staring at herself in the mirror for a second and meeting her own frank gaze. A dreadful feeling of finality swept over her. Time was running out for her, and much worse was knowing that soon the children were going to have to get used to another person looking after them. Although she'd said to Freya during their very revealing talk the other night that she might stay on for a while, Lily knew that it would only prolong the agony if she did. It was time, she thought, to move on—to find the elusive 'something' that would give her fulfilment, help her to reach the goal in life that she hadn't yet put a name to.

Thanks to her lightly suntanned skin, there was hardly any need for her to wear much make-up, but she did brush a little colour on to her cheeks and lips, patting her hair into place for a final time. She'd decided at the last minute not to leave it loose, but to wind it up into a knot on top, letting one or two wavy strands escape around her face. Then, last of all, she massaged some of her precious perfume into her neck and behind her ears.

It was already gone nine when Theo tapped lightly on her door, and when she opened it her mouth dried. He seemed even taller tonight, as he stood there in the dimly lit corridor, his shoulders broader in the expensive, immaculate evening suit he was wearing, his hair dark and glossy, enhancing the strong forehead, the penetrating, searching eyes as he looked down at her.

In one brief moment he took in her appearance, too. To him, she resembled a dainty fairy princess…she only needed a tinselled wand in her hand! He cleared his throat.

'That's a very nice dress, Lily,' he said rather formally, as she locked her door.

'Is it OK…? Will it do?' she asked innocently.

He smiled briefly. 'It will do very well,' he said.

As they went towards the lift they met the nanny who kept constant watch on their floor when parents were absent, and she smiled across at them as they passed.

'Have a good evening,' she said pleasantly.

'You won't hear a thing from our three,' Theo said easily. 'I almost had to wake them up to get them ready for bed.'

As they entered the dining room Lily's breath was almost taken away. It had been transformed, with small tables now surrounding a space in the centre from where the carpet had been rolled away. And practically the only lighting in the room was provided by numerous flickering candles.

'Goodness—doesn't it look…beautiful?' Lily said, as they stood for a moment waiting to be seated.

In another time in his life Theo might have replied, *As beautiful as you*. Instead, he said, 'Barry has a very shrewd idea of the theatrical—this is supposed to be a treat for busy parents, perhaps to take them back to earlier, more romantic times.' He paused. 'Barry likes this to be a memorable last evening for everyone.'

A waiter appeared then, and they were shown to a table just a little way behind the ones nearest the centre of the room. Almost at once the band began taking up position, briefly tuning their instruments, and Lily looked across at Theo.

'I suppose people dance?' she asked, nodding towards the polished oak floor.

'Some do,' he said casually. 'If they want to.'

Lily picked up the menu which the waiter had just given her, feeling relieved. There was obviously no obligation to join the dancers, she thought, which was just as well because she didn't have a clue. She'd never danced with anyone in her life. But she wondered about Theo. She looked at him quickly over the top of her menu. He would be very stylish, elegant—and was no doubt competent in any arena. She imagined him gliding effortlessly around the dance floor, with Elspeth held protectively in his arms.

Lily's eyes misted for a second. They'd have been the most glamorous couple in the room, she thought. How he must miss her. Especially on this particular evening. Instead of his wife being here he had to put up with the children's nanny instead, and, stupidly, Lily wished she could, just for a short while, magic herself into someone else.

But if Theo was feeling nostalgic he certainly didn't show it as he looked across at her over the candlelight, his eyes glistening. 'Have you chosen what you'd like, Lily?' he asked, forcing her gaze to remain locked in his. He paused. 'You know, I'm ashamed to admit it, but it'll be something of a pleasure not to have to make up my own mind every evening next week. It'll be good to be presented with whatever you've cooked for us— knowing that I'll enjoy every bit of it.'

Lily coloured up at his words, and returned her attention to the menu. 'Thanks for that,' she said lightly. 'And I'm happy to say that I shan't mind being back in harness again.' She paused. 'This has been a great holiday, Theo… Thank you so, so much for inviting me to come as well.' She didn't say, *and for footing the bill, paying for every single thing*—because that would have spoilt it.

He didn't answer immediately, but looked at her with such an expression in his eyes that Lily's colour would have deepened even further if she'd noticed it. There was so much he wanted to say—so much he *could* say— but there were no words, and again, for the second time in his life, Theodore Montague felt helpless. Then he shrugged, a slight frown creasing his forehead, his masculinity taking over. This situation *would* be dealt with—*he* would deal with it. Experience was a good teacher, and it had shown him before that every problem became solved eventually, one way or another. It would be no different this time.

'By the way, I must say again that I was impressed

at how you sorted Freya and her toe out,' he said casually. 'Have you had nursing experience, Lily—or first aid?'

Lily smiled at that. 'No—'fraid not. I suppose my reaction to the situation came out of long experience of having to look out for myself—to keep on my toes and not to get fazed under pressure, that's all.'

That was something of an exaggeration, she thought, because she often *did* get fazed. The trick was in not letting it show.

Once the band were ready, the music started playing at just the right level of sound, making sure that the diners could communicate without having to shout at each other, and once again the menu was varied, the food perfectly cooked.

'That pheasant was superb,' Lily said appreciatively as she put down her knife and fork. 'It can be a tricky beast to get right, but the chef has managed to pull it off—as usual.'

Theo nodded. 'I shouldn't think that Barry has many complaints,' he said.

Lily shook her head. 'You'd be surprised. You can bend over backwards to please everyone, and sometimes there are still those who nit-pick. I've known one or two in my time,' she added. 'But it's an occupational hazard we were taught to accept.'

As soon as the main course had been eaten, one or two couples began to take to the floor. The music was simple, rhythmically, and, studying them as they moved, Lily observed that there didn't seem to be any particular pattern to the steps. It seemed more or less a question of moving from one foot to the other, keeping time with the music. If she was really forced to, she thought, she could probably join in with that without falling over or making a fool of herself.

Suddenly Theo leaned forward, his elbows on the table, and Lily turned her attention away from the dancers for a moment.

'Tonight I feel as though all my birthdays have come at once, Lily,' he murmured, and Lily's heart jumped in her chest. He was clearly going to say something important, she knew that at once, but what was it? And could she deal with it?

'Oh?' she said uncertainly. 'Why?'

He waited for a moment before going on. Then, 'Because I've got my little daughter back at last,' he said simply. 'And it's completely blown me away.' He reached for his glass of wine. 'I'd got them all into their pyjamas tonight—Tom was actually already asleep, and Alex was cleaning his teeth in the bathroom—and I was sitting out on the balcony for a moment.' He paused. 'Freya came up to me and climbed onto my lap. She put her arms around my neck…and told me that she loved me.' He drank quickly from his glass. 'She has not got that close to me, nor uttered those words, since Elspeth died. I…I…feel as if a huge shadow has been moved away, letting in the light again.'

Lily found it hard to speak for a moment. So Freya had taken everything she'd said the other night to heart, and had begun to understand her father. Involuntarily Lily reached out and touched Theo's hand, and he immediately responded, curling her fingers in his.

'It was only a matter of time, Theo,' she said gently. 'Children, especially little girls, feel things more deeply than anyone realises. Of course she loves you. She's never stopped loving you.'

'I was getting a bit worried,' he confessed, not letting Lily's hand go. 'And—to make it even better—she's asked to give up on boarding at school. She wants to come home each night, as she used to do. Which pleases me more than I can say. Now we'll be complete again… Well, not quite…' he added quickly. 'But you know what I mean.'

Lily felt a huge wave of emotion well up inside her. It was almost too good to be true, she thought, but the expression on Theo's face said it all. Freya had come back to him.

Just then their waiter brought the dessert menu, and they were both glad to concentrate on that for a moment—to distance themselves from the briefly charged atmosphere. After they'd placed their order, Theo leaned forward again.

'I have to say, Lily, that I feel your hand in this—in Freya's turnaround—' he began, but she cut in.

'Oh, I doubt it, Theo. Don't forget we've all had a super holiday. Everyone's relaxed and…'

'No, it's more than that,' he said. 'That couldn't account for it. I've made sure that the children have had good times, plenty of diversions since they've been without their mother. But it's only since you've been with us that I've seen a distinct change in Freya. And tonight my daughter confirmed what I've been hoping for for so long.'

Listening to his words, Lily felt that all *her* birthdays had come at once, too. It was so touching to see Theo's relief—and if she had been responsible for somehow bringing that about then she could only be glad. Theo was a good man—a loving, caring, generous father, who deserved to be loved totally in return. It must have been agonising for him to feel rejected by the daughter he clearly worshipped.

'Well,' she said brightly, determined not to let any residual sadness cloud the evening, 'that puts the icing on the cake, doesn't it? We won't ask for another thing!'

Suddenly, slowly, he got to his feet and came over to stand beside her. She looked up at him, her eyebrows raised slightly.

'May I have the pleasure of this dance, Lily?' he said, and she answered quickly.

'I don't know how to... I've never danced with any-one before...' she began.

The thought of a man holding her close had always filled her with dread, but Theo took her by the arm gently, raising her to her feet.

'There's really nothing to it, Lily,' he said quietly. 'I'll show you.'

He led her onto the floor—which was by now crowded, with practically everyone in the room joining in.

'Just let your body move with mine, with the rhythm,' he said softly.

And Lily found that it was a lot easier than she could ever have imagined, with Theo's strong arm around her waist, his hand holding hers firmly. Amazingly, her dreaded horror of feeling a masculine form melding with hers had evaporated, and what she was feeling at that moment was not only acceptable, but terrifyingly attractive and desirable. And as he eased her more closely to him, so that she could feel the warmth of his body penetrate the fine fabric of her dress, Lily felt an exciting tremor ripple through her, making her momentarily literally weak at the knees.

The dance, such as it was, demanded nothing more

than to keep time with the beat, and as they swayed together, neither speaking, Lily smiled faintly to herself. This was her very first experience of being with a man in this situation, and she knew that it would never happen again. This was a one-off, and for these precious few minutes Lily felt herself transported to some un-dreamed-of world—a world far away from anything to do with *her*.

When the music stopped no one moved back to their tables. Almost at once it began again, and the dancing continued. Lily could just feel the touch of Theo's chin resting on the top of her head as they swayed together, and the slight, intimate sensation she felt set her emotions rocketing again, sent the blood coursing through her veins at breakneck speed.

After a while they returned to their table, just as the waiter was bringing their coffee, and Theo leaned towards Lily again.

'Of course,' he said, his tone serious, 'there's another very plausible explanation for my daughter's change of heart.'

'Oh?' Lily stirred sugar into her coffee, glancing up at him.

'Yes, I wonder—have been wondering—could it possibly be Jasmine weaving her magic again?'

Lily was nearly caught off guard at that. Oh, no! she thought. How embarrassing! Those fairy stories of hers were not meant for adult ears! She clicked her tongue. 'What have the children been telling you?' she said.

'Well, I've had all the stories you've told faithfully recounted,' he said, 'and I know that when your Eve starts to play on the swing in her garden a fairy called Jasmine suddenly appears and they have long talks. Tell each other everything. And I know that Jasmine makes wishes come true…makes frightened people brave… makes horrid people become nice people.'

Lily covered her mouth with her hand. 'Oh, honestly, Theo… I'm sorry if the children have been wasting your time telling you all that stuff…all that nonsense…'

'It's not nonsense, Lily,' he said. 'Your stories took them to a land of make-believe, made them feel happy and contented before going to sleep, made them think that wonderful things can sometimes happen.' He paused. 'My problem is that I was expected to go on with it—to make up some myself. I told them that those particular stories belong to you, and that you are the only one who knows what the endings are.' He smiled. 'I'm relieved to say that they understood that and stopped pestering me.'

Lily shook her head briefly. 'I'm sorry—I'm afraid it's a legacy from my own childhood,' she said. 'I used to get myself to sleep at night by pretending that there were knights in shining armour to rescue me, or animals who could lead me out of danger in a dark wood…stuff like that.' She made a face. 'And I take full responsibility for Freya letting herself out into the garden that night,' she went on seriously. 'That *had* to be my fault.'

He shrugged. 'She was perfectly safe,' he said. 'The only harm done was to poor Bea, who got a bit worried. But it was short-lived.'

He held her gaze for a moment, and that slow, slightly crooked smile played around the elegant mouth. 'Actually,' he said, 'I'd very much appreciate it if you would tell *me* a story, Lily… You know, one with a happy ending.' He leaned towards her again. 'D'you think that if I wished really hard Jasmine would wave her magic wand in *my* direction?'

CHAPTER TWELVE

'WHEN are you going to be cooking all this food, Lily?'
Freya asked, as the three children helped her to lift the
supermarket bags into the boot of the car.

'Oh—I'll be preparing most of it tomorrow, I expect,'
Lily said, 'and the rest on Sunday morning.'

'Are we going to have some of it, too?' Alex asked.
'Or is it just for Daddy's friends?'

'Of course you'll have some, too!' Lily exclaimed.
'We'll have ours in the kitchen—but you can help me lay
the table in the dining room for Daddy and his guests.'

They had been back from their holiday for almost
two weeks, and the next day Oliver and his girlfriend
were due to visit. Although Lily was not looking forward to seeing the man again, she was determined that
the meal she presented for their Sunday lunch would be
special. In fact, she was looking forward to thinking it
out and preparing it. For Theo's sake.

Since their return life had very quickly returned to
normal, with Theo absorbed in his work and Lily automatically reverting to employee mode. Even though life was
good, with the children quite content to be back home, the
easy familiarity of those sun-filled days between her and

Theo had sort of eroded. It was as if a switch had been thrown, bringing them back down to earth.

She had thought so much about their time away, and Lily was honest enough to admit that one of the high points had been that last Friday evening. As she and Theo had danced together she'd felt so blissfully content, so cherished, so protected—she'd wished they could have stayed there like that for ever. It had been an incredible sensation which she had never expected would ever enter her life. And she'd been conscious that when they'd returned to their table he had been as briefly subdued as she was—as if something precious had been theirs for those few moments, only to slip away, like quicksilver, just out of reach.

Theo had been so busy since their return—not only leaving early most days for the hospital, but also spending hours in his study preparing lectures. Some evenings he came down so late for his supper that by the time he did Lily had already had hers. But she realised that he was having to clear the huge backlog which had piled up while they'd been away. So when he eventually did appear, looking thoughtful and preoccupied, she would put his meal in front of him, wish him goodnight, then go and leave him in peace.

That evening, as she went past him, he put out a hand and caught her arm briefly. 'Are you avoiding me, Lily?' he asked, half-jokingly. 'As I come in, you go out.'

She glanced up at him quickly. 'Of course I'm not avoiding you,' she said. 'I… I just thought you needed time for yourself, that's all. Without having to engage in pointless chit-chat.'

'What we usually talk about is seldom pointless,' he

said. 'Stay and talk—unless you've other things you have to do?'

Lily turned immediately to do as she was told, making herself a cup of tea before sitting opposite him as he began his meal.

'I've hardly had a chance to see anything of the kids,' he said ruefully, reaching for his glass of wine and looking across at her. 'Have they been behaving themselves?'

Lily smiled, helping herself to one of the shortbread biscuits she'd made and arranged on a dish for him to have with his coffee later. 'Your children are never any trouble,' she said firmly. She noticed that he was eating rather slowly, and she said hesitantly, 'Is everything all right, Theo? The meat hasn't dried, has it?' Well, it wouldn't be her fault if it had, she thought. It had been waiting to be eaten for some time.

'No, of course it isn't dry—it's good, as usual.' He paused. 'I was just thinking that we really must get this nanny thing sorted soon… It's sort of…not exactly slipped my mind…but gone on the back burner lately, shall we say?'

Lily sighed inwardly, hesitating before responding to his remark. Then, 'Look, Theo—you've clearly got enough to be thinking about at the moment,' she said. 'If necessary I can delay my departure—at least for another month, if that'll help. Don't worry about the children for now…we'll get it sorted all in good time.'

His expression cleared straight away. 'Well, that would take the heat out of the situation if you could—would— stay on for a bit longer,' he said. He stopped eating and looked straight into her eyes. 'Thank you,' he said simply.

Neither of them spoke for a few moments, then Lily

said, 'I've been thinking about lunch on Sunday, Theo—' she began, but he interrupted.

'Oh, there's no need for you to beat yourself up about that, Lily,' he said. 'Olly and Alice are known for their healthy appetites—I know that whatever you put in front of them will be hoovered up in five minutes flat.'

Lily shrugged. 'Well, anyway, I thought I'd give them asparagus mousse to start, followed by steak and stilton royale with baked tomatoes. It presents very well, and is really delicious.'

'I'm sure it is,' Theo replied, somewhat dryly.

'I usually serve it with new potatoes and fresh green vegetables,' she said.

He looked across at her as she spoke. She obviously really enjoyed cooking, and she was so good at it—good at everything, including looking after other people's children—which she'd said she did *not* enjoy. He glanced at her as she sipped at her mug of tea. If only she could see her way to staying with them permanently he wouldn't have a care in the world. But how could he expect that of her? She was young. She had her own life to live in the way *she* wanted—not to please others.

'And then I thought I'd do a favourite of mine for dessert,' Lily went on, leaning her elbow on the table and cupping her chin in her hand. '*Gâteau Meringue de la Forêt Noire*—it's full of cherries and almonds and fresh cream. It's an indulgence, I admit, but you haven't asked me to do any special entertaining since I've been here, so I'd be happy to push the boat out. And to keep my hand in at the same time.' She paused. 'You never know, I might have to return to the cookery world one day. If my dream of finding that special something I'm looking for never comes true.'

* * *

It was very late on Saturday night when Theo's friends came back from their function. Lily, who'd gone to bed early but hadn't yet managed to sleep a wink, heard Theo greet them. Glancing at her bedroom clock, she saw that it was gone one. Even though her room was on the second floor, she could clearly make out Oliver's rather rough voice—so unlike Theo's cultured tones, she thought instinctively—and a woman's strident giggle. They were all obviously chatting in the hallway. There was a sudden burst of laughter, then she heard the sitting room door being closed firmly, and the sounds became inaudible.

They were probably going to spend half the night going over old times, Lily thought, turning over and giving her pillow a thump. She frowned slightly. The room set aside for them was on the first floor, almost next to the boys. She hoped they'd come up quietly and not disturb them…

The next morning Lily was up early, as usual. She went into the bathroom and ran a brush through her hair, staring at herself in the mirror. Was it her imagination, or was she looking a bit tired this morning? she asked herself. She shrugged. How she looked was of no importance—her presence would be swallowed up by that of Theo's friends, she knew that for sure. She hadn't yet made Alice's acquaintance, but if Oliver was any indication Lily knew exactly what the woman would be like. Just hearing her giggle and her high-pitched voice had been enough.

In spite of those preconceptions, Lily decided to make the best of herself, even though she wouldn't be with the adults much… Her flimsy cotton floral skirt teamed with a low-neck cream blouse would be light and unrestricting. She knew that the outfit suited her in an understated way, and worn with flat, strappy sandals it gave a slightly peasant-like effect. Perfect to wear on a warm Sunday morning, busy in the kitchen, she thought. And although leaving her hair loose would have looked good, Lily decided to tie it back in a ponytail as she was cooking.

She switched on the shower, biting her lip for a second. She wondered whether Oliver remembered the rather embarrassing incident between them the last time they had met. He had been very drunk at the time, she mused, and probably hadn't given the matter another thought… She wished she could say the same. She could still feel the man's presence overcrowding her.

She could hear that the children were awake, so she went down to the boys' room. Freya was there, too, and they all leapt up to hug Lily as she went in.

'Have Daddy's friends arrived?' Alex asked.

'They have,' Lily replied. 'So don't make too much noise, because they're probably still fast asleep.'

'I'm telling the boys one of your stories,' Freya said importantly. 'I've nearly finished it.'

'Good for you,' Lily said. 'And don't forget it must have a happy ending!'

After they'd got ready for the day, the children went on down to the kitchen. Just as Lily was about to follow them, she bumped into Theo at the top of the stairs.

'Good morning, Lily,' he said quietly, taking in her appearance at a glance.

'Morning, Theo,' she said lightly, going past him and running down the stairs. 'I expect you're ready for some coffee?'

'Oh, I've had mine,' he replied, coming down and following her into the kitchen, where the children were doing some colouring. He went over and kissed the top of each of their heads. 'I hope we didn't disturb you last night?' he said. 'There was a bit of noise, I'm afraid.' He glanced at Lily, who was busying herself getting the breakfasts. 'I shouldn't bother with anything for Olly and Alice,' he added. 'They won't surface until midday.'

She glanced up at him. 'Oh? Well, that's OK, then. We'll concentrate on lunch instead.'

'Yes—we're helping Lily to lay the table and everything,' Freya said.

'Don't overdo it,' Theo murmured affectionately.

After breakfast he went out into the garden with the children, leaving Lily in peace. She felt perfectly relaxed about her lunch party—she'd cooked this particular menu many times before, and it had always been well received. She found herself humming a little tune as she lifted the ingredients from the fridge and switched on the oven. She really did enjoy cooking for people, she thought. It gave her great satisfaction to present good, appetising food attractively.

Suddenly a voice right behind her made her start, and she turned to see a woman standing there. 'Oh—hello—you're… You must be Alice?' she said pleasantly.

The woman's black hair, hanging in untidy curls down to her shoulders, framed a rather hard face, and she was clad in a bright green shiny housecoat. She gave a barely perceptible smile as she went across to the sink. 'Yes, I'm Alice,' she said, 'and I'm badly in need of a glass of water to take a couple of tablets.' She put her hand to her forehead. 'We did have rather a good time at the do last night. I have no idea when Oliver will see the light of day. He's virtually unconscious at the moment.'

Lily took a tumbler down from the cabinet and filled

it with water, handing it to the woman, who made a grimace as she swallowed the pills.

'Ugh—the smell of cooking is getting to me in here,' Alice said. 'Sorry—but I'll have to leave... Where's Theo? Is he up?'

'Yes, he's outside with the children,' Lily said shortly, turning back to what she was doing.

Alice came to stand beside her for a moment, looking her up and down, taking note of what she was wearing. 'Theo was telling us what a wonderful find you are,' she drawled. 'He hasn't had much luck with staff before, apparently, and suddenly you appear out of the blue. Not only good with his kids, but a great cook to boot. Well, well... Very convenient for him.' She paused. 'But do be warned...Lily. It is Lily, isn't it? In case you've been wondering, Theo is not on the market. Nor ever will be, I'm afraid. It's a sad loss to the female race in general, but there you go. I wouldn't want you to have any false hopes.' She smiled a superior smile. 'I expect you have an eye for the main chance—but don't get your hopes up, will you?'

Lily was angry at the woman's words, and turned to stare at her, her face hot. 'I take offence at your remarks,' she said, her voice steely. 'I am an employee here. I am not looking for anything more. I have no plans—at least not the sort you've just alluded to.'

'Well, that's all right, then,' Alice said smoothly. 'We go back a very long way, you know... Theo and I were...close at one time...and I know the guy. Shop's shut, I'm afraid.'

She left the kitchen then, and Lily stood rooted to the spot, shaking inside at what had just been said. How could *anyone* think that she had designs on Theo, or that she was looking for a relationship? That a complete stranger should make that assumption was insulting—and degrading. If only they knew—if only any of them knew—just what her feelings were in that direction!

For a few moments she felt unable to carry on with doing the meal, then she pulled herself together. Why was she letting the wretched woman get to her like this? Alice whatever-her-name-was was a complete nobody, and her unlooked-for comments and advice were of no interest whatsoever.

Almost at once Lily calmed down and got on with the job in hand. She heard someone coming down the stairs—it could only be Oliver, she thought—and then heard him go through into the garden. Just so long as he didn't come in here, bothering her, she thought.

After a few moments Theo came in and stood watching her for a second or two.

'I'm going to make some coffee for them,' he said briefly. 'They don't want anything to eat, apparently. Anyway, I told them to save their appetites for lunch.'

'Fine,' Lily said coolly. 'Will one-thirty be about right?'

'Perfect,' he replied, wishing with all his heart that it was just going to be the five of them, as usual. He was already tiring of his friends' company.

Just then the children came in as well, and Lily said, 'Yes, it's about time we laid the table. Freya—fetch the napkins from that drawer, please.'

Lily had to admit how attractive it all looked by the time they'd finished. The expensive glassware and cutlery on the snowy white cloth looked like something from an advertisement.

When it was nearly time to serve the meal Lily sent the children upstairs to wash, just as Theo came into the dining room to fetch some drinks to take out into the garden. He glanced down at the table, frowning.

'Why only three places?' he asked.

Lily shrugged. 'Because there are only three of you,' she replied.

'And what about you?' he demanded—almost curtly. 'Why aren't you eating with us?'

'Because I always have my lunch with the children,' she pointed out patiently, not bothering to add that the thought of having to sit and talk to Theo's guests filled her with distaste.

'Then in that case the children will eat with us as well,' he said, in a tone of voice which brooked no argument. In a sudden, unusual gesture he caught Lily's wrist firmly. 'You are not a kitchen maid, Lily,' he said. 'Please don't act like one.'

The determined expression on his face made Lily catch her breath for a moment, but she merely nodded. 'OK—fine,' she said. 'The children will enjoy being with everyone, I'm sure.'

She was right. They were thrilled to be invited to be part of the occasion, and they all behaved impeccably— which was no surprise to Lily. Even little Tom was made to feel important by not having to wear his bib but being given a napkin like everyone else.

Although the meal had turned out perfectly, with Theo and Oliver doing it great justice by clearing their plates, Alice merely toyed with her food, leaving most of it untouched. She looked over at Lily.

'So sorry not to be able to eat much of this,' she said, 'but I'm afraid I have no appetite today… We ate—and drank—too well last night.'

'Don't worry about it, Alice. The rest of us will make up for it,' Theo said easily, glancing over at Lily and winking at her briefly. 'That was absolutely fantastic, Lily—you're a genius.' He smiled at the children. 'Not a crumb left on the plates over on that side of the table,' he observed.

'It was deeeeelicious!' Alex said, scraping around his dessert bowl. 'Can I have some more, Lily?'

'I think you've had enough for now, Alex,' she said. 'But you can have some more for supper.'

Oliver lounged back in his chair, lacing his fingers across his ample stomach and staring at Lily, who was sitting immediately opposite him.

'Are there any more where you come from, Lily?' he asked lazily. 'I think you're the sort of woman we should all have in our homes.'

Lily looked back at him quickly. She had been conscious of him staring at her now and again during the meal, with a strange look in his eyes, and she wondered if he *did* remember how she'd almost thrown him away from her that night. She shivered involuntarily, hating the sight of his thick, podgy fingers as he held his wine glass, hating the florid face and double chin.

'I can tell you now, Olly, that people like Lily are not to be found—she is a rare treasure. So hands off!' Theo said.

'I wouldn't say no to a bit of hands-on,' Oliver said crudely, and at once Theo got up from the table.

'Come on—I found that book I was telling you about. It's in the sitting room.'

After a few minutes Alice took herself back to bed— she hadn't even bothered to get dressed—while Oliver went into the television room to watch the motor racing. Before joining him, Theo put his head around the kitchen door.

'Thank you again for that super meal,' he said. 'And by the way, they're staying over tonight as well… Alice is apparently not well enough to go home.' He made a face as he said it, but Lily ignored that—they were his guests, and they could stay as long as he wanted them to. But she groaned inwardly. She didn't feel comfortable with either of them—especially after the things Alice had said to her earlier.

'I've promised to take the children to the park this afternoon,' she said. 'So we'll be out of your hair.' She paused. 'There are two freshly made cakes in the pantry if they need something with their tea.'

Theo held up his hand. 'I shouldn't think any of us need much more food for the rest of the day,' he said. 'I'll look after them now, Lily. You've done more than your fair share.'

Thankfully, Lily didn't see much of Theo's guests after that. Oliver spent the afternoon snoring in front of the television, while Theo apparently went to his study to work. And it wasn't until much later that Alice emerged to join the men in the sitting room.

To Lily, it had seemed one of the longest days of her life. Although Alice had said she wasn't well enough to eat lunch, Lily felt that the woman had been deliberately picky—pushing the food around her plate, and leaning back in her chair and staring at the children. Even though everyone else had enjoyed it, her attitude had put a noticeable damper on the occasion. Thinking about it, Lily couldn't imagine that Alice had ever meant anything special to Theo, whatever she'd said. She knew him well enough to know that the woman wasn't his type. But then, did she *really* know? she asked herself. She knew nothing of Theo's past—as he certainly didn't know anything of hers.

It was almost midnight when Lily, only half-awake, thought she heard Tom whimpering in the room below. She had been so tired at bedtime that she'd fallen into the deepest sleep she could ever remember—a sleep full of words and faces, of anxieties about the future, about the children, and about Theo. And in amongst all that there was Alice, sneering at her, and Oliver, who kept on touching her face and neck, but she couldn't tell Theo about it because they were friends and it would upset him.

At last, she managed to drag herself into a sitting position, and, yawning, pushed her hair away from her face, listening again for the sound which had woken her. It was quiet now, but just to make sure Lily slid out of bed. Not even bothering to put on her dressing gown, she padded in her bare feet down the stairs to the boys' room. She pushed open the door gently and looked down at them, at their sleeping, peaceful faces. There was nothing wrong, she thought. She must have imagined it. Or dreamed it.

Turning, she crept out of the room—and was confronted by Oliver, who stood there dressed only in a pair of boxer shorts, his hairless chest gleaming slightly with perspiration.

'Oh…' Lily gasped, overcome with embarrassment at being there wearing just her short T-shirt nightie. She recoiled at his large figure barring her way. 'I hope I haven't disturbed you,' she said, moving away quickly. 'I thought one of the children was awake, that's all.'

She could smell the overpowering odour of whisky on his breath, making her teeth chatter slightly in alarm. The familiar edginess crowded in on her, making her eyes huge with fright as she tried to go back up the stairs to her room.

'Don't go—don't run away,' he said, his voice thick. 'I like you, Lily. I liked you before, didn't I? Only you didn't seem to like me.' He paused, grinning down at her. 'We could have some fun.' He moved towards her slowly. 'You're not shy, are you, Lily? Pretty woman like you must have had quite a few experiences…'

He leered down at her, and Lily was so terrified that she couldn't even swallow, her throat was so dry. He had made it impossible for her to get back to her own room, and she glanced desperately towards Theo's door. She'd go in there and wake him if she had to. Anything to get out of this situation.

Following her gaze, Oliver smiled slowly. 'Theo was called out on an emergency at the hospital,' he said, 'just as we were all going to bed. Said he'd be back by the morning.' He cupped her chin in his hand. 'I like you, Lily,' he said again, stupidly.

Lily's heart was thumping so loudly now that she thought it would choke her. She pushed at his chest with her fists. 'Get away from me,' she breathed. 'How dare you behave like this? You're a guest in this house— get out of my *way*.'

She was shaking so violently that she thought she was going to faint. She knew she had to do something now, before he went any further and there was no time. No time. Quick—quick, go *now*… Without thinking, she turned and ran quickly down the stairs, thrusting open the front door and running away—running, running, her emotions wildly out of control, tears pouring down her cheeks. But she was free, she was out of his orbit, she could escape…

As she pelted blindly along, Lily wasn't even aware of the pavement's rough surface under her feet. The street was completely deserted, and there was no traffic… There was nothing and no one to witness her terrified flight. But after a minute or two the cool night air on her flaming face began to calm her down, and her steps became a slower walking pace. Then, abruptly, she stopped by a lamppost, putting her arms around it and hugging it for support, resting her forehead against its cold surface, waiting and waiting for the passing of time to restore her senses.

Then she stood stock still, the realisation of what she had just done hitting her like a brick. She had left the children alone…left them alone with that man in the house… In her own frenzied panic she had abandoned them! How *could* she have done that?

After a moment, realising that she could actually stand unaided, she let her arms slide down, away from the lamppost—just as Theo drove alongside her. He pulled up sharply with a screech of brakes and got out—and without a word he wrapped his body around hers, almost lifting her off her feet. For several moments he just stared down into her tear-soaked face.

'For God's sake, Lily…what's going on?' he said.

And Lily clung to him, letting the feel of him through her scanty nightwear warm and console her. 'I'm so sorry,' she whispered. 'I'm sorry…'

He said no more, just half-lifted her into the car, then

drove rapidly the few hundred yards home. Lily sat with her head back against the seat, her eyes closed.

They reached the house. The front door was still open, as she'd left it, and there was no sound. Without a word Theo ran up the stairs two at a time, to check on the children. Then he came back down more slowly, and with his arm around Lily's waist led her gently into the kitchen, closing the door behind them. He put his arms around her again tightly, tucking her head under his chin, and began rocking her gently. And as Lily's heart-rate began to slowly return to normal the tears began to flow freely.

Once the worst was over he led her to one of the arm-chairs and sat her down, then knelt on the floor beside her, looking up at her. Her hair tumbled untidily around her face, which was pale and wet with tears, and her eyes were huge. Every now and then a discernible tremor rippled through her slight body. He took a hand-kerchief from his pocket and wiped her cheeks tenderly.

'Talk to me, Lily,' he said gently. 'Talk to me, please.'

Lily knew that if she started unburdening herself to Theodore Montague her tears would begin again—but she knew that she had to do it. Surely he deserved an explanation for tonight's behaviour? But could he ever understand?

He tried to help her. 'What frightened you, Lily?' he asked. 'What were you running away from?'

Lily took a deep breath, her innate common sense and self-control taking over at last. 'It was all my fault—' she began. Well, what else could she say? Oliver hadn't actually done anything—he'd barely touched her. All he had done was revive the past that she'd spent so much of her life trying to forget, to push away from her. And he'd done it so well! For those few awful moments she'd been a helpless child again, subject to adult expectations, demands and desires. And she'd been trapped—as she'd been so many times before. 'I went down to the boys' room because I thought one of them was awake,' she began.

'And someone else was there as well?' he offered.

She hesitated. 'Oliver was standing there, and…' She couldn't explain.

Theo's expression was grim. 'What did he do, Lily? Did he try it on?'

Theo's perceptiveness made it easy, and now Lily's words came quickly.

'Well…sort of…' she said. 'But…what he's proved to me again is that I still can't cope. I will never be able to cope…' She looked down anxiously into Theo's eyes.

'Cope with what?'

'With life. With myself,' Lily said simply. 'I'm lost, Theo. I'm only half a person. I'm useless.'

He couldn't stand seeing her distress any longer, and he pulled her to her feet, enfolding her in his arms again, letting the silence wash around them for a few moments.

'Will you marry me, Lily?' he whispered. 'I want you…so badly.'

His unbelievable declaration, made in this unbelievable situation, made Lily draw back in amazement—and dismay. He didn't know her—not really. Emotionally she was a complete stranger.

'Why would you want a wife like me?' she asked him hopelessly. 'You don't know me, Theo, and I know nothing—*nothing*—of love. I only know lust. I'm damaged goods. Not a sound investment for any thinking man. I'm not a whole person. I'm only half a person. Who wants to settle for fifty per cent of anything?'

'Go on,' he said quietly.

And for the first time in her life Lily was able to unburden herself to a man—to a man she could trust utterly.

'Sam and I never knew our parents,' she said slowly. 'We were given up as babies by our mother—a single parent. Sam was fostered—happily, I believe—while I…' She swallowed, choking back the dark years. 'I went from one home to another. In one particular place I was forced to fend off the unwanted attentions of a man who was supposed to be protecting me…a man who seemed so kind at first, but who wanted more… more.' Lily shivered, her teeth chattering uncontrollably for a moment, and Theo's hold on her increased gently, his expression becoming even grimmer as he began to get the picture.

'Didn't you tell anyone?' he said softly. 'Wasn't there anyone to help you?'

'I tried a couple of times,' Lily said. 'But no one believed me—or they preferred not to believe me. In the end I didn't really believe myself. I gave up trying to explain—stopped trusting any man who came near me. I just ran away all the time. I was soon categorised as an impossible, difficult child that no one wanted to know. But even when I went into a children's home it didn't stop. Every man I came across I saw as a potential danger… even though most of them were not. I lost all my grip on reality. My only obsession was staying…pure.' That last whispered word was almost inaudible.

Theo's voice was gruff. 'I can't bear to think of it,' he said. 'I can't bear to believe it.'

'I know,' Lily said. 'And that was the prevailing attitude. There was no one I could turn to.' She looked up into his face. 'So you see, Theo…I know I would be useless as a wife—because I would be afraid to have feelings, to love you. I am afraid of myself.' She paused. 'I wouldn't know how to please you…'

Theo held her even closer to him. 'Well,' he said, 'you're doing all right at the moment, Lily.' He smiled gently. 'We all have to start somewhere—and I can wait for you. There's no rush. And I'll show you the way, if you'll give me the chance.'

Then, as she continued looking up at him, his mouth closed softly over her parted lips. And Lily didn't pull away—didn't want to pull away, letting his masculinity overpower her, take her over completely, in the first awakenings of a new life, thrilling her mind, body and soul. She was alive at last—alive to love and to be loved.

And his obvious physical need for her as she felt the hardening of his body against her vulnerable frame didn't repel or disgust her. It only made her want to know him fully, as her lover.

Neither of them wanted to move, or to break the spell which bound them at that moment, then he whispered in her ear, 'You have become everything to me, Lily. I don't know what I've done to deserve this second chance—if you'll have me—but I know I could make you happy. I just know that we could be happy together.' Then he paused. 'But I'm forgetting something, aren't I? Forgetting that you have other plans—that you're looking for another answer in your life.'

She put a finger over his lips gently. 'I think I've already found it,' she said. 'I think it's been here all the time.' She closed her eyes, praying with all her heart that she wasn't going to suddenly wake up.

'So...do I have to go down on one knee, Lily Patterson? To beg you to be mine?' he said.

She nestled into him, loving the strong, handsome face, the searching gaze, the seductive mouth.

'No need for that, Theodore Montague,' she said dreamily. 'I'm yours already. Now and for ever.'

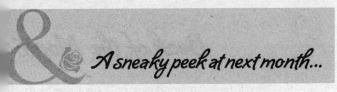

A sneaky peek at next month...

By Request

RELIVE THE ROMANCE WITH THE BEST OF THE BEST

My wish list for next month's titles...

In stores from 15th February 2013:

☐ His Defiant Mistress – Catherine George, Carole Mortimer & Sandra Field

☐ Baby on Board – Liz Fielding, Patricia Thayer & Raye Morgan

3 stories in each book - only **£5.99!**

In stores from 1st March 2013:

☐ The Wilders – Marie Ferrarella, Mary J. Forbes & Teresa Southwick

Available at WHSmith, Tesco, Asda, Eason, Amazon and Apple

Just can't wait?

Visit us Online

You can buy our books online a month before they hit the shops! **www.millsandboon.co.uk**

0213/05

Book of the Month

MILLS & BOON

We love this book because...

A dramatic, gloriously sensual family saga. Descendants of a proud warrior Viking, the Brunson brothers and their sheltered sister rule the Scottish borders. It's a time of danger and treachery—and emotions run high!

On sale 1st March

Visit us Online

Find out more at
www.millsandboon.co.uk/BOTM

0213/BOTM

Special Offers

Every month we put together collections and longer reads written by your favourite authors.

Here are some of next month's highlights— and don't miss our fabulous discount online!

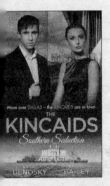

On sale 15th February

On sale 15th February

On sale 1st March

Save 20%
on all Special Releases

Find out more at
www.millsandboon.co.uk/specialreleases

Visit us Online

0313/ST/MB407

The World of Mills & Boon®

There's a Mills & Boon® series that's perfect for you. We publish ten series and, with new titles every month, you never have to wait long for your favourite to come along.

Blaze®
Scorching hot, sexy reads
4 new stories every month

By Request
Relive the romance with the best of the best
9 new stories every month

Cherish™
Romance to melt the heart every time
12 new stories every month

Desire™
Passionate and dramatic love stories
8 new stories every month

Visit us Online

Try something new with our Book Club offer
www.millsandboon.co.uk/freebookoffer

M&B/WORLD2

What will you treat yourself to next?

Ignite your imagination,
step into the past...
6 new stories every month

INTRIGUE...

Breathtaking romantic suspense
Up to 8 new stories every month

Captivating medical drama –
with heart
6 new stories every month

MODERN™

International affairs,
seduction & passion guaranteed
9 new stories every month

n o c t u r n e™

Deliciously wicked
paranormal romance
Up to 4 new stories every month

RIVA™

Live life to the full –
give in to temptation
3 new stories every month available
exclusively via our Book Club

You can also buy Mills & Boon eBooks at
www.millsandboon.co.uk

*Visit us
Online*

M&B/WORLD2

Mills & Boon® Online

Discover more romance at
www.millsandboon.co.uk

 FREE online reads

 Books up to one
month before shops

 Browse our books
before you buy

...and much more!

For exclusive competitions and instant updates:

 Like us on **facebook.com/romancehq**

Follow us on **twitter.com/millsandboonuk**

Join us on **community.millsandboon.co.uk**

Visit us Online Sign up for our FREE eNewsletter at
www.millsandboon.co.uk

WEB/M&B/RTL4